OUT
LAWYERED

OTHER BOOKS AND AUDIO BOOKS
BY CLAIR M. POULSON

I'll Find You

Relentless

Lost and Found

Conflict of Interest

Runaway

Cover Up

Mirror Image

Blind Side

Evidence

Don't Cry Wolf

Dead Wrong

Deadline

Vengeance

Hunted

Switchback

Accidental Private Eye

Framed

Checking Out

In Plain Sight

Falling

Murder at TopHouse

Portrait of Lies

Silent Sting

OUT LAWYERED

a novel

Clair M. Poulson

Covenant Communications, Inc.

Prologue

"You know I can't do that, Kara. I about faint when Abbie looks at me," I told my sister for at least the tenth time.

"She likes you, Saxson. If you ask her, she'll go out with you. Please. She's my best friend. Do it for me. You aren't afraid of me, so you have no reason to be afraid of Abbie," Kara said with a pleading voice.

I may be seventeen, and I might be athletic and smart in school, but by my very nature I am afraid of girls. I can't help it. Shyness around them is just how I am, and Kara knows it. But she won't let up on me. Finally, after telling her as firmly as I could that I wasn't going to ask her best friend out on a date, she got that sneaky look in her eyes that warned me that I was about to get blindsided.

Sure enough. "Then I'll ask her for you, and when she says yes, you'll have to take her out," she said with a grin. "It would be mean if you didn't. And you are not a mean guy."

I opened my mouth to protest once more, but before I could get the words out, she said, "Ollie asked me out, and I'm going with him. We'll make it a double date. Mom says I should only date if I'm with another couple. You and Abbie, and me and Ollie. That would be perfect."

"But . . . but Ollie . . . he's my best friend. That would be weird. And anyway, he would've told me if he'd asked you out. I think you're fibbing, little sister," I stammered, but I had a terrible feeling in the pit of my stomach that she wasn't.

Kara laughed and threw her head back, her long brown hair flying and her blue eyes sparkling. "Saxson, you aren't the only one in the Cartwright family that Ollie likes." Before I could speak again, she said, "I'll call Abbie right now, and then I'll call Ollie and let him know our plans."

I hate to admit it, but I threw up about an hour before my date with Abbie. Now, don't get me wrong. It's not that I don't think she's cute—because she is. I think she's the cutest girl in the whole school. I've always enjoyed having her around the house with my sister, but that was different. She was almost like a second sister then. I guess it was good that my stomach was empty because when I saw her at her door that evening, she was gorgeous. I stuttered and stammered and generally made a fool of myself. But she didn't seem to notice.

Ollie drove his pickup. Kara sat in the front with him, and I was in the backseat with Abbie. It was wonderful and terrible at the same time. Somehow I made it through the movie and dinner. If I said ten words the whole evening, I couldn't tell you what they were.

It might seem weird, but Ollie took me home first. That was because Abbie and Kara were spending the night at Abbie's house. I think when I got out of the truck Abbie said something to me about how much fun she'd had. If I said something in return, I don't know what it was. Probably just as well. It would have been something really dorky, I'm sure.

Kara went to the house with me to get her packed bag to take to Abbie's. She grinned when we went inside and said, "She just told me she hopes you ask her out again. She likes you, Saxson. So you better ask her again."

I reminded my little sister that I hadn't asked the first time, but she just giggled, flipped her hair over her shoulder, and ran upstairs to her room. I went to my own room and sat on my bed, wondering why I had to be such a blubbering idiot. Abbie was cute and sweet, and I think she even liked me, but I was quite sure I'd never go out with her again. I just couldn't.

It was almost midnight when I put my pajamas on. I went to bed and couldn't sleep. I kept seeing Abbie's smiling face, her dark blonde hair, and sparkling blue eyes. When there was a tap on my door, I looked at my alarm clock. It was a little after one. "Yeah?" I called out.

It was my dad, and something about his voice scared me. "You need to come to the living room. Bishop Arnold is here and says he needs to talk to us."

Something was terribly wrong. I scrambled into my pants and a shirt and hurried to the living room. I felt a chill pass over me when I saw not only the bishop but two deputy sheriffs. Mom was sobbing into Dad's shoulder, and his broad shoulders were shaking.

After the men delivered their message, I felt like my whole world had just crashed. I was numb with grief and disbelief.

My little sister, my best friend, and sweet Abbie were all dead!

Ten minutes after they left our house, Ollie's pickup truck was struck head on by a drunk driver in a large truck. The drunk, a man of about thirty, was not badly hurt. I was enraged at the injustice of it all and horrified over the deaths of three special young people.

Looking back, I know I wasn't to blame for what happened that night, but for a long time, I blamed myself. If I hadn't allowed myself to be roped into that date, Abbie, Ollie, and my little sister would still be alive. I cried bitter tears and suffered terrible nightmares for weeks. The loss and the guilt almost consumed me. But with the loving help of my bishop and the support of my grieving parents, I gradually began to heal.

The other driver was charged with automobile homicide. My parents tried to talk me out of it, but I insisted that I was going to attend every day of his trial. He refused to accept responsibility, but I was assured that he would be convicted and go to prison. Those who assured me couldn't have been more wrong. The lead officer had made some big mistakes in his investigation. But worse than that, the prosecutor was a total idiot. Despite the officer's errors, I felt that the prosecutor should have been able to prove the case. But he blew it. I wasn't the only one that felt that a killer walked free because of the terrible job that man did and the expert job the defense attorney did. Many felt the same way, but that didn't change the fact that this man got away with killing three innocent people who were very dear to me.

I couldn't do anything about that terrible injustice. But when that "not guilty" verdict was returned by the jury, I decided what I would do with my life. I was determined to get a law degree and become a prosecutor. I swore to myself that I would never do the sloppy, lazy job this man had done. I couldn't get justice for Abbie, Ollie, and Kara, but I could do my best to see to it that others didn't have to go through what my family and I did.

One

Nine years later

A COLD WIND SWEPT ACROSS the frozen earth, and the sun struggled in vain to spread its warmth on my back as I rode along a barren ridge. I looked at the deep blue sky overhead and thought about how the wind could turn an otherwise beautiful day into one of discomfort. I had experienced it often while growing up on a Wyoming cattle ranch. I pulled gently on the reins, and Midnight, my black Fox Trotter gelding, stopped. I dismounted, stepped up to his head, and rubbed him fondly.

I looked to the south and spotted my truck and horse trailer, little more than a speck in the distance. I judged that I must have ridden five or six miles. I needed to be getting back or I'd be riding in darkness. I gave Midnight's broad neck a gentle pat as I moved again to the saddle and swung up. I nudged him gently with my heel and started forward, turning him back toward the south. The March wind picked up. It reminded me of my youth and the rides I'd often taken, moving cows or checking springs and fence lines on my father's ranch. My life now was very different from what it had been back then. Unbidden, the face of my friend, Ollie Reardon, appeared in my mind. I smiled as I recalled his unruly red hair, dark green eyes, and freckled, constantly smiling face. He and I had ridden together more times than I could remember. His father had owned a ranch just a few miles from the one my father still operated. If we weren't riding on one ranch, we were riding on the other—or from one *to* the other. I'd been almost as close to Ollie as to my own brothers.

The pleasant memory faded, and I saw that face, pale and still, eyes closed, hair neatly combed, hands folded across his chest as he reposed in a dark cherrywood casket. Even now, nine years later, a tear slipped from one eye. I wiped it away with a gloved hand. His face slowly faded, and that of my little sister, just a year younger than me, appeared. I choked back a sob as I thought of her, dead because of a drunk driver. And her best friend, the only girl I'd ever been on a date with, appeared in my mind. I squeezed my eyes tightly, trying to erase that beautiful face from my head as I'd done hundreds of times before. Abbie Pearlman had been Kara's best friend, and I had secretly admired her every time the girls were together in our home. If I'd ever had a crush on a girl, Abbie was the one.

Abbie had both frightened and enchanted me. My terrible shyness had kept me from viewing her as anything other than my spunky little sister's friend. I could see Abbie's face in my mind as she too lay in a shiny casket, her dark blonde hair curled around her silent face, her eyes closed to the happy life she'd lived.

I had often thought I'd forget her, but I had never succeeded in doing so. I didn't want to forget her or Kara and Ollie, even though their untimely, senseless deaths still haunted me. I opened my eyes and urged Midnight into a smooth trot, hoping to rid myself of the memories that had driven me to the life I now lived.

Twenty-six years old, I was the youngest of three deputy Duchesne County prosecutors. I had yet to prosecute a case like the one I watched in a Wyoming courtroom following the deaths of three innocent teenagers, but I still held tightly to the determination that I would never fail *anyone* the way the incompetent, lazy prosecutor in that case had done. He'd allowed the drunk driver to walk with a cocky swagger from the courtroom.

I urged Midnight to a lope. I had to finish preparing a talk I'd been asked to give in sacrament meeting the next morning. Of all the topics I might have been assigned, the one the bishop requested is a principle I still struggled with: *forgiveness*. Many times I thought I'd forgiven the man who killed Ollie, Kara, and Abbie. But had I really? How many times had I dreamed of seeing him sitting at the defense table in one of the courtrooms I worked in, the cocky sneer wiped off his face as he was convicted of some crime, any crime, that I prosecuted him for? I had a long way to go, I admitted to myself, as I pulled Midnight to a walk. I'd never seen that man since he walked from that courtroom that had so forcefully set me on the course my life now followed. *I had to totally forgive him.* Maybe this talk would help me do that.

I just hoped I wouldn't see the teenage girl who reminded me so much of Kara or the pretty woman who I'd been told was her Laurel advisor. I saw her in the hallway after church from time to time. Each time I saw her, I was reminded of Abbie, and I'd often thought that had Abbie lived, she might have looked much like Wyanne Grice. On several occasions, her eyes had met mine, and a smile not unlike Abbie's had lit her face. But each time, I had turned awkwardly and hurried away. Unfortunately, Sister Grice and the young Laurel, Angelica Keen, reminded me enough of Abbie and Kara that just seeing them brought back memories that made the task of forgiveness that much more difficult.

How could I speak on forgiveness if I saw either of those two in church that day? I pulled Midnight to a stop, dismounted, and knelt near a stubby pine tree. I needed help if I was going to exercise the very principle I was assigned to speak on the next morning. After a heavenward plea, I felt a little better, remounted Midnight, and urged him on his way again.

***

I crossed paths with Sister Grice and Angelica on the sidewalk outside the church the next morning. They both said hi as I passed them, and Sister Grice's face lit up with a gorgeous smile which displayed two cute dimples. It was hard for me to smile back, but I tried. I mumbled something, but I couldn't keep my thoughts straight. I stopped and looked back at them, their heads huddled as they talked. It was none of my business why they weren't in their classes, but I heard Angelica thanking Sister Grice for something that they had apparently just retrieved from the teacher's car. Oh, how her sweet voice reminded me of Kara.

I choked back a sob, returned to my truck, prayed for help from the Lord, and finally found some solace. I *could* forgive the man who killed my friends and sister. I committed to the Lord that I would.

I don't know how my talk went, but several people complimented me. Perhaps I did okay. If I did, it was because the Lord was changing my heart.

I saw Sister Grice once more when I was leaving sacrament meeting. Her ward's meetings had just concluded, and she was standing in the hallway, holding someone's fussy baby. Angelica was again talking to her, and both of them crooned lovingly to the child. I hurried past the two of them, mumbling again when they both said hi to me. I felt like the idiot that I am. Why did I have such a hard time socializing even briefly with those of the fairer gender? Was it to be my lot in life? Probably.

It was only after I had entered the classroom that I realized that seeing the two of them and hearing their cheery voices had not caused me to swell with bitterness. The Lord had heard my prayer. With His help, I could do this. I could forgive.

I entered the Relief Society room where the gospel doctrine class was taught. A couple in their midthirties sat next to me. The woman leaned over and said something to the effect that I should ask that pretty Grice lady out, that she'd heard that Wyanne wished I would.

I felt my face flush. I was attracted to her. I had to admit that, but there was no way I could ever ask her—or any other woman—on a date. When I didn't reply, the lady gave me a strange look and said nothing more.

At least she didn't say anything else to *me*, but I heard her whisper to her husband that someone should set me up with Sister Grice. I suppose she didn't think I'd heard, but I had. And I prayed that it would not happen. If my sister hadn't set me up with Abbie, that sweet girl would still be alive. I know, long ago I was persuaded that her death wasn't my fault, but I still couldn't shake the feeling that if someone forced me to go out with Sister Grice, something bad would happen to her.

I was relieved when class began and my attention was drawn to the lesson.

Two

"Saxson, there's been a fatal accident. The investigating officer asked me to come to the scene as he was certain we'd be prosecuting the driver for auto homicide. But I can't make it over there. You're close. The accident is just outside of Duchesne," my boss, Duchesne County attorney Dave Padrick said. "I'd like you to go in my place. Just observe the scene, but get a good picture in your mind. I'll need for you to fill me in later."

I would rather not have been asked to do it, for I didn't relish the idea of seeing a terrible accident scene. I knew it would bring back old and haunting memories. But I did as Dave asked, and ten minutes later I parked my red Ford F250 pickup truck and approached the twisted wreckage. A light snow was falling, and it was very chilly.

Corporal Bardett Kingston of the Utah Highway Patrol spotted me when I drew near to a mangled yellow vehicle. "The EMTs are still trying to get the victim out of the car," he said. "I think she died instantly. The driver was thrown out, and he's not badly injured. He reeks of alcohol. I wanted you guys to get a feel for how bad this is. Dave told me he'd send you. Thanks for coming."

"Yeah, it looks pretty bad," I said, my voice husky. *I knew what a drunk driver could do.*

"The fatality is a girl from Duchesne. She's only seventeen. You may know her."

"I hope not," I said earnestly.

"She was a spectacularly beautiful girl before her date, Jarrod Miano, rolled his flashy yellow Corvette on this curve," he said bitterly.

The curve where we were now standing was just a few miles east of Duchesne. The snow was picking up. I knew that early March storms could be terrible. This one was showing signs of being just that. I shivered.

"I don't recognize the name of the driver," I said.

"He's not from Duchesne," Kingston responded. "This is one of those rare cases where someone was saved because of not wearing a seat belt. He wouldn't have survived if he hadn't been thrown from the car. The ambulance left about ten minutes ago. They're taking him to the hospital in Roosevelt. I asked them to have blood drawn to determine his alcohol level. I think he was pretty loaded. That might have also been part of what saved him from serious injury."

"The girl," I said, gesturing to where the EMTs were busy with the Jaws of Life, trying to get the body out of the wreckage of the yellow Corvette. "What's her name?"

"I haven't actually seen her up close yet, but a couple of kids who stopped said that the driver, Jarrod Miano, had taken an Angelica Keen out this evening," Corporal Kingston said.

That name hit me like a raging bull. "Angelica," I muttered hoarsely.

"Beautiful girl," he said. "So you do know her?"

All I did was nod. I could see my little sister in her casket. I fought back the urge to scream out.

Apparently Kingston also knew the victim—at least he knew who she was and had seen her on many occasions. He shook his head. "She was a senior at Duchesne High School. She was not just a beautiful girl, but a bright and good one. Why she had ever agreed to a date with a rich young man who, I am told, has less than a stellar reputation is anyone's guess."

I heard an anguished scream, and as the officer and I turned, he said with a sigh, "Oh no. It looks like her parents are here. I wish her body wasn't still in the car. Mrs. Keen will probably fall to pieces."

He was right about that. Angelica's mother became so distraught when she saw the EMTs working to remove the bloody, mangled body that Corporal Kingston tried to get her husband to take her away from the scene. He refused to leave but agreed to let one of the officers take his wife to the hospital in Roosevelt to see if she could be given a sedative.

"I'll go get Nayla after they get my daughter out of that horrible car," Shelby Keen, Angelica's father, promised. Then he turned his full attention to the work at the Corvette, his face filled with anguish.

A couple of minutes later, however, he approached Corporal Kingston and me. "He was drunk," he said, angrily pointing a finger at the wrecked car. "Angelica texted us three times. She had demanded that the Miano kid take her home. She said he was angry at her, but he was headed in that direction. Her last text was the most frightening one."

"What did she say in that one?" the highway patrol officer asked.

"She said he was driving really fast, that it was starting to snow, and that he refused to slow down. I want nothing more than to get my hands on him."

"You won't touch my little brother." We all turned to see the new-comer who had spoken. "Jarrod doesn't drink, and he doesn't speed. He loved that Corvette and would never risk damaging it."

Corporal Kingston turned to the man. "Who are you?" he asked.

"I'm Jarrod's brother Micah," he said with an angry growl. Then he squared himself off at Shelby Keen. "And you better quit telling lies about my brother, or so help me I'll tear you apart with my own hands."

Shelby drew back a fist, but before he could plant it in the man's face, Corporal Kingston stopped him. "I'll make sure he is brought to justice, Mr. Keen," he said firmly. "I'll need copies of those texts. In fact, I'll try to find her cell phone in the wreckage. It will be good evidence."

"That kid needs to be in jail. Make sure you arrest him tonight," Mr. Keen snapped.

"You better *all* quit accusing my brother of anything," Micah said, his face flushed and his fists bunched. "That slut he was with must have caused the wreck. I'm sure she did something to Jarrod that made him lose control."

The officer had to literally wrestle Shelby Keen back this time. "I'll—" Keen began, but Kingston managed to get him to say nothing further and turned him away from Miano.

"I think you should leave," I told Micah.

"Who are you?" he demanded.

"Saxson Cartwright," I said.

"What business do you have here?" he demanded.

"I'm here to assist in the investigation. I'll make sure it's thorough," I told him without revealing that I was with the county attorney's office.

"Well, you guys aren't going to pin anything on Jarrod. Our parents are rich," Micah said. "They'll get him the best attorney money can buy if anyone tries to arrest him."

"Where are you folks from?" I asked Micah.

"We're from San Diego, but we live in Vernal now."

"How long have you lived in Utah?"

"Less than a year, but we still have our place in California. My parents are loaded. Believe me. They'll get Jarrod off of whatever you jerks charge him with."

Once again, I told him to leave, and he finally did. I was relieved because I wasn't sure how much more of his mouth I could take without punching him.

Angelica's lifeless body was finally removed from the wreckage and was taken away in a hearse. Shortly after, Corporal Kingston formally introduced me to Shelby Keen, informing him that I was a prosecutor. "You better make sure this kid goes to prison," he said, shaking a thick finger in my direction. "I know the Mianos have lots of money, and they'll hire the most ruthless attorney they can find. I expect you to make sure this kid pays for what he did. You have no idea how it feels."

"Actually, I do," I said to him as he withdrew his finger from in front of my face. I briefly told him about my sister and our best friends, and then I said, "If I have anything to do with it, Jarrod will go to prison for a very long time."

"He better," he said. Then for a moment, his eyes looked beyond me. When he finally focused on me again, the anger had been replaced with intense sadness. "Nayla and I really weren't happy when Angelica told us she was going out with him, but you know how teenagers are. She had stars in her eyes when he asked her out." Mr. Keen paused. "I don't care how much money they have, he belongs in prison."

"Don't worry. I'll build a solid case against him," Kingston promised.

"I'm counting on it," Keen said. "I better go take care of my wife. This could kill her, you know. She's a tender woman. She . . . we . . . loved our daughter." As the grieving father turned toward his pickup, I could see his broad shoulders shaking.

"I'll get this guy," Kingston softly promised to no one in particular and then turned back to me. "Thanks for coming out, Saxson. Now that the girl's body is gone, I have a lot to do."

I didn't leave right away, and when a man with long black hair beneath a red ball cap showed up, I was glad I hadn't. I watched him approach Corporal Kingston. They talked for a couple of minutes, and then Kingston signaled for me to join them. "This is Darrius Chaudry," he said, indicating the stocky man in his midthirties. "He says he saw the accident."

It turned out that Chaudry was more than willing to testify that the yellow Corvette was driving recklessly, passing him at a yellow line at an extremely high rate of speed. That's when Jarrod lost control and rolled the car. Darrius had stopped, along with a couple of other cars. He was the one who'd called 911. He'd been watching from his car since the officers and EMTs had shown up, and finally, as the crowd at the accident thinned, he came forward to tell his story. "This kid was bound to crash," he concluded after explaining to me what he'd seen. "I'll be glad to testify if I'm needed in court."

I stayed a few more minutes after watching Mr. Chaudry drive off. Then I finally drove home in what had become a blinding spring snowstorm. I got very little sleep that night. All the horrors of that terrible accident nine years ago had returned. I grieved like Kara's death was fresh. And I grieved for Angelica Keen. If I had anything to do with it, Jarrod Miano would face justice in a way the man who killed Kara, Abbie, and Ollie had not.

Three

I CAN COUNT AS WELL as the next guy. So when the jury filed into the courtroom, it was pretty clear that a juror was missing. A few days before, we had seated eight jurors and two alternates for the automobile homicide trial we expected to last four or five days at the most. Two days into the trial, one of the jurors was injured in a traffic accident and had to be excused. One of the alternates took her place. That's why we had alternates. No worries. We were still good to go.

The following Monday, the second alternate was hospitalized with appendicitis. That left us with the required eight jurors. We could not afford to lose another one. I counted again. Seven. That's not enough. Now I was worried. The vacant chair was where juror number six should have been seated. The judge called the bailiff forward and inquired regarding the missing juror. The officer had no idea why there were only seven present.

This far into the trial I could easily picture each juror. A man in his early seventies, a retired car salesman, was the missing juror. He was one of the ones I was counting on to go my way and bring the others with him. He had seemed both interested and sympathetic to my witnesses and had a look about him that told me he was a leader.

The judge, the Honorable Cooper Feldman, was shaking his head. "I don't want to declare a mistrial," he said, frowning at the bailiff as though it was the young deputy sheriff's fault that the juror was missing. The bailiff raised both hands, palms up, clearly repeating what he had just told the judge. He had no idea where the man was.

I jumped to my feet. "Your honor, the prosecution requests a recess of a day while the sheriff's department locates the missing juror."

The defense attorney, Malcom Glazebrook, was also on his feet. True to what the defendant's brother had said at the accident scene six months ago, Jarrod Miano's parents had found a high-priced, sleazy, but very experienced attorney. Glazebrook's eyes met mine briefly, and I swear I could see dollar signs in his pupils. "I demand a mistrial, Your Honor," he said in his normal commanding manner.

Frankly, I didn't like the guy. As a prominent Salt Lake attorney, he seemed to have the attitude that he could run right over the top of us small county lawyers. He'd certainly shown that attitude throughout the trial. He'd done everything he could to discredit my witnesses and to discredit me personally. It had not been an enjoyable trial, though I felt strongly that we were winning despite Glazebrook's efforts to destroy my case. I was determined not to let Angelica's killer go free like my sister's killer had.

I don't know how much Mr. Glazebrook was charging his client, but I had a feeling that it was a lot. A mistrial would mean we'd have to start the whole process over and Mr. Glazebrook could rake in even more money from the defendant's family. Little wonder he wanted a mistrial.

Judge Feldman looked over the top of his glasses at me for a moment and then at Glazebrook. His face was expressionless. I was thinking he meant what he said about his desire to keep this trial on track. "Mr. Glazebrook," he said after a short hesitation, his deep voice seeming out of place in a man who was only five-foot-five and couldn't possibly be an ounce over 140 pounds. He paused, and Glazebrook glared at him as if daring him to rule in my favor. "We will be in recess until Monday morning."

"You can't do that, your honor!" Glazebrook thundered. "My client is entitled to a speedy trial. Monday is four days away."

The judge sat back, pushed his glasses up on his nose, and said, "Mr. Glazebrook, a delay of a few days will get this matter resolved a lot faster than a mistrial. It could take weeks to get this case scheduled again. I'll see you all Monday morning at eight sharp." Judge Feldman looked at the bailiff, ignoring Glazebrook's glare. "Tell the sheriff to find juror number six and have him in court on Monday."

I sat back down, but Glazebrook wasn't through yet—he had more to say. "I think tomorrow morning would be enough time to allow the officers to find him," he said. "And if they don't, I demand a mistrial." His glare grew fiercer as he stood at his full six feet four inches. He was a commanding figure with piercing, dark blue eyes and coal black hair. Frankly, I think his hair was dyed black, but I supposed his eyes were their natural color. His long moustache was also black, but it could have been dyed too. I shook my head. The vanity some people had. The man was in his midsixties and was undoubtedly going gray.

Judge Feldman might be a small man, junior to Glazebrook by a good ten years, but he was not intimidated by the glowering defense attorney who was rubbing his moustache like it was a magic bottle. No genie jumped out to aid him—there was no magic in that pampered moustache. The judge rapped his gavel and stood. He'd already called the court adjourned for the day, and he didn't bother to say it again. He gathered his robe as he turned from his chair and moved off the bench.

Glazebrook angrily shook his finger in the direction Judge Feldman had disappeared, and I thought it was a good thing Judge Feldman didn't see him or he might have been held in contempt of court. I would have enjoyed seeing that. I think the case officer, Corporal Bardett Kingston, was thinking the same thing. We sat down, and he leaned over to me. "That guy's a real peach, isn't he?"

I couldn't help but chuckle. "He thinks us country boys don't know a doggone thing. We'll find the juror, and we'll convict this guy. You've done a good job putting this case together, so unless I mess up, we have a great case. Miano's family's money won't get him out of this one."

"Thank you, Saxson," he said. "I think I'll go see if I can help the deputies find the missing juror. He probably just slept in or is a bit under the weather. He is an older fellow, you know."

"Do you know where he lives?" I asked.

He shook his head. "No, but I can find out. He's from Roosevelt. He's a retired car salesman and moved into the county with his wife a couple of years ago. We'll find him."

Suddenly the defense attorney loomed above me, and Kingston slipped away.

"You got lucky on that one, cowboy," Glazebrook said. "But you don't have a chance of beating me. Make me a reasonable offer, and maybe we can settle this case." That was interesting. A settlement would mean he'd get less from his client. I think he was just egging me on for the pure fun of it.

"Not a chance. They'll find the juror, and you can get on with your defense on Monday," I said as I got to my feet, sliding my chair back. I stood four inches shorter that Glazebrook's six foot four, and he outweighed me by a good twenty pounds, but he did not intimidate me. I'd ridden bucking horses and bulls that were a lot scarier than him. I smirked at him and couldn't help but notice how he bunched his right fist.

"*If* you find him," he said, glowering down at me. He stood a moment that way before easing a grin onto his face. "You got no chance, buckaroo." Then, without another word, he turned and started toward the door. But he stopped and stepped back beside me. "I've never lost a case to an attorney who wears boots and Western-cut suits. You are getting seriously out lawyered on this case." He shook his head and snorted like an old bull. He still wasn't through berating me. "You'll want to go back to punching cows by the time I'm through with you, Cartwright."

He started away again. My face was burning, and I had a half dozen retorts I could have thrown at him—one of which was that I was quite certain I was beating him—but I didn't bother. He was only trying to intimidate me. I might have inherited a TV cowboy surname and been raised on a cattle ranch in Wyoming, but I was a good lawyer. I'd save my energy to beat him in court when we resumed on Monday. I watched him go through the door at the back of the courtroom.

I had to win this case. There was no doubt in my mind that his client was guilty of automobile homicide. And young Angelica Keen deserved justice, as did her family. The evidence against Glazebrook's client was rock solid. Corporal Kingston and the officers who assisted him had done an excellent job. Our witnesses had proven to be unshakable in their testimonies despite the badgering they'd received from Glazebrook. One of them, Darrius Chaudry, hadn't even flinched when Glazebrook tried to browbeat him during cross-examination. The evidence I had presented was compelling.

Prior to trial, I had spent many hours on the case as I assisted my boss, Dave Padrick, the Duchesne County attorney, prepare. Little did either of us know that he would not be able to try the case himself due to a sudden heart attack and subsequent open-heart surgery. I had, at his direction, attempted to have the trial delayed, but the judge was adamant that we would proceed. So it became my case by default. The other attorneys in the office had more experience than I did, but they hadn't been involved in this case the way I had, beginning with my presence at the accident scene. They were ready and more than willing to give me advice, but they were tied up with the office's heavy caseload. The outcome of this case was in my hands.

I was a graduate of the J. Reuben Clark Law School at Brigham Young University in Provo. At age twenty-six I still didn't have a lot of trial experience, but I was confident that I was competent to try this case, and so far I felt like I was doing very well. I gathered my papers and put them in my briefcase.

Corporal Kingston had enough experience to make up for my lack of it. He was in his early thirties and had a spotless reputation as an accident investigator. He had more than ten years of experience with the Utah Highway Patrol. We got along well. I'd tried a couple of other cases, minor ones, that he had initiated. We'd won every single one of them.

Back in my office, I took a few minutes to look over my case notes—not that I needed to. I'd gone over everything so many times I could almost recite the facts verbatim. We had a blood alcohol test that was more than double the presumptive level. It had been admitted into evidence, and the jury had heard testimony how and when his blood was drawn and about the calculation made at the lab that established the level. Texts that were sent to her parents by the victim, young Angelica Keen, and ones sent back to her by her mother shortly before her death were solid evidence that the defendant was both drinking alcohol and speeding excessively. Those text messages had also been admitted into evidence, infuriating Mr. Glazebrook.

The speed at the time of the accident had been calculated by an accident investigation expert at a little over 100 miles per hour, and that fact, over defense counsel's objection, had also been admitted into evidence. Darrius Chaudry had testified that he witnessed the accident, that the Corvette had passed him at a solid yellow line at an exceedingly high rate of speed and then missed a curve and rolled several times. He had given his statement to both Corporal Kingston and me right there at the scene. We also had a witness that had testified to selling Jarrod beer at a store in Vernal, and she had watched him put the beer in his car. Still another witness had seen him throw a beer can from the car window as he was leaving Roosevelt and driving toward Duchesne just a few minutes before the crash.

I had submitted evidence that the young female victim had not been drinking, that she was an intelligent, law-abiding girl. I was even able to get evidence admitted about the defendant's character, *or lack thereof.* I went over a few more items from the file, including what the defense counsel had told the jury he would present. He'd been scheduled to begin his defense today as soon as I finished presenting the last of my case, but of course that didn't happen. I couldn't see anything Glazebrook had that would hurt my case, including any surprises that he might spring on me, although I knew I couldn't rule that out. If he did throw something at me, I'd just have to deal with it when he did it.

After putting the file down, I called my boss's cell phone. I spoke to Dave Padrick every day after court. He was recuperating from his open-heart surgery at home but wanted to be kept in the loop. "I would have thought you'd be in court right now," Dave said as soon as I'd identified myself. "I hope you're not calling with bad news."

"Just a delay, I think," I said. "We were short a juror this morning, and as you know, we are out of alternates."

"Did Judge Feldman give you a continuance?" Dave asked.

"I have until Monday. Corporal Kingston and some deputies are looking for him. The missing juror is an older gentleman but a very attentive juror. I'm sure there's a good reason for his absence today," I said.

"I hope you're right. Are you holding up okay against Glazebrook?" he asked. "I would imagine he would have asked for a mistrial today."

"He did, and after the judge left the bench, Glazebrook tried to intimidate me. It's not going to work." I chuckled. "I guess he has a thing against guys who wear boots to court."

"I don't doubt that you can handle him. Keep me posted, Saxson," he said, and the call was terminated.

An hour later, I got a call from Corporal Kingston. "We haven't found Mr. Morberg yet. His wife said he left home last night shortly after coming home from court yesterday. She said he told her he had some kind of an emergency involving his former business partner, a Mr. Graham Pease. She didn't know what it was, but he'd assured her he'd be back in time to go to court. She has no idea where he is. She's tried calling his cell phone. She even called Mr. Pease in Salt Lake. He claimed he hadn't heard from Mr. Morberg, that there was no emergency. As you can imagine, she's pretty worried."

"Is there any chance he was in an accident?" I asked.

"There haven't been any wrecks anywhere in the county today," the corporal told me. "I checked and didn't find any that involved him between here and Salt Lake or even anywhere on the Wasatch Front. "His wife tried calling his cell phone again at my request, but it went to voice mail. We've got everyone in the state looking for his car. So far, we haven't heard a thing."

My stomach stirred uneasily. I could still visualize the sly look on Malcom Glazebrook's face when he had said, "*If you find him,*" to me in the courtroom. I had a dark thought, but I pushed it aside. Glazebrook might be a shady lawyer, but surely there was no way he'd chance losing his law license or worse by causing a juror to miss court. And what would that accomplish anyway? There would simply be a retrial, an expense to the county, an inconvenience to my witnesses, and a lot of extra work, but it wouldn't affect my case. Glazebrook should know that.

"Call me, Bardett, if you learn anything. I don't care what time it is," I said as I attempted to tamp back my worry.

***

I left the office at five, having heard nothing more from the highway patrolman or the sheriff's office. I went to my apartment and wondered what to do about dinner. My nerves were on edge. The mystery of the missing juror was worrying me more than I cared to admit. It just didn't feel right. No phone call from him to my office, the court, or his wife just wasn't normal behavior for an honest juror. I looked in my relatively bare cupboards. Nothing looked good to me. I looked in the refrigerator with the same dreary result. I finally decided to go eat at Cowan's Café.

I had ordered and was waiting for my salad to arrive when my phone rang. I looked at the screen and saw that the call was from Corporal Kingston. "Bardett," I said, "I hope you have some good news for me."

"Sorry," he said. "I'm afraid I don't. Our missing juror's car was just found in the parking lot of Day's Market in Heber. The keys are in the ignition. The doors are unlocked. The officers who found it waited around for an hour to see if Mr. Morberg would return. They checked in the store and even had him paged. They checked all the businesses in the surrounding area. They finally impounded the vehicle and are conducting an inventory of the car now."

"You don't know what they found in the car, then?" I asked.

"Not yet, but the troopers that impounded the car promised to call if they find anything of interest."

"Thanks. Let me know what you learn," I said.

I was just finishing a slice of pie when Corporal Kingston called again. "They found his wallet in the car. There was no money and no credit cards in the wallet. His driver license, Medicare card, and some other cards were there," he reported.

"Somebody robbed him?" I asked. "Is that what you're suspecting?"

"Someone definitely took everything of value from his wallet. We don't know what else may have been taken from his car. The question now is what did they do with Mr. Morberg?"

"What about his cell phone?" I asked.

"Oh, yeah, that was in the car," Bardett answered. "It's got over two dozen missed calls from his wife and several from sheriff's deputies and myself. We've got an all-points bulletin out on Mr. Morberg. I'll call if I learn anything else."

I sighed, looked at the ceiling and then back at my half-eaten pie. It had tasted really good a minute ago, but I couldn't finish it now. My appetite had just fled the scene. This wasn't looking good, not good at all. I called my boss and gave him the bad news. I still couldn't take another bite of the pie, so I boxed what was left of it, paid for my meal, and went home.

***

I didn't hear anything more until late the following afternoon. When I did, it was devastating news. Our lost juror had been found in a remote area of Duchesne County—with a bullet in his head.

Four

It was Detective Sheldon Shelburn from the Duchesne County Sheriff's Department who had called me. He asked me to come out to the scene since it was clearly going to be a murder investigation—no one would shoot himself in the *back* of the head—and because the victim had been on my jury. And even if our late juror was physically able to pull that trigger, the gun would be right there with the body and there would be a vehicle nearby. His, we already knew, was in Heber City. Detective Shelburn had assured me that there was no gun anywhere in the area and no abandoned vehicles.

"Where are you?" I asked him.

"I'm still at the crime scene," the detective said. "The mortuary is sending someone out, but I don't want the body moved until we get the scene processed."

"And where exactly is the scene?"

"Oh, sorry, I guess you do need to know that. It's northeast of Duchesne at a place out on Blue Bench that some of the old-timers call Little Egypt. It's about ten miles from town." He gave me directions and then concluded with, "You'll see our vehicles parked alongside the old road. The body is just a little way through a bunch of juniper trees south of the road."

"I'll be out there in a little while," I promised. Before I left I called my boss and explained what was happening.

"This guarantees a mistrial," he moaned. "And it adds a murder case to our workload. Would you mind going out there and taking a look at the scene? Make sure it is who the officers think it is? Didn't you say last night that they found his wallet with his driver's license in his car?"

"That's right," I said.

"I wish I could go with you, Saxson, but there's no way right now.
I can't even leave the house yet except to walk around the block—with
my wife holding my arm."

"I'm glad to go," I said, not mentioning that I had already promised
Shelburn that I would. "Detective Shelburn says the reason they believe
it is him is because of what he was wearing. He is dressed as his wife
described from when he left to meet someone in the Salt Lake area."

"I'm sure he's right, but I'd like you to look at the guy's face and
make certain."

"I'll do that," I promised.

The road was a decent graveled road. After a few miles, I spotted the
top of a small hill that looked like a gigantic anthill. To someone with a
lively imagination, it might bear a faint resemblance to the pyramids of
Egypt. That had to be where the name Little Egypt came from. I came
to the end of the improved road and spotted a bunch of county sheriff
vehicles parked on both sides of the narrow road not too far beyond the
last oil well. I parked behind the last vehicle and got out.

Detective Shelburn met me as I walked through short but thick
sagebrush to where I could see officers. "Who in the world found the
body? This doesn't look like a place many people would be visiting," I
said as I looked around.

"That's for sure. Maybe an occasional rabbit hunter. There's traffic
going to and from the dozens of oil wells out here, mostly trucks
hauling crude oil and people maintaining the wells. But as you can
see, this is beyond the last well, and oil field workers would have no
reason to come here. I suppose the killer counted on that," Shelburn
answered. "What he didn't count on was an elementary school teacher.
She's a marathon runner and decided to come out here on a run as soon
as school was out. She had turned off the road and was jogging down
through the brush when she more or less stumbled over the body."

"Is she still here?" I asked, wondering who it was.

"Yes. She's pretty shook up. I have her sitting in my Expedition.
It's the third vehicle up there if you want to talk to her," he said as he
pointed to the unmarked gray Ford Expedition.

"I suppose you have taken a statement from her," I said.

"Yes," Detective Shelburn responded. "But I plan to interview her more thoroughly back at the office in the morning. She's quite traumatized right now."

"I would like to talk to her, but why don't you show me the victim's body first. The county attorney wants me to identify it if I can, since I knew him," I suggested. "It looks like the sun will be setting before too much longer."

It was a warm, beautiful, sunny afternoon. September was my favorite month. It was never as hot as the preceding weeks and yet was still warm enough to comfortably work outside or ride horses—or run. When I had time, it was riding that I preferred to do. I did run some, but not the marathon thing. In addition to my black gelding, I had a red roan mare. Both horses were boarded at a place called the Blue Rock Ranch just across the road from the jail/courthouse complex in Duchesne. I didn't get a lot of time to ride them, but I'd planned to ride the following day, Saturday. I hoped I still could. In fact, I might just ride out this way if I had time.

I followed Shelburn through the brush and into the grove of junipers. The ground was pretty much bare and sandy once we got into the trees. There were a lot of small rocks scattered about. The trees were thick in places and sparse in others. The ground fell away to the south in a gentle slope. I could see a canyon of some sort a short distance ahead. That would lead into Arcadia, I thought as I ran through what little I knew of the geography of this part of the county in my mind.

The body of the missing juror was only about two hundred yards from the road and almost directly in front of a fairly large juniper tree. The deputies had the area taped off. The body had a blanket over it. "We'll remove the blanket when the hearse gets here," Detective Shelburn said. "It was attracting a lot of flies."

"If you don't mind, I'd like to take a look," I said. "I'll know him when I see him."

"Sure thing," the detective responded. "Just watch where you step. We have found a few partial footprints, and we don't want to spoil them, although I've already taken pictures of them."

There was crime scene tape on the ground surrounding several areas where I assumed the tracks were located. I was careful where I walked.

I stopped a couple of steps from the body and waited while Detective Shelburn removed the blanket.

The body was lying face up. A bloody hole where the bullet had exited had removed most of his forehead, but despite that I didn't have any trouble recognizing the face. It was definitely Evan Morberg, the missing juror.

"I don't suppose you have any idea how long ago he was killed?" I asked.

Detective Shelburn looked at me. "The medical examiner should be about to tell us for sure, but I don't think he'd been dead long when the jogger discovered him."

"Why do you say that?" I asked.

"She stumbled when she saw him, and her hand touched the guy's arm. She thinks he was still warm, but she couldn't say for sure as she was so shocked."

"Poor lady," I said.

"Yeah, she was pretty shook up. She threw up over there," he said, pointing to the left. "She'll have nightmares about it for a long time, I'm sure."

"Okay, I've seen enough for now," I said with an uncomfortable stirring in my stomach. I looked around for a moment without moving from the spot where I stood. "Have you found any evidence besides the partial footprints?"

"Not much. And the footprints aren't great. Right around the body, where prints would have shown the best, the ground was smoothed over with a branch. There was also a cigarette butt a few feet from the body, but it looks old. I don't know if the victim smoked or not, but Wyanne doesn't. Maybe the killer did, but I'll be surprised if we learn anything from it since it isn't fresh."

Wyanne. I certainly knew who she was. "Is that the woman who found him?" I asked, trembling slightly, knowing I'd have to talk to her.

"Yeah, Wyanne Grice. Like I mentioned, she's an elementary school teacher. This is her second year. She's not from around here, and she is single." Detective Shelburn grinned. "Not too bad to look at, Counselor."

I already knew that, but I didn't respond. There were always plenty of people trying to set me up with single women. Frankly, even though I got lonesome at times, I wasn't even thinking about getting married.

I'd always had a hard time talking to girls and especially asking them out, so I just didn't. "I'll talk to her for a minute before I go back to town," I said. That I could do. In connection with work, I was okay talking to anyone, even to the woman who reminded me of Abbie. At least I hoped I could.

I spent the next several minutes talking to other officers. When the hearse arrived, I watched while the body was eventually bagged and carried from the scene. The hearse was parked directly behind my red F250 pickup. But what caught my eye wasn't the hearse or my truck. It was Wyanne Grice, the attractive young woman who'd been Angelica Keen's Laurel advisor. She had apparently left the officer's patrol car, for she was leaning against my front fender. I hadn't been aware that Detective Shelburn was walking right behind me until I stopped. He said over my shoulder, "What did I tell you, Counselor? She's nice looking, isn't she?"

"Yeah," I agreed as I studied her for a moment. Her long, dark blonde hair was pulled into a ponytail, which stuck through the back of a light blue ball cap. She was a short woman, maybe three or four inches over five feet. She was curvaceous but slender. I judged her to weigh about 125 pounds. Dressed in blue running shorts that came to just above her knees and a matching shirt, she looked really good. Even though I'd seen her many times in the hallways at the church and at Al's Foodtown, I had never done more than said a mumbled hi to her. At the moment, Wyanne was slightly hunched over and had her hands over her face. It made me feel bad for her. There was something about her that I'd been drawn to from the first time I'd seen her. And it was more than just the slight resemblance to Abbie.

I pulled my eyes from her and started moving toward my truck again. Wyanne looked toward me as I approached. There was a flicker of recognition but no pretty smile like she usually cast my way. She dropped her eyes. They were red from crying, and she looked quite pale. "Hi, you must be Wyanne Grice," I said as I stopped near her.

"Yes," she said without looking up.

"My name is Saxson Cartwright." I held my hand out to her, and she looked at it and then reached out with hers.

"I know who you are," she said. "I've seen you at church lots of times." Her hand was damp and soft, but her grip was firm. She looked at me with light blue eyes that were almost a perfect match for her hat and the sky beyond her. After pulling my hand back and while maintaining eye contact, I said, "I am a deputy county attorney. The man you found was serving as a juror on a case I'm prosecuting."

She nodded her head. "That's what Detective Shelburn told me. Jarrod Miano. He killed one of my Laurels." Her lips began to quiver, and she pulled her eyes from me. She rubbed at them with her fingers.

"I'm sorry you had to find him, Miss Grice," I said.

She sniffled and then mumbled, "Me too. I was having a decent run until I stumbled over his feet. They were sticking out from behind a tree. I've never seen anyone dead before."

"I know it's not pleasant," I said.

She looked back at me, and a minuscule smile tugged at the corners of her mouth revealing two deep and cute dimples. "You know what I mean, I'm sure. I've seen plenty of people at viewings, even my own mother and . . . and . . . Angelica Keen. But this is different."

She looked away again, but I had a hard time taking my eyes from her face. Wyanne wasn't model beautiful, but she was certainly attractive, and I found myself drawn to her in a way I'd never experienced before. I did finally turn my head and look back at where a group of deputies were talking a short distance away, and I tried to shake off the spell that the witness had cast on me.

Detective Shelburn caught my eye, and I'll be doggoned if he didn't wink. I felt my face turn warm, and I looked back at Wyanne. To my surprise, she was watching me. Her eyes shifted, and she lifted a bottle of water she'd been holding and took a sip. Then she put it in a fanny pack she wore around her slender waist. Before either of us spoke, Detective Shelburn joined us. "Miss Grice," he said. "I'm sure you won't want to head back to town now. The sun is going down, and it'll be dark soon."

"That's for sure," she said. She pushed herself away from my truck and then spoke again. "I'm going to have a hard time going on runs like this again, at least alone. I was having a great run until . . . you know."

"Yes, we know," the detective said. "And we certainly don't blame you one little bit. I would like to see you in my office at nine in the morning if you don't mind. I'll need to take a complete statement from you at that time. In the meantime, make a written note of anything that comes to your mind about what you saw out here."

"Okay, Detective, I'll do that, and I'll be there," she said.

"Now, since you are on foot, I'll bet the counselor here will give you a ride home. The other officers and I are going to be here a little longer, and I'm sure you don't want to wait here any longer than you already have," Detective Shelburn said. "Oh, and you don't have to worry about his wife getting jealous. *He doesn't have one.*" With that the officer flashed me a grin. "See you around, Saxson," he said and strode quickly back toward the other officers.

"Thanks, Sheldon," I said just a bit snidely to his retreating backside. I turned back to Wyanne. "Is that okay with you? You're more than welcome to ride back to town with me."

"Thanks, I appreciate it," she said. "Where's your car?"

I nodded and said, "Right behind you. I'm a country boy at heart, and I drive a truck."

She blushed. "Oh, I'm sorry. I've been leaning against it."

"You can lean there anytime you want to," I said and then realized how corny it was. "Here, I'll get the door for you." There was a reason I was still single. I didn't say the right things to women, especially young pretty women.

"Thanks," she said, and I got the full effect of those deep dimples. I was glad she could actually smile after what she'd been through.

I opened the door and offered her my hand. She took it and climbed gracefully in, and I shut the door. After I turned the truck around and started back toward Duchesne, she asked, "Who would want to kill a man like that? His poor wife. It breaks my heart for her."

I looked across the seat as Wyanne rubbed her eyes. "I believe he was a good man, and I also believe he was a good juror. I really needed him on the jury."

"So you'll have to finish the trial without him?" she asked.

"Without Evan Morberg, we can't finish the trial," I said. "We need eight jurors, and we're left with seven now."

"So what will you do?" she asked. "You can't let that guy get away with killing Angelica. That would destroy her family."

"I suppose that the judge will declare a mistrial on Monday and the new trial will be scheduled. That will be weeks or possibly even months away, and it will mean seating a whole new jury and starting the case over. It's a bit of a bummer because I had just about finished presenting my case. Frankly, that's what the defense attorney would like, I think."

I was finding Wyanne fairly easy to talk to. Maybe it was because I was thinking of her as a witness instead of the attractive woman I had been so uncomfortable with in the past. I spoke with witnesses all the time.

"Why is that?" she asked. "How would that help him defend that Miano guy?"

"There are two things. First, he knows what my witnesses will say and how they will say it since he's already heard them once. That means he can think about ways that he might be able to trip them up. The second reason is financial. He can charge his client more if we have to try the case again. It means more money in his pocket," I replied, glancing at her. "As you probably already know, the defendant is a spoiled and wealthy young man. His rich parents will pay whatever the defense attorney asks."

"Can they win the case?" she asked.

"Not unless I do a really bad job prosecuting it. Or if the delay somehow causes evidence to be lost or witnesses to disappear," I said. "We have a rock-solid case."

I told her a little more about the case against the defendant, and then I said, "Now, since you'll be a witness in a murder trial if they find the person who killed Mr. Morberg, I'd like you to tell me what happened this afternoon. Of course, this isn't your official statement. You'll be giving that to Detective Shelburn in the morning."

"I'm afraid there's not much to tell," she said. "I was just running like I do quite regularly. I mean I run a lot. I've run out here before and liked it. There is very little traffic, and for the most part, the road is pretty good. We get out early on Fridays, so I hurried home, put on my running clothes, and headed out. Now I wish I hadn't."

I looked over at her. "I can certainly understand that."

"Yes, it turns out it was a mistake. It's going to make it hard for me to go running anywhere that there aren't lots of people around. I keep thinking that whoever killed him might have killed me if I'd been there a little earlier."

"If you'd run up right when he was doing the deed, that could be. But he wouldn't have singled you out otherwise," I said and told her about the juror's car being found in Heber.

She looked across the truck's cab at me, a question in her eyes. "Do you think he was killed because he's on the jury?"

"I don't know what to think," I said. "The timing is very suspicious, but I don't see how killing a juror would benefit anyone. I suppose there could be a motive that has nothing to do with the trial. Detective Shelburn will look into that."

"So what you do know is that whoever shot him brought him out here in their car," she said.

"Had to have," I agreed.

"This is really creepy," she said with a frown.

"Miss Grice," I began in an effort to learn more about what she did and saw, "did you see any vehicles out here when you were jogging?"

"Detective Shelburn asked me that. I saw a couple of big trucks that looked like they were hauling oil," she said. "I also saw a few other vehicles, but I think most of them had to do with the oil wells . . . except for maybe one." She drew silent and scrunched her eyes.

I waited while she thought. I slowed down when a jackrabbit ran across the road in front of me.

After I sped up she spoke again. "It was a black SUV. The windows were tinted, and it was hard to see inside—although I wasn't trying to." She hesitated again.

"What direction was it going?"

"West, toward me. It was headed to the highway."

"Could you see the driver?" I asked.

"Yes, but I didn't really look at him. The front windows weren't tinted," she said. "So I could see inside a little."

"So it was a man?" I asked.

"I think so, but I'm not sure. I really didn't look closely at all. I didn't see anyone else in the vehicle. That didn't mean there weren't any in the back, but there was no passenger beside the driver. I'm pretty sure of that."

"Did the driver have a hat on?" I asked, attempting to prod her memory.

She scrunched her eyes. "Yes. It was a baseball hat, but I'm not sure what color it was."

"That's good. Did he wear glasses?"

"That I remember clearly. He was wearing dark glasses," she said without hesitation. "Quite large ones."

"Hair?" I asked.

"I'm sorry; I can't remember."

"About where were you at along this road when you saw the SUV?"

"I was only a couple of miles from the highway," she responded. She looked out the window. "Pretty close to where we are now."

"You say it was a black SUV. Could you tell what make it was?"

"I *think* it was black. It was a dark vehicle. I'm sure of that. It was a really nice one," was her answer. She was thoughtful for a moment. Finally, she said, "It might have been a Cadillac Escalade. It was definitely a luxury SUV."

"That's good to know," I said.

"Do you think the killer might have been driving that car?" she asked, a quaver in her voice.

"I suppose it's possible," I said. I thought for a moment, and then I asked another question. "Miss Grice, Detective Shelburn told me that you touched the body and that—"

She broke in before I had finished my question. "It wasn't on purpose," she said. "I tripped over his legs." She shuddered. "I fell right beside him, almost on top of him. I accidentally touched his arm when I was trying to get up."

She didn't add anything else, so I said, "The detective said that you thought the arm was warm."

She nodded. "Yeah, that's right. I thought dead bodies felt cold and stiff. His was neither."

"Meaning he hadn't been dead very long," I said.

I looked across at her and saw her shudder. Her arms were folded tightly across her chest. "I know this will sound crazy, but I thought maybe he was still alive—until I saw his head, and I knew he couldn't be. I got up and stumbled away. I got sick to my stomach," she said. "I even threw up."

"As would anyone," I told her.

We rode in silence for a while. I had left the gravel road and was southbound on the highway before Wyanne spoke again. "I can't believe this is happening. I probably saw the killer, didn't I?"

"It's possible," I had to agree.

"You said the Miano family is rich," she said quietly.

"Very," I agreed.

"So someone in his family might drive a Cadillac," she went on.

"I'm sure Detective Shelburn will look into that." I thought about what I had learned for a moment, and then I asked, "Wyanne, could you give me an estimate of the age of the guy driving the SUV? I know he had dark glasses and a ball cap, but could you make an educated guess?"

She was thoughtful for a moment. "I have no idea, honestly. It could have been an older person, or it could have been someone about your age. I just didn't pay close attention."

"You don't know how old I am," I said, trying to lighten the atmosphere.

"You're older than me, and I'm twenty-three." Those adorable dimples made a comeback. "I'd say you are probably about twenty-six."

"Not bad," I said with a grin. "I am exactly that." Then on an impulse that was totally out of character for me, I asked, "Are you hungry?"

"Yeah, I threw up, remember? But my stomach is pretty much settled now. Are you?"

I grinned at her. "I didn't throw up, but I haven't eaten since lunch. Maybe we could have something together," I suggested. I couldn't believe I was saying that. She must have cast some kind of spell on me.

"I'd like that," she said. "I don't think I want to be alone right now. But I would like to change clothes first. Do you mind?"

I didn't mind at all. It seemed that I had just arranged a date of sorts. I hadn't been on a date since . . . since Abbie. I shivered. I looked over at Wyanne.

She was grinning. "I've noticed that you're shy," she said.

She had me there, and I didn't mind at all. But my flaming face probably did. Wyanne Grice had just morphed from a witness into a beautiful woman that tied my tongue in knots.

Five

I PULLED UP IN FRONT of her apartment and forced myself to get out and open the door for her, the way a gentleman would. She stepped out and said, "Thanks. It won't take me long."

"I'll wait here," I said.

She smiled. "You don't need to do that. Why don't you come in?"

I started to stutter. I tried, but I was unable to say no. I felt awkward as I walked to the door with her. She inserted her key and opened the door, and I followed her inside. Her living room was neat and orderly, quite the opposite of mine. She invited me to sit down while she changed. She pointed to a beige love seat.

My mind went places that disturbed me while I was waiting. Wyanne might have seen the killer. In fact, she very likely did. That could put her in danger. The thought made me shudder. If the murder of juror number six had anything to do with my prosecution of Jarrod Miano, then it wasn't a big leap to think that whoever did it would not want to let a potential witness testify if the killer was caught—or even to keep the killer from getting caught. For that matter, even if the murder wasn't connected to my trial, the killer wouldn't want anyone to identify him. I wiped the sweat from my face.

When Wyanne came back into the living room, she looked amazing. She'd apparently done more than change her clothes. She'd let her hair down. It fell in soft curls clear to her shoulders. She must also have touched up her face. Wow! She was most definitely attractive. She had on some tight blue jeans and a pink shirt, Western cut no less. Her eyes were shining.

I stood up and should have said, "You look really nice," or something else complimentary. But that wasn't me. I don't think I'd ever told a girl that she looked good. Instead I said, "Ready?" *Lame.*

"I am," she said, and without any hesitation, she asked, "Saxson, are you all right?"

"Sure, why?"

"You look kind of pale. If you don't want to—"

"I'm fine. Let's go," I broke in. But she was right; I was feeling kind of shakey. I didn't want her to be in danger. I didn't know this girl very well, but she had affected me in a way no one but Abbie ever had before. I was scared for her. Honestly, I was scared *of* her—not like I might be scared of someone pulling a gun on me but *relationship* fear. Put me with a pretty woman in a strictly professional manner, and I'm fine. But with someone like Wyanne Grice outside of a professional atmosphere, I'm toast. I don't mean to be like I am; I just can't help it.

She looked at me kind of strangely for a moment, gave her head a tiny shake, but said nothing more. We went to Cowan's Café and sat at the corner booth on the west side. "I'm buying," I said after we were seated.

"You don't have to do that," she protested.

"I think I probably make more than you do," I said awkwardly.

"All right, you have a point," she said. "I'll let you."

Did that make this more of a date? What was wrong with me?

We talked while we waited. Mostly, she talked and I listened. My natural shyness was part of the reason, but my worry about her was eating at me something awful. Once our meals came and we settled in to eating, we didn't talk much, but I couldn't help but notice how she kept looking at me. I ran through my mind what she was seeing. I'd never thought of myself as a handsome guy, but I suppose I wasn't ugly either. I knew my blond hair wasn't messy because I kept it short, not much more than a butch cut. I was six feet tall and weighed 180 pounds. I was in great physical shape. My eyes were probably a close match to the blue of hers. My face was clean-shaven, showing the full effect of my square jaw.

She said nothing but put her fork down, watching me the entire time. When she spoke, it was evident to me that this teacher was not only pretty, she was also perceptive. "Saxson, I know I don't know you very well, but I can tell something is worrying you. Let me guess: you think that since I saw the likely killer and he saw me I might be in danger."

I tried to shake my head, but it turned into a nod. "I don't want to scare you, but I have had that thought."

She smiled. Her dimples were deep, but the smile did not touch her blue eyes. "I'll be okay. He doesn't know who I am," she said, but it was not spoken with conviction. "And how could he possibly know that I found the . . . the dead guy?" There was still no conviction in her tone. She picked up her fork again, and once more we both began to eat, but I had a feeling that she had lost her appetite, just like I had.

Later, when I walked her to her door, she again invited me in, but I declined with a stutter.

She didn't take no for an answer. "Please, Saxson. I'm sorry, but I could use company for a little longer."

That was all it took. My masculinity prevailed. I like feeling needed. I went in with her. We watched TV together while sitting on the love seat and ate some ice cream. We talked, her a lot, me not so much. She talked a lot about Angelica. She had clearly been very close to the girl. She also spoke of Angelica's parents, and what they must be feeling. By the time I finally left, it was after ten. And at the door, she made me blush when she said, "Saxson, thanks for staying. I'll be okay now." Then she reached up and kissed me on the cheek. That was a first for me. I might be twenty-six years old, but no one of the female persuasion, excluding my mother and a couple of aunts, had ever done that to me before. Despite my worry, I think my feet barely touched down as I walked to my truck. I looked back as I opened my door. She was standing at the window, smiling and waving. I waved back, my face flaming.

***

The next morning, I was up early. I spent a few hours doing my laundry, shopping for some groceries to fill my pathetic cupboards and refrigerator, and attempting to make my apartment presentable, if not really clean. I tried not to admit that my efforts, feeble though they were, were an attempt to make my place as much like Wyanne Grice's as possible. By the time I finished, I felt like things were in much better

38 CLAIR M. POULSON

shape on the home front. I had to admit that my apartment was still far from clean and orderly. It was, however, vastly improved.

When I had finally finished all that I felt like doing, I looked at my watch. It was ten thirty. I thought of Wyanne. By now, she should be well into, if not completed with, her interview with Detective Shelburn. The sun was shining brightly, there was no wind, and I felt the urge to saddle up one of my horses and take that ride I'd been thinking about.

I grabbed several bottles of water, made some sandwiches, dug a couple of apples from the refrigerator, and packed it all into a sturdy leather packsaddle. I put on my hat; pulled on my boots; and headed, saddlebags in hand, out to my pickup.

I was driving toward the small ranch where my horses were being stabled when my cell phone rang. I answered it as soon as I saw on the screen that it was Detective Shelburn calling. "Good morning, Detective," I said.

"Hello," he responded. "I have Wyanne Grice with me here in the office. Do you have a moment that you could come up and speak with us?"

"Sure, I can do that. I was just heading that direction to get one of my horses and go for a ride," I said as I wondered what was going on that required my attention. I felt slightly unsettled.

"Thanks. Just come into the office, and I'll fill you in on a problem that has come up," he said.

A problem? I was afraid of that. What could the problem be? I hoped everything was okay with Wyanne. I'd worried about her all morning. My worry, it turned out, was justified.

As soon as I walked into Sheldon's office, I could tell by the look in Wyanne's eyes and the lack of a smile that something was bothering her.

"Good morning," I said, trying to keep my voice light and nodding at Wyanne. "What can I do for you, Detective?"

"It's not for me; it's for Wyanne," Sheldon said. "She found a rather disturbing note taped to her door this morning."

I felt a knot form in my stomach. I caught her eye for a moment. She said nothing, but she didn't need to. I could see worry in those pretty blue eyes. I turned back to Detective Shelburn. "What did the note say?"

He held out a clear plastic evidence bag. There was a piece of paper inside with a few words written on it. I took it and, leaving the note inside, read it. Then I turned to Wyanne. "I'm sorry about this," I said.

"It's a threat, isn't it?" she asked, her voice quavering.

I looked at it again, and then I read it aloud. "Miss Grice, you didn't see anything or anyone. Don't forget that." I looked back up at her. "Yes, I would say it's a threat. Wouldn't you, Detective?"

"No question about it," Sheldon agreed.

"But it doesn't mention the murder yesterday," she said as she twisted her hands in her lap. "Maybe it's just a joke." There was no conviction in her voice, and she didn't smile at the thought.

I shook my head, handed the evidence bag back to Sheldon, and then said quite firmly, "Miss Grice, this is a threat. We all have to take it seriously. And frankly, I think it confirms what we already believed. The driver of the SUV killed Mr. Morberg."

She looked from me to the detective.

He nodded. "I agree with Saxson," he said.

She looked back at me. "That was what I was afraid of," she said. "I don't know what to do."

"What do you want to do?" I asked.

"I want to go to my apartment and pretend it never happened," she said. "But that's all I could do is pretend."

"I'll ask the sheriff to increase patrols around your apartment," Detective Shelburn said.

"That would make me feel better," Wyanne responded. "I guess that's all that can be done. I can't just quit my job and go into hiding somewhere. And anyway, I saw what I saw. An innocent man was murdered. I wouldn't want my fear to allow someone to get away with that. Nobody should get away with murder. Nobody!" She seemed adamant in her opinion. But I guess after what she'd seen the day before, that was not too surprising.

"We haven't caught anyone yet," Detective Shelburn reminded her. "But we do have some suspicions."

She nodded and looked at me. "It is someone who is either related to or a friend of Jarrod Miano."

"That's very likely," I agreed. "On the other hand, it could be totally unrelated to Mr. Morberg's service as a juror."

"That's right," Sheldon said. "I'll look into Mr. Morberg's personal life. Who knows? He may have enemies from something that has happened in his family or that happened before he moved to Roosevelt. He owned a small car dealership. Maybe he made enemies related to his business. The call he got to leave his house was reported by his wife as having something to do with the business he sold, or so she thinks."

Wyanne nodded and said, "I guess that's possible, but you guys don't really believe that, do you?"

The detective slumped. "You're right," he agreed. "But we'll figure it out, me and the other deputies who are assisting."

"So what do I do?" she asked.

I was watching her face as she spoke, and I again did something that was totally out of character. "Do you know how to ride a horse?" I asked.

"Of course I do," she said, showing those dimples for the first time since I'd entered Sheldon's office. "I grew up on a little farm. Why do you ask?"

"I was going to go for a ride today, and I wondered if you would like to, ah . . . to come, ah . . . with me."

"Now that's a great idea," Sheldon said with enthusiasm. "Why don't you two go relax today. My colleagues and I will work this case."

"I would like that, but there is one problem. I don't have a horse," she said. "My mother and I sold my horse when I went to college. She couldn't afford to feed it when I wasn't home and working."

The detective, who I think was fancying himself a matchmaker, jumped right in with, "I happen to know that the good attorney here has two of them and they aren't but a few hundred yards from where we are sitting right now."

Wyanne looked at me. "Was that what you had in mind?" she asked.

"Yes," I said as I felt my face get warm. "Would you, ah, like to do that?"

"I would," she said, and she grinned at me. "There is one condition, however."

"What would that be?" I asked, puzzled.

"Is the horse you want me to ride well broke? I don't want to get thrown."

"Yes, Miss Grice," I said. "She is very well trained."

She suddenly looked very sober. "I don't have a saddle," she said.

"Actually, that's not a problem. The guys who stable my horses have a tack room in their barn that has plenty of saddles. They've told me I can borrow any saddle I need at any time. So, ah . . . should we go?" I asked. Sheldon grinned at me. I smiled back. I could read the approval in his face.

"There is one more problem," Wyanne said, but she was smiling, so I wasn't too worried. I said nothing, just looked at her. She said, "I'm not dressed to ride."

"Do you have what you need at your, ah, your apartment?" I asked.

"Of course." She stood up, and Sheldon and I did the same. "Thanks, Detective. I'll be okay."

"We'll keep an eye on your apartment," he reaffirmed. He turned to me. "Where are you going to ride?"

"I was thinking about going out across the bench to Little Egypt. If it's okay with you and with Miss Grice," I said.

"It's okay with me. How about you, Wyanne?" he asked.

Her face was a little pale, and her recent smile was gone, but she swallowed hard then said, "As long as I'm with Saxson, it'll be okay. In fact, it might be therapeutic."

"Will you be armed?" Sheldon asked me. "I know you have a permit to carry concealed weapons."

"I'll be armed," I said. I turned back to Wyanne. "I'm a crack shot, in case you, ah, you wonder."

"Then let's go riding," she said as her smile returned.

Thirty minutes later, Miss Grice was wearing a pair of well used riding boots, old blue jeans, and a slightly faded blue Western shirt. A white felt hat sat atop her blonde head. She looked like a dream come true. Together, we approached my horses. At the sound of my voice, they both trotted over. I put a halter on Midnight and then offered the lead rope to Wyanne. She took it and held him while I caught Raspberry, my red roan mare.

As we led them to the barn to saddle them, she said, "You have really gentle horses, Saxson. And they are good looking."

If I was not so miserably shy, I might have said, "Just like the girl who's about to ride one of them." Of course, that wasn't possible for me, but the thought was there. I did say, "I think you'll like riding this mare. Raspberry's a really good horse." I patted the roan's nose as I spoke.

The very fact that I was here with this pretty girl and was about to spend several more hours alone with her would have made my mom and dad proud—or, more likely, driven them into a state of shock. I think they had long since given up on me when it came to the female gender. Not that this ride with Wyanne was anything more than just that, a ride. I doubted, even if we had a good day, that I would have the courage to ask her out again. But I was enjoying her company. I had no idea how she felt; although I honestly didn't think she saw me as anything more than a guy who was helping her through a tough time.

I began saddling my gelding. To my surprise she said, "I can saddle Raspberry, if you don't mind."

I pointed into the tack room and said, "Pick one out. You obviously know what you're doing." She grinned and stepped into the room. After we had saddled the horses and I was fastening my saddle bags behind my saddle, she said, "I guess we should take some water."

I patted the saddle bag. "I have several bottles in here and some sandwiches, cookies, and apples. There's enough for, ah, for both of us."

"Thanks, Saxson. You're a thoughtful guy. I think this is going to be fun."

I strapped my rifle scabbard to my saddle and slid in my loaded 30-30 rifle. My .38 caliber revolver was strapped to my side, and I had spare bullets in the saddle bags. I didn't anticipate any trouble, but I wasn't taking any chances.

In a few minutes, we rode up the road, past the small municipal airport, and then alongside the highway to the graveled road that would lead us to Little Egypt. We rode beside the road where the ground was softer so that the horses wouldn't have to walk on the gravel and so we wouldn't have to move for the oil trucks that frequented the road.

We didn't talk a lot, but we rode side by side. Miss Grice was clearly very much at home in a saddle. That made me feel good. It was silly because I barely knew her and would probably not have the courage to ask her out on a *real* date. And that being the case, I doubted I would see much of her in the future. But for now, for this day, I could try to ignore my shyness and enjoy the time I was spending with a woman that I was very much attracted to.

It was a gorgeous day. The sun was shining, there was no wind, and the temperature was just right. The horses were full of spirit but didn't give us any trouble, even though I could tell they would both have liked to open up and run hard for a while. They didn't know, though, that they had a long trip ahead of them. They'd be ready for a drink and hay by the time Wyanne and I got back to the small ranch that was their home.

There were a hundred questions I would like to have asked Wyanne—about her family, about her past, about her education, about herself—but I didn't have the nerve. However, after riding for three or four miles, she began to talk. She wasn't handicapped like I was—no shyness that I could perceive. Much the opposite, truth be told.

"Tell me where you grew up," she said. "You must have come from a farm or ranch of some kind."

I could answer her questions. Her asking them made it easier for me. "I was raised on a cattle ranch in Wyoming," I said.

"Wow! That's cool. My family had a small farm, but all we had were a few skinny cows, a couple of dogs, and some chickens. My dad had a job in town," she explained. "When I was in high school a neighbor gave me a horse. I had it until I went to college. Did you like being raised the way you were?"

"I did. I loved the ranch, the cattle, the horses, even the hard work."

"Why did you leave?" she asked, looking over at me and smiling. "Am I being too forward in asking that?"

"Not at all," I replied, wishing I could be so forward. "I still return to the ranch quite often. One of my younger brothers stayed and helps my father run the ranch now. And I think my youngest brother will stay on the ranch after his mission and college. But I was interested in the law. I wanted to be a prosecutor."

"And now you are one," she said. "And I'll bet you're good at it."

"I try," I said. I hoped I was good at it and that in time I would become much better.

"Was there a reason you wanted to prosecute?" she asked.

She must have been reading my mind, for there was a reason and I was thinking about it. "Yes," I said.

"Do you want to talk about it?" she asked. "I hope I'm not being too nosy."

"Of course not," I responded. I didn't admit she was making it easier for me to talk to her. I appreciated it, but there was no way I could tell her that. At the same time, however, talking about the tragedy that led me to where I was in life was hard because of the emotions it evoked. "There was a prosecutor that was a bumbling fool," I began. "He did such a sloppy job on a case I watched, one I was very, ah, interested in, that I swore I would be a prosecutor someday and I'd do my best to never let a man go free that had done what the man in that case had done."

She looked over at me. "What kind of case was it?"

Without looking at her, I said, "Auto homicide. Three counts."

"Oh my gosh, Saxson. The guy killed three people and got away with it? They must have been people you cared about."

"They were," I said.

We rode in silence for a couple minutes. Finally, Wyanne asked, "Can you tell who they were? Unless it's too hard."

I swallowed hard, and then with a grief-filled voice, I said, "It was my little sister, my best friend, and my sister's best friend."

"I'm so sorry, Saxson," she said as she reined her horse so close to mine that our knees were touching. With her that close it was hard for me to talk. Not that I didn't like her proximity, because I did, but I wasn't used to having someone who was so pretty so close to me.

When I didn't answer for a long minute, she said, "It's hard for you to talk about, isn't it? If you don't want to tell me any more about it, that's okay. I understand."

I didn't have the courage to tell her that it wasn't only the loss that was hard to talk about; her nearness made it difficult too. I nodded and she smiled. I guess it was her shining eyes and deep dimples that loosened my tongue at last. "They were killed by a drunk driver only a few minutes after I got out of the truck," I said. "And that stupid lawyer let him get away with it." That old anger came back even though I was trying so hard to forgive him. "That drunk driver killed Kara. She was sixteen. And Ollie was my age. He was like a brother to me. And Abbie . . ." I couldn't finish that thought.

"She was your friend too, wasn't she?" Wyanne asked.

I nodded. "I'd been on a date with her that night. She was the only girl I ever took on a date. My sister set it up. Anyway, that's where my desire to become a prosecutor began."

"And the man that did this is free because of a poor prosecutor?"

"That and a cop who didn't do his job very well either," I told her.

We rode in silence for several minutes again. Finally I felt the urge to tell her more. "My sister looked a lot like Angelica. She was beautiful and a really good girl. She liked my buddy as much as I did. And Abbie . . ." I cut myself off and looked straight ahead. "She was very pretty and as sweet as Kara. And she, ah, she had long . . ." I trailed off, and we rode in silence for a couple of minutes.

"The guy that did this to juror number six will be caught, and he will be tried," I finally said. "Only I hope we'll do a whole lot better job than the prosecutor did on the case against the guy that killed Kara and Ollie and Abbie. He got off, and it was because the prosecutor was lazy or stupid or something. I watched most of the trial, and when I could see what a bad job the guy was doing, I thought that someday I would have that job, and when I did, I would do better. I read quite a bit," I went on. "And I'd read a lot about both fictional and real trials. Even though I was only seventeen at the time, I felt like I knew a little bit about how it should be done. I know now that the prosecutor in that case did even a worse job than I thought at the time. He should have been disbarred."

Wyanne's horse had drifted away from mine, but she brought the mare close again. I was glad she did because I wouldn't have dared. I was really getting to like her, and with liking her, I could feel that old fear of girls pressing on me. Still she was making it a lot easier. That scored her huge points in my eyes. I just wished . . . I banished the thought and listened to the question she was asking.

"So from then on, you wanted to become a lawyer and put the bad guys in jail?"

"That's right. And I enjoy it."

We rode in silence for a while. From time to time, I'd glance at her, and many of those times she'd be looking at me. Wow! This was a new experience, and I was loving it. I just wished it would continue.

After maybe fifteen or twenty minutes, she again rode her horse close to mine and asked, "Were you happy growing up?"

"Yeah, I was. It was good. I have great parents, and I got along well with my siblings," I said.

"You mentioned two brothers," she said, "one on the ranch and one on a mission. And you told me about Kara. Are there others?"

"I have an older sister and a much younger one," I said. "We stay in touch. We're a close family. I think losing Kara did a lot to make us want to stay close."

We drifted apart again as we rode through a small patch of sagebrush. She didn't attempt to get close again after we were past the brush. She looked deep in thought, and suddenly she lifted a hand and brushed a tear from her eye.

"Are you okay, Miss Grice?" I asked, wishing I had the courage to call her by her first name. "We'll get this killer. I promise."

"It's not that," she said, and to my delight she rode close again. "I just wish I'd had close-knit family. My childhood was . . . not happy."

I was stunned. She seemed like such a happy, delightful person that I had assumed she'd grown up much like I had, especially after she mentioned her farm. I wanted to ask her about it, but I couldn't find the words.

She again made it easy on me. "My dad was mean—mostly to my mom but sometimes to my brother and me. We were poor. Dad didn't bring much money home. He drank up most of what he earned in the bars in town."

"I'm sorry," I said.

"Yeah, so am I. Anyway, Mom worked as a waitress, and we mostly lived on her income. When I was old enough, I worked at the same café Mom did. Actually, I wasn't old enough. I was only thirteen, but I worked when Mom did, and the owner let me. It helped when I had some money of my own. I gave most of it to Mom to buy groceries, but I did get something just for me sometimes, something inexpensive. I never let Dad touch what I earned. I had to hide it from him, or he would have taken it. I even had to hide my tithing jar. We had a garden, too, that my brother and I took care of. It wasn't great, but it helped keep us from starving. And we did occasionally sell a calf. But Dad usually took that money even though we took care of the farm without his help."

She grew silent, and I glanced at her. She was looking ahead, but I don't think she was focusing on anything. She finally looked over at me again, brushing a tear from her eye. "I used to get bullied at school because I wore clothes we bought from Deseret Industries. I think Denny, that's my big brother, was bullied too, but he never talked about it. DI clothes were all Mom could afford. But she kept us clean, and she always took us to church. And when she could, she'd have prayer with us. But Dad would get really mad if he caught us praying. So usually we would only do it if he wasn't home. Of course, she taught us to always have our personal prayers. I still do, but I'm not sure about my brother. Probably not."

She quit talking when a large oil truck roared by on the gravel road, throwing up a dust storm in its wake. After the dust had cleared, she continued. "My brother ran away from home when he was sixteen. Dad had come home drunk one night, and I guess my brother had taken all he was going to. He told Dad that if he couldn't come home sober that maybe he shouldn't come home at all. Dad told him that it was his house and that if Denny didn't like it, he was the one that didn't need to come home. They argued while Mom and I just hung on to each other. Finally Dad hit him, and then they fought. It was horrible. My brother was faster and stronger. He ended up knocking Dad out cold. They both had blood all over them. I still get a sick feeling when I think about it."

"I'm sorry," I said awkwardly.

Wyanne rubbed her eyes with the hand that wasn't holding her reins. "Thanks, Saxson. You're a great listener. I feel like I can talk to you and you won't judge me. I appreciate it."

"No problem," I said. "So your brother left?" I was curious now, and I wanted her to keep talking.

"Yes. He ran away that night. I haven't seen him since. I was fifteen then. He's a year older than me. I have no idea what happened to him after that. Mom did get a letter from him about a year after he left. He didn't tell her where he was, but he told her that he was okay, that she didn't need to worry about him. Of course, that didn't help," she said with a sad smile.

"My mother talked about leaving Dad after Denny left, but she didn't have to. He got arrested one night after he beat her so badly that I had to take her to the hospital. He assaulted one of the cops when they were arresting him, so he got charged with that too. And when he was in the jail in Richfield, he . . . he . . ." She couldn't go on.

I wanted to take her in my arms, but of course there was no way I could do that. So I just reached out and touched her elbow. She looked over at me, and for the next couple of minutes, she cried softly. Then finally, she gained control of her emotions. She wiped her eyes with the back of her hand and said, "You must think I'm a terrible boob."

I shook my head. I had no such thoughts, and I dug deep and finally found the courage to say, "No, I don't. I think you are a great person."

Her red-rimmed eyes grew wide. "Do you really mean that?"

"Yes, I do," I said, and she smiled at me.

"Thanks for listening," she said. "You're the only person I've ever talked to like this except for a roommate. She's my best friend."

Curiosity was getting the best of me. My shyness was overridden by my aggressiveness as a prosecutor and my interest in seeing justice done. "Do you want to finish telling me about your father?" I asked.

She nodded, pulled her horse close to mine again, and reached out to me. I shifted my reins to the left hand and allowed her to take hold of mine. I felt a jolt not unlike electricity run up my arms and through my whole body. I made no attempt to pull my hand from hers. I had never held a girl's hand before, not even Abbie's. It felt wonderful. It was also very frightening.

We rode that way for a minute or two before she said, "Dad beat a man up in jail. The guy died. Dad went to prison for life on the murder charge, so at least we didn't have to testify about what he did to Mom."

"Oh, Miss Grice," I said. "This whole thing must be really hard on you. I had no idea."

She nodded and squeezed my hand. "Thanks for understanding."

"Where is your mother now?" I asked.

"She died a year ago. The doctor said it was a heart attack. I think it was a broken heart."

"But she had you," I reminded her.

"Yes, she did, and I tried to make her proud."

"I'm sure you did," I said.

"I hope so. I'm just grateful that she lived long enough to see me realize my dream to become a teacher," she said.

"So you sold your horse when you went to college. Have you ridden at all since then?" I asked.

"My roommate, the one who is still by best friend, is from a ranch family—not a big ranch like the one your family owns but a nice one.

They have horses. She used to take me riding," she said. "That's why my boots are so scuffed. She and I rode quite a lot."

After a couple of minutes, she let go of my hand. I hoped that wasn't the last time she'd ever hold my hand.

Six

We talked more as we rode. Mostly she talked and I listened. She told me about a lot of things, mostly about college, her roommates, and her mother. But as we rode past the site of the last oil well, she mentioned her father again. "I suppose I can thank Dad for two things. First, it's because of him that I became a runner. I began running even before my brother left home. I would do it just to get away from the house. And I learned that I enjoyed it, and pretty soon I was running competitively in high school. The second thing I owe to him is my profession. I had such a scarred childhood that I wanted nothing more than to help other kids enjoy life. I figured teaching elementary school was a way to do that. And it is. I love it."

"I'm glad, and I'll bet your students love you, Miss Grice," I said.

"That's all I can ask for," she said. Then she grinned. "Miss Grice? Really? You keep calling me Miss Grice. That makes me sound like an old spinster schoolteacher."

"What do your kids at school call you?" I asked.

"Miss Grice, but you're not one of them," she said, again pulling her horse close to mine and punching me on the shoulder. "You are my, ah, my . . ." She didn't complete her sentence.

Despite my shyness, I wanted to know what she was thinking, and I stammered, "Your . . . your what?"

Her face turned a pretty shade of red. "My new, really good friend," she said. "Saxson, I really enjoy being with you."

I felt my face as it made an effort to match hers. "I, ah, I like being with you too," I managed to stammer.

She grinned, and those dimples were so deep I felt like I could drown in them. I'm afraid I was in a bad way. I really did care for this girl, this new *really good friend*, and I wasn't sure what to do about it. But there was one thing I could change; I could start thinking of her as Wyanne instead of Miss Grice. And maybe I could even call her Wyanne. It really was a pretty name.

She looked to the right then. "We are almost to where I found Mr. Morberg. Do you care if we ride over there? I had a nightmare about finding him last night. I worry that it'll get worse. I think it would help me to see the place without his body being there."

"Sure, if you want to, Wyanne," I said.

"I do," she answered without hesitation, and she turned her horse in that direction. "And thanks for using my first name." I followed as she wove between the trees. I couldn't take my eyes off her back. She was wearing her long, dark blonde hair loose. As she rode, her hair swayed gently back and forth beneath her cowgirl hat. She had beautiful hair, I decided. In fact, at this point, I couldn't think of anything about her that wasn't beautiful.

Except her scream!

Wyanne screamed so loudly that Raspberry leaped to the side and then bolted ahead. I spurred Midnight and quickly caught up. I thought for a moment Wyanne was going to tumble from the mare's back as we tore through the trees, but I was able to reach out and steady her. Then I let go of her and grabbed Raspberry's bridle, and we gradually slowed to a walk. We rode a little farther, and her horse calmed down. Finally, we both pulled our horses to a stop.

She looked at me, her eyes wide with what could only be terror.

"Wyanne, what is it?" I asked. "What happened?"

"Didn't you see it?" she asked as tears filled her eyes.

"See what?" I asked. "All I could see was Raspberry bolting. I was afraid you might fall off."

"I would have if you hadn't steadied me," she said. "You didn't see that man?"

I looked quickly around. "What man?" I asked as I grabbed my sidearm.

"The dead one," she said, pointing a trembling hand back the way we had just ridden.

I holstered my revolver. "I didn't see anyone."

"It's because you were busy trying to catch me. I'm sorry I spooked Raspberry."

"She's okay now, Wyanne. But I think we better go take a look back there."

She said, "Let's walk. I'll lead Raspberry."

She started to dismount, but before she could, I was on the ground and reaching for her. She slid off, and in one surprising move, she put her hands around me and tucked her head neatly into my chest. I slowly reacted by putting my arms around her. Raspberry's and Midnight's reins fell free, but I knew the horses wouldn't go anywhere—unless Wyanne screamed again, but I figured that was unlikely now. I'll admit that I was tempted to use the horses as an excuse to pull free of Wyanne, but something deep inside of me wouldn't let me do that. So for a couple of minutes, we held one another tightly.

I could feel the wild beating of her heart against my chest. And I wondered if she could feel mine, although mine was beating wildly for a much different reason than hers. My fear was not of a dead body but of what I was doing. Which was stupid. I shouldn't be afraid of holding a wonderful woman in my arms. It was the natural thing to do. But I was afraid. Despite that, I clung to her until she finally released her tight hold on me. And when she did, a new fear developed in me. I was afraid that I might never get to hold her that way again. Good grief, I was twenty-six years old. I needed to get over my shyness. Especially with Wyanne. There was nothing about her that I needed to fear.

We finally pulled totally apart, and she looked up at me. "Thank you, Saxson. You're so patient. I've never met a guy quite like you before."

No, I suppose she hadn't. I was not a normal guy, at least not when it came to romance. My heart was racing at her nearness. I was afraid of her. Or was I afraid that I was falling for her? And for a guy like me, that could be a disaster in the making. But I cleared my head and said, "We better go have a look at this, ah, man you saw."

"I know, but I'm scared. Will you hold me again for just a minute, then maybe we can go look?" Her fear-filled eyes bored into mine.

I guess the natural man beat out the normal Saxson Cartwright, because I took her in my arms, and for another couple of minutes, I held her. Finally she said, "Okay, I guess I'm ready now." At that point it was almost as hard for me to release her as it had been to take her in my arms in the first place. But I did, albeit reluctantly.

I led both horses with one hand and held her hand with the other. We walked back through the trees that Raspberry had charged through. As we emerged in the very same small clearing where Mr. Morberg had died, I saw what she had seen. She pulled in tight against me, but she did not scream again. We moved toward what was most definitely another dead man. He was on the ground, on his back within just a few feet of the place that she had stumbled over juror number six. But this man had no face left. The bullet that had entered the back of his head had blown his face away as it exited.

I stared dumbly at the corpse. Wyanne said, "I'm going to be sick," and pulled away from me. I let her walk away, and while she threw up in the sagebrush, I pulled out my cell phone and began to make a call.

When I reached Detective Shelburn, he asked, "How's the ride going, Counselor?" in a cheerful voice.

"It was going great," I said truthfully, "until Miss Grice began to scream and her horse bolted."

"Good grief. Is she okay?" he asked.

"She's physically all right, or at least I hope she will be as soon as she finishes throwing up."

"What's going on?" the detective asked suspiciously. "I take it something's wrong."

"You could say that. There's been another murder," I said. "There's another dead man in almost the exact spot where our missing juror was found."

There was silence on the other end of the line for a long moment, but I could hear the heavy breathing of the officer. Finally, Detective Shelburn said, "You wouldn't be pulling my leg, would you, Counselor?"

"I wish I was, Sheldon."

"There's a dead man there?" Sheldon asked. "A dead body?"

"I'm afraid so."

"Who is it?"

"I have no idea," I replied. "His face is missing. But it is a man, not a woman. I'm sure of that."

"Okay, keep the scene secure until I get there," he said, all business now. "I'll be right out, and I'll get some others on the move as well."

"Okay, I'll do that," I replied.

"Saxson, what about Miss Grice? Is she really going to be okay?"

"I hope so. We rode over here so that she could face her fears. She said she'd had a nightmare about finding the juror there yesterday. She thought it would be easier for her if she could view the spot without a body in it. I hope this doesn't make it worse. But I know this much—Miss Grice is a strong girl. She's been through a lot of trauma in her life. And I do mean a lot," I said.

"Take care of her, Saxson," he said. "She likes you; she trusts you."

He ended the call before I could make a bumbling reply. I glanced toward Wyanne. She was rubbing her mouth with the back of her hand. She looked up and saw me watching her. She shook her head sadly, and I led the horses toward her. She met me halfway.

"I'm sorry, Saxson," she said. "I'm such a sissy. It's good I'm a teacher and not a nurse. You must think I'm awful, the way I scream and throw up and all."

I didn't think that at all. And to my total amazement, I said something that I would have normally never dared say. "I think you're amazing," I said. And I opened my arms. She stepped into them, dropped her head against my chest, encircled my waist with her arms, and let out a gentle moan. Oh my, what was I letting myself in for? I thought as my heart again began to beat out of control.

A few minutes later, after we'd led the horses a short distance from the scene and I'd tied them to a couple of trees, we heard sirens approaching. "Sounds like the cavalry is on the way," I said.

She looked up at me, and in such a solemn tone that it made me chuckle, she said, "I thought *we* were the cavalry. We have horses and guns."

"That we do," I agreed.

"Could I try one of those bottles of water now?" she asked. "I think my stomach is finally settled."

She drank a little bit, and I asked as the sirens grew closer, "Can you eat anything?"

"Did you say you had apples?" she asked.

"I did." I retrieved them from my saddlebag. We sat on the ground near the horses, side by side, very close, and I didn't panic—not much anyway. We ate the apples and fed the cores to Raspberry and Midnight.

The cops arrived and went to work. After telling Detective Shelburn our story, I said, "We'll hang around for a while, but maybe not too close, if you don't mind." He nodded his approval, and I turned to Wyanne. "Would you like to walk for a few minutes?" I asked, waving my arm to the east.

"I'd like that, but what about Midnight and Raspberry?"

"They'll be fine right here," I assured her.

I suppose I should have been brave enough at this point to reach out and take her hand, but I was losing my courage already. Wyanne saved me from myself again. As soon as we were out of sight of the officers, she reached over and took my hand in hers. Neither of us let go as we walked for several minutes. We soon arrived at the edge of the hill overlooking Arcadia, a large agricultural area. "There are more of those pointed hills," she said as she swung her arm to the north. "So that's why this place is called Little Egypt?"

"I guess so," I said.

We strolled along the edge of the hill until we reached an old road that led down from the flat area where we stood, winding to the bottom some distance away. It was narrow and rutted but looked passable.

"I don't think I'd like to drive on that thing," Wyanne said.

As she spoke I noticed something. "Someone did," I said as I released her hand and knelt on the ground. "There are car tracks here. I think they're fairly fresh."

"I wonder . . ." she began and then stopped.

"If the killer went this way?" I asked.

"Yes," she said. She knelt beside me and studied the tracks. "Are there two sets here? Maybe the same vehicle drove up the hill and then left by driving back down."

"I see what you mean; there are two sets of tracks. I think you may be right," I said. "The tracks look to me like they were made by the same vehicle. We better go back and let Detective Shelburn know what we've found. Let's follow this old road back but maybe not walk on it. We don't want to ruin any tire tracks that he might be able to photograph."

We started back, and once again, Wyanne took my hand. It was beginning to feel quite natural. She looked over at me and said, a hopeful look in her eye, "Maybe I didn't see Mr. Morberg's killer. Maybe he drove this way yesterday and that was just someone who happened to be on the road that I saw."

I hated to burst the small bubble of hope she'd found, but I decided it was best to face the facts now rather than let it build only to be burst later. So I said, "I'm sorry, but I didn't see any other tracks, did you?"

Her face fell, and she looked away. "No, and there would have been if he'd come this way yesterday." She looked back at me, forced a smile, and said, "At least it was a thought."

I nodded, smiled at her, and said, "I don't know if these are from today or not, but I wish there were four sets of tracks instead of two."

She was thoughtful for a moment, and once again I saw hope shining in her eyes. "Okay, so maybe the tracks we found were from yesterday. Maybe I really didn't see the killer. Maybe whoever killed this guy came in on the main road."

"Maybe," I said, but not for a minute did I believe that.

She rubbed at her eyes with her free hand, and then she said quite firmly, "I need to face the facts, Saxson. I have been threatened. I did see the killer."

"I wish you hadn't," I told her.

She responded with a shrug and said, "As long as we're wishing, I wish I'd never come out here yesterday. Mostly I wish nobody had murdered those two men."

I didn't add any wishes. It wasn't doing either of us any good. We walked on and soon arrived back near the murder scene, and before we got too close, I called the detective's name. He walked over to where we were now standing, and I said, "We thought you might want to take a look at something, Sheldon. There's been a vehicle on this road. It went down the hill over there." I pointed to the west. "The road down to Arcadia is rather poor, narrow and rutted. I wouldn't think a person would try it without four-wheel drive."

"It went both up and down," Wyanne added. "But there are only the two sets of tracks, so it probably wasn't the guy from yesterday."

The detective nodded and cleared his throat. "Let me talk to the other officers for a minute, and then we'll see if we can get some good pictures."

He rejoined his colleagues, and he pointed in our direction as they talked. Then he came back to us. We walked a short distance together along the edge of the narrow, rutted road, and he was able to get some fairly good photos of the tracks we'd found. "It's quite a ways over to the edge of the hill, isn't it?" Sheldon asked.

"Yes, it is," I agreed.

"Let's drive over. We can keep to the side of the road, and then we'll walk down the hill," he suggested.

"Do you need us here still?" I asked.

He looked at me, then at Wyanne, and back at me again. "I guess not," he said. "You probably want to get started back to town with your horses."

"We would like to," I said, "but if there's anything else we can do before we go, just say so."

He took off his hat, ran a hand over his head, and then put it back on. "Maybe, if you don't mind, you two could ride your horses to the bottom of the hill and see which way the tracks go from there?"

"Are you up to it?" I asked Wyanne. "It'll add quite a bit of distance to our ride. I don't want you to be so sore you can't even move tomorrow."

"I'm fine. Let's do it," she said.

After we had finished our inspection at the bottom of the hill, I spent a few minutes with Detective Shelburn and his boss, the sheriff, who had just arrived.

"I think it's rather obvious that the same killer is responsible for both deaths," Shelburn said.

"I don't suppose you found any identification on the body?" I asked.

"None, but the medical examiner should be able to help us identify him—you know, dental records, fingerprints, and so on."

I had been thinking about the body, and an idea suddenly surfaced. I asked, "Is the body gone yet?"

"No, why?" Detective Shelburn asked.

"I'd like to see it again," I said. "I'm probably wrong, but I have an idea who it could be."

"By all means, Counselor. Let's go have a look."

By the time we got back to where the vehicles were parked, the body was on a gurney, but it had not yet been loaded into the hearse. I turned to Wyanne. "You don't have to look, but there's something I need to make sure of."

"I'll hold the horses and stay back here," she said. "I don't want to look at him again." She trembled slightly as she spoke. I was afraid a lot of nightmares were in her future.

The body was already in a body bag, but the mortician zipped it open at my request. "Is there something in particular that you're looking for?" Sheldon asked. "I mean, you know how the face looks. It's pretty much gone."

I was looking at what was left of it as he spoke. It was pretty bad. "It's not his face, but I did want to see his ears, at least his right one," I responded. I stooped down and quickly found what I was looking for. My heart began to race, not the kind of racing that Wyanne caused but a stressful, worried racing. "Would you take a close-up photo of this ear, the one with the ring in it?" I asked Sheldon.

He did, and then he stepped back. The dead man was wearing a long-sleeved shirt. What I was looking for was on the victim's right shoulder. I asked the mortician to work his sleeve up if he could. He worked for a minute with gloved hands. And then I again stooped close. There on his shoulder was a small tattoo. It was of a football with the words *state champions* beneath it. I stood back up and turned to the detective. What I had suspected was right on target, and I wasn't happy. "This is, or was, a man by the name of Darrius Chaudry. He witnessed the accident that killed Angelica Keen. He testified earlier this week in my trial."

"Are you sure it's him?" the detective asked.

"Oh yeah, I'm positive. The earring isn't distinctive, but Darrius wore one like this. The tattoo—that's the clincher," I said. "Chaudry was part of a high school championship football team several years ago. He showed me the tattoo and actually bragged about it. There is no doubt that this is him."

"Oh my." Detective Shelburn took a deep breath. "So both victims are tied to your automobile homicide trial."

"I'm afraid so," I said. "This isn't good."

"For the case against your auto homicide defendant it isn't, but it does narrow down our search for the killer. This has to be related to the wreck and the trial. You're going to have to have a mistrial, and you'll be short a key witness when it goes in front of a jury again," Sheldon said.

I shook my head. "This is a blow; that's for sure."

"Where is this victim from?" Sheldon asked.

"Somewhere in the Salt Lake area. I have his address as does Corporal Kingston of the highway patrol," I said. "I'll get it to you after I get back to town."

***

Wyanne and I were back on the horses and had been riding west for several minutes when she said, "My stomach is settled now. I think I could eat a sandwich."

I was hungry too, so I pulled them out, handed one to Wyanne, and unwrapped the other one for myself. After we finished, I said, "I have cookies too."

"That sounds good, but do you have any more water? I could use a drink."

I handed her a bottle. She drank and handed it back. Then she accepted a couple of cookies. I ate one and then decided it was time to quit stalling on making the call I needed to make. I pulled out my phone and dialed my boss.

"I'm calling Dave Padrick," I said to Wyanne as the phone began to ring. "He's my boss, the Duchesne county attorney."

She nodded and said, "He probably won't like this."

"That's for sure. I've been putting it off because I hate to make his recovery more difficult. But I've got to let him know before someone else does.

Dave answered the phone a moment later. "Hey, Saxson," he said, sounding at least somewhat like his normal, cheerful self. "I thought you were taking a day off. What's going on?"

"I don't know how to tell you this, Dave, but one of our witnesses on the case against Jarrod Miano won't be available for the retrial," I said.

"Why not?" Dave asked before I got the bad news all delivered.

"He's dead, murdered. He was shot in the back of the head, just like our missing juror. His body was lying near where Miss Grice found the body of juror number six. From the brain and blood splatter, it's obvious he was killed right there, just Like Mr. Morberg was. Both men died execution style. But both of their bodies were turned so their faces were looking at the sky. Well, not looking, but you get the picture. It's downright sick."

For a moment, my boss seemed to be at a loss for words. But he finally asked, "Who found him? Did the cops go back out there or something? That's not a place that's frequented."

"It was Miss Grice," I said. Wyanne playfully leaned toward me and punched me on the shoulder.

"What?!" he exclaimed. "Why was she back out there?"

"I was with her," I said. "We were riding my horses. She wanted to see the scene without a body there. It didn't work out so well, I'm afraid."

Again Dave was silent for a moment. When he spoke he said, "It sounds like you're trying to take good care of our latest witness. From what I hear she's a right nice-looking gal. Is she okay after another trauma?"

I repeated what I'd earlier said to Detective Shelburn. "She's a strong girl, Dave. She'll be okay."

I was looking at her as I spoke. She mouthed quietly, "Only if you make sure I am."

I nodded and then talked to Dave again. "We're on our way back to town now. I'll let you go. I'm sorry to have to deliver such bad news."

"It is what it is," he said glumly. "Now, Saxson, you take care of that pretty teacher. It would seem to me that whoever killed our juror also killed our witness and she saw him. Do whatever it takes, but keep—her—safe."

"I'll do that," I said, wondering just how I could. The county attorney was right. She could very well be in a great deal of danger.

Seven

Early that evening, Wyanne and I met with Detective Shelburn at his office at his request. He'd told me he needed some things clarified by the two of us. He looked stressed and tired. We discussed possible motives and even suspects. Finally, he sat back in his chair and said, "I think the most likely scenario is that either young Jarrod Miano personally committed the killings, or he hired someone to do it for him."

"He or his father," I said.

"Yes, I agree," Sheldon said. He started to rise to his feet. "I need to get to work." But he settled back into his chair again, a worried look crossing his face.

"Is there something else?" I asked.

"Yes," he said, looking at Wyanne as he said it. "We've got to figure out how to keep you safe, Wyanne."

"I'll be okay. I'll keep my doors locked," she said, sounding very uncertain.

He picked up his phone. "I need to make a call."

He spoke with his boss, the sheriff. "I have Miss Grice in my office," he said.

Wyanne looked at me and grinned. "I'm glad you don't call me *Miss Grice* anymore."

Sheldon spoke to the sheriff for a moment, and then he put the receiver down. "Okay," he said. "We have a plan. The sheriff thinks that you should sleep on Miss Grice's sofa."

I choked. Wyanne turned a deep shade of red. Sheldon laughed. "Just kidding," he said, slapping the desk with his hand. "You should have seen your face, Saxson." He laughed some more. "But seriously, the sheriff's going to have a deputy posted outside the apartment. That's a short-term plan, but it'll give us time to come up with something more long range."

I would never have admitted it, but I honestly felt that being close by would be the best way to keep her from harm. But that wasn't possible, and I knew it. "What about when she goes to church tomorrow? She can't just sit in the apartment," I said. "She has her Young Women's class to teach."

Wyanne looked at me and then back at the detective with a slightly cocked eye. "I'll be okay, guys. I'll be safe in church. And it's not that far from my apartment to the chapel."

"No, that won't work. Our killer could be waiting for you to be alone for even a minute or two," Detective Shelburn said.

I had a solution to the church problem. But I felt a stutter coming on when I tried to suggest it. Wyanne, as if reading my mind, turned her pretty blue eyes on me and in perfect seriousness asked, "Our wards meet at different times. I know you'd have to miss some of your meetings since my sacrament meeting starts before your priesthood meeting is over, but would you be able to go to church with me, Saxson?"

"Sure, that would work," I said, feeling myself flush.

"Then, after church, if you don't mind terribly, maybe I could fix dinner and we could eat at my place," she went boldly on.

"Well, I guess—" I began.

Detective Shelburn again slapped his hand on the desk, cutting me off short. "It's a plan," he said. Then he grinned that silly grin of his and added, "Unless of course, you have made other dinner arrangements, Counselor."

Wyanne's face fell. "Have you?"

"Of course not," I said. "Thanks, Miss Grice."

Sheldon laughed loudly and rose to his feet as Wyanne punched me on the shoulder. "I need to get to work. Take good care of her, Saxson. And we'll make sure there's someone nearby—as a little extra protection."

Wyanne and I walked out to the parking lot. We'd left her car at her apartment before our ride. So I opened the door of my truck for her and said, "I'll give you a ride home."

"Thank you, *Mr. Cartwright*," she said, unable to keep from grinning. And as she stepped up into my truck, she said, almost under her breath, "*Miss Grice!*"

I shut the door, went around, and got in on my side. After I was belted in and the engine was running, I said to her, "You are quite amazing, Wyanne. You can joke despite all the, ah, the danger you are in."

"To be totally honest, I'm scared to death. But there's no sense in just hiding in a shell. Life goes on," she said with a slight quaver in her voice.

"Yes, it does. Would you like to go somewhere and eat?" I asked, even as I was thinking that I wasn't the same Saxson Cartwright I'd been just twenty-four hours earlier. All I'd need right now would be for her to turn me down—that would set me back for sure.

I needn't have worried. She laid a soft hand on my arm and said, "I'd love to. Would it be okay if we go to Subway or Burger King? We could take our sandwiches to my place and eat them there if you don't mind."

I didn't mind at all. Boy, would my folks be proud of me. And my siblings would all be rolling their eyes.

***

Wyanne unlocked her door while I held our Subway sandwiches— footlong for me, six-inch for her. I followed her into her apartment and put our sandwiches on her kitchen table. She disappeared down the hallway with a quick wave of her hand. When she came back, she'd changed out of her riding clothes, and her hair had been brushed until it shone. She grinned and said, "Sorry. You'd probably like to change too."

"After we eat," I said.

She looked at her phone. It was flashing. "Looks like I have a message. Do you mind if I listen to it before we eat?"

"Go ahead," I said.

She punched a button, and for a moment there was no sound, then an electronically altered voice came on. "Miss Grice, you are a stupid little fool. You apparently don't take me seriously. I'm not a patient person. I won't continue to warn you. Forget what you saw, or you will pay for it." The message ended. Wyanne collapsed into my arms, ghost-white.

It was several minutes before we finally started eating our sandwiches. We had both finished before she said, "I guess I better call Detective Shelburn. I promised to let him know if anything happened."

"I'll call him," I said, and she nodded with relief.

He answered his phone a moment later. "Counselor, I take it something has happened or you wouldn't be calling," he said.

"I'm afraid it has," I responded. "Wyanne had a message on her landline phone when we got to her apartment. It was—"

"A threat?" he asked as he interrupted.

Wyanne gripped my arm tightly.

"Very much so," I said. I recited what the voice mail had said.

"Was it a man or a woman?" he asked.

"I assumed it was a man, but now, as I think about it, I can't be sure. The voice was electronically altered. But it was a fairly deep voice. It was probably a man."

"You didn't erase it, did you?" he asked.

"Of course not. Remember, Detective, I'm the one who needs evidence to be preserved."

"Sorry," he said. "Are you still at Wyanne's apartment?" I answered in the affirmative, and he told me he'd be right over.

Detective Shelburn made a copy of the voice mail, discussed its implication with Wyanne, and told her that she needed to be doubly careful. She was subdued and said little while he was there, but she did say that she understood the seriousness of the situation. After he left, she invited me to stay longer, but I needed to get home, shower, and put on clean clothes. I checked before I went home to make sure a deputy was in place in front of her apartment.

"Call me if you need me," I said as I opened her door.

"I wish you didn't have to go," she said, frightened.

I hugged her. "You'll be fine."

"Before you go, would you . . . would you mind giving me a blessing? I need extra strength, Saxson. I may act brave, but I'm falling completely apart inside."

I shut the door again and said, "Thanks for asking." She sat on a chair in her kitchen, and I placed my hands on her head, praying silently that the Lord would help me say what He wanted me to say. I'd given quite a few priesthood blessings in my life, but I felt very inadequate at that moment. I asked her what her full name was.

I started the blessing with a few stutters, but then I felt the Spirit settle over me, and I spoke clearly the words that came to my mind.

When I finished, she stood and hugged me. "That was beautiful, Saxson. Thank you."

"I'm glad I could do it," I responded. I looked deeply into her eyes and felt strongly that something was bothering her. "What is it?" I asked. "Was it something I said?"

She looked away from me and then said, "You said something about some hard decisions I would have to make. You said I would know what to do when the time came."

I did remember saying that, but I had no idea why, other than that the words were put in my mouth. I told her that and then said, "You'll be okay, Wyanne. I do need to go, but call me if you need anything. Otherwise, I'll pick you up for church at 10:45 or so in the morning."

She nodded, thanked me for the blessing, and saw me to the door. I stopped and spoke for a moment with the deputy outside. I stressed the seriousness of the situation and left, unsure if he clearly understood. I prayed that he did.

We got both stares and comments when we walked into her ward the next morning. One of my biggest weaknesses is my ridiculous shyness. But I was not in the least hard of hearing. So I heard every whispered word from one of her ward members, who tugged Wyanne a couple of steps away and asked her how she'd managed to persuade the handsome *Mr. Bashful* to escort her to church. I didn't recognize the woman, but she seemed to know me. The handsome part missed the mark, but *Mr. Bashful* couldn't have been truer.

Wyanne giggled and, looking at me, said, "I didn't give him a choice." She left the older lady looking puzzled as she stepped close to me. "Sorry about that," she said. "Should we go in?"

"Who is she?" I asked. "I don't recognize her."

Wyanne chuckled. "I know her to see her, but I honestly don't remember her name."

We were together until it came time for her to go to her meeting and for me to go to priesthood meeting. "Are you okay?" I asked.

"Of course I am," she responded. "Are you?" She grinned as she said it.

I grinned back, but I was honest with her. "I am a bit uncomfortable. I don't do well in crowds and especially when they're people I don't know well. But I can do it."

She touched my arm gently and said, "I'll meet you in the foyer after the meetings are over."

My meeting was out before hers, so I waited by the front door. A gray-haired fellow of about sixty approached me. "I'm Rod Ledden," he said as he offered his hand to shake. "You are that young prosecutor, aren't you?"

"Saxson Cartwright," I said as we shook. "And, yes, I am a deputy county attorney."

He was short and stocky and looked up at me as he went on. "My wife and I live on the same block as Sister Grice. Is everything okay with her? I noticed a sheriff's vehicle parked near her apartment building last night. Is there something that we neighbors should know about? I mean, you know, sometimes some rather unsavory characters live there. Maybe you don't know, but I wondered if it was a stakeout of some kind—you know, watching for drug deals or something."

"I'm not privy to the comings and goings of the sheriff and his deputies," I said, not about to tell him why the deputy had been parked there.

"I guess you wouldn't be," he said. "I just wondered." He started to turn away and then stepped back toward me and said, "You might have them watch for a white car. I don't know the make. The wife and I were late for church today. She has a hard time getting ready on time. You know how it is with women."

Actually, I didn't know. That was part of my problem. But I said, "Yes, sometimes they have a hard time getting ready on time." I had no idea if that was true or not. My mother and sisters had always been punctual.

"Yes, well, we were late, but I noticed this white car parked there, an older car. There was a guy sitting in it. He was a ways south of the officer. He was not right in front of the apartment building, but he seemed to be watching it. If the cop is there when you take Sister Grice home, you might want to mention it to him in case he didn't notice," he suggested. "It could be a drug dealer."

"I'll make sure the officer knows if I see him," I said. I was thinking that Rod Ledden must watch too much TV. "Thanks for telling me." I didn't add that the white car's presence there did concern me. The safety of *Sister Grice* was what mattered to me. I determined that I'd keep an eye out for the white car.

He leaned a little closer as his wife joined him. "That car was there yesterday too—in the late morning. And the guy was just sitting in it, watching the apartment building."

That worried me more. I glanced around for Wyanne, ready to be rescued from this guy and get her home. I didn't see her. The Laurels must still be in class, I thought. "I'll keep it in mind," I said.

"Okay, Brother Cartwright. I appreciate it. I try to be a good citizen."

"Thank you for that," I said. "Did you see the driver?"

He leaned forward again. "The guy was young, and he was wearing a blue shirt and a red baseball cap. The car had Nevada plates. I did notice that, but I didn't get the number."

"Thank you. You are very observant," I said again as I finally spotted Wyanne and turned toward her.

The Leddens said hello to Wyanne as she joined me, and then they walked out the door.

"Should we go?" she asked.

I was more than ready to leave, and I quickly opened the door for her. After we were outside and heading down the walk, she asked, "What did Brother Ledden want?"

"Do you know him well?" I asked.

"They live near me. His wife brought me a loaf of fresh baked bread just a couple of days after I moved in last year. She's really sweet. And he seems like a . . . a good man," she said tentatively. Then she wrinkled her nose a little and grinned. "He is a little strange." Then she got a look of shame on her face and said, "I'm sorry. That was rude. I shouldn't say things like that. What did he want?"

"He is concerned about drug trafficking at your apartment building." I grinned at her. "He says there's a deputy sheriff staking the apartments out."

A shadow crossed her face. "If he only knew," she said. "But why was he asking you about it?"

"He apparently knows who I am, and he thought that since I was a prosecutor I'd know what the deputy was doing." We reached my truck. I unlocked it with my key fob and then took hold of the door handle. "He asked me to tell the deputy about a suspicious car he's seen near your apartments." I opened the door, waited while Wyanne got in, and then shut it.

As I walked around the truck, I saw a white car driving slowly past the church. And to my dismay, the driver was wearing a red ball cap. That caused me to pay closer attention. It was a Chevy Malibu, older model. I quickly glanced at the back of the car as it passed by. It had Nevada plates. The driver was looking right at me, or at my truck at least, as he passed. He was frowning and sped up a little as soon as he had gone by. I couldn't help but notice that he was wearing a blue shirt. My stomach gave an uncomfortable roll. Something didn't feel right. I was glad Brother Ledden had told me about the car.

I got in the truck but said nothing about the white car until we were on our way down Main Street. And then it was only because Wyanne asked, "You were saying something about Brother Ledden and a white car?"

My stomach rolled again. "I don't want to worry you, and it's probably nothing," I told her. "But he says a white car has been hanging around your apartment. He's seen it a couple of times, and both times the driver was sitting in it, just looking toward your apartment building."

"I don't like that," she said. "Did he say what kind of car it was?"

"No, he didn't seem to know." I did not mention the older model Chevrolet Malibu, but I was determined to find the car again and see what I could learn. It might be a coincidence that it happened to pass the church right as we were getting ready to leave. But I don't like coincidences.

She looked thoughtful as I turned onto the street that led to her apartment. "I don't think anyone who lives there has a white car," she said.

I pulled up and parked. I got out and walked around to help her out, looking up and down the street as I did. A white car stopped along the street about a block away. I walked slowly around the back of my truck, watching the Malibu, for I was certain it was the same car. The driver did not get out.

I pasted on a smile when I opened the door for Wyanne. She'd apparently been thinking about the mysterious car, for the first words out of her mouth were, "Did he say anything else about the car?"

"He says it had out of state plates," I responded. "He thinks they were Nevada plates."

A cloud again passed over her face. But all she said was, "Oh."

As we walked to her door, there was not another word about the car, but I had a feeling that there was something she wasn't telling me. Could she have seen it around here?

We were inside her apartment before I brought the subject up again. I asked, "Wyanne, have you noticed a car like that drive by or park near here the past couple of days?"

She shook her head, but instead of answering the question, she said, "I stirred up a casserole for lunch. Is that okay?"

Eight

I stuck around after lunch for a few minutes. But for some reason, Wyanne seemed a little off. I wasn't sure if it was something I'd said, or if she was just becoming despondent over the danger she'd so innocently been thrust into. When, a little after three in the afternoon, I said that I should be going, she didn't ask me to stay longer.

She did follow me to the door, and I glanced out to make sure a deputy was in place, and I was relieved to see that Tyrell Barnes, a rookie deputy, was sitting in one of the sheriff department's gray SUVs. He was parked across the street. "Looks like the sheriff is good to his word," I said. "There's a deputy out there. He's a rookie, but he's a good officer."

She nodded but said nothing. If I were most guys, I'd have asked her what the problem was, for there clearly was one. But I'm not most guys. I simply could not pry. I was reaching for the door when I saw something that disturbed me. The white Malibu with the driver wearing a blue shirt and a red ball cap pulled up directly in front of her apartment. It definitely had Nevada plates. But contrary to what Rod Ledden had stated about the man's earlier behavior, he did not sit in his car for more than a couple of seconds after he'd parked. He climbed out, looked directly at Wyanne's door, and then started toward it.

I looked at her, but she wasn't looking out the window. She was simply standing morosely in front of the door. The sadness on her face was breaking my heart, but I couldn't think of a single thing to say, so I did what I did best around pretty girls: I kept my mouth shut. But I did not open the door. I wasn't leaving until I determined what the man in the red cap was up to. I noticed that Deputy Barnes across the street was also on high alert. He got out of his truck and was moving across the street at a jog.

The man disappeared from my sight, and a moment later there was a loud pounding on the door. Wyanne jumped, and her face went pale. But she still didn't speak to me. Something was bothering her a great deal.

"I'll get the door," I said. "Why don't you step into the kitchen, Wyanne?" But she didn't move; her eyes were glued to the door.

The pounding came again, and at that moment Deputy Barnes joined the man outside the door. With him as backup, I opened the door, preparing mentally for a confrontation. The deputy, who was both shorter and a whole lot lighter, had his hand on the stranger's arm. My mental preparations proved to be insufficient. The man in the red baseball cap shook free of the deputy's grip and stormed through the door. He stopped and thrust his face forward until his nose was only inches from mine. He was slightly taller than me and probably outweighed me by a good forty pounds. He was a big man, and his fists were bunched. His eyes bored into mine, anger shooting from them like bolts of lightning. My fists were also bunched—I expected there was about to be a fight.

I heard Wyanne give a little gasp, but before I could turn and look at her, the man in front of me snarled, "You. You're the reason my girl-friend is in trouble. You better leave her alone or you'll wish you had."

I was confused. What girlfriend? Was it someone I had prosecuted? Who was he talking about? I didn't wonder for long. Behind me, in a soft, quaking voice, Wyanne said, "Jimmie, what are you doing here?"

My heart sank. Wyanne was the girlfriend.

"I heard this guy got you into all kinds of trouble, and I'm here to take care of the problem," he growled as his eyes shifted past me. Then he looked back at me as the deputy again grabbed his arm.

"Get out!" the man said as he raised one hand and shoved a finger in my face. "Get out now."

The deputy spoke up then. "Sir," he said, "you need to come with me. I'm not supposed to let anyone bother Miss Grice."

Jimmie again shook his arm free and spun until he was toe to toe with the deputy. "Then get this man out of here, right now!" he demanded. "He's the one bothering her."

"Jimmie, please don't. He's helping me," Wyanne said from behind me, prompting me to turn. Her face was white, and her eyes were full of tears.

"Who is this guy?" I asked angrily. I'd never had a hard time speaking when I was mad.

"Jimmie Martin," she said softly, her eyes failing to meet mine. "He won't hurt me."

I was crushed, to say the least. It seemed pretty clear that Jimmie was a boyfriend. It was time for me to leave.

But Deputy Barnes didn't see it that way. "Mr. Cartwright is just helping keep Miss Grice safe," he said. "You're the one that needs to leave."

The big man turned on the deputy, transferred his finger from my face to his, and said, "Don't you even try to tell me what to do. This is my girlfriend, and I will protect her. If you don't get out of here right now, I'll make a complaint against you."

"It's okay, Deputy," Wyanne said. "I'd like to talk to Jimmie. He seems to misunderstand any relationship he and I ever had." She looked up at Jimmie, held herself a little taller, and said, "I was never your girlfriend. We dated, but that was all."

His face darkened. "That's not true, Wyanne," he said through gritted teeth.

"You guys can go. I'll be okay. Jimmie and I need to talk, I guess. I can straighten this out."

"Are you sure?" the deputy asked.

"Yes, I'm sure."

"I'll be right outside like the sheriff told me to."

"That won't be necessary," Jimmie said. "I can take care of her."

Deputy Barnes simply shook his head. "I have my orders," he said, and he turned to leave. I followed him out, and the door slammed behind me so hard it made the living room window rattle.

We both walked down the sidewalk in silence. I was angry, but I was also hurt. The first time in my life I had developed serious feelings for a woman and had been able to actually talk to her turned out to be a farce. She'd been nice to me, held my hand, hugged me, and withheld the fact that she was still embroiled in a relationship—a complicated relationship, maybe, but a relationship. Yes, Wyanne had said the guy wasn't a boyfriend, but his attitude told me otherwise.

Deputy Barnes said, "I'm sorry, Mr. Cartwright. I shouldn't have let the guy approach the door. It's my fault."

"It's not your fault," I said as I stopped and looked him in the eye. "I think you handled things well, and I'll tell the sheriff that if I need to. So don't you worry about it."

"Thanks, but I think the guy's a jerk," Barnes said.

"Seems like one, doesn't he?" I agreed. "But Miss Grice apparently isn't afraid of him, so I suppose he can't be too dangerous." So much for not calling her Miss Grice. She was that to me from now on. Whatever might have been, in my mind at least, was not going to be. If I saw her again, it would be in court, and my relationship with her would be like any other witness, strictly formal. I would not refer to her as Wyanne. What a fool I'd been.

"So you don't think he's the one making threats?" Deputy Barnes asked me.

"No, he's not the one," I said. "If it was him, she would never have asked us to leave. Whoever left the threats is still a danger to her. Keep a close eye on her."

He agreed, and I went to my truck and drove toward home. The disappointing thoughts running through my mind were such that it seemed that I was doomed to be single forever. But that was okay. I'd been doing just fine until I met Miss Grice.

My cell phone vibrated. I hadn't switched it off vibrate since church. I pulled it from my pocket and looked at the screen. Deep down, I had hoped the call was from Miss Grice, telling me that she'd worked out the *misunderstanding* and that Jimmie had left. It wasn't her.

"Counselor, I just talked to Tyrell Barnes. He's pretty upset," Detective Shelburn said. "What can you tell me about this Jimmie Martin character?"

"Nothing more than Tyrell told you, I'm sure. He says he's Miss Grice's boyfriend. Apparently he thinks I have put her in danger," I said, unable to keep the bitterness I was feeling from my voice.

"He talked to me earlier today," the detective revealed.

"Jimmie Martin did?" I asked, stunned.

"He called dispatch, demanding to speak with me. I met him at the office. He didn't tell me what his relationship with Wyanne was, but he did indicate he knew her and that he'd heard she was a witness to a murder and wanted to know what it was all about," Sheldon said.

"How did he know that?"

"I guess it's all over town by now. He said he was having dinner last night at a café. He said someone mentioned her name and that she was in danger," Sheldon told me.

"What did you tell him?"

"As little as I could get by with. And I didn't mention you at all. I simply told him that she may have seen something, but I didn't take it beyond that. I know it made him angry because he stormed out of my office. I was wondering what his interest was until Tyrell called me. Are you sure he isn't connected to the killing, Counselor?"

"She clearly knew him and wasn't afraid. She said they just needed to talk. I suppose he's worried about her. It's probably just that simple."

"Maybe," Sheldon said. "And maybe not. I'm going to do a little checking on the guy. His name is Jimmie Martin, right?"

"That's what Miss Grice said."

"Okay, I'll let you know when I learn anything," he promised. "I guess you have to be in court on the Miano case in the morning."

"Yes, and of course it will be delayed," I said. "And I'll be short a witness when we start again."

"Can you still make a case without Darrius Chaudry?" he asked.

"Oh yeah, I'm sure I can. He was just a nice bit of icing on the cake, so to speak. I can still put Miano behind the wheel, and our accident reconstruction expert can still show excessive speed. Corporal Kingston did an outstanding job on the case. We'll have no trouble proving Miano was drunk. I'll still convict Jarrod Miano," I said, and I was confident I could. "I can't help but think that whoever killed both of your murder victims is thinking that without them, the case is dead, but that's not true."

"That's something else I needed to talk to you about, Saxson," he said, sounding a bit tentative.

"What?" I asked.

"There's another suspect in the murder of Evan Morberg," he revealed, stunning me.

"You've got to be kidding," I said.

"I'm afraid not. Do you have a minute? I'd like to tell you about it."

"I'm all ears," I said.

"If you remember, I told you that Morberg owned a car dealership before he retired and moved to Roosevelt," he said.

"Yes, I remember. He was supposedly going to a former partner or someone about that business when he disappeared."

"Well, it seems that the partner thinks he was cheated when Morberg sold the dealership. From what Mr. Morberg's wife told me, the guy was pretty angry, and just a few days ago, she got a call from him while Morberg was in court." Sheldon paused, and I waited to see what was coming next. Sheldon spoke again. "The man's name is Graham Pease. He's in his midfifties, according to Mrs. Morberg. He only owned a third of the business, but apparently he thought he should get half the proceeds from the sale."

"Anybody would know that a third ownership would only bring a third of the proceeds of the sale."

"Or less," Detective Shelburn said. "Morberg accused Pease of stealing from the business, so he only gave him a fourth of the money when they sold, and Pease told Mrs. Morberg, when he called, that he would make her husband pay. That is a threat, although it could be interpreted a couple of different ways."

"Meaning," I began, "that Pease could have meant that he would sue Morberg for what he believed he was owed." I paused for a moment. "Or he may have meant that he would kill him or something else drastic."

"She believes it was a physical threat," Sheldon said. "But Morberg didn't, and when he got the call that lured him from town, he didn't hesitate to go, despite protests from his wife. So I've got to consider Pease a suspect."

"Of course. But if he were Morberg's killer, how would you explain the killing of my witness?" I asked.

"That's what makes me lean toward our first theory, but I have to follow this lead. I'm going to find this Pease guy and see what he has to say. He could have an alibi. And he may not have a black Cadillac Escalade or something like it," he said. "I'll keep you up to date on what I learn. But regardless of who the killer is, one thing remains the same: Wyanne Grice most likely saw him, and she has been threatened by him. Her life is very much in danger."

"And I doubt she wants my help anymore," I said bitterly.

"I'm sorry, Saxson. I thought she really liked you," he said. "And maybe you'll find out shortly that she really does."

"I kind of doubt it, but that's okay. Just make sure your guys keep a close eye on her."

After ending the call, I got out of my truck, went in the house, and sat on my sofa. I thought about what the detective had just told me. He'd promised to find out more about Jimmie Martin. Suddenly, I got up and went into my spare bedroom where I kept my computer. I wasn't waiting for Sheldon. I could check on Martin myself. I booted my computer up.

Ten minutes later, I shut the computer down again and leaned back in my chair. Jimmie Martin was who he said he was. He lived in Las Vegas, where he worked in a casino. But there was more. He'd gone to school at Southern Utah University in Cedar City, the same place where Wyanne had told me she'd earned her bachelor's degree and teaching certificate. So she had to have met him there. It seemed strange to me that a girl as sweet as Miss Grice would have dated him. I couldn't find evidence of him having completed his degree, but I suppose he could have. But why, if he had a degree in anything, would he be working in a casino at a blackjack table? But that's what he was doing. I know I had the right guy because I found a picture of him, and the face was one I wasn't likely to forget. The only difference between the photograph and the face that had been inches from mine was a leering smile instead of a frown filled with glaring hatred.

I was restless. There were still a few hours of daylight left, and I had to get out of my apartment and do something, something to get Wyanne—Miss Grice—off my mind. I drove up to the Blue Rock Ranch and spent an hour with my horses. I could talk to them, and they would listen. That hour calmed me down. Horses were great therapy. There was only one downside. I couldn't look at Raspberry without thinking of Miss Grice. That was an image I would have to get out of my mind. And I was determined that I would.

Nine

Judge Cooper Feldman was scowling as he took his seat on the bench. He addressed me and said, "Mr. Cartwright, I watch the news. It seems we've lost a juror. You know what that means, don't you?"

"Yes, sir," I said, but I didn't say what it meant.

The lawyer for the defense rose to his feet. "Your Honor, I know that a mistrial is inevitable, but I have a motion for the court."

"State your motion," Judge Feldman said.

"The defense moves to have the charges against my client dismissed," he said with a sly grin.

I jumped up. "On what grounds?"

"You know perfectly well on what grounds," he said, peering at me like I was some lesser form of life he'd like to squish beneath his highly polished black shoes. "You lost your key witness." He turned his attention back to the bench. "The state cannot possibly hope to prevail without Mr. Chaudry. You heard his testimony. Our young cowboy here," he said, gesturing dismissively at me, "can't make his case without him, and his case, even with the witness, was weak at best."

"I can still make my case, and I don't need Mr. Chaudry to do it. He was not a key witness, just a helpful one. I strongly oppose the defense's motion," I said.

Judge Feldman was shaking his head. "Am I missing something here?"

Glazebrook shook his head. "I thought you said you watched the news," he said in a deprecating tone.

"Not since Friday night," he said. "My wife and I spent the weekend with our daughter in Salt Lake. What did I miss?"

"Mr. Chaudry is dead," he said with a malicious grin. "Sorry. Thought you knew he'd been killed. So as I said, I move to dismiss."

Judge Feldman's face darkened, his eyes narrowed, and he glared at Glazebrook. Then he looked at me, not quite so darkly, and asked, "Is that true, Mr. Cartwright?"

"Yes, Your Honor," I said. "He was murdered. But I can still proceed at a new trial. Mr. Chaudry is not critical to the state's case."

He nodded and looked back at Malcom Glazebrook. "Your motion is denied, Counselor," he said. "We'll set a new date for trial."

"I think that the cowboy and I need to sit down. In light of recent developments, I think we can reach an agreement of some kind," Glazebrook said with a smirk.

"Mr. Glazebrook, just because Mr. Cartwright wears a Western-cut jacket and boots to court does not give you license to call him a cowboy. He is an officer of this court. And I warn you—I am not afraid to find you in contempt of court and let you cool your heels for a few days in this county's fine jail."

The defense attorney jerked. He said, "Yes, Your Honor," and sat down.

I suppressed a smile.

"Get your calendars out, gentlemen. We're going to set a new trial date right now, and then I will have the bailiff bring what's left of our jury in so I can thank them and excuse them from further duty in this matter," the judge said.

We set a date about six weeks away. After the judge had spoken to and excused the jury, he rapped his gavel firmly and adjourned court.

I turned to Corporal Kingston and said, "We'll review everything in a few days. We're going to beat this man."

He nodded, leaned in toward me, and whispered, "Could he or his client have had anything to do with these murders?"

Before I could tell him that that was exactly what I was wondering, Malcom Glazebrook, no longer cowed by the judge, said, "I'd like to visit with you in your office for a few minutes, cowboy."

I stood up and faced him. "I guess you can get away with that as long as court is adjourned. Anyway, just so you know, I really am a cowboy, so I don't mind the nickname. I'll see you in my office in five minutes."

"I'll need a little longer than that," he said. "I need a few minutes to confer with my client. I'll see you in about fifteen minutes."

Angered, I said, "I won't be in my office in fifteen minutes. I'll be leaving for the day. If you want a minute of my time, it will be in five minutes."

He rolled his head back and laughed. "Like you have someplace else to go," he said. "We both have the rest of the day off. Fifteen minutes."

I looked pointedly at my watch. "Four," I said and pushed my way past him, headed for the exit, signaling to the highway patrolman to follow me.

"He's a real jerk," Corporal Kingston said as soon as we entered my office.

"He is that. Now, to your statement a moment ago," I began. "I do suspect that the defendant's hands are not clean when it comes to the murders, but you do need to know that Detective Shelburn has identified another suspect. So it may be purely coincidental."

Kingston shook his head. "You don't believe that, do you?"

"No, but we'll wait and see what Shelburn turns up," I said. "In the meantime, watch your back."

The corporal's face grew concerned. "If they killed me, you wouldn't have a case, would you?" he asked.

"I don't care nearly as much about the case as I do your well-being. Two men connected to this case are dead. A witness to the murder of our missing juror has been threatened. "Don't let your guard down for a minute."

Just then, one of the legal assistants tapped on my door. I opened it, and she told me that Mr. Glazebrook was waiting to see me. "Right on time, I see," I said, winking at the patrolman. "I'll be in touch, Bardett. Be careful."

He nodded and left. A moment later, Malcom Glazebrook, in all his glory, entered and took a seat in front of my desk. I sat down behind it and said, "So what did you want to talk about?"

"I have an offer for you," he said. There was no smirk. His face was perfectly serious. "I want to show you that I am a fair man. This matter is weighing heavily on my client and his family. My client will plead no contest to driving too fast for conditions. We can do it today before the judge leaves."

I tried not to show my shock. That was a ridiculous proposal, and I knew that he knew it. But I said, "Make it a guilty plea instead of no contest, and I'll talk to the family of the victim."

"No contest or no deal," Glazebrook said, almost acting as if it was me making him an offer.

"Why no contest?" I asked even though I knew what his answer would be.

He shook his head with a sad expression on his face. "I wonder how you ever passed the bar exam. I know you're an inexperienced attorney, but you know very well that Miss Keen's family will try to sue my client, and by pleading no contest he admits no guilt and simply puts this silly criminal matter behind him." I thought about how to respond to him without letting my growing temper get the best of me. But I hadn't said a word before he said, "I won't even bill you for what I just taught you, Counselor. Now you know the difference between a guilty plea and no contest. Try not to forget it."

I bit my tongue. I didn't want a scene. So I simply said, "There is no deal. Thanks for coming in, Mr. Glazebrook." I stood, more than ready for him to leave my office.

But he remained sitting. "Sit down, Cartwright. I do have something else. But first, let me say that you will regret turning down this offer. There's no way you can beat me. I can out lawyer you any day of the week and on any case. And I will prove it when you and I face off on the Rutledge case in less than two weeks."

I did not sit but rather rounded my desk. "That's not your case," I said as I pointed to the door.

"It is now. Rutledge fired his attorney and hired me just this morning. I cleared my calendar so we don't have to change the date. When I finish with you there, maybe you'll reconsider my offer on the Miano case."

He stood up then and shook his head. All I could say was, "I'll be ready. You do know it's set as a bench trial."

"Of course I do. It's in front of your local-yokel justice court judge, Clyde Dunson," Glazebrook said with his trademark smirk.

"Judge Dunson is a good judge," I protested. "He's fair, and he's extremely conversant with the law."

"For not having a law degree, he's okay, I suppose, but he's part of a dying breed. I will say this though—he's honest, from what I've been told. He won't find someone guilty just because the case is brought by the local prosecutor's office," Glazebrook said. "I'll beat you in that case, and then we'll talk about Miano again."

He stepped through the door, but he stopped and turned back. "Maybe you would consider an offer on Rutledge. It's a DUI, but I would consider something less, way less."

I shook my head. "I've been through this with his previous counsel. This is a second offense in less than two years. There will be no plea deal."

"See you in court then, buckaroo," he said and finally left.

I pulled out the file on Rutledge and began to thumb through it. Karl Rutledge was fifty-eight years old. In addition to the current DUI and the one from about eighteen months ago, he had three others that spanned a period of several years about ten years ago. The arresting officer wasn't a strong witness, and unless he was really good in court, he could get tripped up by Glazebrook. If that happened, I might lose. But in good conscience, I had to try. Rutledge needed help before he killed someone by his drunken behavior.

The file was still on my desk, and my door was open when Dave Padrick limped slowly toward me.

"Hey, what are you doing here?" I asked. "I thought you were supposed to stay home."

He waved a hand dismissively. "I had to get out of the house for a while. My wife drove me over. I'm doing a lot better. But I better sit down," Dave said and eased himself into the chair recently vacated by Malcom Glazebrook.

"Well, it is good to see you," I said as I pulled a chair up next to him. It didn't feel right to me to sit behind my desk. He was, after all, my boss.

"How did it go this morning?" he asked. "Were you able to reschedule the auto homicide case?"

"Six weeks," I said. "Maybe by then you'll be able to take it."

"I suppose I could, but it's yours, Saxson. You can handle it as well as I can. Did Malcom try to get you to take an offer?" Dave asked.

I rolled my eyes. "He did—after Judge Feldman denied his motion to dismiss because one of our witnesses is dead."

"That doesn't surprise me," Dave said, slowly shaking his head. "What did he ask you to consider?"

"A no contest plea to speeding too fast for conditions."

"That figures."

"I turned him down flat. The Keens have made it clear to me that they don't want to hear any offers. Glazebrook also told me that he's taking over as defense counsel for Karl Rutledge. It's set for trial in a couple of weeks in Judge Dunson's court," I informed Dave.

"Rutledge, the drunk?"

I nodded.

"He has a history, that guy does," he said.

We discussed the Rutledge matter for a few minutes. Unfortunately, Dave had the same concerns with that case as I did. "That young trooper could lose that one for you," he said. "But I agree. We can't reduce it. Work with Trooper Still closely. Maybe if you prepare him well enough he won't let Glazebrook get to him."

I agreed, and then I said, "Detective Shelburn has another possible suspect on the murder of Evan Morberg." I spent a couple of minutes explaining.

"Well, I guess we'll see what he turns up. I agree that Morberg's partner might have a motive to kill him, but I can't see how our dead witness—what's his name again?" Dave asked.

"Darrius Chaudry."

"Yes, that's right. I don't see how there could be any connection other than the Miano case. But we need to be open to all possibilities," he said. "I don't want anyone to be able to accuse us of sinking our teeth into one theory of a case to the exclusion of other possible scenarios." Dave winced. "I probably better let my wife take me home. I'm worn out already."

I stood and walked with him to the door. But he stopped beside the legal assistant's desk and looked at me. "How's our witness holding up? Miss Grice, is it?" He grinned as he asked his question.

I had no smile to offer in return. "Let me tell you what's happening while I walk to your car with you." I explained about Jimmie Martin on the way out.

"Have you called her today to see how she's doing?" he asked as he leaned against his car, his wife walking around to support him. "I don't like the sound of this Jimmie fellow."

Nor did I, but I didn't say so. I just said, "No, Miss Grice is a big girl. She'll call someone if she needs help."

He cocked an eyebrow. "I know it's hard for you to talk to young ladies, Saxson, but force yourself. Call her. I suspect there's more to this matter with her old 'boyfriend' than meets the eye. And when the sheriff's deputies find the killer of our juror, her testimony will be critical. I told you to take care of her, Saxson, and I'm telling you again."

I wanted to, that's for sure, but I wasn't sure what I could do to keep her safe now that her former boyfriend, or whatever he was, had come to town. "I don't have her cell phone number," I said lamely.

"Talk to Detective Shelburn. I'll bet he has it. I mean it, Saxson. I don't want anything to happen to that girl. And I'm sure you don't either. So swallow your pride and take care of her," Dave said. He was not smiling. "I mean it."

Instead of returning to my office or even leaving for the day, I decided to see if Detective Shelburn was in. He was, and I was directed back to his office. He looked tired and worn as he stood and greeted me. "I guess your case has been reset," he said as we shook hands.

"We try again in six weeks," I said. I smiled wanly. "Dave Padrick was just in. I tried to pawn it back off on him. He should be back to work by then."

"Let me guess," Sheldon said as he waved me to a seat. "He wants you to keep it."

"That's right. But I'm not so sure that's a good idea," I said as I sat down.

Detective Shelburn returned to his chair behind his desk and then leaned forward. "Would you like a little advice, Counselor? You're perfectly capable of winning against Malcom Glazebrook. Don't sell yourself short. And you can do it without Darrius Chaudry. You said it yourself. You've already put most of your case on once, so you've had practice. Bardett Kingston is an outstanding officer. Together you can put that little hotshot in prison." He sat back.

I thought about what I'd told the corporal earlier. I repeated it to Detective Shelburn. "I warned Bardett Kingston to watch his back.

That older brother of Jarrod's, Micah, looks like he could be dangerous. I met him the night of the accident. He's not a nice character. I'm sure that both he and the rest of the Miano family know that if Kingston were, ah, sidelined, my case would be over."

Sheldon frowned. "You have a thought there. The last thing we want is an attack on the trooper." He was thoughtful for a moment. "He's not the only one that needs to be especially careful. The killer, if it is someone from Miano's camp, could go after you as well."

"I've thought of that." I patted my coat. "I keep my pistol handy."

Ten

DETECTIVE SHELBURN TOLD ME HE believed there was a good chance that the killings had nothing to do with the Miano case. He said, "Let me tell you what I've learned today, and you'll understand where I'm coming from. I am more inclined now to believe that Morberg and Chaudry were killed by Morberg's ex-partner, Graham Pease. Let me explain."

A protest that had just left my brain was arrested as it reached my lips. I decided to hear what he had to say before I spoke.

He rubbed his chin, looking thoughtfully at me. When he could see that I wasn't going to comment, he went on. "I have some friends with the police in Salt Lake who have been trying to locate Pease. It seems that he and his wife are not at home and haven't been for three or four days."

"Maybe they're on a trip," I suggested.

"Maybe," he agreed without enthusiasm. "But get this, Counselor; Graham Pease drives a black Cadillac Escalade."

"Whoa!" I said. "Now you've got my attention. But remember, Miss Grice only thinks it was an Escalade."

"That's right, but there's more. The car that your dead witness, Mr. Chaudry, was driving was purchased from Morberg Motors."

"Whoa and double whoa!" I exclaimed.

"Yeah, that's what I said. Now I just need to see if Pease had a beef of some kind against Darrius Chaudry," he said. "I'm working on that now."

"I hope you find something," I said. It could just be a coincidence, but I've never really placed a lot of stock in coincidences. There could be something there.

"At any rate, Saxson, even though I still think both you and Kingston need to be very careful, I'm leaning toward Pease as the killer," he said. "That, however, doesn't help Miss Grice. Whoever the killer was, if in fact he was driving a black Escalade, he might think that she can testify against him when we catch him."

I sat and worried. All I could do at that point was hope and pray that she was taking care of herself and that the sheriff made sure she was constantly being guarded by his deputies. I said, "Miss Grice should be teaching today. How are your men keeping track of her while she's at school?"

Sheldon frowned. "Have you tried to call her?"

"That doesn't answer my question," I said.

"No, I guess not. Well, I've tried to call her cell phone, but I get no answer. I also texted her," he added. "There has been no response to my texts."

"Is there a deputy at the school?" I pressed.

He slowly shook his head. "Not anymore. I called the school. She didn't come to work today."

A huge knot formed in my stomach. "Is she at home?"

"No, but her car's there. Jimmie Martin's car is gone. I talked to the principal just before you came in." He paused and drummed his fingers on his desk.

"And . . ." I pressed anxiously.

"Wyanne called him this morning. She told him her life was in danger and that she wouldn't be able to come to work for a while," Sheldon revealed to my dismay. "She told him she was staying away from Duchesne so the people who were looking for her couldn't find her."

Was she feeling safer with Martin than with us trying to protect her here? Maybe so. "She'll lose her job," I said.

"That's what the principal told me at first. But when I explained what was happening, that she really was in mortal danger, he promised he'd try to keep it open for her for a while, that he'd cover her class with substitutes. But he made it clear that he couldn't justify doing that for very long," Sheldon said. "I'll keep trying to reach her, but I think you should too."

"I don't have her cell phone number," I said.

"I do, and I'll give it to you. Get your phone out."

He read her number from his phone, and I entered it into mine. I was feeling sick. I knew what I'd learned about Jimmie Martin, but I asked Detective Shelburn what he'd learned about the guy. He told me exactly what I'd already discovered in my own search.

"Does he have a record anywhere?" I asked.

"Not that I can find," he said. "He seems to be clean."

"He's a jerk," I said. "He probably scared her into leaving town."

"I'm sure he did, although I have to admit that if you and I can't find her, neither can the driver of the black Escalade," he said.

I forced a smile. "If that's supposed to comfort me, it doesn't."

"I didn't think it would. Maybe if you call, she'll respond. I'm telling you, Sheldon, the girl likes you."

"Sure she does," I said bitterly. "That's why she ran off with her old . . . whatever he is. I'll try to contact her."

I didn't return to my office. Instead, I went home, changed my clothes, and went for a ride on Midnight. I rode hard, but I couldn't get Miss Grice from my mind. I had ridden through town, across West Bench, and was approaching Starvation Reservoir. I was sweating and so was Midnight. I pulled up and dismounted. I had not yet tried to call Wyanne. Though I felt that "Miss Grice" was more appropriate, it was hard not to think of her as the sweet friend I'd made. I had a strong signal on my iPhone, so I punched in her number. It rang until it went to voice mail. I debated for a moment but decided I'd leave a message. I said, "Miss Grice, this is Saxson Cartwright." *Lame.* Saxson would have done the job. "I'm worried about you. I have some information you need. Call me when you get a chance."

I put my phone in my pocket, but after a moment I pulled it back out and sent a text. I wrote the same message on the text that I'd left on her voice mail. I was just about to send it when, on an impulse, I added: *Dinner yesterday was great—thanks.* I sent it off.

For several minutes I sat on a rock overlooking the lake. I suppose I thought I'd get a message back from her. At least I hoped I would. But I finally got back on Midnight and headed for home. I'm not sure which tormented me the most: my worry about her safety or her seeming rejection of me. One thing seemed certain. She would be the last girl to ever reject me. There was no way I could ever let another woman get as close to me as she had. But even though I feared that there was no future with her, if something happened to her, I would be deeply hurt.

I was riding down the lane to the barn on the Blue Rock Ranch a couple of hours or so later when my phone began to ring. I pulled it from my pocket and looked at the screen. I was almost dizzy with relief when I saw it was from Miss Grice. I answered it.

"Mr. Cartwright." It wasn't Wyanne's voice. "I already told you once, and I don't want to have to tell you again. My fiancée has nothing to say to you. Don't call her again—ever!"

"Let me hear Miss Grice say that," I said angrily. "She knows that her life is in danger, and I—"

Jimmie cut me off. "She is in danger because of you, you jerk. I don't know why you think you're so important, but she doesn't want to talk to you."

"Again, Mr. Martin, at least have the courtesy to let her tell me that herself," I said. The call was terminated before I could get out another word.

It was beyond my ability to understand why a woman as sweet and kind as Miss Grice would have anything to do with the likes of Jimmie Martin. If he was any kind of a decent person, he would have let her talk to me, to tell me for herself. That call concerned me. Maybe she hadn't rejected me but was under some kind of duress. I wished I knew.

I called Detective Shelburn as I continued down the lane. "I left a message on Miss Grice's phone," I said as soon as he answered. "I just got a call back, but it wasn't from her; it was Jimmie Martin. He made it clear that I was not to try to call his *fiancée* again."

"Did she tell you that?" he asked.

"No, he said she didn't want to talk to me," I said. "That doesn't ring true to me. Anyway, I'm not sure what you'll do when you get your suspect in custody, whoever that turns out to be. I just hope you can build a case without Miss Grice's testimony."

"She'll come around, Counselor," he said, but I wasn't so sure. It seemed to me that Jimmie Martin had somehow convinced her that I was the enemy—or that she was no longer free to think and act for herself. I was no longer as convinced as I had been that she had rejected me.

Eleven

I ENTERED THE COURTROOM AND put my file on the table. No one else had yet arrived. I'd climbed out of bed early that Wednesday morning. As was the case the past several days, I hadn't slept well. I was trying to keep from thinking about Wyanne, but I was experiencing something that I was totally unfamiliar with. Never in my life had I been distracted by thoughts of a woman. It was affecting my sleep and my ability to do my job.

I needed to be sharp today. In a few minutes, others would enter the courtroom. In thirty minutes, the DUI trial of Karl Rutledge would get underway. I expected to see Malcom Glazebrook any minute now. And with him, the fifty-eight-year-old defendant who looked more like seventy-five or eighty would also appear. I'd asked Trooper Ferron Still to come in early so we could once again review his testimony and prepare him better for the grilling he was bound to get from Malcom Glazebrook, but so far, he hadn't appeared. I'd expected him forty-five minutes ago. When I headed for the courtroom, I'd left word in my office to have him join me there as soon as he showed up.

His tardiness didn't exactly give me confidence on how he'd perform on the witness stand. I'd met with him a couple of times already, and those meetings hadn't exactly left me feeling comfortable. But I could only do my best and hope that Judge Dunson would see it my way.

I went over my notes until, five minutes later, Trooper Still sauntered in, looking spit shined in his uniform. He seemed perfectly at ease, but I wasn't fooled. I was afraid that five minutes with Malcom Glazebrook would reduce him to ashes. "Where have you been?" I asked him tersely. "I was hoping you would take this trial seriously. You arrested a man who needed arresting, but your job isn't finished until we get a conviction."

"You worry too much, Saxson," he said. "I know what I did, and I'll just tell it exactly like it happened."

I had to give him credit for confidence. I prayed he wouldn't let me down. We talked for a couple of minutes about the case. He seemed sure of his answers to my questions. He looked up when Malcom Glazebrook and the defendant, Karl Rutledge, walked in.

"He cleans up well," Trooper Still said. "I mean the defendant. He sure wasn't dressed like that when I arrested him." For the first time, his confidence seemed a little bit shaken. "Will Judge Dunson think he's not the drunk I arrested?"

"Don't worry about the judge. He's experienced. He was a cop once himself," I whispered as Glazebrook showed his client where to sit. "What you need to worry about is the defense counsel. He is not a particularly polite man, and he'll be very aggressive, even insulting, when he cross-examines you. So remember, Trooper, whatever he asks you, think before you answer and don't contradict anything you've already testified to. Just stay calm, don't get mad, and above all tell the truth. And again, don't expand on any of your answers. Answer my questions and his, but don't add anything beyond the simplest answer."

"I got it, Counselor," he whispered as his confidence seemed to return. "How hard can it be?"

I whispered one more warning. "Under pressure, it can be very hard. Now, is there anything you can think of that you haven't told me? Anything at all."

"I don't think so," he said. "I think we've got this guy."

I wished I was as confident.

He looked back as someone came through the door. "Hey, that's Corporal Kingston. What's he doing here?"

"Does that bother you?" I asked.

"A little. He's had a bunch of experience on the witness stand."

"Don't worry about him. He's here to observe. And if you do make any mistakes, I'm sure he'll help you avoid them in the future," I said. "He's the lead officer on the Miano auto homicide case that I am prosecuting."

"The one that got postponed because of the murders?" he asked.

"That's the case. He's testified once, but the mistrial means he'll have to do so again. I suggested he may want to be here today just to watch Glazebrook. That will help him better prepare for when he goes back on the stand," I explained.

Just then, Malcom Glazebrook stepped from his table to mine and leaned past me. "So this is Trooper Ferron Still," he said with a sneer. "My goodness, you are still a little boy. You're even greener than the prosecutor. Prepare to be taught." He chuckled and addressed me. "I've got you, Cartwright. You don't have a chance."

"We'll see," I said. I was not intimidated, but a quick glance at the trooper's red face told me that he was. That wasn't good. Only seconds ago he'd been very confident. Malcom Glazebrook could have that effect on people. It was one of the things that had made him such a successful defense attorney.

Katherine Ingram, the clerk of the justice court, entered and fiddled with the computer equipment for several minutes. One of her deputy clerks, Yolanda Montez, joined her for a moment and then left after smiling and greeting Trooper Still and me. A uniformed officer, Leland Rusko, the bailiff, joined Yolanda next. The two of them tested the sound equipment and appeared to be satisfied. The bailiff left for a moment, and then he reentered and nodded at Katherine. The judge appeared on the bench, and the bailiff called out, "All rise."

We all duly stood. The judge sat as the clerk said, "The justice court for Duchesne County is now in session with the Honorable Clyde Dunson presiding."

"Please be seated," Judge Dunson said. For a moment he looked over the courtroom. There were a couple of spectators in addition to Corporal Kingston in the gallery, but other than them, all he could see were the defendant, the defense attorney, the trooper, and me. I didn't recognize the spectators. I assumed they must be friends of the defendant.

Judge Dunson then said, "The case before the court today is State of Utah versus Karl Rutledge. He looked at his computer screen and began to read the information.

"We know the charges," Malcom Glazebrook interrupted. "Defense waives the reading of the information."

"Very well, then. Briefly, for the record, the defendant is charged with driving under the influence of alcohol, a class B misdemeanor, enhanced, and for driving with a suspended license, a class C misdemeanor. Mr. Cartwright, are you prepared to proceed?"

I stood up. "I am, and if it's okay with the court, I'd like to waive making an opening statement."

The judge looked at Mr. Glazebrook. "Counselor?" he said.

"Whatever the cowboy wants is fine with me. I'll waive my opening as well," Glazebrook said.

Judge Dunson looked a little startled, and then he frowned. "Mr. Glazebrook, let's get one thing straight at the outset. We are all grown-ups, and I expect us all to act like it. There will be no snide remarks, and you will address the prosecutor properly," he said. "Is that clear?"

"Got it," Glazebrook said cockily. Had we been back in Judge Feldman's court, he would probably have been found in contempt, but he had not been warned in this court before, so he apparently thought he'd test the limits. Well, now he knew what those limits were. It remained to be seen how he would act.

"I call Trooper Ferron Still," I said.

The judge instructed the clerk to swear the trooper in. After that, Still was directed to the witness stand. I moved to the podium and asked the trooper to state his name and occupation. He did so, and then I asked him how long he'd been a trooper.

"Almost a year," he answered. I was beginning to worry. The rookie confidence seemed to have vanished since his little encounter with defense counsel.

"Is this the first time you've testified in court?" I asked, trying to elicit a little sympathy from Judge Dunson.

"Other than moot court while I was in the police academy, it is," Trooper Still replied.

"Well, all I can say is relax. Your only job right now is to answer the questions you are asked by me and Mr. Glazebrook."

He nodded. "No problem," he said, trying to show the confidence he'd exhibited when he first entered the courtroom.

I smiled reassuringly and then asked him about his training. I had him not only talk about the police academy, but I got into the specifics of his training in handling arrests involving driving under the influence. He relaxed slightly and recited what the court needed to know. Then I asked, "How many times have you arrested persons for driving under the influence? I don't expect an exact number but as close as you can recall." I was trying not to make him any more nervous, but I knew that if I didn't ask this question, the defense attorney would.

He thought for a minute. "Probably a dozen or so."

"Okay, now let's talk about the case before the court today. First, Trooper Still, do you see the defendant, Karl Rutledge, in the courtroom? And if so, would you point to him and describe what he's wearing?"

"That's him right there," he said, pointing to the defendant. "He's wearing a blue suit with a white shirt and red tie."

I couldn't help but wonder where Rutledge had gotten the suit. I doubted that the guy had the need of one very often. I continued, "I want you to think about May 17 of this year. What were you doing that day?" I'd forewarned him about the questions I would ask. He was ready for this one.

"I was on duty, working a day shift."

"Would you tell the court what happened that day as it relates to the defendant?"

"I was dispatched to an accident on North Fork Road above Hannah, the road that leads to Defa's Dude Ranch and the trailhead to Granddaddy Basin."

"When did you arrive at the scene?" I asked.

"It was about two o'clock in the afternoon."

"What did you observe when you arrived there?"

"A blue Dodge pickup, an older model, was lying on its side at the edge of the road."

"Describe the road," I prompted.

"It's a dirt road, quite rough with a lot of curves, but it's wide enough for two-way traffic."

"What was the weather like that day?"

"It was raining a little. The road was muddy and quite slick."

So far Trooper Still was doing very well. But the tough stuff was yet to come. I asked, "Did you see the defendant at the scene of the accident, and if so, what was he doing?"

"He was sitting in a blue car with another man. They were waiting for me."

"What did you do when you got there?" I asked.

"I approached the blue car and asked which of the two men was the driver of the wrecked truck. Mr. Rutledge said that he was. I asked the other man if he'd witnessed the accident. He told me he hadn't, that he was just keeping Mr. Rutledge warm and dry while he waited for someone to come and investigate the accident," the trooper testified.

"What did you do next?" I asked.

"I had Mr. Rutledge get out of the car and walk over to my patrol car."

"So did you speak to Mr. Rutledge when you got back to your car?" I asked.

"I did," the trooper said.

"Did the defendant have any injuries from the accident?"

"Not that I could see. I asked him if he was hurt, and he told me that he wasn't," Trooper Still testified.

The trooper answered each of my questions as I led him through what had transpired over the next few minutes of his investigation. He explained that he had detected the odor of an alcoholic beverage on Rutledge's breath. He testified that Rutledge had admitted to drinking two beers at the bar at Defa's Dude Ranch at noon. The defendant had told him that a deer ran across the road and he rolled the truck when he dodged to miss it. Trooper Still further testified that he saw several empty Coors beer cans and a full six-pack inside the overturned cab of the Dodge pickup. Finally, the trooper testified that he tried to run some field sobriety tests at the scene, but due to the rain, the muddy road, and the rough surface he skipped a couple of them. But he did require the defendant to submit to the gaze nystagmus test, the single most effective test there was to determine sobriety.

I was impressed with how accurately he explained that test and exactly what occurred when he administered it. In short, the defendant failed that test badly. He also had Rutledge submit to a couple of other tests, simple ones that should not have been affected by the weather and road conditions. Finally, I asked, "What did you conclude when you had finished the sobriety tests?"

For the first time since we had begun the trial, Malcom Glazebrook jumped to his feet and shouted, "Objection. This trooper does not have the experience to draw conclusions about the sobriety of my client. He has only made a handful of DUI arrests. He shouldn't be allowed to answer the question."

"Your Honor," I began, but before I could state my position, the judge waved me off.

"Overruled, Mr. Glazebrook. I will hear his answer," Judge Dunson said. "And I will determine what weight to give his response." Then he turned toward Trooper Still. "You may answer the question."

"I concluded that he was under the influence of alcohol," Trooper Still said.

Next I had him recite questions he had asked the defendant and the answers given. One was, "Did you ask the defendant if he had consumed any alcohol following the accident?"

"I did," he answered.

"And what was the defendant's response?"

"He said he hadn't had anything to drink since the accident."

"Did you get the name of the man whose car the defendant was sitting in when you first arrived at the scene of the accident?"

"No, he was in a hurry to leave, and since he hadn't witnessed the accident, I let him go," he said. This was one of the rookie mistakes that had worried me going into this case. He should have obtained the man's identification and asked him a few questions about what was said between him and the defendant while they waited. But he hadn't, and there was nothing I could do about it. I did, however, feel a slight sinking in my stomach as the trooper's eyes left my face and looked at something or someone behind me.

"What happened next?" I asked.

"I placed Mr. Rutledge under arrest for driving under the influence of alcohol and for driving while his license was suspended and advised him of his Miranda rights. He said he was willing to answer whatever questions I had. I put handcuffs on him and had him sit in my patrol car until the wrecker arrived from Hannah. Then I took him to the jail in Duchesne." Once again, Trooper Still looked beyond me. Something in the gallery had caught his attention. He appeared nervous. I didn't like the feeling of this.

I had him tell the court what was discussed during the ride back to the jail. Mostly it was small talk, although the defendant did admit to drinking before the accident, denied having anything to drink after the accident, and admitted that his driver's license was suspended. At the jail, he submitted to a breath test. At that point, I asked the judge to admit the results of the test.

For the second time, Glazebrook bounded to his feet with a loud, "Objection, Your Honor! You can't admit this without first receiving testimony that the machine was working properly. Surely there's an expert here to testify to that," he added snidely.

Apparently Glazebrook hadn't read the file he was given by preceding counsel, or he'd chosen to ignore some of it. I patiently said, "Your Honor, I have in my file a written waiver of the expert witness by defense counsel accepting the result of the test."

His Honor worked the mouse on his computer for a moment and then said, "I have it on my screen now. It was scanned into the file by my clerks. It looks good to me."

"That was prepared by the defense counsel that I took over for. I don't consent, Your Honor. I demand that you do not allow the test results to be admitted," Mr. Glazebrook said. He turned to me. "You should have known I'd object to that, Cowb . . . Counselor," he said.

"Your Honor, I have to disagree. It's too late now to change that waiver," I said.

"Mr. Glazebrook, I warned you. Mr. Cartwright is an officer of the court, not a cowboy," Judge Dunson said sternly. Actually, I liked to think of myself as a cowboy—but not in the sense that my opponent was using the term.

"I called him 'Counselor,'" Glazebrook said.

"You started out saying *cowboy*. I'll ignore it for now, but it better not happen again. And now to your objection; it is overruled, and the breath test is admitted."

"But, Your Honor—" Glazebrook started.

"Sit down, Mr. Glazebrook. I have ruled," Judge Dunson said sternly. Then he told the clerk, Kathrine Ingram, to mark the test and hand it to him.

As soon as that was done, I asked, "Trooper Still, what was the result of the breath test?"

"Objection!"

"Now what, Mr. Glazebrook?" Judge Dunson asked with feigned patience.

"I object to the breath test being testified to by the officer."

"I already have the results," Judge Dunson said as he held up the marked document and waved it. "I can read. Overruled. Answer the question, Trooper."

"It was an even .10," he said.

I had a few more questions concerning the officer's DUI report. Then I brought up the matter of the defendant's suspended license. I introduced his driving record after the officer testified that he'd checked and discovered that his license was in fact suspended. I offered the driving record as an exhibit. With no objection from the defense, the judge admitted it and ordered that it be marked as state's exhibit two.

I held up a large plastic evidence bag holding several empty Coors beer cans. Trooper Still testified that he'd taken them from inside the cab of the wrecked truck. I established the chain of evidence, and that was also marked and then admitted as state's exhibit three. Finally I produced a full six-pack of Coors. Again, the officer testified that he had removed it from the truck. It was also marked and admitted.

I checked through my notes and concluded that I had asked Trooper Still all the questions I could think of. I turned to Malcom Glazebrook.

"Your witness, Counselor." I felt like I'd thrown a goldfish to a barracuda, a feeling not unlike the one that was festering in me for leaving Miss Grice with Jimmie Martin. I didn't have a great deal of confidence that the trooper could handle the challenge. That feeling eroded more as I walked back to my seat and caught a grin on the face of one of the two men sitting behind the bar.

Twelve

As a child, I used to be fascinated watching cats on our farm. When one had a tasty bird in sight, it would slink down until its belly was on the ground and its tail was straight out behind it with only a slight twitch giving away its designs toward the bird. It would then take a few slow steps and stop and watch its prey again, its eyes never once wavering. Then it would slowly crawl closer to its unsuspecting lunch. Finally, when it was close enough, the cat would spring like an arrow from a bow, and a moment later it would proudly prance off with the poor little bird in its mouth.

Malcom Glazebrook was the cat. Trooper Ferron Still was the bird. Malcom, clearly sensing the unease of the witness, was very gentle as he asked a few mundane questions. I was nervous as I saw the trooper relax. Like the bird of prey, he thought he was safe. I wanted to jump up and shout, "*Look out, Trooper! You are about to become cat food.*"

Glazebrook was good at what he did. After three or four minutes, he had the witness at ease. He hadn't asked a single damaging question. I guess Dunson thought he was not going to. I knew full well that he was. I just didn't know when or what the question would be.

At one point, the defense attorney turned around and walked back toward his table. As he did so, he gave me a sly grin. He picked up a piece of paper and returned to the podium. He studied the paper for a moment—or at least pretended to. Then he looked up at Trooper Still and smiled. I could envision that barn cat slithering closer to its prey. Then Malcom asked, "Now, you testified that you asked my client if he'd had anything to drink following the accident. Is that correct?"

"Yes, sir, it is."

"And what did you say his response was?"

"He said that he had not." The cat was getting closer, but the foolish bird didn't see it.

"I understand. Now, he also told you that he'd had two beers at Defa's. Is that also right?"

"Yes, sir," the trooper said.

"Now, you also testified that he had a blood alcohol level of .10 when you tested him at the jail. Is that also true?" Glazebrook asked, still smiling charmingly. The cat appeared ready to pounce.

"That's right," Trooper Still agreed.

"You told the court you had been trained on how to handle DUI cases. I suppose that included learning about the burn-off rate of alcohol in the human body and also how much alcohol it would take for a person of a certain weight to reach the level we discussed here. Correct?"

Trooper Still nodded.

"I didn't hear you," Glazebrook said. "This trial is being recorded. You'll need to answer verbally."

"That's correct," Still said.

"It's correct that you need to answer verbally?" Glazebrook asked.

"No. I mean, yes, I do need to answer verbally."

Glazebrook was toying with him now. The cat's tail was moving back and forth ever so slightly. "So what is your answer, Trooper?"

"My answer is yes."

"Yes what? Yes you need to speak up?"

I rose to my feet and said, "Your Honor, I object. The defense attorney is badgering the witness."

"Sustained," Judge Dunson said firmly before Glazebrook could respond. "I understood that the witness was agreeing to what you said about the amount of alcohol it takes to reach a certain level and what the dissipation rate is. Your question was asked and answered. No more games. Go ahead with your next question."

Trooper Still was getting nervous. It was like the bird was suddenly sensing danger but didn't recognize the source yet. Trooper Still kept wiping his brow. He looked down at me, and I mouthed, "Don't get upset."

He nodded and listened as Mr. Glazebrook asked, "From your training, can you tell the court if two beers many hours before the test would be enough to cause a test of .10?"

"It wouldn't," he said slowly, unknowingly stepping into a cleverly laid trap.

"That's right. So that means that the defendant must have consumed some alcohol after the accident, doesn't it?"

The trooper must have remembered my coaching at that moment, for he didn't answer quickly. Instead, he appeared to think the question over for a minute. Finally, he answered, "Not necessarily. He might have—"

I knew what he was thinking, and I knew that Judge Dunson did too, but Mr. Glazebrook didn't want him to say it. He said, "Just answer yes or no. That's all."

"No," he said firmly.

"No? Are you saying that you were wrong when you said two beers could have caused my client to achieve a .10 test? Yes or no." The cat had sprung, and the bird was in its claws.

"No," the trooper said as I could see confusion clouding his face. The bird was struggling, but it was too late.

"So he must have clearly consumed some after the accident, right?"

"No, he might—" Trooper Still began.

"Thank you. Let's move on to another matter now," Glazebrook said.

The trooper gave a visible sigh of relief. I knew it was premature, but all I could do was wait to help him clarify his answer on redirect examination. I'd warned him that something like this might arise. I could only hope he remembered. I could still help the trooper recover.

The defense attorney again turned back to his table. At that moment, my cell phone, which was sitting on my desk to the side of my legal pad, buzzed. I glanced at it. There was a text message. I quickly read it, and as I did, my blood pressure spiked. The message said, *It's me, Wyanne. I'm okay. Are you? I'll call you when I can. Please, please don't hate me.*

Thoughts of her had been attempting to intrude on my thoughts during the trial, and I'd managed to tamp them down most of the time. I didn't need the distraction. I had to give my full attention to the case.

But now I was distracted. Many questions ran quickly through my head. Where was she? Was she really okay? What did she want to call me about? Why didn't I recognize the number the message came from? How soon could I get a recess and try to call the number on the screen? Did I hate her? No! No! No! But . . .

The deep voice of Malcom Glazebrook brought me back to the matter at hand. "Trooper, did I understand correctly that you didn't get the name of the fellow that stopped to help my client?"

"That's right," he said, twisting uncomfortably in the witness chair while looking into the gallery.

Glazebrook asked a few more questions, clearly attempting to get the trooper to change his testimony about the field sobriety tests. But Still didn't budge. Finally, after a few more things that didn't amount to much, he said, "No more questions, Your Honor."

He went back to his seat. I got up and approached the podium with my legal pad in my hand. "Trooper Still," I asked as I fought to tamp down the temptation to worry about Wyanne . . . Miss Grice. I got my thoughts back on track and asked, "Mr. Glazebrook asked you if two beers would be enough to cause a test of .10, which of course is above the presumptive level in Utah of .08. He didn't give you a chance to clarify your answer. I'd like you to do that now."

"Objection!" Glazebrook shouted as he came to his feet.

"Mr. Glazebrook, that microphone in front of you works very well. You don't need to shout for the recording to be made. Tone it down," Judge Dunson said. "Now, what are you objecting to?"

"There is nothing to clarify," he said. "You heard his answers. Two beers won't produce that test in a man the size of my client. The prosecutor needs to move on to a different topic."

"Overruled," Judge Dunson said. "And remember, you are not testifying. Don't try to add to what the witnesses say in my court. I can hear them for myself. You may clarify, Trooper."

Glazebrook remained on his feet as Trooper Still began to speak. "What I wanted to say was that it is well known that a standard answer to the question of *how much have you had to drink* is two beers. He could have had—"

"Objection," Mr. Glazebrook said.

"Overruled. Sit down, Counselor," the judge said firmly.

Glazebrook sat.

"You were saying," I prompted the witness.

"He could have had many more than two. In my experience the answer 'two beers' is an admission of drinking, nothing more," he said.

"As if you have any experience," defense counsel mumbled just loud enough to be heard but not loud enough to unduly raise the ire of the judge.

I asked a few more questions just to make sure the trooper's testimony was clear, and then I said, "No more questions."

"Anything further of this witness, Mr. Glazebrook?" Judge Still asked.

"No, Your Honor."

"You may step down, Trooper," the judge said. Then to me he instructed, "Call your next witness, Mr. Saxson."

"The state rests, Your Honor," I said as my eyes wandered to my iPhone.

"Very well." The judge looked at his watch. "It's a little early, but I think we'll wait to hear the defense case this afternoon. We will recess for lunch," he said. "Be back and ready to go at one o'clock sharp."

"All rise," Deputy Rusko, the bailiff, said.

The trooper and Corporal Kingston were following me back to my chambers. As we walked, Trooper Still said, "That wasn't so bad. Thanks for letting me clarify."

"That's my job," I said, my thoughts on Miss Grice.

"I think we've got it, don't you?" he asked.

I stopped and faced him. "You did okay, Trooper, but it's not over yet. I'll see you after lunch. Come back a little early."

"Sure thing, Mr. Cartwright," he said. "I won't let you down."

I nodded, smiled, and said nothing. He didn't realize it, but he already had. I was not looking forward to the defense presenting its case.

Corporal Kingston said, "You did fine, Ferron. Why don't you and I go to lunch? Maybe I can give you an idea about what to expect from Mr. Glazebrook when he puts on his defense."

Back in my office, I spoke with our legal assistants, Becky Proctor and Josie Miller, for a moment and then shut the door and sat down at my desk. I opened the text message from Miss Grice and typed a reply. I thanked her for contacting me and said I would try to call her. I summoned all the courage I could find and typed that I missed her, and before I could change my mind, I hit the send button.

I then dialed the number on the text. It rang several times before it was finally answered. When the voice was that of Jimmie Martin, I quickly hit End and stared at my phone.

A couple of minutes later, as I was still sitting, deep in thought, I got a text. It was from the same number. It read: *Wyanne apologizes for the text. It won't happen again. And once more, Mr. Attorney, do not attempt to contact her again. Consider this fair warning.*

That was it. But it told me a whole lot. I could read between the lines as well as the next guy. And what I read was that Wyanne wanted to talk to me and that Mr. Martin was doing all he could to stop it. In fact, I viewed the message as a threat. And yes, I had just used *Wyanne*. She had texted me. It wasn't a mistake. I wasn't going to give up on her. I could only hope now that she would find a way to call me.

I punched in another number and waited until Detective Shelburn answered. "Hello, Sheldon," I said after he spoke into the phone. "It's Saxson. I thought you should know that I just got a text from Wyanne. I was wondering if you'd heard from her too."

"No, I haven't. Are you in your office?" he asked.

"I am. We're on a lunch recess."

"Then you probably want to go eat," he said. "I was going to offer to come over."

"I don't need lunch," I told him. "Come on over."

I opened my door, and in response to Josie's question about where I was going to eat, I said, "I'm not going to lunch. I need to meet with Detective Shelburn. He'll be here in a moment. Send him right in when he gets here, please."

I sat back down and reread the texts. A minute later, the door opened. "Detective Shelburn is here," Josie announced.

I thanked her, and Sheldon stepped in and shut the door behind him. I held my phone out to him as he sat across the desk. He read, frowned, and then handed the phone back to me. For a moment, he didn't speak, but he did appear to be thoughtful. Finally he said, "So it's Wyanne again, not Miss Grice." He grinned.

"Maybe," I said. "We'll see."

"I don't like what I read, Saxson. This tells me that Wyanne isn't acting of her own free will." He reached out. "Let me see that phone again."

I handed it to him. The texts were still displayed. "This isn't the number she gave me," he said as he handed the phone back again. He pulled a little notebook out of his pocket and wrote for a moment. As he put it away, he said, "I just wrote the number down."

I held the phone out to him again. "Here, make sure you get it right."

He waved it off. "I've got it. I'm good at numbers." As if he needed to prove the point, he smiled as he recited my number and then the number of the phone in Wyanne's apartment. Then he frowned. "I'm not sure Jimmie Martin is who he claims to be."

"What?!" I exclaimed.

"That's right. If I had fingerprints, we could run them and see if he pops up under a different identity."

"But Wyanne called him Jimmie," I objected.

"If I'm right, and I have a strong feeling that I am, she would have only known him as Jimmie Martin. The deceit may have begun before he ever met her," he said. "The question is how can we get his fingerprints? His car is gone. Any ideas?"

I thought for a minute. "I'll bet he left his fingerprints in Wyanne's apartment. He wasn't wearing gloves when he came that day, and he surely touched something."

"But how do we get in?" he asked.

"A search warrant?" I asked.

"Based on what?"

"Miss Grice is a witness in a homicide case, and she's missing. If we word it right, I think we can get the on-call judge to sign off," I said. "Judge Feldman is on call if I remember right. And it's one of his jurors that was murdered. He'll go for it." I sat back for a moment and rubbed my chin as I thought it over. After a moment I said, "For that matter, Detective, maybe we don't need to bother him. There might be an easier and quicker way. Jimmie Martin's prints could be on the outside doorknob. Or, if that doesn't work, maybe the manager would let you in without a warrant. After all, Wyanne is missing."

"Sounds good to me, Counselor," the detective said. "I'll work on it this afternoon. Call me when you get out of court. I'll start with the doorknob. If that doesn't do it, I'll talk to the manager. If I have to, I'll try to get a warrant, but I think you're right. I should be able to get it done the quicker way."

"Sounds good," I said. "And I appreciate it."

"Hey, Saxson, I may not have all the same reasons for wanting to find her as you do." He grinned knowingly and then went on, "But I do need to find her. I'm going to get to the bottom of this homicide mess, and when I do, we'll need her. Besides that, she could be in danger just being with this Martin guy."

"Do you know if she's called the school again by any chance?" I asked.

"I don't know, but I'll find out," he replied. "So how's it going with Malcom Glazebrook today?"

"He's got something up his sleeve. I have a sneaking suspicion what it is, but I'll find out for sure this afternoon. I've rested my case," I said.

"You can beat him, Saxson. I have faith in you."

"Thanks, but in this case, you might be wrong. I'll do the best I can. It's just that the young trooper made some mistakes, kind of big ones. We'll see how it goes."

After the detective left, I went over my notes from court, made some notations, and reread the texts. And read them yet again. Wyanne's text was a cry for help, but at the moment, I didn't see what I could possibly do other than pray for her. And I did that.

Finally, at quarter to one, I headed back to the courtroom. Trooper Still was already sitting at the table, and Corporal Kingston was standing next to him. I put my file down and sat beside him. "Hey, you're looking a little down, Trooper," I said.

"It might be my fault," Kingston said. "I've been talking to him about Glazebrook, warning him what the guy might be capable of."

"Which is why you are here as well, Corporal," I said. "All three of us need to learn all we can today about the defense attorney."

Kingston walked back in the gallery and sat down as I opened my folder. Trooper Still glanced over at me and asked, "Are you mad at me, Mr. Cartwright?"

"Good grief, no. Why would I be mad at you?" I asked. "Does Corporal Kingston think I am?"

"Oh, no, not at all."

"Then why do you wonder? I don't look mad, do I?"

"Well, I think you think we're going to lose today. Did I do that bad on the stand? I mean, you know, he did rattle me a few times, but I tried to remember what you told me."

"You did fine. We are both up against one of the wiliest defense attorneys in the state," I explained. "Win or lose, we can learn a lot from this guy."

"I don't like him. He's a jerk," he said sullenly.

"I don't like him either, but we don't have to like him to learn from him. You got unlucky by having to go to court for the first time against an attorney like Malcom Glazebrook. But remember this—there is a place, an extremely important place, for defense attorneys. Our legal system is a system of checks and balances. Defense attorneys keep guys like you and me in line. They make sure we do our jobs right. And when we don't, we have no right to get mad at them.

"What we have to do is learn from experience and do better the next time. Everybody that is accused of a crime has the right to a good defense. I believe in that. Believe it or not, sometimes cops get it wrong, and sometimes prosecutors get it wrong as well. I'd feel terrible if I sent an innocent person to prison. And believe it or not, sometimes a good defense attorney uncovers things that people like us miss. So don't dislike defense attorneys. We need them."

"I understand," he said. "I just don't see why they have to be such jerks."

"Most of them are great folks. You just had the bad luck to come up against one of the arrogant ones. You'll meet a lot of good ones as well. Take my word for it. Now," I concluded as I saw Glazebrook and his client come in, "we'll end up today having done the best we could. If we win, that's great. If we lose . . . well, so be it. And remember this too, Ferron. Don't be mad at the judge if he rules against us. He has a tough job, and he takes it seriously, but if we come up short, he'll do what he is supposed to. Now, just relax. It's up to me now. You've done the best you can. Now I need to do my best."

"Thanks, Mr. Cartwright," he said. "Corporal Kingston's right. You're an okay guy."

"Yes, the cowboy's all right, Trooper. He's just inexperienced," Malcom Glazebrook said, eavesdropping. "Today and the next time as well, he'll lose to me." He chuckled. "He's out of his league, and so are you for that matter."

The trooper didn't reply, and I said nothing either. After Glazebrook was seated again, Trooper Still leaned over and whispered, "He really is a jerk." But to his credit, he grinned. He'd be okay.

Thirteen

THE JUDGE TOOK THE BENCH, and Malcom Glazebrook called his first witness, the defendant, Karl Rutledge. He asked Rutledge about what I expected he'd ask. He confirmed that Rutledge had consumed some beer at Defa's. But Malcom then asked, "Now think, Karl, was it just two beers, or might it have been more?"

"Oh no, it was only two. I've learned that I can't handle more than two, so I always limit my beers to two," he said, looking rather smug as he talked. He'd been well coached during lunch.

"Now, let's make sure we are clear here. You did drink, but you were not under the influence of alcohol, is that right?"

I thought about objecting that his opinion should not be allowed. I changed my mind.

"You know it is," the defendant answered.

"You admit that you were driving, is that right?"

"Yeah, I was driving."

"If you were not under the influence, why did you have an accident? What caused you to lose control of your truck and tip it on its side?" Malcom asked.

The defendant relaxed in his chair and said, "Well, you see, it's like I told the kid that arrested me. This here deer, a great big buck, a four-point, ran right out into the road in front of me. Boy was he a beauty. It would have been a shame to hit a pretty buck like him with my truck. I have a bullet waiting for him come hunting season. Anyway, I slammed on my brakes. I'd've been okay if it wasn't raining so hard. The road was muddy, and I hit a rut and flipped my truck on its side. I wasn't driving very fast, and it's good I wasn't 'cause I woulda killed that beautiful deer."

I groaned silently. This guy was sure of himself.

Malcom said, "I'm sorry you damaged your truck, but I'm glad neither you nor that big buck was hurt."

"Yeah, me too," Rutledge said with a smirk.

"Now, as you know, the state's witness, Trooper Still, says that in his *opinion*, you were under the influence of alcohol. Is he right?"

"I dunno," he said. "I wasn't when I wrecked, but the beers I drank afterward, you know, while I was waiting for the cop to come, might have affected me some."

I had been expecting something like this. I swallowed hard and listened.

"Wait just a minute here, Mr. Rutledge. The officer testified that you told him you hadn't had anything to drink after the wreck. Was he lying?"

"I dunno," he said again. "I thought he meant if I'd had anything to drink from my truck. I had some Coors there, but I didn't touch none of them. But by the time Mr. Clark came along, I was cold, and when he offered me some Bud, I took it."

"So you did drink after the wreck but before the officer arrived," Glazebrook asked.

I looked over at Trooper Still. He looked as defeated as I felt. And I had a feeling that there was more to come.

"So why didn't you tell Trooper Still that you drank some beers while you were waiting?" Glazebrook asked.

"He didn't ask. If he'd have asked if I drank some of *Mr. Clark's* beer, I'd've told him that I did. If he'd have asked Mr. Clark, he'd have told him too. It was chilly, and the beer warmed me up."

Glazebrook wrapped up the direct examination of his client after only a few more questions. It was my turn, and I stepped to the podium, my legal pad in my hand. I tried to appear like I wasn't defeated. Who knew, maybe I could trip the defendant up. My first question was, "Mr. Rutledge, you do admit that you were driving. Is that right?"

He hung his head. "Yeah, I was. But I thought my license was still good."

"But of course it wasn't. Isn't that true?"

He tried to look remorseful. "Sorry. But nobody told me it wasn't. How was I supposed to know? I thought it was good."

"I see. You said the road was slick and that you weren't going very fast," I said. "Tell us how fast you were driving."

"Not very," he said.

"Did the speedometer in your truck work?" I asked.

"'Course it did. I take good care of my truck."

"How fast were you driving?" I asked again.

"I don't know for sure, probably about 15 or 20 miles per hour."

I wasn't getting anywhere with that line of questioning, so I changed my tactics. "How many times have you been convicted of drunk driving?" I asked.

"Objection!" Glazebrook roared. "What may or may not have happened to my client in the past is not admissible."

"Your Honor, you admitted the driving record of the defendant as a state exhibit. It not only shows that the defendant's license is suspended, but it also shows his previous traffic convictions. And as you know, I charged this as an enhanced offense. Furthermore, there is some discrepancy in the witness's testimony. Prior offenses might show a reason for the defendant to be less than truthful regarding his testimony today."

"That's ridiculous," Glazebrook countered. "This is clearly prejudicial."

"Your objection is overruled," Judge Dunson said. "Answer the question, Mr. Rutledge."

"What was the question?" the witness asked.

"How many times have you been convicted of driving under the influence?" I repeated.

"I renew my objection," Mr. Glazebrook said.

"I have already overruled your objection. Now sit down and let the witness speak," Judge Dunson said. Then he again directed the witness to answer my question.

"I'm not sure. Maybe two or three," he said.

"Thank you. That's all."

I sat down. The witness was excused. Mr. Glazebrook said, "The defense calls Thomas Clark."

One of the men in the gallery stood up. Beside me, Trooper Still moaned.

The man being sworn was short, fat, and had ruddy cheeks. I guessed that he'd had way more than his share of beer in his day. He took the seat, and then I stood up and said, "I object. This witness was not disclosed to me by the defendant."

"He's a rebuttal witness. I didn't know I'd need him, but when the trooper testified that my client said he hadn't had any drinks, it became important for me to call him," Malcom argued.

"He was here in the courtroom, so you clearly intended to call him," I said.

"That's not true. I didn't know who he was until my client told me at lunch. I guess I just got lucky."

I wanted to call Glazebrook a liar, for that was exactly what he was. But I refrained. I simply told the judge that it was unfair to allow him to testify.

"I'll allow him to testify," Judge Dunson said. Then he looked directly at Malcom. "But he is to testify only in rebuttal. Is that clear?"

"That's what I intend," Glazebrook said with a smirk back at me. He asked the witness to identify himself and establish that he was in fact the driver of the blue car. And then Malcom asked, "Did my client, Karl Rutledge, drink anything while he was waiting with you for Trooper Still to arrive?"

"Yes. I had a couple of six-packs of Bud in my car. I let him drink a few cans," Mr. Clark answered.

"No more questions," Glazebrook said. The dagger had been thrust.

I stood and walked to the podium. The only thing I could do was try to discredit the witness. "Mr. Clark," I said, "how long have you and Mr. Rutledge been friends?"

"Objection!" Malcom shouted.

"Overruled, and you don't have to shout," Judge Dunson said. "Answer the question."

"We've been buddies for years. I don't know for sure how long," Mr. Clark said.

"Drinking buddies?"

"Objection!"

"Overruled."

"I guess you could say that," he said.

"Isn't it true that you and Mr. Rutledge were drinking together at Defa's earlier that day?"

"So what if we did?" he asked belligerently.

"I'll take that as a yes. How much did you drink when you were there with the defendant?"

"Objection!"

"Overruled."

"Two beers."

"Of course," I said. "How much did you drink while you and the defendant were waiting for the officer to arrive?"

"Two beers," he said.

"How many times have you been convicted of driving under the influence?" I asked.

"Objection, Your Honor. You can't just let the cowboy keep asking these kinds of questions," Malcom Glazebrook said.

Judge Dunson's face grew dark; he leaned forward and pointed at Malcom. "I warned you twice, Mr. Glazebrook. I hope you have your checkbook with you. You are in contempt of this court. When we are finished here, you are to write a check for $500.00. Now to your objection, you are again overruled. You sprung this witness on the prosecution. I am going to give him a lot of latitude."

Glazebrook, fuming, sat down.

"Mr. Clark, how many times have you been convicted of driving under the influence of alcohol?" I asked again. "And remember that you are under oath, and my legal assistant can quickly and easily get me a copy of your driving record."

The smugness was gone from Thomas Clark's face. "I think maybe four," he said.

"And were you under the influence on the day of your friend's accident and arrest?"

"I don't think so."

"What is your date of birth?" I asked.

"Objection!"

"Overruled."

I wrote down Mr. Clark's birth date and then said, "Nothing further," and returned to my seat.

Mr. Glazebrook stood, but he sat right back down again. "Defense rests," he said.

Trooper Still leaned over to me as the witness was returning to his seat. "Wow, you sure did a good job with him."

"Don't get too excited, Trooper," I said. "It might not have been enough. All Mr. Glazebrook needed to do was create a reasonable doubt."

"Mr. Cartwright, do you have any rebuttal witnesses?" Judge Dunson asked.

"No, Your Honor, I'm ready to argue," I said.

"Do we need a recess first?"

"I do," Glazebrook said. "I'd like to work on my closing statement."

Judge Dunson rapped his gavel. "We will be in recess for fifteen minutes." He turned and hurried off the bench.

"I'll see you in a few minutes," I said to Trooper Still.

As I entered the office, our lead legal assistant, Becky, asked me how it was going. "I think we might lose this one. The trooper made some mistakes that I'm sure he'll never make again."

I stepped into my private office. Josie stuck her head in and said, "Detective Shelburn would like you to call him as soon as you can."

"Okay, but while I do that, would you run a driver's license check for me? I'll need it before I go back into court in a few minutes." I gave her the full name and birth date of the surprise witness.

"I'll have it," Josie promised.

I dialed Detective Shelburn's cell phone number. He answered right away. "Hi, Saxson. How's it going in court?"

"Not as well as I'd like," I said. "Did you have something for me?"

"I lifted some prints from the doorknob, but I also persuaded the apartment manager to let me into Miss Grice's apartment. I got some better ones in there. Of course, I don't know which are hers, which are yours, which are Martin's, and which might be from a friend or neighbor."

"Mine are on file," I said. "I don't know about Wyanne's."

"I'll sort through it. I just wanted you to know we wouldn't need a search warrant. But that's not all," the detective said. "I dialed the number Miss Grice texted from."

"Did anyone answer?" I asked.

"Jimmie Martin did, and he told me to bug off."

"Why am I not surprised?" I said. "I won't be in court much longer."

"Call me when you're back in your office," he said.

I made a short outline for my closing argument, took the driving record of Thomas Clark from Josie, and returned to the courtroom. I noticed that the surprise witness, Thomas Clark, whose record I held in my hand, wasn't in the courtroom. I asked Deputy Leland Rusko, the bailiff, about him.

He grinned. "He's being booked. I arrested him for intoxication. I should have caught it before, but I wasn't the one that screened him when he came into the courthouse."

"Does Judge Dunson know?"

"I'm sure he does. I told Yolanda, and you know how she is," he said. "She was jumping up and down when she said she'd tell the judge." Yolanda Montez was one of the deputy clerks in Judge Dunson's court. She was a spitfire. "The judge wants him brought back as quick as he's booked. They'll be along with him shortly."

"Maybe I won't need this," I said, waving the driving record. "His record is as bad as his buddy's."

In my closing argument, I simply covered the main points of my case and told the judge that I thought that Mr. Clark, the surprise witness, was not reliable and that his testimony should be discounted. I made the same argument about Mr. Rutledge. I pointed out that they both had a motive for lying. In Clark's case it was to help his friend. In the defendant's case, it was in his own self-interest to lie. Finally, I pointed out that the defendant admitted that he was driving while his license was suspended.

Malcom Glazebrook spent more time speaking than I did. He tried to hammer home the fact that the judge had been given reasonable doubt as to the defendant being under the influence at the time of the wreck. He also brought up the suspension charge. He stated that it was a reasonable defense that Mr. Rutledge did not know that his license was suspended. He then told the judge that there was no way he could do anything except find his client not guilty on both counts.

I had the last word, as the prosecution always does. But all I did was point out that it was not a valid defense if the defendant truly didn't know he was on suspension. I urged the judge to find Karl Rutledge guilty on both counts and sat down.

"I wonder where Corporal Kingston is going," Trooper Still said.

I turned just in time to see Kingston leaving the courtroom with his phone to his ear. "He must have gotten some kind of call," I said.

"But he's off duty," he reminded me.

"Maybe his wife needed a gallon of milk or something."

We turned our attention to the judge as he began to speak. "I have listened carefully to the evidence," he said. "And I have made a decision."

Malcom whispered loud enough that I could hear him say, "We should stand up, Karl. But don't worry; we've got this one." The two of them stood and faced the judge.

"Mr. Rutledge, I find you guilty of driving with a suspended license." The judge paused as the door that connected the courtroom to a holding cell opened. An officer escorted Thomas Clark in and pointed to one of the jury chairs. Clark, wearing an orange jumpsuit, was sullen as he sat down. "Mr. Clark, I'll get to you in a moment," Judge Dunson said. Then he again addressed the defendant and said, "To the charge of driving under the influence, I find you not guilty."

"Thank you, Your Honor," Malcom Glazebrook said.

"Let me explain why I have ruled the way I have," he said. He looked at me as he spoke. "I honestly suspect that Mr. Rutledge *was* driving while under the influence, but I am bound by the law, and the law says I must find 'beyond a reasonable doubt,' and I think there's a very good chance that Rutledge was drinking while he was waiting for Trooper Still to arrive. That creates reasonable doubt about his alcohol content at the time of the accident."

He addressed the defendant again and said, "You have the right to be sentenced in not less than two nor more than forty-five days to the suspended driving conviction. Also, you are entitled to appeal my decision on that matter, but it must be done within twenty-eight days."

Glazebrook whispered something to his client, and then said, "We waive time for sentencing. We'd like to proceed today. And there will be no appeal."

Trooper Still whispered, "So he gets a $310 fine and walks. I really messed up."

I didn't comment. The judge directed the defendant and his client to stand at the podium. As soon as they were there, he asked, "Counsel, would either of you like to make any recommendations before I pronounce judgment?"

"Standard fine, a week of suspended jail, and a short probation is reasonable," Glazebrook said.

I countered with, "I think a fine of $1,000 and thirty days in jail would be more likely to help Mr. Rutledge learn that he shouldn't be driving while suspended. He has a number of previous convictions for that offense."

"Thank you, gentlemen. Karl Rutledge," he began, "I have your driving record on my monitor here. Let's talk about it for a moment. I see three driving-under-the-influence convictions. And I see that you are an alcohol-restricted driver. That means you can't drive with *any* alcohol in your system."

"He wasn't charged with that," Malcom said quickly.

"No, he wasn't," Judge Dunson said, "but there's nothing to preclude me from taking into consideration his admission to two beers before he got into his truck."

"You're the judge," Glazebrook said snidely.

"Yes, as a matter of fact, I am. Now, back to the driving record." He studied it for a moment. Finally, he sighed and looked at the defendant again. "You have been convicted of driving while either suspended or revoked *twelve* times. I also see two convictions for driving without an interlock ignition device. I won't get into all the moving violations and driving without insurance that I see here. The fine, including surcharges, is $1,000. And I am giving you 180 days in jail of which I will suspend 120. Bailiff, the jail sentence is to begin today. You are to take him into custody as soon as I adjourn this court."

The judge set up a schedule for payment of the fine and gave him a two-year probation. He rattled off some pretty stiff terms, and then he said, "Mr. Glazebrook, you and your client may sit down. Bailiff, would you escort Mr. Clark to the podium? Mr. Clark, I understand that you testified in my court after you'd been consuming alcohol. Is that true?"

"Just two beers," he said.

"You are in contempt of this court. I am ordering you to serve five days in jail starting now. Bailiff, both of these men are to go to jail right now. And Mr. Glazebrook, don't forget the $500 you owe. Pay it to my clerk at the window before you leave. We are adjourned." He rapped his gavel and left the bench.

Fourteen

As I shuffled my papers back into the file, Trooper Ferron Still said, "Wow! Judge Dunson really hammered him."

I picked up the file and looked at him with a grin on my face. "I guess you could say that we lost but we also won. You did okay, but you'll do better next time."

"I sure will. I've learned a lot today."

Malcom Glazebrook stepped toward me and held his hand out. "I am surprised, Cartwright," he said. "You got lucky today. You managed to get something out of nothing. I'd like to meet with you before I leave." His face broke into an uncharacteristic smile, and he added, "First I have to give the court five hundred bucks. But it was worth it. I had fun today. And of course, my fee to my client just went up by $500." He laughed. "I'll see you in your office in a moment. I have an offer to discuss with you. And Trooper Still, did you learn anything today?"

"Yes, sir. I did," Trooper Still said.

"Good. The next time we meet in court, I'll expect to have to work harder to beat you. But I will beat you. Of that you can be sure."

I watched as Glazebrook left the courtroom.

The trooper said, "For a minute there, I almost believed he was human."

"We both learned some things today. I better get to my office."

"I still wonder where Kingston went," he said. "I wanted to talk to him."

"Give him a call," I suggested.

Still dialed his cell phone. We walked to the back of the courtroom together, and he clicked off his phone. "It just went to voice mail," he said. "I hope everything's okay."

I felt a flutter of worry. I hoped so too. He was a good officer and a smart man. I decided to call him myself in an hour or so.

As I walked toward my office, I pushed Kingston from my mind and finally allowed thoughts of Wyanne to linger there. I was anxious to find out where she was and find a way to get her away from Jimmie Martin—or whoever the creep was. One thing I was quite certain of was that he was not her fiancé or even a former boyfriend.

Josie said, "Detective Shelburn got called out on a case. I don't know what. But he stuck his head in and said to tell you that he'll call you when he gets a minute."

I was disappointed. I was hoping he'd learned something about Martin. "Thanks," I said. "Malcom Glazebrook will be in as soon as he pays his contempt fine over in justice court."

"Did you say contempt?" Becky asked as she entered from another office. "Who's in contempt?"

"The sweet Mr. Glazebrook," Josie replied with a wicked grin. "Can you imagine that?"

Becky's eyebrows went up. "Have you ever seen Judge Dunson find anyone in contempt before?"

"No, but I think he has. It's rare, yet he did it twice today." I explained about Thomas Clark. We had a good laugh, and I went to my office to await the visit from Glazebrook. I assumed he wanted to try another offer to get me to reduce the case on Jarrod Miano.

I switched my phone off vibrate and willed it to ring with Wyanne at the other end. It remained ominously still. I thought about calling Dave. I knew he'd want a report on the case I'd tried today. But just then Josie stuck her head in and said, "Malcom Glazebrook is here."

I sighed. "I guess I better see what he wants. Send him in."

Malcom stepped in, offered his hand to me, and said, "I think you'll find what I have to say to be of interest to you."

I'd see about that. I didn't say that out loud. I did say, "Have a seat, and I'll listen. And by the way, congratulations on your win today."

"Thanks, Saxson, I appreciate that," he said as he settled his lanky frame into a chair and began to stroke his long black mustache. "I meant it when I said you did a good job," he offered. "You didn't have much to work with, but you did okay. That brings me to my offer. And I hope you will seriously consider this. How much do you make working here?"

That caught me off guard. "Why do you want to know that?"

"Tell me what you make, and then I'll tell you what I have to offer," he said.

"I don't usually discuss my salary, but I live fine on what I make. And I like my job here," I said. "That's worth a lot in and of itself."

"Okay," he said as he twisted slightly in his seat. "I have to assume it's not very much. I have two other attorneys in my office. We need another one. I'd like to offer you a position, and I can guarantee that you'll make several times what you make here."

I was stunned. I guess my face must have shown it because he said, "You didn't see that coming, did you?"

"No, quite honestly, I didn't," I said. "But why would you want me? We are very different."

"Saxson," he said, "you have spunk. You're smart. You can learn. I can teach you. We may be different, but we could use a nice guy like you, a nice but ambitious young lawyer who's not afraid to work."

"You don't want me," I said after a long pause. "Let me tell you why I went to law school in the first place." I told him about my sister and our friends and about the prosecutor that did a lousy job on the case. "To my parents' chagrin, I decided to be a lawyer and to prosecute instead of stay on the ranch."

"So you really are a cowboy," he said. "Do you ride bucking horses and all that stuff?"

"I've done it all, Malcom," I said. "And frankly, I miss it, but I keep a couple of horses here and ride whenever I can."

"I'll be darned," he said.

"All that aside, I went to law school to become a prosecutor," I said. "I appreciate the offer, but I'm right where I want to be."

"I'm sorry to hear it," Malcom said. "I'd like to have you on my side so I wouldn't have to keep beating you up in court." He smiled pleasantly. "Okay, I guess that means you'll be prosecuting Jarrod Miano again. So, that being the case, I have something more to discuss with you. I have decided that you are better than I thought you were. I'd like you to consider letting Jarrod plead no contest to reckless driving. Of course, there would be nothing in the plea about alcohol. And a guilty plea is out of the question as I'm sure he'll be sued, and I want to be able to show that he did not admit guilt. You understand that, I'm sure."

"I do," I said.

"Okay, what do you think?"

I pretended to think it over, although I was opposed to the idea. Finally, I said, "Let me talk to Miss Keen's parents. If they agree to it, I'll do the same, but frankly I think they want to go to trial again."

"Well, as long as you let them make the decision." He stood up. "This case today was a trial run, you might say. You did okay for a young buck, but don't get cocky, Saxson. I out lawyered you today, and I will again. But in all honesty, I'll expect more of a fight from you than I did before. Short a witness, you'll have to work harder. " He held his hand out again. I shook it. Then he said, "The offer of a job is still on the table. Let me know if you change your mind. And let me know what Miss Keen's parents say. I have a feeling they'd like this thing to be wrapped up. And I know my client would." He moved to the door, and I stepped around the desk.

"Thanks for coming in. I think both the trooper and I learned something today," I said. "I thank you for that."

"You're welcome. And I'll teach you and Corporal Kingston a few more things in a few weeks—unless you change your mind, of course. And I sincerely hope you do. I'm sure we could find a place for your horses somewhere in the Salt Lake Valley. Oh, and one more thing. About the reckless driving offer. I won't oppose a reasonable jail sentence," he said.

"Exactly what do you mean by reasonable?" I asked.

"Thirty days max," he said. "Tell the Keens that. Maybe they'll agree to save both you and me some trouble."

"I'll tell them," I said. "Drive careful going back to the city."

We walked together to the parking lot. I watched as he climbed into his vehicle. A black Cadillac Escalade. My stomach did a summersault, and as I walked back into the office, I felt chilled. *Black Escalade.*

My cell began to ring as I stepped into the reception area of the office. I pulled my phone out as I walked into my office and shut the door. Not until then did I look at the screen, willing it to be Wyanne.

It wasn't. It was my boss. "Hi, Dave," I said.

"I figured you'd be through with your trial by now. How did it go?" he asked.

"Won one and lost one," I said.

"That means you lost the DUI. Did it surprise you?" he asked.

"Not really," I responded. I explained in some detail how the case went, including the sentence Judge Dunson imposed and the two citations for contempt of court. "It was an educational day," I concluded.

"Did Glazebrook attempt to discuss the Miano case with you?" he asked.

"He did. He asked me to consider a no-contest plea and up to thirty days in jail for reckless driving. He wants no mention of alcohol and won't even consider a guilty plea."

"You better take it to the victim's family," he said.

"I will, but I'm pretty sure they'll turn it down."

"Of course. Even without our murdered witness, we have a solid case. We can go to court on this, and we can win," he said. "Have you heard anything from Miss Grice, or has Detective Shelburn?"

"I got a text from Wyanne. She promised to call, but so far nothing," I said. "Both Detective Shelburn and I tried calling her. I also texted. We both heard back from Jimmie Martin." I told him what Martin had texted and what he'd told Sheldon. "Something is terribly wrong. I'm afraid she's being held against her will."

"Is Sheldon working on it?"

I assured Dave that he was, and then I asked him how he was feeling. "I'm getting there, Saxson. It's just taking me longer than I'd like. But I trust you and the other guys to keep the office running."

"And Becky and Josie," I said. "Those gals are on top of things."

We said good-bye, and I leaned back in my chair. I was mentally exhausted. I checked the time. It wasn't quite four o'clock yet. I had time to go for a ride on Midnight or Raspberry if I left soon. I didn't have to be sitting here when Wyanne or Sheldon called; I could take their calls anywhere.

I straightened things on my desk and was about to leave when Josie said, "Do you have a minute to speak with Judge Dunson? Katherine Ingram was just in here, and she said the judge would like to speak with you before you leave."

"I was just leaving, but I'll talk to him first. I'll stop by his chambers on my way out."

Judge Dunson's three clerks were giddy about the check for five hundred dollars from Mr. Glazebrook. I visited with them for a moment before I stepped into the judge's chambers.

"Hey, Counselor," he said. "How are you?"

"I'm fine," I said. "You surprised me today. I didn't expect you to throw the book on Rutledge after I lost on the DUI."

"The defendant is out of control. He needed some jail time. I'm sorry I had to find him not guilty on the DUI."

"Hey, Judge," I said, "you did what I would have done had I been in your shoes. And honestly, I think Trooper Still learned something from today's trial. I think he'll be more thorough in the future."

He agreed. We had only visited for a few minutes when my cell phone rang. I pulled it out and looked at the screen, disappointed that it wasn't Wyanne. "I need to take this," I said. "It's Detective Shelburn."

He nodded, and I took the call. "Saxson, I think you may want to meet me out here."

"Out where?" I asked.

"I'm in Indian Canyon, about ten or twelve miles from town," he said. "We've got a situation here. It's not good. Someone shot Corporal Kingston."

"What?!" I exclaimed. "He was in my courtroom this afternoon. What in the world happened?"

"We don't know yet. They flew him by helicopter to the hospital. He was wearing his vest or he'd already be dead. Someone meant to kill him, Saxson."

"I'm on my way," I told him. I clicked off and said to Judge Dunson, "Corporal Kingston of the highway patrol has been shot. I'm heading to the scene up Indian Canyon."

"How bad is it?" he asked, concern in his eyes and his voice.

"He's alive, but that's all I know," I said as I exited his office.

"What's the matter?" one of the clerks, Yolanda Montez, asked.

"The judge can fill you in. I've got to hurry."

As soon as I was in my truck and on the road, I called Dave back via the truck's Bluetooth.

"But I just talked to you," he said, stating the obvious.

"Sorry, boss, but I'm headed to the scene of another shooting. Someone shot Corporal Kingston. He's alive and in the hospital. Detective Shelburn asked me to come out there. I just wanted to make sure it's okay with you. Both of the other guys are in Roosevelt."

"Go for it, Saxson. I hope this doesn't have anything to do with the Miano case. If it does, we've got a serious problem," he said.

"I'm afraid it might have. Kingston was off duty and on his phone when he left the courtroom toward the end of the trial. I'm wondering if it could have been a setup."

"Saxson, watch your back. You could be next."

That thought had already occurred to me, and it was very unsettling.

I drove faster than I should have up the canyon. Trooper Still's worries about Corporal Kingston, and for that matter my own, had been valid. I silently prayed that he would live. I needed him for the Miano case, yes, but that was nothing, really. He had a young family. They needed him far worse than I did.

Detective Shelburn waved me over to where he was standing when I pulled up behind a line of parked vehicles. Several officers were taking pictures and measurements, and others scoured the area around Kingston's patrol car. "He was apparently standing right here in front of his car when he got shot," Sheldon said.

"You say his vest saved him?" I asked.

"Possibly," he said. "The first person to stop after he was shot was a Mr. Bill Rambler. He's from Vernal. He's still here. He's sitting in his car writing a statement."

"So was he shot more than once?" I asked as I stared at the blood on the pavement.

"Yes, he was shot three times: once in the leg; once in the chest, right over his heart; and once in the neck. The one in the leg bled badly, but the one in the neck is the most serious. I'm not sure he'll survive. They took him by Life Flight to the Intermountain Medical Center in Murray."

"This scares the heck out of me," I said. "It has to be related to the Miano case."

"I'm still looking at a couple of things with Mr. Morberg's partner, but this has me thinking more than ever that this has to do with keeping Miano from getting convicted."

He showed me around the scene for a moment, and we talked about the shooting. Finally, I switched gears. "I was offered a job today by Malcom Glazebrook."

Detective Shelburn jerked his head around. "You're not seriously going to consider it, are you?"

"You know me better than that. But here's what I thought you should know. I walked him to his car after he'd made the offer—oh, he also offered to plead Miano to reckless driving, no contest, of course, and to agree to thirty days in jail."

"Are you going to take it? At this point, you may have to. If Kingston can't testify, what choice do you have?" he asked.

His observations mirrored my own. "Glazebrook will hear about this, and when he does I expect he'll withdraw the offer. I don't have a case without the corporal."

"Boy, this looks bad, Saxson. I've got to find out who's behind all these shootings." He looked at me with a question in his eyes. "You walked out to Glazebrook's car? I got the feeling there was something else you were going to tell me."

"Have you ever seen what he drives?" I asked.

"No, I don't have any idea what he drives."

"Would you like to guess?"

He began to shake his head. "Don't tell me it's a black SUV."

"An Escalade. But of course, even if we did suspect him of the other shootings, he didn't do this one. He was with me until just before you called."

Sheldon looked into the distance for a moment. I guessed that he was thinking exactly what I was. When his eyes met mine again, he said, "This one was different from the others. Someone could have done it for him." He shook his head. "I hate to even think something like this. Surely no attorney would be so corrupt as to murder people to win a case."

"I'd hope not," I said, "but we can't rule it out. The Miano family is loaded. I mean, they have so much money there's no way they could ever spend it."

"So if they offered their attorney a huge bonus if he were to win, perhaps he would resort to murder to get the money. Greed does awful things to people, Counselor."

"Maybe when he told me I'd be out lawyered, this is what he meant. He beats me by killing my case, literally," I said. Then I shook my head. "I hope we're on the wrong track here. Glazebrook was actually halfway nice to me after the trial was over. Even though he got the guy off, he told me I'd done a good job with what I had to work with. And he encouraged Trooper Still to have a better case the next time they met in court."

When we got back to where Kingston had been shot, a man of about forty approached us. He was dressed in tan pants, a light brown shirt, and a red tie. He had a light yellow jacket over it all. He was about six feet tall, was slender, and had short red hair. As he turned toward me, his blue eyes glistened. Detective Shelburn introduced us. "Mr. Rambler, this is Saxson Cartwright with the Duchesne County Attorney's Office. Saxson, this is the man who was first at the scene, Bill Rambler. Bill is a trauma nurse. If Kingston survives, it will be because of what Bill did when he got here."

"How long had Kingston been down before you arrived, do you think?" I asked Bill.

"Not long. In fact, I think the black car that was just going around that curve was probably your shooter," he said as he pointed south. "I came from that way." He pointed back to the north, toward Duchesne. "The car was really hauling."

"Black, you said? Could you tell anything other than that?" I asked.

"Not really," he said. "But I'm pretty sure it was black. Well, maybe a real dark blue. It might have been an SUV of some kind, but I can't really say."

I looked at Detective Shelburn, and he nodded. "You're thinking the same thing I am."

"Probably," I agreed. I addressed the witness again. "So it had barely happened when you arrived."

"By the grace of God, yes," he said reverently. "The officer was conscious, but he didn't speak. I saw instantly that I had to stop the bleeding from both his neck and his leg, or he would bleed out in a matter of a minute or two."

"Most people wouldn't have known what to do," Sheldon said.

"Most people would have thought he was already dead. I would have thought that as well if it hadn't been for the way the blood was pumping out of his leg and his neck. The shooter may have thought he was dead, especially with that shot to the chest. Without his vest, that bullet would have hit his heart."

"But Kingston never spoke to you, right?" I asked.

"No, but one eye opened when I spoke to him," Bill said. "I would swear that he gave a sigh of relief. You know, like he might have thought I was the man who'd shot him and was going to finish him off. He apparently realized I wasn't. He passed out shortly after that."

"If anyone but you had been here first, he would have died," Sheldon said.

"I did what I could for him," Bill said softly. "I just pray it was enough."

I heard and felt a text come in on my iPhone. I quickly retrieved it from my pocket. *Help me,* I read on the screen.

Fifteen

My knees felt like they would buckle. I felt the blood drain from my face. My hand started to shake. Detective Shelburn held out his hand and said, "Let me see that."

I released my iPhone to him and put my hands over my face.

Bill Rambler said, "Let's get you sitting down. You look like you've just had a shock."

Had I ever! Those two words had hit me right between the eyes. I didn't see the number that the text came from, but I knew as surely as I'd ever known anything that the message was from Wyanne. She was in serious trouble.

Bill was steering me toward a nearby car, but I shook him off. "I'll be okay," I said. "I'm not a weakling, really. I just got that text, and it . . ." I didn't finish.

Sheldon joined us. "Forward this to me," he said as he handed my phone back. The screen was black now, and I had to touch it with my thumb to open it. Steadier now, I read the message again. Nothing had changed. It was still a cry for help, but I didn't recognize the number. I fumbled for a minute in an attempt to send it to Sheldon's phone.

He reached out and took the phone back. "Let me do it now that the phone is unlocked," he said. He worked quickly. "It's the same number she texted you from before."

"Are you sure?" I asked.

"I told you I'm good with numbers, Counselor," he said with a forced smile. "I don't forget phone numbers."

"That's a rare gift," Bill Rambler said. "Does that text have anything to do with what happened here today?"

Before I could answer, Sheldon said, "There. It's on my phone now."

He handed it back to me. I read the text again and then put the phone away. "In answer to your question, Bill," I said, "it could have something to do with this shooting. A loose connection is all though." A thought ran through my mind. It prompted me to ask, "Is there any chance the driver of the black car may have seen you?"

Before he answered, Sheldon picked up on my thought. "This is very important. Think hard. Did you notice the car before you pulled up here?" he asked.

Bill slowly shook his head. "I was stopping, and I just looked to make sure my car wasn't going to be in a spot that would endanger other drivers. That's when I saw the black car. But I only looked at it for a moment because I could see that the officer needed help immediately."

"It was driving very fast, you said," Sheldon observed. "So if he happened to look south as he left the scene, he might have seen your car coming, right?"

Mr. Rambler looked up and down the highway, and then he said, "Yes, that's possible."

"But he couldn't have seen you get out of the car?" I asked.

"Oh no, he was around that curve by the time I had parked," he responded. "Why? Do you think I'm in some kind of danger?"

"If he didn't see you, you should be okay," Sheldon said. He waved the phone that he still held in his hand. "The young woman we believe this text came from saw a black SUV a few minutes before she found the body of a murder victim. She soon started getting threats."

The man's color faded, and the freckles on his nose and cheeks stood out. "So is there a connection between that murder and this shooting today?" he asked astutely.

"Most likely. The dead man was a juror in a case Mr. Cartwright was prosecuting. Corporal Kingston was the arresting officer," Sheldon revealed. "And it gets worse. A key witness in the case was also murdered."

Bill Rambler was a smart man. "And now the officer could die. He was meant to die. What would that do to your case, Mr. Cartwright?"

"It would effectively kill it, no pun intended," I said.

"Someone wants the person you were prosecuting to get off," Bill added. "It must have been a serious case."

"If he's convicted, he would almost certainly spend time in prison," I said.

"And his family is very wealthy," Sheldon added.

"I guess I better hope the guy didn't see me," Bill concluded and rightly so.

"Just be watchful," Sheldon said to Bill. "If you do get any threats, call me. Don't take any chances." Then he turned back to me. "I think I can wrap it up here and let the others finish with the crime scene. You and I better get back to town. Maybe by the time we get there we'll know more about Jimmie Martin."

"Is that who might be after . . . who might have shot the officer?" Bill asked. "Jimmie Martin?"

"You have nothing to fear from Martin. He's a different threat to the girl who saw the car that may have been driven by the killer. We don't know much about him yet, but we don't think there's any way he could be related to the family of the man Saxson is prosecuting."

"What about you?" Bill asked me. "Are you in danger too?"

"I've been threatened," I told him honestly, "but my concern is for the girl who sent me this text. I can take care of myself."

"That's what Kingston said," Sheldon reminded me.

I felt a chill come over me. We had some work to do.

***

An hour later, Detective Shelburn and I were sitting in his office looking at a couple of printouts. He'd hit pay dirt with one of the fingerprints taken from Wyanne's apartment.

"Martin Jameson," Sheldon murmured. "He changed his name but kept it close." He swiveled around to face his computer. "Let's see what we can learn about Jameson."

What we learned was not good. In fact it was very, very bad. Martin Jameson had served time in a Nevada prison for aggravated assault and armed robbery. He also had previous offenses on his record before that. But from the time of his release from prison, the only thing Sheldon could find was that he had successfully completed his parole.

"He may have changed his stripes," Sheldon said as he looked up from his computer. "But *I'm* guessing he's still the same vicious tiger that went to prison." He once again started working his mouse and keyboard. "Let's see what else we can find—maybe an old address or one for his parents."

I was feeling quite helpless. I could think of nothing I could do to contribute. All I could do was worry about Wyanne. I got a distraction when my phone rang. It was my boss again.

"Saxson, what's going on?" he asked. "Is the highway patrolman going to make it?"

"I don't know. Detective Shelburn called the hospital after we left the scene. He was told that Kingston's in surgery, and that's all we know." I stepped out of Sheldon's office so I wouldn't distract him. "He was meant to be dead." I explained in some detail about Bill Rambler, the shot to the heart that was stopped by the bulletproof vest, and the sigh of relief when Kingston apparently realized that it wasn't the killer who was standing over him.

"There's no doubt Kingston's shooting and the previous ones are all an attempt to stop the trial. And if Kingston doesn't make it, young Mr. Miano walks free," he said, the bitterness in his voice matching the bitterness in my heart.

We talked for a little longer before I told him, "I got a text from Wyanne Grice."

"Really? Is she still okay?" he asked.

"No," I answered flatly. "She sent two words from the same cell phone number as before."

"Which means Jimmie Martin will figure out that she sent it," he concluded. "What did she say?"

"Help me," I responded. "But I don't know what to do. I feel so helpless."

I heard Dave groan, and then he said, "Is Detective Shelburn working on it, or is he too busy on today's shooting?"

"He is working on it and is making some progress," I told Dave. "We now know that Jimmie Martin is actually an ex-con by the name of Martin Jameson."

"Brilliant," Dave said facetiously.

For the next little while, I told him what little we knew about Jameson, none of which was positive when it came to Wyanne's predicament. "Let Sheldon work on it," he counseled me. "I need for you to talk to the family of Angelica Keen. At this point, it would be best if we settled the case. But see what they think. Maybe that will get your mind off Wyanne for a little while. Then if Kingston comes through the surgery, I think I'll have you go to Murray and see if you can talk to him. I'm sure Sheldon will want to go, but I doubt he'll push you away from his case."

"He'll be fine, and frankly, I'd like to stay on it as much as I can," I said.

"What have you got on your calendar next week?" he asked.

"I have district court on Monday, and then on Tuesday, Judge Dunson has a pretrial calendar and a couple of bench trials that will probably be settled."

"I'll have one of the other guys cover for you, Saxson. I might even be able to come in myself. I can work on the pretrial calendar if I need to," he said. "You work with Sheldon in any way he'll let you. And frankly, if Sheldon makes an arrest on the killings, I'll want you to be in the trial with me. We'll work it together."

"You need to take care of yourself," I reminded him.

"I will. If I need to, I'll have one of my civil attorneys at the county building help out on the juvenile and district court calendars next week. You concentrate on the Miano case and Miss Grice's situation. Do whatever you need to do to see to it that our killer comes to justice and that she is found," he instructed me. "And, Saxson, watch every move you make. I'm sure Kingston was lured into a trap. Don't let the same thing happen to you."

When I went back into Sheldon's office, he looked up and flashed a tired smile. "Jameson's parents have an address in Vegas. I just got off the phone with an officer down there. He is going to go have a talk with them. Then we can decide what to do. I wish we had more officers in the department. I'm feeling overloaded," he said as he rubbed his temples. "At least, for now, I think I can quit looking at the dead juror's former partner for the killings. There's no way he would be after Kingston."

"I probably can't do much, but my boss said that if you could use my help, he'd clear my calendar for me," I said.

He brightened up. "That would be great. If I have to go to Vegas, I'd like you to go with me," he said.

"I'll do it," I responded. "Dave also wants me to visit Kingston when he comes out of surgery and is alert enough to talk. However, if you'd rather I didn't talk to Kingston until later, let me know."

"Hey, if Dave Padrick wants you to talk to him, then you do it. But I'm sure that won't be until tomorrow morning sometime—if at all."

"We've got to believe that he's going to make it, Detective," I said.

"I'll keep trying to trace Martin Jameson. Our top priority right now is finding Miss Grice."

I couldn't have agreed more. "Before I do anything else, Dave wants me to talk to the Keens. He thinks that we need to settle the Miano case at this point. But they've got to be on board before we do that."

"I understand," Sheldon said. "I'll keep you in the loop. And if Kingston is up to it, we'll go to the hospital together. We could talk to him and still make it to Las Vegas tomorrow if we need to."

"I'll be available for whatever you need," I told him. I turned back to the door. Then I stopped and looked back at Sheldon. "If the Keens agree to a deal, I'll want to stop at Malcom Glazebrook's office tomorrow and let him know. The sooner we can pull Miano back into court for a plea, the better."

"We'll make the time," he said. "I'd like to take a look at Glazebrook's SUV if it's there," he said. "He's on my list of *people of interest.*" He smiled, but I knew he was quite serious.

When I visited the Keens' home, I was welcomed warmly by Nayla, a pretty woman with dark brown hair and brown eyes. She was slightly overweight, but as I observed her, I was sure she'd lost weight over the past few weeks. It was undoubtedly a rough time for her. Her face was pinched, and she moved like a much older woman than the forty-five-year-old woman she actually was. It was heart wrenching.

"Shelby will be home any moment now," she said, forcing a smile. "It's nice of you to come by."

"There is something I need to speak to you and Shelby about," I said. "Would it be better if I came back later?"

"No, I just talked to him," she said. "He'll be here shortly. Why don't you sit down. Would you like a soda?"

"Thanks, I'm fine," I said. We visited for the next few minutes. I asked her about her other children, and she told me that they were doing as well as could be expected.

It wasn't long before Shelby walked in, a frown on his face. He was a burly man, about five ten with hair that needed to be cut. Like his wife, I think he'd lost weight since the death of his daughter. I stood and shook his hand. He didn't appear glad to see me. His first comment confirmed that.

"You wouldn't be here if there wasn't a problem of some kind," he said.

"I'm sorry, but I do need to speak with both of you. I was in court on another matter with Malcom Glazebrook today." They didn't need any clarification. They knew very well who Malcom was, and they had made it clear on several occasions that they didn't like him. I didn't blame them. "He asked me to speak to you about a proposal he has."

"No need to talk to us, Saxson," Shelby said angrily. "You know we aren't interested in any kind of deal. We want that rotten rich kid in prison, and we won't settle for anything less."

"I understand how you feel, but when a serious offer is made, I am obligated ethically to let you hear it. It can't be my decision alone," I explained.

"Well, you're here, and you can go back and tell him we said no. And that we mean it," Shelby said.

Nayla touched his arm gently. They were sitting side by side on a love seat. I sat at an angle from them on a padded chair. My eyes met hers. She tipped her head slightly as she said, "I think we need to listen before we tell him we've turned it down." She turned to me. "I agree with my husband that we aren't interested, but we'll listen."

Shelby ground his teeth, but he didn't comment.

"He told me that Miano would plead no contest to reckless driving, but there would be no mention in the conviction of alcohol," I said.

"No deal," Shelby said firmly.

"That's not all of it. He says that he would agree to thirty days of jail time," I added.

"We think thirty years would be more like it. Even that would be less than he deserves," Shelby said. "The answer is still no."

"I understand, but there is something I need to tell you," I said.

"What, is someone else dead?" Shelby asked bitterly. "I'll never believe that the murder of that juror and the guy that saw the wreck wasn't the handiwork of Glazebrook and the Miano clan."

Nayla must have seen the look on my face that I thought I'd suppressed, because she said, "What's happened? Please tell us."

"I'm sorry, but Corporal Kingston was shot today. He's still—"

Shelby cut me off as he angrily burst to his feet, "They've killed him too? This is just too much!"

His wife stood up and again put a gentle hand on his arm. Shelby clamped his mouth shut, although he looked like he was about to say a lot more. Nayla asked, "I'm sorry, is he dead?"

"No, but he's in critical condition. And I've got to be honest with you," I said. "If he doesn't make it, we no longer have a case."

"So they win?!" Shelby thundered. He stared at me for a long moment, and then he said in a softer, wavering voice, "The only thing we can hope for now is for the cops to find the killer and bring him to justice. Like that will ever happen."

"Will he die?" Nayla asked as her eyes filled with tears. "He has such a beautiful little family. His poor wife."

I was also on my feet, but I said, "Why don't we sit down again, and I'll tell you as much as I can about what happened today."

Shelby shook his fist, started to say something, but when he looked at his wife, he calmed down. She was crying softly. He pulled her back to the love seat, and they sat. I sat too and then gave them a moment while Nayla composed herself.

"Where did it happen?" Shelby asked. "Was it in that same location, what did you call it, Little Egypt?"

"No, it was in Indian Canyon, right on the highway. He was with me in court today. I'd asked him to observe since Glazebrook was defending the guy I was prosecuting. I thought it would be good for him to watch before he has to take the stand against Glazebrook again when we go back to trial," I explained. "He got a phone call and left the courtroom just before my trial was finished. It wasn't long after that when I was notified by Detective Shelburn that Corporal Kingston had been shot. Shelburn asked me to come to the scene."

"But he's still alive?" Shelby asked, much more subdued now.

"He's in surgery," I said. I told them about his injuries and how someone had saved his life or at least stabilized him enough to be flown to the hospital in Murray.

"Even if he lives, he might not be able to testify. We pray that he will live, but we might not have a chance now," Shelby said, shaking his head.

"That's right. I think we could delay it if we had to. It would be hard for Glazebrook to argue against me," I said.

Shelby stood again. His wife and I watched as he paced the room for a moment, continually running his hand through his hair. Finally he stopped. "If we don't take the deal, who will die next?" he asked, looking at me. "Probably you, huh?"

I said nothing, but it's good I'm not a poker player because my face must have given me away.

"You are in danger, aren't you?" Shelby asked as his wife covered her mouth.

"I'll be fine," I said with more confidence than I was feeling. "I can take care of myself."

"I would have thought that Bardett Kingston could have taken care of himself as well. And he carries a gun," Shelby said.

I pulled my jacket back, revealing my shoulder holster. "So do I."

Nayla looked at me for a long moment, deep in thought, and then she asked, "Have you been threatened? We heard that Wyanne was threatened because she might have seen the guy that killed poor Mr. Morberg."

"I hear she's disappeared," Shelby said as he stepped back toward the love seat. "Is she okay, or do you know?"

"We are worried," I said after debating with myself about what I should say and what I shouldn't. "We don't know where she is."

"She's our little boy's schoolteacher," Nayla said. "And she was Angelica's Laurel advisor. She's a wonderful person."

"Let's sit down," Shelby said. "We need to talk, I guess."

We sat down again, and then he said, "What was the offer? I didn't listen very well."

I went over it again, and he looked at Nayla. She nodded, and he looked back at me, crestfallen. "Would you mind if we talked privately for a moment?"

I nodded, and they disappeared into another room. When they came back, Shelby spoke softly but bitterly. "It's a far cry from what we want, but we think we should agree with the offer." His face hardened again for a moment. "Jarod Miano should go to prison for what he did. But I . . . we don't want anyone else to get hurt."

"We don't want you or Miss Grice to get hurt," Nayla said softly.

"She's in danger because of the murder of Mr. Morberg, and that has no bearing on the Miano case," I forced myself to say.

"It's related to what happened to our Angelica," Shelby said with a firm shake of his head. "She was such a sweet girl. She had a very tender heart. She'd want us to settle this thing now. It goes against my grain, but tell Glazebrook we agree," he said.

"Let's do something a little different," I suggested. "I'd feel better if I could tell him that we want a guilty plea instead of no contest. I want Jared to have to admit to what he did. And I think we should go for a longer jail sentence."

"How much longer?" Shelby asked.

"Let's begin with six months. I can always drop down if I have to," I suggested.

"Mr. Cartwright, you're a good man," Nayla said. "We can agree to that, can't we, Shelby?"

"Yes," he said firmly. "But if we have to accept the no contest and thirty days, we will. Just do the best you can for us—for Angelica."

I stood to leave. Shelby stopped me at the door. "Will you let us know about Corporal Kingston? We'll be praying for him."

Sixteen

I CALLED AHEAD THE NEXT morning to see if Malcom Glazebrook would be in his office in Salt Lake. I was told that he had a matter at the Matheson Courthouse in the afternoon but that if I could be there by eleven, he could see me. His receptionist wanted to know what I wanted, but I simply said, "I'll tell him when I see him."

That would work perfectly for both Detective Shelburn and me. Bardett Kingston had survived the surgery, but he was still in critical condition. We were told that we shouldn't even attempt to speak with him until after twelve. So with that in mind we headed for Salt Lake in Sheldon's unmarked gray Ford Explorer.

We both had overnight bags with us in case we needed to go to Las Vegas. So far, we didn't know. The officers down there had located the home of Martin Jameson's parents, but they had gotten no response when they knocked on the door in plain clothes. They had been told the importance of not giving the people inside any idea that the cops were interested in the place. Sheldon had also talked them into setting up surveillance on the home to see if anyone entered or exited the residence. They also agreed to see if Martin showed up at his job in one of the casinos. Our plan was to wait, but if we heard of any activity at the house or if we learned that Martin was at work, we'd catch a flight to Las Vegas. The officer Sheldon talked to had agreed to pick us up at the airport and give us whatever assistance we needed.

I was tense over the whole situation. I hadn't received any further texts. The last one was a desperate plea. My prayers could be said to be the same—desperate pleas to the Lord for Wyanne's safety.

We reached Malcom Glazebrook's office about ten thirty. His Escalade was in the parking lot, so we were sure he was there. Sheldon agreed to stay outside while I went in. "I'll get some pictures of his Escalade," he said. "I want his license number and some shots of his tires. If we happen to get a match to the tracks in Little Egypt . . . well, then we'll arrest the good attorney."

"Just don't let anyone catch you," I said. "Glazebrook might get nasty if he thinks we are doing anything nefarious."

"I can be discreet," he said with a grin. "Good luck in there."

When I was ushered to Malcom's private office, I had to suppress a whistle. Everything about his firm's decor shouted of money. If I were so crazy as to accept his offer of a job, I would obviously have a much nicer office than Duchesne County provided for me. But I still wasn't tempted.

Malcom welcomed me with a hearty chuckle and a firm handshake. "Decide to take the job, did you? Why don't I show you around the place, introduce you to the staff?"

"Actually," I said, "that's not why I'm here. Sorry. I *am* impressed with your office, but I don't think I'd fit in too well here. Like you're always saying, I'm just a cowboy."

"Not a problem," he said enthusiastically. "We can decorate your office with Western things. We could get some Western paintings or whatever you want."

"Thanks, Malcom," I said. "But I don't think I would work out well for you."

"I'm sorry to hear that, Cartwright," he said. "We'd love to have you." He waved me to a chair and then moved around his massive oak desk. After we were both seated, he leaned forward, petted the huge black mustache on his lip—one that looked like he'd dyed it using a black permanent marker—and said, "So if you aren't here to take the job, why are you here?"

"I met with the parents of Angelica Keen last night. They asked me to make you a counter offer."

"Very good," he said. "Spell it out for me."

"They can live with reckless driving, but they want a guilty plea," I said. Malcom slowly shook his head, but I pushed on anyway. "They would also like six months in jail."

"I don't know if my client would go for that, especially considering the unfortunate accident of your investigating officer."

"That was not an accident," I said as I felt my temper check in. "It was nothing short of attempted murder."

"Really? I hadn't heard that." I knew a bald-faced lie when I heard one, but I let Malcom go on. "That's too bad. I hope the guy pulls through."

Do you really? It was good I only thought that. "I think he will. I'm going to see him this afternoon. I hope to get a chance to talk to him if he's conscious."

"Well, I really am sorry," he said. "And to show you that I care, let me say this. You drop the guilty plea nonsense, and I'll go up to the thirty days we talked about before."

"Six months," I said.

Malcom smiled. "I really like you, cowboy. You got grit. I won't ask my client to agree to six months, but I'll see if I can get him to accept ninety days. If he does, do we have a deal?"

I looked at him for a moment and finally nodded. "How soon can you let me know?" I asked.

He waggled a finger at the door. "Step out for a moment and shut the door. I'll make a call, and when you come back in, I'll have your answer. And while I'm on the phone, feel free to look around the office and say hi to the staff. My job offer still stands. I'll guarantee you three hundred thousand annually," he said.

"Are you kidding me?" I asked, stunned at the figure.

"You got it, Saxson. I'll even put it in writing for you. Think about it."

I did as he suggested and looked around the office. The receptionist was an attractive girl of about twenty who introduced herself as Missy Bevans. She had short, light blonde, curly hair and a very curvaceous figure. She was probably about five six. She batted her blue-shaded eyes at me and spoke in a husky voice. "I hope you come to work here. It would be nice to have a good-looking younger man around, especially a single one."

That was too much for me. I was no kind of a flirt. My professional visit had just turned to a flirty one. I stuttered as I responded to her. "I, ah . . . don't know . . . if I . . . ah . . . will take the offer." I'm afraid I was blushing even though I was not attracted to the girl, pretty though she was.

"You are cute," she said with a grin as she came out from behind her desk and stood way too close to me. "Please join us," she said, her husky voice teasing. "I need someone here closer to my age. We could go to lunch together and maybe, you know, get to know each other." She smiled seductively at me. "Did Mr. Glazebrook make a good offer to you? I think he really wants you to come."

"Ah, yes," I said. "I'll be . . . ah . . . thinking about it." I took a couple of steps back. I was ready to move on and meet someone else. I had not lied to her. I would think *about* it. But I would not think about *accepting* it. The last thing I needed was to work in an office with a pretty girl who would probably try to hang on me every time I was in the office. "Good to . . . ah . . . meet you."

I stepped past her desk and saw that there was an attorney I judged to be in his late forties sitting at a desk in an office. He was watching me through narrowed eyes. "You must be the cowboy Malcom's been telling us about," he said. "Why don't you come in for a minute." He stood as he spoke. I stepped into his office, and he stepped past me and shut the door. "I'd like to talk to you for a minute," he went on, "but I don't need the receptionist to hear us." He nodded as he spoke toward Missy Bevan's desk. "She's a doll, but she's also a flirt."

He wasn't telling me anything I hadn't already discovered. "Yeah, I noticed."

"Sit down, cowboy," he invited.

I thought about the fact that Glazebrook's title for me had already been shared with his staff. He stepped back behind his desk and lowered his heavy body into his chair. I had evaluated him quickly. He was probably about five eight, but he easily weighed more than two hundred pounds. His dark hair was slicked back, and he had a ducktail that passed over his collar in the back. He looked at me with small hazel eyes that didn't seem too friendly now that the door was closed. I took an instant dislike to the guy.

"Lionel Gancina," he said. He did not offer to shake hands. "Malcom said he was trying to get you to come to work here. I don't think that would be such a good idea."

Taken aback, I asked, "Why not? Because of Missy?"

"That too. She'll pester you constantly," he said. "But no. The reason is that I frankly don't like you. All you'll do is track horse manure in here."

"You don't even know me," I said, shocked at his words and the anger that was shooting from his eyes.

"I know your kind," he said. "You'll do whatever it takes to be Malcom's number-one attorney. I won't stand for it. I'm second-in-command here, and no one is going to interrupt that arrangement."

"So you're his favorite now," I said.

"I'm the best attorney in the office. The other guy's okay too. You would be in the way," he said, glowering more fiercely as we spoke.

I stood up. "Nice to meet you," I said and turned for the door.

"I didn't dismiss you," he said angrily as he hoisted his bulk from his chair.

I returned his glower. "I don't know who you think you are, but if I decide to accept Malcom's invitation, you'll just have to live with it."

"What did he offer you?" he asked.

I took a step toward the door. "That, Mr. Gancina, is none of your business."

"I think it is," he said.

"Then ask Malcom," I retorted and opened the door.

"I'm not finished, cowboy," he said.

"Yes, you are. And if I decide to take Malcom's offer, you better be prepared for me because I won't take your nonsense," I said and swung through the door, slamming it behind me.

"He's a jerk," Missy said. "He asked me to marry him. I turned him down, and now all he does is harass me."

"He's twice your age," I said. "And more than twice your size."

"Yeah, and he's already gone through three wives. He's creepy," she said with a scowl and a touch of what? Fear? I thought so.

It was easier talking to Missy when it was about someone else, someone I already disliked. We had moved into the professional category now. "Why do you stay here if he mistreats you?" I asked.

"Mr. Glazebrook likes me. And he told me that if Lionel hurts me, he'll fire him," she said.

Just then Malcom came out of his office. "Hey, I see you've met our lovely receptionist."

Two other ladies had appeared from a large office just beyond Lionel's. They were both older women—over fifty, I'd say. Malcom introduced me to them and then said, "I'm still trying to talk the cowboy here into joining the firm."

"I hope he does," Missy said, batting her eyes at me again. The other women laughed and said something about how I would like it here if I joined the firm. Then Malcom nodded toward his office as he said, "Did you meet Lionel?"

"Yes," I said and suppressed the temptation to tell him what I thought of the guy.

"The other lawyer is a lot nicer than him," he said. I guessed he knew what an arrogant jerk Lionel was. It would be all I could do to work in the same *building* with him let alone the same *firm*.

Malcom said, "I talked to my client. I sold your offer."

As I walked back with him to his office, I said, "Are you sure?"

He smoothed that awful moustache. "Just like we talked," he said as he ushered me ahead of him into his office. "He'll serve ninety days." And then leaning in close and whispering in my ear, he said, "It would do the cocky little bugger good." Then he straightened up and asked, "Have you reconsidered my offer?"

"It's tempting," I said. Despite the reasons I knew I could never work here—Missy being one and Lionel another—I had decided I wouldn't turn him down cold until I had the Miano matter closed. "May I have a few days to consider it? If I change my mind and decide to accept, I'd like to have the Jarrod Miano case behind me first. I don't want to spring it on Dave Padrick until that matter is over."

Glazebrook must have bought my bluff, for that was all it was. I had an ulterior motive. I gently eased into it now as Malcom waved me to a chair and sat down behind his desk again, a big smile on his face. "I think you'll like it here. Don't worry about Lionel, and as for pretty little Miss Bevans, I think you'll come to like her."

"Probably," I said as I hoped that he would rise to the bait. "Like I was saying about Dave Padrick, I also don't want to spend too much time before I tell him." I tried to appear deep in thought.

"Well, since we've settled the case, there's no need to wait until the day of trial to enter the plea. If I call the judge and set a date that meets my schedule . . ." He let the thought linger for a moment. Then he continued, "Would you be able to make your schedule work?"

"I can do it," I said. That was exactly what I was hoping for. I wanted to get the matter moved way up. "Did you have a date in mind?"

"It'll be next week if I can convince Judge Feldman. If I tell him you have agreed to it, I think he'll work us into his calendar," Malcom said confidently.

"Let's do it, and then I'll let you know if that money is enough to win me over," I said. "And your receptionist." I forced a grin. "I really didn't expect such a good offer."

"I'm serious, Cartwright; you'll give us some balance in the firm. I really need you," he said. "And I assure you that Lionel Gancina will not be a problem. He's a brilliant attorney with a rotten personality, but he does a good job for me. So will you."

As I rode the elevator down to the first floor a couple of minutes later, I thought about what he'd just said. He needed me for balance. If I were fool enough to accept, I suppose he was thinking that I could overcome the conflicting images that he, Missy, and Lionel had created. I wasn't sure that I, or anyone else, could balance out the likes of those people. And there was no way I'd ever put myself in a position where I had to try. But I wasn't going to let him know that yet. I had decided to play along with his offer and act interested.

As we had agreed, I met Detective Shelburn around a corner a block away from Glazebrook's office. I didn't want Malcom or any of his staff to see me with Sheldon. Frankly, I wouldn't be surprised if either Missy or Lionel were watching me right now. He cranked up the car as soon as he saw me, and when I jumped in and started to fasten my seat belt, he gunned the SUV. We sped off to the south, keeping Glazebrook's office out of sight. A block later, my phone indicated that I had just received a text. Before I said anything to Sheldon about what had occurred in Malcom's office, I dug out my phone and looked at it.

I felt a jolt.

Please help me. I'm in Vegas. I wasn't the whiz with numbers that Sheldon was, but I did recognize the number this time. Sheldon glanced my way. I showed it to him.

"We're going to Vegas. As soon as we've talked to Kingston, we'll head for the airport," he said.

We were headed south toward Murray, away from downtown, on State Street. For a few minutes, we didn't talk. And I was glad, because I wanted to think. Sheldon seemed as deep in thought as I was. He was the first to break the silence. "Saxson, I wonder if that text is really from Martin. He could be setting a trap for you."

Surprised, I said, "That is exactly what I was thinking. Otherwise, why would Martin let her use the phone to contact me?"

"I suppose she might have been able to slip it away for a moment or something," he said, glancing at me. "Frankly, I doubt it, but if she did send the message, she probably deleted it as soon as she sent it."

"And she would be expecting me not to reply considering what Jameson did before when I did," I reasoned.

We discussed the matter further, but we both knew that we had to go to Las Vegas. Even if Martin Jameson was setting us up, it was a chance we would have to take, but we'd do it with plenty of backup and an abundance of caution.

I changed the subject. It was killing me to think about the terrible situation Wyanne might be in. "Did you get a look at Glazebrook's tires and license plate?" I asked.

He nodded. "There were two black SUVs in the lot. I checked them both out even though only one of them was an Escalade."

"What was the other one?" I asked.

"It was also black, a Lincoln Navigator," he answered. "I remember Miss Grice saying that the car she saw was a black SUV and that she only thought it might be an Escalade."

"Yes, I suppose it could have been something like a Navigator. She was quite sure it was a luxury vehicle. She told me it could have also been something else as well."

"At any rate, I ran the plates of both vehicles and got good pictures of the tires. The Escalade was the same one you saw Malcom driving. The other one is registered to a man by the name of Lionel Gancina," he said.

"Good old Lionel," I said snidely.

"You know him?" he asked.

"I'm afraid I do. He's a cold, evil-looking man if I ever met one," I said. "I'd be likely to peg him as a Mafia hit man if I were to meet him on the street."

"Who is he?" he asked.

We pulled into the parking area of the IMC. He found a parking spot, and as we walked toward the hospital, I filled him in on my visit to Glazebrook's office. I told him first about Gancina and then about the agreement Malcom and I had reached on the Miano case. Finally, I told him of the huge offer he'd made in an effort to get me to join his firm.

"I suppose you made it clear you weren't interested," he said.

I chuckled. "Actually, I told him I'd give him an answer as soon as the Miano matter was closed. I hinted that it would be nice if we could set an earlier date to let Miano enter his plea. He's going to try to set it for next week," I said. "Once the Miano matter is laid to rest, then I'll tell him what he can do with his job offer."

"I like the way you think, Saxson," Sheldon said. We entered the hospital lobby and looked for the elevators. "Let's hope that we find Kingston on the mend," he said. "If he were to not make it, heaven forbid, and you hadn't yet gotten the plea on the record, Glazebrook just might change his mind," Sheldon said.

"My thought exactly," I agreed as we entered an elevator.

Sheldon looked crossways at me as we rode up. "Why does Malcom Glazebrook want you in his firm?" he asked. "I am really puzzled by that."

"Balance in the office is what Glazebrook said he was after," I told him

The elevator stopped, and we stepped off. It was time to visit the patrolman. "Let's hope he's able to talk and that he can remember what happened," I said.

"And that he is going to live. I'll tell you, Saxson, when a cop you know gets shot, it's almost like it was a member of your own family."

Seventeen

CORPORAL BARDETT KINGSTON WAS IN a great deal of pain, but he was able to speak. His neck, which had been so badly injured, was bandaged, and he was restrained so he couldn't move it. His leg was also bandaged. He was being fed intravenously. He had tubes all over the place, but he was able to force a smile. I was just grateful he was alive. His wife was sitting with him along with a man and woman who were introduced to us as his parents. The three of them excused themselves, telling us that they would let us speak with Bardett in private. However, we were warned that he would probably not be able to speak much, as he tired very quickly.

"Sorry, Saxson, I really messed up the Miano case, didn't I?" was the very first thing the officer asked as I stepped to his bedside. His voice was raspy, and it was obvious that it hurt to talk.

"You didn't mess anything up," I said.

"They tell me I'll live," he said. "They also say I'll be in here for quite a while. But I will testify if I possibly can," he said. "At least I can talk, even if it's not very well."

"You won't have to," I told him. "Jarrod Miano is going to plead no contest to reckless driving next week, and he has agreed that he won't oppose serving ninety days in jail."

Bardett cringed and closed his eyes for a moment; then he opened them again. "He killed Angelica," he said. "He should go to prison."

"I agree," I said, "but at this point we are lucky to get this much."

He moaned. "It's my fault I got shot. You told me to be careful, but I wasn't. You need to be careful too. You were threatened."

"This deal with Miano should remove the killer's incentive to shoot anyone else," I said, "or to come after you again."

"Detective," he said, "let me tell you what happened if I can talk long enough."

It sounded like Kingston's voice was going to give out very soon. We had to make this easy on him and be fast. Sheldon and I exchanged glances. We traded places, and he turned on a small digital recorder.

"I will try to make it so you don't have to talk too much," Sheldon said. "So don't try too hard. It sounds like we've already worn you out. Let me do some guessing, and you just say yes or no. Let's start with the call you received in the courtroom. Do you think it was the killer setting you up?"

"Yes. The voice was weird," Bardett said. Then he winced in pain and again closed his eyes.

Detective Shelburn waited for a moment before he asked, "Was it electronically altered?"

"Possibly," Kingston said.

"Did he tell you to come to where he shot you?"

"Yes."

"Did he make some kind of excuse to make you think you had to go, maybe something to do with your family?"

"Yes." He paused and again closed his eyes for a moment. Sheldon waited. Bardett kept his eyes closed as a spasm crossed his face. Finally, he was able to speak again. "Said my . . ." His voice faded. We waited. "My wife." A long pause.

"Your wife is from Price. Is that right?" Sheldon asked.

"Yes."

"I understand she was in Price that day with your kids. Is that right?"

"Yes."

"Did the caller tell you your wife was in some kind of trouble?"

Bardett shuddered and then said, "Broke down."

"He told you your wife's car broke down and she needed your help?"

"Yes."

Sheldon turned to me and said, "Whoever this is seems to know all about Bardett." He turned back to the patient. "Is that what you are thinking, Bardett?"

"Yes."

"Did you see the person who shot you?"

"Yes."

"Did you recognize him?"

"No. He . . . was dressed in black. Masked."

"The person was wearing a mask?"

"Yes."

"Did he speak?"

"No."

"So he just came up and shot you?"

"Yes."

"Where did you get hit first, in your leg?"

"Yes."

"Was he some distance away when he fired the first time?"

"Yes."

"He was coming toward you as he shot, is that right?"

"Yes."

"And the second shot. Was it in your neck?"

"Yes."

"Did you fall down after the second shot but before the third?"

"Yes."

The longer the interview went on, the harder it was for Corporal Kingston to speak and the more difficult it was for us to understand him. "We need to wrap this up," I said to the detective. He nodded then looked at Kingston again.

Detective Shelburn asked, "Did he think he'd killed you when he shot you in the chest?"

"Yes."

"A motorist came along just moments after you were shot. He was a trauma nurse. He told me that he thought at first that you were dead. He said you looked dead but that when he told you who he was and that he was there to help you that you sighed. Were you pretending to be dead until you realized that he was not your assailant?"

"Yes."

"That was brilliant, Bardett," I chimed in.

"It really was. One more thing and then we'll let you rest," Sheldon said. "Did you see the car the shooter was driving?"

"Yes."

"Was it black?"

"Yes," Bardett said after thinking for a moment.

"Was it an SUV?"

"Yes," he answered. His eyes were closed, and they hadn't opened for a while.

"You've been a big help," Detective Shelburn said. "You can rest now. Thanks for seeing us."

He didn't respond, and we quietly slipped out and told his family that he had been a big help but that he was very tired now. I told them we had reached a plea agreement on the Miano case and that Bardett would most likely not have to testify. They were clearly relieved. None of them asked what the agreement was. It didn't matter to them. What mattered was that their son and husband would recover.

We got lucky and were able to book a flight to Las Vegas that would leave three hours after we had seen Kingston. If it had been much longer than that, we may have simply driven down. We stopped for a late lunch before we went to the airport. We were eating when Sheldon received a call from his contact in Las Vegas. He spoke on the phone for a couple of minutes. Since I could only hear one side of the conversation, I didn't pay a lot of attention to what the detective was saying. But as soon as he ended the call, I asked, "I heard you tell him what time we would be there. What was he telling you?"

"Okay, here's what's going on. Jameson has not been at the casino where he works for several days. An officer finally talked to someone there, a woman who was apparently his supervisor. He told the lady that she was not to say anything to Martin about their conversation. He says he thinks the lady understood that if she didn't do what she was told that she would be subject to arrest. He was pretty stern with her."

"What did she tell him about Jameson?" I asked.

"Jameson called in sick a week ago. He called again this morning and told her that he was still in pretty rough shape but that he should be able to be back to work in three or four days. The supervisor at the casino told him that wasn't good enough, that they needed him back right away. He said he'd try. The lady asked him if he was in the hospital. He said he had been but that he wasn't anymore."

"Did she ask him what hospital he'd been in?" I asked.

"She says she didn't but that if he calls again, she will. She says she thinks he's faking it, and if they confirm that, they'll fire him. Of course, you and I know he isn't sick. I hope we can charge him with something when we catch up with him, but if not at least we can get him fired for lying to his employer," Sheldon said.

That wasn't a lot of comfort. What I wanted was to know that Wyanne was safe and could return home. But then, like a kick in the gut, I remembered she was still a witness in a murder case and would still be in danger until the killer was caught. Settling the Miano case did not change the fact that someone had murdered Evan Morberg and Darrius Chaudry and had attempted and almost succeeded in killing Corporal Kingston.

Detective Shelburn was watching me across the table. "You're thinking about Wyanne, aren't you?" he asked.

"I am. Even if we find her and get her away from Martin Jameson, she is still very much in danger," I said.

"I'm afraid that's true. But let's take it one step at a time. We're getting closer, I think," he said. "Jameson has been spotted. He's in his parents' house now, and they're watching to see if he comes out. There are officers all around the area, but they're keeping out of sight."

"So the question is does he have Wyanne in there with him?"

"All we can do is wait and see," he said.

A few hours later we were met by Sheldon's contact, a detective by the name of Clint Reeves with the Las Vegas Metropolitan Police Department. He had my six-foot frame bested by a good four inches. He was in excellent shape, probably weighing around 210 pounds. He was waiting for us near the baggage collection area, as arranged, even though we both only had carry-ons. He was dressed in gray slacks with a black turtleneck shirt and a gray sports coat. His brown hair was cut in a butch. He waved when he spotted us. I guessed that Sheldon must have given him a good description of us.

He introduced himself and then said, "I have a brother who lives in Vernal and works in the oil field. He says the press is all over the killings you've had up there."

"I'm afraid he's right. We've tried to keep things low profile, but that's impossible when we have a case like we do," Sheldon said.

We discussed the Miano case with him as well as the three shootings as he led us to his car. Once we were on our way downtown, he said, "Martin Jameson, your suspect, has never come back out of his parents' house. And our officers haven't seen anyone else go in—or come out."

"I don't suppose there's any way you might have talked to some of the people in the neighborhood?" Sheldon asked.

"We were afraid that it would raise too much suspicion and tip the perp off if we sent officers door to door, but that doesn't mean we haven't done anything," he said. "Through tax records, utility companies, and the like, we've learned who lives in all of the houses in the area. We've had a couple of officers making phone calls to the neighbors."

"That's great," I said. "Have they been able to learn anything?"

"Yes, they have. We've only been waiting for you to arrive before we decide what to do," he said. "The lady across the street was sitting on her porch one night. She can't remember which night, but it was in the past week or so. She said it was dark and cool out, but she had a shawl wrapped around her. She told us that she likes to sit in the dark and listen to the sounds of the night. She had no lights on. She's an older lady, a widow, but she is in reasonably good health and her eyesight is good.

"At any rate, she saw Martin and someone else enter the house that night. She couldn't say if it was a woman for sure, but she says that whoever it was had fairly long hair and that it wasn't very dark, maybe dark blonde. Even though it was dark, there is a streetlight not too far away. She said that Jameson, and she is sure it was him, kept looking around like he didn't want anyone to see him. She said she's seen him enough that she knows his build, the shape of his head, and so on. She also explained that where she was on the porch, she was shaded from the streetlight and he most likely wouldn't have been able to see her.

"Anyway, she said the person with him appeared to be highly inebriated. Those were her words, not mine. My guess is that Jameson had drugged Miss Grice, and I am quite sure that's who he had with him. Nothing else makes any sense."

I felt a wave of anger go through me. I guess I clenched my fists because the detective said, "I know how you feel, Mr. Cartwright. You'd like to punch his lights out, and I don't blame you. Anyway, Miss Grice, if that's who it was, was stumbling, and Jameson almost had to carry her. He'd parked his car, an old white one, out front, and they went up the walk and to the front door. The sidewalk is quite long, so our witness was able to observe them for a minute or more, she claims. Finally, he opened the door while holding his victim with one arm around her waist and then dragged her inside and shut the door. At that point, lights were turned on inside.

"That was probably several days before you called us," Detective Reeves went on. "The morning after you called, our officers went to the door disguised as salesmen and received no response to their ringing of the doorbell and knocking. That was before we'd learned that the neighbor had seen Jameson take someone inside."

"So if Jameson was there he didn't answer the door," I said. "And Wyanne, if it was her, was in no condition to do so or was stopped from doing so by Jameson."

"That's my assumption as well," Detective Reeves said. "Back to the neighbor's story. She said that the car he was driving that night was not the one she usually sees him use. In fact, she told our officer that she'd never seen the white car before. The officer that had been on the phone with her called me to see if there was anything else he should ask her. I instructed him to have her come down to the station. It was about an hour after that that I spoke with her. My impression is that she was accurate in what she saw and that she remembered the details very well."

"What did she tell you?" Sheldon asked.

"She told me that about an hour after he went in with this *inebriated person* that he left again. She went in the house and went to bed after that, and she hasn't seen Jameson since. She didn't see him when he arrived a while ago because she was in her utility room doing laundry, she thinks. But our officers did see him, and that time he was driving a different car, one registered to his father. It's a dark blue, late model Prius. He drove it into the garage, and it hasn't come out since. Our witness hasn't seen anyone else leave, and for that matter, neither have any of the other neighbors or officers."

"Okay," Detective Shelburn began, "this is what we have. A person who may have been drugged, probably a woman, was taken into the house by Jameson, the man who took Miss Grice from Duchesne. She is most likely still in the house. She's clearly in danger if she is still alive, and we pray that she is," he said, glancing at me with a sympathetic look in his eyes. "It also appears that at this time, Martin Jameson is also in the house, but it seems unlikely that his parents are at home. Does anyone know where they are?"

"That's another thing," Detective Reeves said. "Not a single neighbor has seen them for at least two weeks. But we know the blue Prius is in the garage. We have learned that his parents have a second car, a dark blue SUV, a Lincoln Navigator, according to state motor vehicles. The neighbors haven't seen that vehicle for over two weeks either."

Sheldon and I looked at each other. "Dark blue," I said. "Wyanne may have seen a dark blue SUV rather than a black one the day of Morberg's murder."

He was already nodding his head. "Now I have to figure out if he has any connection to the Mianos. Does everyone drive a black or dark blue Navigator or Escalade these days?" he asked facetiously. "I can't afford a vehicle like that."

Detective Sheen was looking very puzzled, so Sheldon took a minute to explain about the killings and that Wyanne had seen what we believe may have been the killer driving what she described as a black luxury SUV, possibly a Cadillac Escalade. "But she wasn't positive about that make," he went on, "and now I'm wondering if she also may have been wrong about the color."

"Detectives," I said as my heart began to thud, "if Jameson was Morberg's killer and he saw Wyanne, he would have recognized her, and that would explain why she received the threats so quickly." I shivered.

"And he had time to have gotten rid of his parents' SUV and steal the white Malibu somewhere, and then return, knowing that Wyanne wouldn't recognize that car," Shelburn said. He turned to Detective Reeves. "That makes it even more imperative that we get in that house." He looked directly at me and added, "We're going to act on the assumption that it is her that he took in that house."

Eighteen

ONE WARRANT HAD BEEN OBTAINED for the arrest of Martin Jameson and another to search his parents' house. I participated in preparing them. A bunch of officers from the Las Vegas Metropolitan Police were gathered just out of sight of the Jameson house. A SWAT team was briefed and ready to attempt to rescue Wyanne and arrest Jameson as soon as the order was given. But I requested one more thing before they actually stormed the house.

None of us knew if the messages I'd received were from Wyanne or Martin Jameson attempting to lure me into a trap. I was seated in a police van with my cell phone in my hand. My call was going to be recorded, and it was also being transmitted to the command van, which was parked right in front of us. With me were Detectives Shelburn and Reeves. I punched in the number that the distress texts had been received from. I was praying that Wyanne would answer, but I wasn't surprised when the voice of Martin Jameson, whom I'd known as James Martin, came on the phone. "Mr. Cartwright," he said. "I'm so glad you called. Is there something I can do for you?"

The tone of his voice sent ice into my veins. I hesitated for just a moment before I said, "I just want to see Wyanne, make sure she's okay."

"I told you before that she's fine. She doesn't want to talk to you," he said. "She told you that herself."

I had the phone on speaker. The two detectives were as quiet as church mice. "Please, James," I said, using his assumed name so that I wouldn't tip him off that I knew who he really was. "Just let me see her, let her tell me for herself that she is fine and that she doesn't want to see me again, and then I'll leave you two alone," I said.

"She already did that," he reminded me.

"But I want to hear her voice again. I want her to tell me she's happy with you," I said.

"Where are you?" he suddenly asked me.

"I'm in Las Vegas. Is that where you are?"

For a moment, he was silent, and the detectives both got worried looks on their faces. "Why would you think that I'm in Vegas?" he asked.

"I did a little checking and found out that you're a blackjack dealer in a casino down here," I told him. "I went to the casino, but I was told that you were home sick, that you've even been in the hospital."

"Oh yes, of course," he said. "I did tell my boss I was sick, but I'm really not. I'm just otherwise engaged." He chuckled.

"Please, just let me meet you somewhere," I said. "I won't even insist on talking to her alone. You can listen to our conversation."

"I'm afraid you've wasted your trip. My wife and I are not in Vegas. We are out of state on our honeymoon," he said. "Right now we're in a beautiful hotel many miles from Las Vegas. I'm sorry you wasted your time and gas."

Sheldon passed a hastily written note to me. *He didn't send the texts. Miss Grice must have found a way to do it,* he had written. I nodded. He began to write again while Detective Reeves typed a text message on his cell phone.

"So you're married now? Where did you two get married?" I asked.

"That really isn't any of your business," Martin growled. "I gotta go now. My beautiful bride is waiting for me at the pool. I need to get down there with her."

The next note was shoved in front of me. It read: *The SWAT team is going in. Keep him on the phone as long as you can.*

I nodded. The text from Reeves to Sheldon was planned as the signal to let them know the operation was about to begin. "The least you could have done was invite me to the wedding," I said. "I would have come."

"I'm sure you would have," Jameson said with a laugh. "But neither my love nor I wanted you there, or anyone else for that matter. It was a nice little affair though. She was quite stunning in her white satin wedding gown."

"I hope the two of you will be happy," I said. "Tell her that I congratulate her."

"We will be happy, I assure you," Jameson responded. "And I will tell her that you are glad she married me."

"Did you at least invite your parents to the wedding?" I asked. "I know *she* has no family, so you couldn't have invited them."

"I told you that no one was invited. I would have had my parents come, but they are indisposed," he said, and he laughed again. It was an evil laugh. I shivered.

Detective Shelburn looked at me and began writing another note. I continued to try to keep Jameson engaged in conversation. I said, "You do know that the police would like to talk to you about that white Chevy Malibu you were driving when you and Wyanne eloped, don't you?"

For a moment, it was silent, giving me time to read Sheldon's latest note. It read, *I'm worried about his parents.*

So was I. The silence stretched on. I could hear him breathing.

Finally, he spoke again. "What about the Malibu?" he asked.

I was taking a shot in the dark, but I decided to bluff. "You know very well why. It's been reported stolen," I said.

"Stolen! No, of course not. That was my car. But it doesn't matter. I sold it already. I needed something a lot classier to take my new bride in on our honeymoon," he said.

"The authorities know you had it," I said. "I saw you in it, and so did a sheriff's deputy in Duchesne. And we know it was stolen."

"If you're trying to worry me, you have failed again," he said.

"The cops will find you," I warned him.

Our conversation ended abruptly at that point. I heard Jameson shout, "What is that?" A fraction of a second later, there was a loud bang. The SWAT team had planned to throw a loud flash grenade into the house and then force their way in. Detective Reeves jumped from the van, leaving the door swinging open.

That bang was welcome. Silence followed. I heard Jameson scream, then it sounded like the phone was dropped, but it was still connected. I listened as one officer told another that he would restrain him. I could hear what sounded like a struggle. Then it was quiet again. A minute or so passed before I heard Jameson begin to curse.

The cell phone on the floor was working fine, and Sheldon and I could hear officers shouting. Someone said something about finding the girl and that she was drugged but alive. Sheldon and I both jumped from the van and raced toward the house, which was around the corner from us and in the middle of the block.

Sheldon's phone rang. He took it out and answered it as we ran. Then he put it away and grabbed my arm and slowed both of us to a walk as we approached the sidewalk that led to the front door of the Jameson house. "That was Detective Reeves," he said. "They've cleared the house. We can go in. Wyanne is drugged, but she seems to be okay otherwise."

Detective Reeves met us at the door. "She's back here," he said as he directed us past Martin Jameson, who was sitting on the floor in handcuffs and leg irons. Apparently the shock from the grenade had worn off, because he was fighting his restraints. He spotted me and shouted, "You set me up, Cartwright. I'll kill you for this."

I ignored him and followed Reeves into a bedroom. Two officers were supporting Wyanne, who was sitting between them on the edge of a king-size bed. Each officer had hold of one arm to steady her. Her head was down and swaying from side to side. Her dark blonde hair, normally so shiny and clean, was a tangle of greasy strands. Her eyes were closed, one of them black, and her face was bruised. She was dressed in a pair of blue jeans and a blue Western-cut blouse that I recognized but that was dirty and wrinkled. Her feet were bare. The pain that hit me at the sight of her was blinding.

My first impulse was to run to her and take her into my arms. My second impulse was to turn around, go back into the living room, and violently plant one of my cowboy boots in the middle of Martin Jameson's face. I went with my first impulse. I knelt in front of her, reached out, and pulled her to me. She didn't resist; her head fell against my chest. Tears stung my eyes. The officers let her arms go.

"Wyanne," I said softly as I stroked her greasy hair and held her tightly. "It's me, Saxson. I'm here. You're safe now."

I had no idea if she heard me or if she understood me. My heart was breaking for the only girl I'd ever held in my arms. The only girl that I'll ever love. Yes, I said love. I didn't think this was something that would ever have happened in my life. But this girl had become the most important person in the world to me. I continued to hold her. The officers at each side got up from the edge of the bed and moved away.

"Wyanne," I said again. "I'm sorry I let him take you away. I didn't know he was dangerous. I'm so sorry. But I'm here now." Not a word, not a movement. I felt my shirt getting wet, soaking clear to my skin. I pushed her gently back and looked at her eyes. They were glazed but also full of tears, and those tears were spilling onto me. "I'm sorry," I repeated.

I felt movement. Her arms, which had been at her sides, slowly rose, and first one and then the other went around my back, and I felt her tug weakly at me. I pulled her close again. Oh, how I loved that girl. Yes, the improbable had happened.

I have no idea how long I knelt there, holding her to me. After a little while her arms gained strength, and she was holding me tightly too. I felt a hand on my shoulder.

"Saxson, the paramedics need to examine her," Sheldon said.

I slowly released my hold on her. Two paramedics, a woman and a man, gently pried her arms from around my back. They finally succeeded, and I rose to my feet and stepped back as they laid her on the bed and began an examination. My eyes did not leave her for any longer than the occasional blink. After a minute or two, I felt a tug on my arm again. "Saxson, let's go in another room. She needs them right now," Detective Shelburn said.

"She cried," I said as I stepped back with him and pointed at my wet shirt.

"That's great, Saxson. That means that she recognized you. She'll have to go to the hospital. We'll go there too. They're taking Jameson to jail."

"I hope he gets charged with everything any of you officers can think of," I said as I stared at Wyanne as the paramedics continued examining her.

"He had a gun on him, but he was too stunned to reach for it. He's an ex-con and isn't allowed to have a weapon, so that's one charge. I'm sure they'll find drugs here too, at least whatever he used to dope Wyanne with. And I suppose we will charge him with kidnapping and maybe more in Duchesne. That will be up to you and Dave Padrick."

"That will happen, believe me. Is Jameson talking?" I asked.

"Not really. Cursing would be more like it. They'll interview him more when they get him to the jail," he said. "Maybe we can wait outside until they bring Miss Grice out."

We wandered to the sidewalk that fronted the street. We talked, we paced, and I worried, praying that Wyanne was going to be okay.

Detective Reeves came out and approached us. "Jameson's parents' dark blue Navigator is in the garage," he said. "Are you going to want to take some photos of the tires?"

"I sure am. I'd like to compare them to the tire prints we took at our murder scene. My bag is in your car. I have a camera in it," Sheldon said.

"We'll go get it in a moment, but first there's something I need to show you fellows," Detective Reeves said rather ominously. "We'll need to go into the garage. If Jameson *is* your killer, you'll have to wait your turn to get him." Sheldon and I looked at each other but said nothing.

The large garage door was closed, and Detective Reeves led us inside the house, through the living room, and then through the kitchen and into the garage. Sure enough, there was the dark Lincoln. It was so dark that it was almost black. But Reeves led us past it. A couple of crime lab techs were standing over a large chest freezer. Reeves told them who we were and said, "I'd like these men to take a look in there."

I almost lost my lunch when I peeked into the freezer. Staring up at me were lifeless eyes of the severed heads of an older man and woman. Other severed body parts filled the freezer below them. I literally stumbled backward. Fortunately, I was able to keep my stomach from totally revolting. I was aware of Detective Shelburn as he stepped back with me. His face was a little white. Detective Reeves was watching us. "Rather shocking, huh?"

"I'll say. Are they his parents?" Shelburn asked.

"It looks like it," Detective Reeves said. "I saw pictures of them earlier. Martin Jameson is one nasty fellow. We're lucky Miss Grice is still alive."

"Let's see how she's doing," I suggested, anxious to escape from the garage and allow my upset stomach to settle.

They were just loading Wyanne into an ambulance when we reached the fresh evening air outside. The paramedics had inserted an IV in one of Wyanne's arms.

As we walked toward her, Detective Reeves said, "I'll impound the Lincoln. Maybe you could get pictures of the tires later instead of now."

Sheldon nodded. "That would be better because I'd like to go through that car with a fine-tooth comb," he said. "I suppose we'll need another warrant to do that."

"Probably not, but I think we'll get one just to be on the safe side."

"If he is our killer, I need to see if I can find anything, besides the tires, that will tie him to the family of the young man Saxson was prosecuting when people started to die," Sheldon said.

"If it was him that shot Morberg and Chaudry, how could he have shot Corporal Kingston? He's been down here with Wyanne," I said. "I'd like to think he's our killer because that would mean that Wyanne is safe now, but I don't know if that's the way it is."

"One step at a time, Counselor," Sheldon said. "We'll figure it out, and if he was our shooter, I promise you I'll give you a rock-solid case to prosecute. Not even Malcom Glazebrook will be able to shoot holes in it when I get done."

Wyanne was in the ambulance now, and the paramedics appeared to be about ready to leave. "I wonder if they'd let me ride to the hospital with her?" I asked as I moved in that direction.

They wouldn't, but Detective Reeves said, "I'll get an officer to take you. What about you, Sheldon? Do you want to go to the hospital too, or do you want to help me here?"

"I better stay with you. Even if Jameson isn't out killer, he abducted a woman from my jurisdiction. I need to follow up on that as well," he said. He turned to me. "You go, Saxson. I'll catch up to you later. I'll rent a car after we finish up here and meet you at the hospital. I'm going to need to interview Miss Grice as soon as she's able to talk. She might know something about the murders if Jameson is our guy."

I had to wait about ten minutes before an officer was available to take me to the hospital, but the officer made good time, and we arrived not long after Wyanne was taken into the emergency room. I talked to the paramedics who had treated her. They both felt like she was going to be okay. I felt some relief, but I would feel a whole lot better when a doctor told me the same thing and even more so when Wyanne herself assured me that she was okay.

I had to wait in the waiting room while an emergency-room doctor examined Wyanne. So with time on my hands, I decided I should report to my boss again.

Nineteen

THE CALL TO DAVE PADRICK took about fifteen minutes. He had lots of questions and concerns. He was as revolted as I was with the gruesome murder of Jameson's parents. He instructed me to phone again after I'd spoken to Wyanne.

After the call had ended, I checked on Wyanne again. She was still in the emergency room, and I was told to wait. My stomach had finally settled after viewing the gruesome find in the Jameson garage, and I was hungry. I found the cafeteria; bought a sandwich, some chips, and a drink; and sat down to eat. I was about halfway through my meal when a call came in on my iPhone. I was surprised when I saw that the call was from Malcom Glazebrook's office.

"Good evening," I answered.

"Cartwright, glad I could reach you," Malcom said in his booming voice.

"If you're calling to see if I've decided to accept your offer, I need a little more time," I said.

"No, it's not that," he said. "But I really do hope you'll accept. I need you here."

"I am giving it due consideration," I said. That was stretching it a bit. But it was on my mind. I just couldn't understand why he would want someone who was so different from him and his current staff.

He chuckled. "It's a good offer, but I know you know that. No, I'm not looking for a decision yet. But my call does have to do with my offer," he admitted. "After you left, I had a talk with my top associate, Lionel Gancina. He told me he was very much opposed to you joining the firm. I asked him if he told you that, and he admitted that he had.

He shouldn't have done that, and I made it very clear to him who the boss is here. I have solid reasons for wanting a young, capable lawyer like you on my staff, reasons that I have no intention of discussing with Gancina."

"I'm flattered, Malcom," I said. "Although I think that if I do decide to join you that Lionel will fight me in everything I try to do."

"No he won't," Malcom said darkly. I could almost feel the heat in his voice coming out of my phone. "He's a capable attorney, but he is not indispensable. I made that clear to him."

Wow! Now that surprised me. Malcom would take *me* over an experienced man like Gancina if push came to shove? That raised my suspicion level. Did Malcom see in me a man he could corrupt? He couldn't be further from the truth if he was thinking that.

"Gee, Malcom," I said thoughtfully. "I don't want to be the source of dissension in your office. Maybe I should just back out now."

"No, don't do that," Malcom said. "You may not be anywhere near the lawyer I am, but you're honest. I like that. I like it a lot. The same can't be said of Lionel. Don't ever tell him I said this, but despite the fact that he's my top attorney, I don't trust him."

That rocked me. "I'm sorry," I said lamely.

"Don't be. I said that you're not nearly the lawyer that I am, but with experience and training, you can be," he said. "I see more potential in you than in anyone that works for me. And your honesty is one of the reasons. I don't mean to give you the impression that you and I might not have disagreements from time to time, but I can always depend on you telling me how you feel and not hiding anything. I can't say that of Lionel or my other associate."

"I'll let you know in a few days," I said. "And I'll see you next week."

"I look forward to it," Glazebrook said, and he ended the call.

I stared at my phone, trying to decide why he really wanted me on his staff. My honesty? I just couldn't bend my mind around that idea. I think I knew Glazebrook well enough now to know that he was not one who cared a whit about honesty. It was something else.

Suddenly, a reason hit me right between the eyes. It seemed rather far-fetched, but the more I thought about it, the more I wondered if I might be on to something. If it turned out that Malcom Glazebrook was in fact the killer or at least in some way tied in with the killer and was charged with a crime, murder or something less, he would need an attorney. I continued to think this through. He knew that I was honest. So if he made me his attorney and then admitted to me what he'd done, I'd be obligated to keep his confession confidential. And any knowledge or suspicions I had now would be essentially buried. I couldn't share them with anyone. And I would have to fight against Detective Shelburn and my current boss, Dave Padrick. The idea of that made me ill.

I finished my sandwich and chips and threw the wrappings in the trash. I drank the last of my soda and threw the cup away as well. All the while my mind was busy. Maybe Malcom really did think that I had the making of an excellent attorney, and if so, I could imagine him putting me in a position where I would have to help him and not fight him. As I walked back toward the emergency room, I thought more about it. Finally, I considered the implications of the way my thoughts were going. Malcom Glazebrook must be considered a suspect in the killings. I could not dismiss Martin Jameson at this point, but in my mind Glazebrook rose to the top of my suspect list.

I was anxious to discuss my thoughts with Detective Shelburn. But in the meantime, I shoved consideration of Glazebrook to the back of my mind and inquired about Wyanne. I was relieved to learn that she had just been moved to a regular room. I spoke briefly with the doctor who had attended to her in the emergency room. He assured me that she should recover fully. He also told me she was already coming out of her drug-induced state and that I should be able to talk to her soon.

With a much lighter heart, I headed to the room where she'd been taken. I wanted *soon* to become *very soon*. I wanted nothing more right now than to make sure she really was okay. I was just stepping off the elevator when my cell phone vibrated. I quickly pulled it out and looked at the screen. It was Sheldon. I took the call as I walked briskly up the hallway.

"Hey, Counselor, how is Miss Grice?"

"She's doing better. I haven't actually seen her yet, but I will in a minute. She's been moved to a regular room, and I'm going there now," I told him. "The doctor told me the drugs are wearing off. I should be able to talk to her soon."

"That's great. Tell her I'll be in to talk to her later. Detective Reeves and I are headed for his impound lot to search the Navigator. By the time we get there, a warrant will be signed," he said.

I reached the room, number 333. The door was closed. "I'm at Wyanne's room. I'll talk to you in a little while," I told him and put my phone in my pocket. I tapped lightly on the door. A redheaded nurse opened it, and I said, "I'm looking for Wyanne Grice."

"Are you Saxson?" she asked.

"Yes, Saxson Cartwright," I said.

"I'm Cecilia Stockam. I'm going to be Miss Grice's nurse for the night. I was just getting her settled. She's been asking for you, so why don't you come in. She'll be glad to see you," Nurse Stockam said.

I followed her into the room and saw Wyanne in the bed with her eyes closed. She looked relaxed. Her hair was still greasy, but it had been neatly brushed. Her black eye stood out on her slightly battered but otherwise serene face. I was suddenly all choked up. I stepped close to her and stood staring down at her. Her eyes opened, and she gasped. "Saxson. You found me," she said softly. Her lips curled up slightly, giving me a glimpse of those adorable dimples of hers.

Both arms had IVs in them, but she moved the one closest to me, wiggling her fingers. I reached down and took her hand. The dimples grew deeper. "I look awful," she said.

"You'll never look awful to me," I told her. My mother would be so proud of me. I didn't stammer or turn red or lose my voice.

"Mr. Cartwright," Nurse Stockam said, "there's a chair in the corner. If you'd like to move it beside the bed, feel free to do so."

"Thank you," I said. "I think I will." I released Wyanne's hand and retrieved the chair. I sat down as close as I could to the bed and again took her hand in mine.

For a long time, we simply gazed at each other. She was smiling. My heart was full. I silently thanked the Lord for keeping her alive and safe and allowing me to find her. My many prayers had been answered.

After a few minutes, Nurse Stockam said, "I'll check on you later, Miss Grice."

"I'm Wyanne," Wyanne said softly as her eyes left mine and caught the nurse's.

"Wyanne. What a beautiful name. I'll leave you two to catch up on things," she added perceptively.

The nurse closed the door behind her as she left. Only then did Wyanne speak to me again. "I'm so sorry," she said. "You must think I'm awful."

"Not at all," I said. "I think you're wonderful. I'm the one who's sorry."

"You shouldn't feel that way," she said. "You did nothing wrong."

I put a finger on her lips. "I shouldn't have let that creep, Martin Jameson, take you away from Duchesne."

"Who?" she asked, looking puzzled.

"Jimmie Martin," I said. "But that's not who he really is."

Her eyes grew wide.

"He knew that if he told you who he really was and what he'd done that you would never have agreed to date him," I said.

"I met him at school," she said. "We were both students at Southern Utah University. I met him in a class we took together. He seemed like he was a nice guy. He told me he'd served his mission in Ohio. He went to church with me. I wouldn't say that I was his girlfriend, and when he started becoming possessive, I told him it would be best if we didn't date."

"How did he take that?" I asked.

"He wasn't happy, but he didn't threaten me or anything like that. I saw him a couple of times after that on campus, and each time he approached me and asked if I was ready to date again," she said. "I told him that I wasn't interested in dating any one guy, that I was concentrating on my school and didn't want any distractions. The truth is I was a little afraid of the guy. Now I understand why."

"He's not a very good guy, that's for sure," I said.

"He disappeared from campus after the last time I talked to him. I never saw him again until he showed up in Duchesne."

"Had you ever seen the car he had in Duchesne before that day when he came to your apartment?" I asked.

"No, he drove a Volkswagen at school."

"I think he was driving a stolen car," I said. "If I had the plate number on it, I could check for sure. But we don't know where it is now."

"I want you to tell me about him, who he really is," she said. "But first, tell me how you knew I was in the hospital. I don't even know how I got here or where Jimmie is now. How did I get away from him?"

"You really don't remember?"

"No, Jimmie kept me drugged. Sometimes it was worse than others. I remember being in the emergency room with a doctor and a couple of nurses. The last thing I remember before that was when I sent you a text message," she said.

"You texted more than once," I said.

"I remember that."

"How did you do it?" I asked her. "When I called or sent a text, it was Martin that responded. He texted me after the first one you sent and told me you didn't want to see me."

"Yeah, he got really mad when he saw what I'd done. It was his phone. I don't know what he did with mine," she said. "I was lucky those last two times I texted you. I was on a sofa, as I recall. The TV was on, and Jimmie was sitting next to me. He was tired or under the influence of something. I don't know which," she said. "Most of the time, he must have doped me up before I became coherent. Those two times I was able to take his phone and send you messages. I was still pretty out of it. It was a miracle that I remembered your number. I think I just typed something like *help me*."

"That's exactly what you wrote."

"Jimmie started to stir, so I deleted the message after I'd sent it and put the phone back," she explained. "It was only after that when I remembered that I hadn't told you where I was or at least where I thought I was. Anyway, after a few minutes, I tried to get the phone again, but he woke up and slapped me. He hit me a lot. Then he held me down and gave me another shot."

"You sent another message," I prompted her.

"Yes. I don't know how long it was after the first one. It might have been days. But it was just like the first time. We were on a sofa, a TV was on, and he looked like he was asleep. I honestly don't remember much of anything after we got to Las Vegas. He brought me here after he . . . well . . . kidnapped me," she said. "I didn't want to come with him, but he made me."

"I want to hear how he made you go with him, but first tell me about that last text message."

"When I woke up, he was asleep. I took his phone again and texted you. I wasn't very coherent, but I knew he'd brought me to Las Vegas. Now that I think about it, I suppose he could have taken me somewhere else after we came here, but all I could think was to tell you I was in Vegas. So I did, and again I was with it enough to delete the message and put the phone back. Is that why you came down here?" she asked.

"That's only part of the reason," I told her. "Before that, Detective Shelburn had figured out who Martin really was—that he worked in a casino as a blackjack dealer and that his parents lived here. To make a long story short, we figured out that you were in the house with him, and so a SWAT team went in and rescued you."

"You were there when they did?" she asked.

"Yes," I answered. "I saw you on a bed, and you and I sat there together for a little while until the paramedics started to examine you."

"I don't remember any of that," she said. Then her face grew very serious. "Where is Jimmie?"

"He's in jail, and with a little luck, he'll rot there," I said, unable to keep the bitterness from my voice. "He's a nasty character. Now, you were going to tell me how he convinced you to go with him," I prompted her.

"I'd say he forced me rather than convinced me," she said with a frown. "He told me he'd kill someone I was very close to if I didn't cooperate. I had to do what he told me to. When he forced himself into my apartment, I honestly thought I could talk to him and convince him to leave me alone. That's why I asked you to leave. I had no idea I was in danger. But I soon realized that he wasn't the man I'd met in college, that he was an extremely evil person. I didn't dare not believe him."

I was puzzled. "Your mother is dead. Your dad's in prison. You haven't seen you brother in years. Who could he hurt, your college roommate?"

"Saxson, he meant you," she said as her eyes met mine. "He's evil, but he's not stupid. He could see that I cared deeply about you."

"You went with Jameson because he threatened *me*?" I asked.

She shook her head and smiled sadly. "Saxson, you are my closest friend in the entire world. All I could do is pray that you'd find me, and you did. Thank you."

I stood up, leaned over her bed, and did that which I would not have dreamed of doing even a few short weeks ago. I kissed her tenderly on her lips. "And you, Wyanne, are my best friend too." I straightened up and gazed into her eyes. They were misty with tears. There was more that I wanted to say, but suddenly my old shy self returned. I tried anyway. "I . . . I . . ." It wouldn't come out.

She grinned then, and those adorable dimples of hers were as deep as I'd ever seen them. "Let me try," she said. "Saxson Cartwright, I love you. Your turn."

I felt a chill of pleasure run from the top of my head to the soles of me feet. That was all it took to loosen my lips. "I love you, Wyanne Grice," I said. I leaned down and kissed her again.

A moment later, as I held her hand and gazed into her wonderful blue eyes, she said, "Now will you tell me about this horrible man I knew as Jimmie Martin?"

Twenty

I TRIED TO TALK HER into letting me tell her about Jameson later, but she insisted. So I began with his prison sentence, back before she'd ever met him. "He changed his name, managed to get false ID, and abandoned his old identity to begin a new life. But he was still the same evil person." I said nothing about the bodies in the freezer or anything about the blue Lincoln Navigator. I thought I'd ease into that later. I wanted Detective Shelburn to be here when we discussed our suspicions regarding Martin being the killer that she saw on the road. I said, "That's enough for now. Let's talk about something other than Jameson."

She didn't argue, and she asked, "How did the DUI trial with Mr. Glazebrook go?"

"He pretty much won," I said, explaining what had happened. "But I guess he didn't think I did too badly. He offered me a job."

"What?" she asked. She got a worried look on her face. "Does it pay better than the county?"

"Way, way better. But I am not even remotely interested." I told her a little bit about my experience in his office much earlier that day. I didn't mention the flirty receptionist.

"You haven't actually turned him down yet?" she asked. "But you are going to soon?"

"I am, but not until I get a plea out of Jarrod Miano, which is going to happen next week. So we won't be going to trial on that case."

"Saxson, the lives that have been lost . . ." She paused, thinking deeply. Then she said, "What's he pleading to?"

I told her, and she frowned. "That's not much for what he did," she said.

"It's the best we can do now." I didn't mention the shooting of Corporal Kingston.

She was thoughtful for a moment, and then a spasm of fear crossed her face. "The guy I saw, he killed for nothing."

"If it was to keep Miano from going to prison—and we don't know that at this point—then he probably figures he won. There will be no prison time, only a stint in the county jail."

"Whoever did it is still after me." The fear hadn't left her face.

"Whoever it is won't get to you," I said firmly. "Let's talk about something else."

So we talked about other things until the nurse came in again well after midnight and told Wyanne that she was going to check her vital signs. "Would you please step out, Mr. Cartwright?" Nurse Stockam asked.

"All right, but I'll be right outside the door, Wyanne," I said and left the room.

Sheldon came strolling up the hall. "Hey, Counselor, how's Miss Grice?"

"She's doing remarkably well," I said. "But she doesn't remember a thing about what happened at the house today. She doesn't remember us being there." I spent several minutes telling him what I'd learned from Wyanne.

The nurse came out and said, "You can go back in, Mr. Cartwright. And who is this?"

"This is Detective Sheldon Shelburn," I said. "He's going to need to talk to Wyanne for a little while."

"It's awfully late," she said. "But she seems to be wide awake and in very good spirits. Just don't stay very long. She is very malnourished. She told me she was starving. I'm going to bring her something to eat in a few minutes if I can get it cleared with the doctor. Then she has got to have some rest."

Sheldon and I went in together. "Hello, Detective," Wyanne said brightly as we stepped near her bed. "I've sure kept you busy, haven't I?"

He chuckled. "I guess you could say that. How are you feeling?"

"Hungry," she said. "And light-headed. Do you have any idea what he drugged me with?"

"A local officer, Detective Reeves, is working on that," he said. "He'll be here in the morning. I'm afraid there is a lot that he'll need to talk to you about. But right now, if you're up to it, I have a few things I need to ask about. I know it's late," he said as he looked at his watch. "If you want me to wait, I will."

"I think I'll be okay," she said. "I don't think I even need to be in here, but the doctor says I have to. We can talk until I get some food."

"You've been through an ordeal," I said. "You need to do whatever it takes to make sure you're okay before you leave the hospital."

"I guess you're right," she said. She spoke to Detective Shelburn. "What do you need to know?"

"First, did Martin Jameson ever say anything to you that might have led you to wonder if he'd had anything to do with the murders of Darrius Chaudry or Evan Morberg?"

Her eyes grew wide. "He didn't do that, did he?" she asked.

"I take that as a no," Sheldon said.

"Surely he wouldn't have had any reason to kill them, would he? I know he threatened to kill Saxson, but he couldn't have killed them, could he?" she asked.

"We don't know, but we intend to find out. Now, I know he doped you a lot," Sheldon said, "but can you recall any time that you were riding in a vehicle with him other than the white Malibu?"

Wyanne squeezed her eyes shut for a moment. I felt her grip tighten. When she opened her eyes again, she said, "I think I was only in the old Malibu. I wasn't drugged until sometime after we reached Las Vegas. I'm not even sure when he drugged me. It might have been when we stopped to eat after we got into the city. I think I remember eating in a fast-food place, but I don't remember leaving it."

"Okay, then—" Sheldon began.

Wyanne cut him off. "Wait. I remember him telling me that he had a nicer car in Las Vegas. That was when we were on the freeway."

"Did he tell you what kind of car it was?"

"Not exactly. He said something about a really nice SUV, but that was all," she responded. Then she asked, "You really don't know where the Malibu is?"

"We think it was a stolen car. It'll probably turn up sometime," Sheldon said.

"You have a reason for asking this, don't you?" she said, looking first at Detective Shelburn and then at me.

Sheldon answered. "There was a very dark blue Lincoln Navigator in the garage of the house we found you in," he said.

"Was the house his?" she asked.

"No, it belonged to his parents," he responded. "As near as we can tell, he doesn't own a house. But according to neighbors, he spent a lot of time with his parents."

"Are you telling me that they were in the house while he was holding me there?" she asked darkly. "If so, they're as guilty as he is."

Sheldon looked at me, and I said, "She needs to know."

Sheldon sighed. "His parents are dead."

Before he could explain, Wyanne asked, "How did they die and when? Jimmie didn't say anything about his parents to me."

"What about when you dated him?" I asked. "Did he ever talk about his parents then?"

"We didn't date much," she reminded me quite firmly. "But yes, I remember him telling me that his parents lived in Las Vegas, where he'd told me he was from. What happened to them?"

"Why don't you tell her," Sheldon said.

"Okay. Wyanne, right before the paramedics took you in the ambulance, Detective Reeves, the officer we've been working with, asked us to come into the garage. The SUV he mentioned to you was there. So was a large chest freezer."

Wyanne shivered. "What was in it?" she asked. "Was it . . ."

"His parents," I said as gently as I could. "We suspect he killed them. The Las Vegas officers are working on that now."

The hand I wasn't holding rose to her mouth and covered it for a moment. When she removed it, she asked, "How did he get them to fit?"

"Let's just say he *made* them fit and leave it at that. Now, about the SUV. It was a—"

"First, how did he make them fit in the freezer?" she asked stubbornly.

"I think you have figured it out." I paused, and she signaled me to go on. "He cut them up," I said.

She gasped, and her hand again flew to her mouth again.

"Be careful," I said. "Don't pull that IV out."

She didn't respond to my caution, although her eyes did flick to where the IV entered her arm on the underside of her right wrist. "I've heard of that being done before," she said. "What a horrible thing to do. Now, tell me about the SUV," she said.

Sheldon took over again. "It was a late-model, very dark blue Lincoln Navigator," he said. "It's registered to his parents."

"Oh . . . I see now," she said. "The SUV I saw that day when I was running was, I thought, black. It was certainly a luxury vehicle. And now that I think about it, I suppose it could have been dark blue, but if so it would have been a real dark blue."

Detective Shelburn reached in his pocket and pulled out his cell phone. He fiddled with it for a minute, and then he said, "I have a picture of it right here." He held the phone out to her.

She took hold of it and looked closely. She nodded. "I suppose that could have been the car," she said.

"Now, let me show you something else," Detective Shelburn said as he took the phone back. He put it in his pocket and then pulled out a small plastic evidence bag with a sheet of paper in it. "I found this in the glove compartment of the Lincoln when I searched it earlier tonight," he said.

I examined it for a moment and then handed it to Wyanne. "It's about like the one we found before, the one that was taped to your door," I said. This one read, *Don't push me. If you don't leave things alone, something very bad will happen to you.* Wyanne read it and then looked back at me, shook her head sadly, and then glanced at Sheldon on the other side of the bed. "Is it the same handwriting as the other one?"

"I would say so, and the paper is the same as well," he said.

She shut her eyes for a long moment. When she opened them again, she said, "Maybe Jimmie, I mean Martin, was going to leave this on the door, and then when he saw you and the cops hanging around my place decided to do the *very bad* thing that he had threatened and forced me to leave with him."

I was digesting this new development. I was still troubled by the timing of everything. I could see how Jameson could have taken Wyanne to Las Vegas when it appears that he did and then returned to Duchesne without her and shot Corporal Kingston. But he would have had to have doped her up so badly that she'd have been out of it for a long time, close to a day.

"We're not saying it was Jameson that killed my juror and witness," I finally said. "It's just one of the possibilities. So far, we know of no connection between him and the Miano family."

"But this note," she said, her eyes on the note that I still held in my hands, "it was in the Lincoln."

"Maybe he found it on your door and took it," I suggested as the idea popped into my head.

"That could be, but it would also mean that at some point he was in Duchesne in the Navigator," Sheldon pointed out.

"Or he might have had it in his pocket and at some point put it in the Navigator," I suggested. "He could even have done that when the Navigator was right there in the garage."

I turned my eyes back to Wyanne's face. "Is there any chance that he could have gone back to Duchesne and left you unconscious here?" I asked.

She shrugged her shoulders. "I can't remember anything about when he had me drugged except those two times I told you about when I sent the texts. So I would have to say it was possible."

To Sheldon I said, "I think we have to consider him in all of the shootings."

"Yes, even Corporal Kingston's."

"Kingston?" she asked, covering her mouth. Her lips quivered, and she began to shake. "Did he kill a policeman?"

"Corporal Kingston is alive. I'm sorry. We should have mentioned him earlier. He was shot, but he had a bulletproof vest on. He's going to be okay," I told her.

"I hope it *was* Jimmie who shot all of them," she said suddenly. "Because he's caught now and can't hurt you or me or anyone else, Saxson." She shuddered again.

"You're tired, Wyanne. We need to let you sleep. We can talk about this later. Your nurse will be here with a snack in a minute."

"Okay," she said and yawned. "But you have to tell me everything, please."

"We will," I promised.

"You look tired too, Saxson. In fact, both of you do," she observed.

"We have a room, and I rented a car," Sheldon said. "We're not far from here. We better get going."

"I'll stay here with Wyanne," I said as the door to the room opened and Nurse Stockam came in carrying a tray.

"This girl needs some rest," she reminded us.

"We were just talking about that," I said. Then I turned to Sheldon. "You go ahead and get some rest. The rooster will be crowing soon."

"I suppose it will," he said with a grin as he looked at his watch.

"But you need to sleep, too, Saxson," Wyanne said.

I pointed to a large soft chair in the corner of the room. "That will do for me," I said.

"No, you need someplace better than that," she protested.

"Wyanne, I'm not leaving you," I said. "And that is final."

She managed a smile. "I was hoping you'd say that."

Nurse Stockam smiled. "He's welcome to stay, but he's got to let you rest. You've been through a terrible ordeal."

Sheldon said his good-byes and left.

The nurse spoke once the door was closed. "You can eat this little snack now, Wyanne. It took a while to get the doctor to okay you to have something to eat."

"Thanks," she said. "And then I promise, I'll try to go to sleep, although that's all I've done for—I don't know how long."

"We can give you something to help you sleep if you need it," the nurse said.

A look of alarm crossed Wyanne's eyes. "No, please, no drugs. I don't want anything. I've been out for way too long already."

Nurse Stockam smiled and shook her head. Her red hair swayed gently. "I'm sorry. I guess you've had quite enough of that." She turned to me. "We will be in from time to time, so you'll be disturbed. I hope you can rest a little despite that."

"I'll be fine," I assured her. "I just want to be near her."

"Of course you do. Can I get you anything?" she asked.

"Nope, I'm fine."

The nurse checked the IVs, read all the monitors, made a few notes on the computer in the corner of the room, and then left. Wyanne nibbled at her snack, said a few things to me, and then she drifted to sleep.

I, on the other hand, could not fall asleep. My mind was busy with all the aspects of the murder case churning about in the gray matter in my head. And there were the practical things I needed to think about and things that needed to get done. I finally pulled out my iPhone and began to make a list of things I had to do before I got back to Duchesne.

My list included such things as having someone get some clean clothes for Wyanne, renting a car so Wyanne and I could take our time going back home, and making sure she was safe. There were a few other simple things that I included. I was hoping I could go to sleep after I had finished it. I tried, but all I could do was watch Wyanne sleep. I enjoyed that, but I knew that I needed rest as well.

Finally, I pulled my iPhone out again and began to make notes on it. A few minutes later, I had a list of all the suspects we had identified and what there was about each one that pointed toward that person's guilt. I had included Martin Jameson; Micah Miano; Malcom Glazebrook; his associate attorney, Lionel Gancina; and the former business partner of Mr. Morberg, Graham Pease. A common thread with all of them was a dark blue or black luxury SUV. Finally, I had simply written that there must be other persons who would kill to keep Jarrod Miano out of jail, like family or friends.

I again put my phone in my pocket, gazed at Wyanne for a few minutes, and then shut my eyes. The next time I opened them there was light coming through the window and Wyanne was awake and watching me.

"You snore," she said with a grin. "But not too loudly. I could get used to it."

Twenty-One

I HADN'T TALKED TO MY parents in days. They knew nothing of the turbulent events that were occurring in my life. And I wasn't planning to call and tell them. I didn't want them to worry.

Detectives Sheldon Shelburn and Clint Reeves had interviewed Wyanne for about an hour. Sheldon had informed me that he was going to catch a plane and fly back to Salt Lake as soon as he had helped me arrange for a rental car that Wyanne and I could drive back to Duchesne. I had informed him that I was not going to hurry; I figured we were safer driving and staying in motels along the way than being in Duchesne, where there could still be a killer that wanted to eliminate the two of us.

He agreed. When my phone rang, a nurse was just helping Wyanne into a wheelchair to be escorted out to my waiting rental car. She was protesting that she felt just fine and that she could walk. I answered my call as the nurse was explaining hospital policy.

"Saxson," my father's booming voice rang out in my ear. "Are you okay, son? Your mother and I are worried about you."

"I'm fine, Dad. Why would you be worried?" I asked as I slipped out of the room, Sheldon following me.

"We got a phone call this morning," he said. There was something in his voice that caught my attention.

"What kind of call?" I asked, glancing at the detective.

"A very disturbing one," my father said. "The voice was strange."

"Was it electronically altered or something?" I asked as a dark dread fell over me.

"Yes, that would explain it," he said. "Whoever it was told me that you were in over your head and that I should tell you to resign from the Duchesne County Attorney's Office. The caller said that if you were smart, you would accept the other offer of employment you'd received. The caller also said that you should see to it that your girlfriend did not go back to Duchesne and that she should forget what she thinks she saw. Son, what is going on down there? I had no idea you had a girlfriend. And what is this other job you could take? Saxson, your mother and I are sick with worry."

"Dad, I'm fine," I said. "Yes, I have been offered a different job, but I don't want it."

"Saxson, you're always welcome to come home. There's plenty of work on the ranch. You know that. And we'd love to have you here."

"I have a good job," I said. "Things are just a little tense right now, but it will pass. Don't worry about me."

"Well, we are worried. We've never had anything like this happen before," he said, the anxiety etched deep into his voice. "Can you at least tell us what's going on?"

"Dad, please listen to me," I said. "I'm okay."

I'd been so engrossed in my conversation with my dad that I hadn't even noticed the nurse wheel Wyanne up beside me. She was looking up at me, her eyes filled with fear. "Saxson, have your parents been threatened?" she asked.

"No," I said. "I'll explain in a minute."

"Who are you with?" my father asked.

"I'm with Wyanne, the girl you've apparently been told about, and a detective from the sheriff's office. Listen, Dad, we need to head for home. I'll call you when I'm on the road and explain things to you. But please, don't worry about me," I said.

"Let me talk to the girl," he said sternly.

"No, Dad, I don't think you need to do that," I said.

"Do what?" Wyanne asked.

"He wants to talk to you, but that can wait."

She held out her hand. "I'll talk to him."

"Put her on, son," he said in the same tone he had used when I was late doing my chores and he was telling me to get them done.

I shook my head and handed the phone over. I was not used to disobeying my father. I walked a few feet away. I really didn't want to hear this conversation. I strolled up the hall with Sheldon and took the opportunity to tell him about the message my father had received.

"Who would know how to contact your father?"

"Anyone. His phone is listed in the directory."

"Not anyone," he said. "There's no way the call came from Martin Jameson."

"That's right. And even if he did make a call from the jail, he'd have no way to electronically alter his voice," I said. "So who would it be? It had to be someone who knew I'd been offered a job by Glazebrook."

"I don't know, but do you mind if I call your father later?" he asked.

"Of course not," I said and recited the phone number, knowing that once it was in Sheldon's head he wouldn't forget it. We headed back down the hall. When I reached Wyanne again, she smiled and handed my phone back.

"Okay, Dad, you've talked to her. We really need to go now," I told him.

"She seems like a wonderful girl," he said. "Your mother and I would like to meet her."

"And you will," I said, "but not yet."

"Saxson, your mother wants to talk to you."

I shook my head. Wyanne was watching me. Her smile had faded, but there was still a sparkle in her eyes. I was thinking that maybe I *should* have listened while she was talking to my father.

"Saxson," my mother's voice came through the phone to me. "Tell me about this girl. I thought you were deathly afraid of girls. She must be really special. We want to meet her."

"Hi, Mom," I said. "She is great. You'll love her just like I do when you meet her. But right now, she and I need to get in a car and head for Duchesne. We've been out of town and need to get back."

"I don't know what you've gotten yourself into, young man, but you take care of yourself and that girl too. What is her name? Tell me a little about her."

"Wyanne Grice. She's a schoolteacher. She's very pretty. She isn't shy, and she's helped me to get over my problem. I love her very much, and you and Dad can quit worrying. I promise, I'll call you later and fill you in. In fact, Detective Sheldon Shelburn will call you and Dad. I'll let him fill you in. Right now is just not a good time," I said. "I love you guys. If you get any more calls, let me know immediately."

"We will, but now, please hand the phone to Wyanne. I want to say hi to her."

Knowing it was no use to protest, I handed the phone to Wyanne. Again I didn't listen to her conversation but spoke with Sheldon. A moment later, she called out, "Saxson, here's your phone. Your mother is still on it."

I took the phone back and heard my mom say, "I can't wait to meet her, Saxson. You two be careful."

"And you and Dad be careful too," I said. "I love you guys."

"Okay, Saxson," she said. "We love you too."

I ended the call and said, "Sorry about the delay," to the nurse. "We can go now."

An hour later, we had purchased Wyanne some clothes. She changed in a public restroom and threw her dirty ones away. She had showered in the hospital, and her hair was shining; her face, even badly bruised and without makeup, was the prettiest face I'd ever seen. I was still wearing the same clothes I'd had on the day before, but I was okay. I'd shaved and didn't think I smelled too bad. She'd been in her clothes for several days and was grateful to be rid of them.

Finally, after seeing Sheldon off to the airport, we left Las Vegas and started east on the interstate driving a bronze Ford Fusion rental car. Wyanne was quiet. I hoped she was okay.

We had driven maybe thirty minutes when she said, "Saxson."

I looked over at her. Her pretty blue eyes were glistening. "I wish I'd had parents like yours."

"They are pretty special, that's for sure. I just wish they would quit worrying."

We drove on in silence for a while. A few minutes later, she said, "How are we going to stay safe? If it was Jimmie, I mean Martin, who killed those people in Duchesne, he wouldn't have been able to call your father, would he?"

"That's right," I said.

"So there's still a killer out there who wants to shut me up," she said.

"And I won't let him," I assured her.

"I'm counting on it," she said and once again lapsed into silence.

***

We'd taken our time returning to Duchesne. We attended church in newly purchased clothes in Provo. We'd also visited with Corporal Bardett Kingston at the hospital in Murray. He was in good spirits and much stronger than when I'd last seen him. As a precaution, a Utah Highway Patrol trooper was with him, out of uniform but fully armed. Every eight hours, a different trooper would relieve the one on duty. That security was going to continue for as long as Kingston was hospitalized or until the person who had shot him had been arrested.

Wyanne and I arrived in Duchesne on Tuesday afternoon. I'd have taken even longer to go home, as we were having a good time, but I had learned that I would have to be in court at ten o'clock on Wednesday morning. That was the time and date that Malcom Glazebrook had managed to set a hearing in front of Judge Cooper Feldman. I wasn't about to miss it even though Dave had offered to have one of the other attorneys cover for me.

We had arranged for Wyanne to stay in the home of Detective Shelburn and his family for a few nights. And a deputy would be stationed outside as an extra precaution. We all felt that she would be much safer there than in her apartment. I had spoken with my parents several times over the past few days. They were fully aware of the difficulties that Wyanne and I were facing and what we'd both been through.

Wyanne was going back to school on Wednesday—with tight security in place. I was going to court. I carried my security in a shoulder holster beneath my sport coat. I took Wyanne to the elementary myself that morning and made sure that the deputy that had been assigned to protect her was fully aware of how serious his duty was. Then I drove to the courthouse.

I had some time before I was to be in court. I spent some of it working with Josie Miller, preparing a warrant of arrest on Martin Jameson. I instructed her to send it to Detective Clint Reeves at the Las Vegas Metropolitan Police. He had already assured me that he would serve it on Martin Jameson at the jail. We both knew it was

CLAIR M. POULSON

very unlikely he would ever come to Duchesne to face the charge, as
Reeves had built a solid case of murder against Jameson, but I wanted
it in place just in case something went wrong with the case down there.

As the morning wore on, I kept expecting Malcom Glazebrook to
walk in. I'd received no indication that he would fail to come. As ten
o'clock approached I hadn't seen him, but the family of the victim,
Angelica Keen, had arrived. I spoke to them for a moment and made
sure they were still okay with what we were doing.

"It's for the best," Shelby Keen said. "We appreciate your efforts."

"It will be nice to get it behind us," Nayla agreed.

"Why don't you folks go on into the courtroom. I'll be in shortly."

They left, and I looked at my watch. "Josie," I said, "have there
been any calls from Glazebrook or his office?" She shook her head.

"No. And I just finished checking messages in case we somehow
missed his call. There are none from Mr. Glazebrook."

"Thanks," I said. I looked at my watch again. "It's ten minutes to
ten right now. I guess I better get in there. Hopefully Malcom will
show up shortly."

I walked over to the courtroom and went in. As I expected, Judge
Feldman was not on the bench. I had been told that this was the only
case on his docket that day. I took a moment to survey the gallery. The
defendant, Jarrod Miano; both of his parents; and his brother, Micah,
were seated in the gallery behind the defense table. Micah looked over
at where I stood. The look he gave me was a deadly one. I shivered.
He definitely belonged on my list of murder suspects. He was full of
hatred, and right now that hatred was directed at me.

I glanced around the gallery again. The Keens were seated on the
back row on the far side of the gallery as far away from the Mianos
as they could be. Three deputies were sitting on the back row as well
but on the other side of the aisle from the Mianos. One of them was
Detective Shelburn. He nodded at me. I nodded back. I didn't see
Malcom Glazebrook. I carried my file to the prosecutor's table and put
it down. Then I sat next to Marv Hanger, one of my colleagues. "Hey,
Saxson," he whispered, "I see your defendant and his family, but I don't
see Malcom Glazebrook."

"I'm sure he'll be here shortly. Maybe he just wants to make a grand
entrance," I said snidely.

The bailiff was the same one who had been in justice court during the Rutledge case, Deputy Leroy Rusko. He sauntered over, leaned across the table, and whispered, "I'll keep a close eye on the Miano family. I don't like the looks of that brother. He had a knife on him when he came through the metal detector. He created quite a scene when we took it from him. He looks like he'd like to cause trouble."

"Yeah, I'll say," I agreed.

"He wasn't here when you were trying this case a few weeks ago, was he?" Leroy asked.

"He was at the accident scene, but I haven't seen him since then until today. I wonder where he's been."

"Well, I'll keep an eye on him."

Just then the courtroom door opened. I didn't bother to turn because I knew that Leroy would know Glazebrook if it was him. But he frowned. "I don't recognize that guy," he said. "But he's gone over to the Mianos. And he's dressed in a suit that must have cost him a couple grand." He grinned and moved away from us.

I looked back just as the man ushered Jarrod Miano out of the gallery. The lawyer, Lionel Gancina, had Jarrod sit; then he flashed me a shark's smile. He stepped over to my table. "I guess I'll be doing the honors today, cowboy. Don't try to pull anything, or I'll hang you out to dry."

"Just let Jarrod enter the plea that Malcom and I agreed to, and everything will be fine," I said. "By the way, why isn't Malcom here?"

"I think he's seen about all of you he can stand," Gancina retorted. "He really doesn't want you to join the firm." He chuckled. "And you know how I feel."

"You can cut the crap, Gancina," I said. "Just tell me where he is."

"He had a slight medical problem," Gancina said. "So I guess I get the pleasure. I don't usually venture out into hick towns like this, but here I am. So no funny stuff."

He took his seat just in time for the judge to come in. Deputy Rusko asked us to rise and announced that court was in session. Judge Feldman told us to sit, and then he said, "The case before the court is State of Utah versus Jarrod Miano."

Lionel Gancina rose to his feet. "Your honor, Lionel Gancina for the defense. I will be handling this matter for Mr. Malcom Glazebrook, who is unable to be here today. I'm an associate of his."

"Very well," the judge said. "This won't take long. We are here today to entertain a change of plea. Mr. Cartwright, would you like to explain for the record?"

I stood up and said, "Thank you, Your Honor. The state and defense have reached an agreement. Jarrod Miano will be allowed to plead no contest to reckless driving, and we will dismiss the automobile homicide charge."

"What's going on here?" Jarrod Miano shouted, jumping to his feet. He swore and shook a fist at me.

Judge Feldman rapped his gavel and said, "Sit down, Mr. Miano," as the bailiff rushed over and grabbed Miano by the arm. "I will not allow outbursts in this courtroom. If it happens again, I'll have the bailiff restrain you. Mr. Gancina, explain to your client what the results could be if he tries anything like this again."

"Nobody pulls this kind of stuff on me," Jarrod shouted, jerking his arm away from Lionel, who had taken hold of him. "What do you think you're doing? I ain't taking none of this from this . . . this hick," he said, pointing a finger at me. "Nobody talked to me about this. Maybe Malcom talked to my father, but he didn't talk to me. So you can all shove this whole thing."

Judge Feldman rapped the gavel again. "Mr. Miano, you are in contempt of this court. Bailiff, remove the defendant from the courtroom."

"Don't you touch me," Jarrod said, shaking a fist. "I'll knock your head off if you do."

Sheldon and the other deputies sprang into action to assist the bailiff. Jarrod swung his fist and connected with one of the deputies. A scuffle followed.

When the officers were finally in control of Jarrod, they got him facedown on the courtroom floor. Detective Shelburn had his handcuffs out and was about to place them on Jarrod's wrists when there was a roar from behind me. Micah, the older Miano brother, vaulted over the barrier from the gallery and into the well with us.

Marv and I grabbed at him, but he was too fast. He kicked Detective Shelburn in the ribs before we could stop him. We each grabbed an arm and wrestled with him until several more officers entered the courtroom at a run. Apparently the judge had hit his panic button. Three of them took over for Marv and me. More of them helped handcuff Jarrod.

When both Miano brothers were secured, Judge Feldman said, "They both go to the jail. Mr. Gancina, you are to go talk to your client. We'll be in recess for one hour, and when we're in session again, I will expect the defendant to be calm and ready to enter his plea. I also want this other man taken back there. I want his name, and I'll make my contempt in his case official and on the record. In addition, the county attorney's office is free to bring whatever other charges against him that they deem appropriate. I'll see both men back here in an hour—*in restraints*." Judge Feldman rapped his gavel. "This court is in recess."

Twenty-Two

SOMEONE MUST HAVE CALLED THE county attorney, because he came into the office just before we were due back in court. He was slightly stooped and clearly experiencing some pain. "I understand I missed a little rodeo in the courtroom," he said with a chuckle. "I didn't want to miss it if we get a repeat."

"I hope they have the guy settled down," I said. "I really wanted to get this matter behind us today, but now I'm not so sure we will."

"What does Glazebrook say?" he asked.

"He isn't here," I said. "He sent that other lawyer, the one I told you about, Lionel Gancina. He's arrogant, but he has his work cut out today. I think the judge has had all he's going to take."

At that moment, Gancina entered our office. "Can I speak with you, Saxson?" he asked.

"Sure," I said. I nodded to Dave and said, "Lionel, this is my boss, Dave Padrick."

"It's good to meet you," Lionel said. "If you want to sit in, feel free."

"I think I will," he said.

The two men followed me into my office. After we were all seated, Lionel said, "I think I have my client calmed down. But he wants me to renegotiate the terms of the plea with you."

I glanced at Dave, but he simply said, "It's your case, Saxson."

"What does he want to negotiate? The offer I made is very generous," I said.

"That's what I told him, but he insists that Malcom didn't talk to him, only to his father. I think you heard him say that in court.

Anyway, he feels he should be able to decide for himself. He says his father doesn't speak for him," Lionel said.

"Very well, here is my offer. He pleads guilty to reckless driving and agrees not to oppose a ninety-day jail sentence. Then the auto homicide goes away. He can take it or leave it," I said.

Mr. Gancina glared at me. "It's no contest," he said.

"Lionel, if you want me to turn down Malcom's generous employment offer, you will convince your client to plead guilty to reckless driving," I said.

"Are you serious?" he asked.

"Dave here is my witness. Get me a guilty plea and there won't be a vacancy in the county attorney's office."

"I'll see what I can do," he said as he stood up. "I'll go back and present this to him. He glanced at his watch. I'll see you back in court in fifteen minutes."

After he'd left, Dave said, "He really doesn't want you to take that job in Malcom's firm, does he? But you told me you were not remotely interested."

I grinned. "I'm not. I love working for you, Dave. But I'd like to get a guilty plea for the sake of the victim's family. Gancina thinks he's a great lawyer. I guess we'll see how good he is. Surely he can convince Miano to meet my terms." I shrugged. "We'll see how it goes. If they insist on a no-contest plea, we can still do that, and I'll still turn Glazebrook down. But who knows, maybe they'll take the guilty plea."

"I like the way you work, Saxson," he said.

We talked about what we'd do if Jarrod refused any kind of deal at all. We hoped that it didn't come to that because we didn't want any more people to be harmed, which could happen if we had to take this to trial again. Finally, Dave got to his feet, winced with discomfort, and said, "Well, let's go in and see what's going to happen."

When we entered the courtroom, it was almost filled to capacity. There were no less than a dozen officers stationed strategically around the room. Some were in the gallery and others in front of the bar, scattered throughout the well. Armando and Tamara Miano were seated right where they had been before. The eyes of both parents were filled with anger. They sat with their arms folded and stared straight ahead.

The Keen family, visibly shaken, were in the same place they'd been before as well—as far from the Mianos as they could get. I recognized a reporter from the *Uintah Basin Standard* in the gallery. There were a number of citizens, who, I guess, had just come to see the fireworks. I sincerely hoped that there wouldn't be any more.

Dave Padrick and I sat at the prosecutor's table. Marv Hanger and our legal assistants were seated on the council bench behind us. I think they expected more fireworks too. Lionel Gancina came in right after we did and took his seat. He looked at me and nodded. I took that to mean that his client had agreed. I hoped that's what he meant.

"All rise," Deputy Rusko called out as Judge Feldman took the bench.

Court was called back into session, and the judge told us to be seated. He stared out over the courtroom for a moment, and then he said. "I hope everyone is in control of their emotions. I will not have another scene like we had earlier. Officers, bring the defendant and his brother in." Apparently he now knew the identity of the second combatant.

Jarrod Miano's hands were cuffed in front of him and attached to a chain around his stomach. In addition, his feet were in leg irons. He shuffled in and took a seat beside his attorney. His brother, Micah, similarly restrained, was directed to a seat in the jury area between two officers.

Lionel leaned over and whispered something to Jarrod. The defendant nodded. The judge asked Jarrod and his counsel to stand at the podium. Once they were in place, the judge said, "Mr. Cartwright, state the terms of the proposed agreement."

"We have offered to let the defendant plead guilty to reckless driving, and in exchange the state will not pursue the auto homicide matter. We also will not require more than ninety days in jail, but we do want at least that," I said.

The judge then addressed the defendant. "Do you understand the terms of the agreement?"

Jarrod nodded.

"Mr. Miano, you must speak verbally so that a record can be made of your response."

"I understand," he growled.

Judge Feldman then spent a moment making sure that the defendant understood the consequences of what he was doing. Finally, he asked, "How do you plead to the charge of reckless driving?"

He glanced at Lionel Gancina, who whispered something to him. Then he looked at the judge. "Guilty."

"Your Honor, may I say something?" someone in the gallery shouted. We all looked back. It was Jarrod's father, Armando Miano. His eyes were shooting daggers at the judge.

"Who are you?" Judge Feldman asked.

"I am Jarrod's father. I am the one who spoke with Malcom Glazebrook about this arrangement. This is not what I agreed to."

"Mr. Miano," Judge Feldman said sternly. "This young man is of age. What you and Mr. Glazebrook might have agreed to is of no consequence. Your son speaks for himself. He has agreed to the terms Mr. Cartwright spelled out, he has entered his plea, and I accept that plea. That ends it. Sit down, please."

Armando shook his fist and said, "I am paying the attorney, and I *will* have some input here."

"Sit down, or I'll have you removed from the courtroom," Judge Feldman said, his voice growing louder.

A pair of uniformed officers stepped toward him. He hesitated, glanced at the officers, and then sat down. His wife looked as angry as he was, and she whispered something to him. He shook his head and whispered back. I heard what he said to her—"Just shut up. I did the best I could. Jarrod brought this on himself. I'm tired of paying to get him out of trouble."

Just then the judge addressed the defendant, and I tuned out the Mianos to listen. "As to sentencing," Judge Feldman began.

Lionel spoke up, "We waive time for sentencing, Your Honor. We'd like to proceed right now."

"All right, I'll do that," the judge said. "Mr. Miano, I sentence you to six months in jail with three months suspended. That means you will serve the ninety days agreed upon. I am also imposing a fine of $1,800.00. You will be on probation for three years." He then spelled out the terms of the probation, which included a no-alcohol clause, and made it clear that it would be a supervised probation.

Jarrod seemed slightly dazed. Finally he shook his head and asked, "Are you telling me I have to serve three months in jail?"

"Yes, you do. And that time will start today."

"I thought the jail was going to be suspended," he said.

"No, that's not what you just agreed to," the judge answered.

"Then I don't plead guilty," Jarrod said in a raised voice.

"You already have. You will also serve an additional thirty days for the outburst earlier for which I found you in contempt. "Officers, you may take Mr. Miano back to the jail."

Jarrod turned and faced the back of the courtroom. "Dad, do something! This guy is about to put me in jail."

"I guess that's your problem, Jarrod. You made the deal, not me," his father said with a red face.

"I'm not going back there," Jarrod said again as three officers stepped forward and forcibly dragged him away from the podium. "Dad, Mom, do something!" he shouted.

"We'll get you out, Jarrod," his mother shouted.

Her husband swung toward her. "We will do no such thing."

"Armando, he is my son. I will not allow him to go to jail. How will that make me look?"

The judge intervened. "There will be order in the courtroom. Remove the defendant and bring his brother to the podium."

Dave rose to his feet. "Your Honor, the state will file an information with the clerk of your court within the hour charging Micah Miano with assault on a police officer, resisting arrest, and disorderly conduct. We would like you to set bail today."

"Bail is set at $10,000. But Mr. Miano, you are also in contempt of this court, and I am sentencing you to jail for thirty days for that offense. You will not be able to be released on bail until that time is served. My clerk will set the matter for arraignment as soon as she sees the information from the state." He then rapped his gavel and declared the court adjourned.

Micah was cursing as the officers dragged him out of the courtroom.

Dave leaned over to me as the judge was leaving the bench. "Good job, Saxson. I'm feeling quite weak. I'm going back to the office now. You may want to stay and speak with the Keens. And I'm sure defense counsel will want to talk to you, to remind you that you made a deal with him." He grinned, slapped me on the shoulder, and headed for the exit.

Angelica's parents were already moving toward me, and Shelby Keen said gruffly, "How did you get a guilty plea out of him?"

"I applied a little pressure," I said.

"Well, we want to thank you," he added. "You're a good prosecutor. We'd tell your boss that, but he left."

"You're welcome," I said. "I just wish I could have done more."

"I would have preferred to see him go to prison," Shelby said, "but at least this is something. I just hope he hates it in there."

"We're okay with what you've done," Nayla Keen said. "He admitted guilt. We thank you for that. That was more than we expected." The Keens then turned and made their way toward the exit.

I stuffed my papers into the file folder. Lionel Gancina stopped me as I went to leave the courtroom. "You did okay, Cartwright," he said. "But I still don't want you in our firm."

"Don't worry," I told him. "We had a deal. You did your part, and now I'll do mine. As soon as I can reach Malcom, I'll let him know that I'm turning down his offer."

"Good," Lionel said with a scowl in place. "I had to apply a lot of pressure to Jarrod to get him to agree. Anyway, you would have been miserable with us. We're not like you, not any of us."

"Is *that* why you wanted me to refuse, or was it really about Missy Bevans?" I asked with a smirk.

His scowl disappeared, and he grinned. "You are pretty smart. Yeah, I saw the way she was flirting with you," he said. "I intend to marry her. I just need time to convince her. You would have made that much more difficult."

"I wouldn't have competed even if I'd gone to work there," I said. "Missy's not my type." Then I changed the subject. "So what is wrong with Malcom?"

"He got beat up pretty badly yesterday. He's in the hospital," he said.

"What? Do you have any idea who did it?" I asked.

Lionel shook his head. "Not a clue. He didn't ever see them. They came at him from the back. He's lucky they didn't kill him."

"Well, give him my regards and tell him I hope he's better soon," I said.

"I will. Do you also want me to relay your job-offer refusal?" he asked.

"Sure, that would be great."

Lionel turned away, but then he suddenly turned back. "I'll tell Malcom you out lawyered him." He chuckled. "He would never have gotten a guilty plea out of the little creep. He was set on no contest." Another chuckle. "Of course, he didn't have the incentive you gave me. I might have strangled the little creep if he hadn't agreed to your terms." He turned away, but before he left he said over his shoulder, "Oh, and Cartwright, no offense, but I won't invite you to the wedding."

Poor Missy Bevans, I thought. She had no idea what was ahead.

Back in the office, Dave was drinking a soda. He looked very weak.

"You shouldn't have come," I told him.

"It was worth it," he said. "You outmaneuvered Lionel and Malcom today. I'm just glad you're not leaving us. By the way, how much did Glazebrook offer you?"

"A minimum of $300,000 a year."

"And you turned that down?" he asked. "You must be crazy."

"Nah. I just like you and the rest of the guys and gals here."

Dave turned serious. "Saxson, I think the killer was in that courtroom. I kept getting this awful feeling, and it wasn't my heart acting up."

"I know what you mean. I did too. But I don't know who it was. There were people there I didn't recognize. At first I thought they were just interested townsfolks, but now I'm not so sure." I turned to the legal assistants. "Josie, Becky, were there any people in there that you didn't recognize?"

"Several," Josie said.

"I agree," Becky confirmed. "There were a couple of guys on the back row. They were tough-looking guys. They both had tattoos all the way down their arms. I wonder if they could have been friends of Jarrod's," Becky said.

"I think I'll go see if Detective Shelburn is in his office. Maybe he recognized them," I said.

***

Sheldon didn't know who they were either; however, he said, "They looked like tough nuts. I watched as the Mianos left. Those guys spoke to them for a minute out in the parking lot, and then they got in a gray car, a late-model sedan, and drove off. Keep an eye out for the car. If you see them in town, get their license number and give me a call. I'd like to find out who they are. Oh, and Saxson, I get the feeling that Jarrod Miano's mother is not happy over the plea agreement. She looked like she was giving her husband an earful."

"That family's lucky they aren't all in jail for contempt. They really pushed Judge Feldman's buttons today," I said.

Sheldon laughed. "It was one crazy day in court, wasn't it? By the way, I'm glad Wyanne is staying with us until we can figure out something more permanent and safe. Our kids really like her."

"I appreciate what you're doing. I'll pick her up after school," I said. "I'll probably stay with her until I bring her to your place in the evening. I'll make sure she has dinner."

"She can eat with us," Sheldon said.

"I'd like to take her to dinner," I insisted.

"I don't blame you," he said. "Are you thinking about what we can do on a more permanent basis?" he asked.

"I'm thinking about it," I said. "I do have an idea, but I don't know if she'll go for it. We'll talk about it tonight." I was about to leave when I thought of something else. "Sheldon, I learned the real reason Malcom Glazebrook wasn't in court today. He got beat up yesterday. He's in the hospital."

The detective's eyes narrowed. "Do you think there's some connection to this case?"

"I don't know what I think, but it does give one pause. Miano's family isn't particularly happy with the plea bargain. Who knows? Maybe someone took it out on Glazebrook or even figured the whole deal would fall through if he couldn't make it to court."

"Perhaps I'll be taking another trip to Salt Lake," Sheldon said thoughtfully. "Do you know which hospital he's in?"

"No, but I'm sure if you call his office, you can find out."

"I'll do that. I want to talk to him. Who knows, he might have some idea of why he got beat up," he told me. "I'll go out in the morning."

"One more thing," I said. "What have you learned on the tire tracks?"

"I don't have a match from any of the SUVs I've examined," he said. "Although that doesn't rule them out. Tires are easily changed."

Twenty-Three

IT WAS A SUNNY AFTERNOON and quite warm. I picked Wyanne up from the school and asked her if she'd like to go to dinner. She agreed. Then I said, "How about if we go check my horses first? There are some things we need to talk about. Do you mind if we drive to Roosevelt for dinner and talk on the way?"

She was in an agreeable mood. We drove to the ranch and walked out to my horses. As we petted and fussed with them, Wyanne asked me how it went in court, and I told her what a crazy day it was.

"So Jarrod Miano is in jail," she said after I'd given her a blow-by-blow account.

"He is, and so is his brother," I said.

She studied my face for a moment. "Maybe they're the ones who did the shootings," she observed. "It sounds like they're violent men."

"That's for sure, but I'm bothered by a couple of guys that were in the courtroom," I told her. "They were driving a late-model gray sedan. Detective Shelburn saw them talking to the Mianos in the parking lot."

She shivered and leaned against me. "Do you know who they are?" she asked.

"I don't have any idea." I described them to her, right down to the tattoos and long, dark hair. "Sheldon thinks I should watch for them. So I will."

Wyanne shuddered. "It just doesn't get any better, does it?"

"I'm afraid not, but Sheldon is working hard, and a couple of other officers are helping him," I told her. "He wants you to stay at his place until we can figure something better out."

"I've been thinking about it," she said. "I can't think of anything except me quitting my job and moving somewhere where no one knows who I am. And I don't want to do that. I like my job. Do you have any ideas?" she asked.

I put my arms around her. "I do."

"What? Tell me," she pleaded.

"I don't know if you'll agree," I said. "We'll talk about it tonight."

"Why not right now?" she asked, her eyes narrowing.

"Later," I said. "After dinner."

She reached up and kissed my lips, a lingering, sweet kiss. "Okay," she said. "I hope it's a good idea."

I thought it was, and I hoped she would agree. We spent a few more minutes with the horses, and then we went to her apartment, where she changed and picked up a few things to take to Detective Shelburn's later. Then we went to my place. I changed my clothes, checked my pistol, and again secured it in my shoulder holster. I didn't mention the gray car I'd spotted about a block away, but I worried about it. I just didn't want to worry her too. It was probably nothing. When we left, I helped her get in my truck and then looked casually up the street. The gray car was still there. It looked like there were a couple of people in it, though it was hard to tell at that distance.

I drove to Main Street and turned east, keeping a close eye on my rearview mirrors. The gray car showed up about a half block behind me when I stopped at the traffic light. When I started up again, I decided to take steps to determine if the car was going to follow me. I turned left and went past the grocery store. The gray car followed.

I made a right turn, drove two blocks, and pulled into the post office.

"What are you doing?" Wyanne asked.

I hated to upset her, but it looked like I had no choice. "We're being followed by a gray car."

She gasped. "Are you sure?"

"I am now," I said as I looked up the street and saw the car pulled off to the side. "I'm going to go in and get my mail," I told her. "Do you need to get yours?"

"Well, yes, but why now?"

"If the gray car is still there when we come back out, we'll know they're following us."

We both went in and got the mail from our boxes. The gray car was still sitting where it had been when we went inside.

"Let's go," I said and helped her into the truck.

I returned onto Main Street and started toward Roosevelt again. "Let's see what they do now."

"What are we going to do?" she asked, a tremor of fear in her voice.

"I'm going to flip a U-turn and drive back toward them. When we're close enough, see if you can read the license plate. Write it down if you have something to write on," I instructed her.

She dug in her purse and came out with an envelope and pen. I suddenly made the turn and drove back toward them. The driver took a fast right turn off of Main Street just before I got to them. But Wyanne had already read the license plate, and I had gotten a quick look at the driver and his passenger. There was no question that they were the two tattooed men from the courtroom.

"Now what?" she asked.

"I could use a roll of duct tape. They have it in Kohl's Hardware."

She gave me a funny look. "What? You're going to get some tape while we're being followed by two guys who probably want to kill us?"

"I want them to think we turned because I forgot something," I said with a smile.

"Okay, but I'm coming in with you," she said.

"Of course you are."

We went inside, and I found the tape. We were alone in the aisle, so I pulled out my phone and dialed Sheldon's number. "Do you have that license number?" I asked Wyanne as the phone rang. She pulled it out and showed it to me.

"The gray car is following us," I said the moment the detective answered. Just then another customer started toward us. I signaled for Wyanne to follow me. We left the aisle and walked to the next one, where we were alone again.

"Saxson, are you there?" the detective asked. "Are you okay?"

"I just needed to move. We're in Kohl's Hardware. I have the license number of the car." I read it to him off Wyanne's paper. "The men are the ones that were in the courtroom," I said. "We're going to head for Roosevelt for dinner."

"Be careful, Counselor. I assume you're armed," he said.

"I am. Let me know what you learn."

I paid for the tape, and Wyanne and I left the store, keeping a close eye out for the gray car. I didn't see it again until we were headed east on Main Street. Wyanne reached over the console and took hold of my arm. "Do you see them?" she asked.

"Yup. It worked. They're behind us again."

"What are we going to do now?" she asked.

"I think we decided on dinner in Roosevelt," I said, glancing over at her and smiling.

"Smarty pants," she said. "What's the tape for?"

"It's normally used to make repairs," I said.

"I figured that, but what in particular?" she asked, eyeing me suspiciously.

"I don't know. I just need it in case I need to tie somebody up or something."

"Of course," she said facetiously. "I should have known that. Are they still back there?"

"Yep. I wonder if they have enough gas to go to Roosevelt and back," I said as I crossed the Duchesne River on the east end of town.

***

They had enough to get to Roosevelt because they followed us all the way there. Sheldon called and told me the name of the registered owner of the car. "It's a Chrysler Sebring, and it belongs to Micah Miano."

"Who is sitting in jail," I said.

"Clearly friends of his," he responded. "We still don't know who they are. But I know where Micah is. I'll go talk to him. Maybe I can learn something."

"Wyanne and I are going to get some dinner. I'll see if they're still here when we're finished."

"Where are you eating?" the detective asked. I told him, and he cautioned, "Watch yourself, Saxson. These guys could be dangerous. I'll have someone from the Roosevelt Police drive by a few times while you're in there."

"I'll be careful," I said as I maneuvered my truck into a parking space. Once again, the gray Chrysler parked a block away, but I was able to see where they were. I discreetly pointed them out to Wyanne.

She appeared nervous and clung tightly to my arm, but she didn't say anything.

While we waited for our order to arrive, Wyanne said, "Okay, Saxson, tell me what your idea is—you know, the one that is supposed to make me safer."

"Maybe we can talk about it while we're driving back," I said. I was worried about what her reaction might be. Procrastination seemed like a good idea.

She folded her arms across her chest and stared at me. "No, I want to hear it now. So out with it, mister." Her sternness made me chuckle. "It's not funny," she said, fighting to keep from smiling. "Talk to me."

"You may not like my idea," I said as I wondered how to say it. I looked around us. There were people at other tables, but everyone seemed wrapped up in their own conversations. I had planned to wait until after we'd eaten, but I guessed that now was as good a time as any. I looked in her blue eyes. I gulped. Oh no! I felt myself clamming up. I wasn't sure my tongue was going to work after all. It had been so easy to talk to her lately. *Why now?*

"Even if I don't like your idea, I'll still love you," she said. "We can be open and honest with each other."

That didn't help. I took a deep breath. She was smiling at me now. Oh, how I loved that smile. I tried to decide how to say what I wanted to say to her. Finally, I figured out a way to ease into it. "Wyanne," I said and stopped. Maybe I could do this—and maybe I couldn't.

"What?" she asked.

"Ah, I, uh, I wondered . . ." My tongue froze.

Those gorgeous dimples of hers grew as deep as I'd ever seen them. "You can do this, Saxson. We know each other."

She really wasn't making this any easier. "Okay," I said, "let me ask you this." The roundabout way was definitely the way to go about it.

"Go ahead, sweetheart," she said.

Oh boy. That really smacked me. She was toying with me. I took a sip of my water. Then, diverting my eyes, I said, "Were you scared tonight? You know, when those guys were following us."

"Of course, but I still felt safe."

"Why did you feel safe?" I asked.

"Because I trust you. I feel safe when I'm with you."

That helped. "Okay, so here's my idea. Maybe you could, ah . . . you know . . . stay with me," I stammered. That didn't come out exactly the way I'd intended.

"I'm not that kind of girl, Saxson," she said very seriously.

"Well, you know, I don't mean that like it sounded," I said. I was floundering.

"Let me see," she said, putting a finger on her cheek and looking quite thoughtful. "I would only live with you if we were married."

There. She'd rescued me. "Yeah, that's what I mean," I said.

She grinned, moved to my side of the booth, threw her arms around my neck, and said, "If you're asking me to marry you, the answer is yes."

"Are you sure?" How dumb was that? I thought.

"Are you?" she asked as she leaned back and looked into my eyes.

My courage returned in the face of her positive response. "Yes, I am, but here's where you might disagree."

"I doubt it, but fire away," she said.

"Well, it would need to be soon," I said.

"Sounds great. Like when?" she asked.

"Like *real* soon," I said.

"I'll only marry in the temple," she responded. "Can people elope to the temple? That soon?"

Goodness, that girl could read me like a book. "Yeah, that soon."

"I'm worthy. I have a recommend. Do you?" she asked.

"Of course," I said.

"Then let's do it as soon as possible."

"Okay," I said, and right there in that restaurant full of people I kissed her.

Then she removed her hands from around my neck and moved to her side of the table again. We both noticed at the same time that a dozen people or more were watching us, grins on the assortment of faces. I felt myself go red. Wyanne, bless her, looked at our audience and said, "What? He just asked me to marry him. And I said yes."

Laughter filled the air, and everyone began to clap. Okay, I think I just did something in a way that no one had ever done before. I could envision Wyanne telling our future family about this night. So far it had been memorable—but we still had to get back to Duchesne with the goons following us. Who knew what lay ahead before this night was over?

Things soon settled down, our meal came, and we began to eat. After a little while, I looked at her and said, "I need to get you a ring."

"I'll help you pick one out, but it doesn't need to be expensive," she said. Then her face dropped. "Saxson, I don't have any family to disappoint by not giving them notice. But your parents will be upset if we do this right away, won't they?"

I shook my head. "Maybe, but they'll get over it when we explain. They had given up on me ever getting married. They know how hard it is for me, you know, talking to girls."

"They don't even know me except for that short conversation I had with them on the phone a few days ago," she said. "They may not be too pleased."

I put my fork down, held her hand across the table, and said, "They will love you, Wyanne. Oh, how they will love you."

"I hate to do this, but I think I'll ask for another week off from school. When I tell my principal I'm getting married, he'll work it out," she said.

"So, are you saying we should meet with our bishops and stake president Sunday and then call one of the temples and arrange for someone to perform the wedding?"

"Yes, if you're sure your parents won't get upset."

"They won't, especially if we do a little honeymoon and include a stop on our ranch. My folks will be so excited."

"Then it's a plan," Wyanne said giddily. "I am going to elope to the temple with the man of my dreams."

I looked across the table at her in wonder.

When I asked for the check, the waitress said, "Your dinner is paid for. The manager said it's on the house. Congratulations."

"Thank you, Betty," I said, stealing a peek at her name plate. "And tell the manager thanks too."

My phone rang.

"Saxson, an RPD officer just told me that those guys are still waiting out there. Are you two about finished?"

"We were just ready to walk out," I said.

"Okay. They haven't approached your truck, but you better be careful," Detective Shelburn said.

Suddenly, the excitement and euphoria of the past half hour vanished.

"Was that Shelburn?" Wyanne asked after I clicked my phone off.

"It was. Those goons are still out there."

"So what are we going to do?" she asked.

"We are going to get married ASAP."

"I mean what are we going to do right now."

"We're not going to let them mess this night up for us," I said as I laid a generous tip on the table for Betty.

Twenty-Four

I SPOTTED THE GRAY CAR as we walked out of the restaurant. Several thoughts ran through my mind. I considered walking behind the car and tapping on the window with the barrel of my pistol. But these men could be killers. And I was with the person I loved more than anyone in the world. I thought about asking for a police escort, but I didn't want to seem like a coward. Finally, we simply got in the truck. The gray car pulled onto the road and followed us, as I expected.

"Saxson, they're back there," Wyanne said with a tremor in her voice.

"You have your seat belt on, don't you?" I asked.

"I always wear my seat belt."

"Okay then, let's see if we can lose them. Are you ready for a ride?"

"You won't wreck, will you?" she asked.

"That would ruin this night for us, and I already told you I wouldn't do that."

"Okay, then do it. I trust you, Saxson."

I turned off the highway and into a neighborhood and then began racing through the streets. I turned left and then right and then right again and then left. I was driving as fast as I dared. "Are they still back there?" I asked.

"They are," she said.

I gripped the steering wheel tightly and glanced in the rearview mirror. They were close. I took another turn and then another and pretty soon we were in Ballard in an open area. I sped up, and then I slammed on my brakes and made a dangerously fast turn back toward the gray car. The driver was coming too fast, and when he swerved to miss us, which I had prayed that he would, he ran off the road and rolled his car. I turned again, driving rapidly back to where they had crashed.

Dust was filling the air, and the gray Chrysler was rocking slightly on its top. I slid to a stop with my headlights illuminating the Chrysler. "Wyanne, we're in Ballard. Call 911."

"What are you going to do?" she asked as I leaned over the seat and grabbed the roll of duct tape.

"I'm going to use this tape," I said.

I bailed out, pulling my gun from my shoulder holster, and approached the wrecked car. One of the men was trying to crawl out through the driver's window, which was shattered. I didn't see the other one. I walked around the car, dropped to my knees, and peered inside. The second thug was trying to follow his buddy.

Wyanne appeared at my side, her phone to her ear. "They're sending the cops," she said. "I tried to describe where we are."

"Okay, hold this gun," I said. "Point it at the guy climbing out."

"I've never shot a gun," she said.

"This is a revolver. All you have to do is pull the trigger. Don't do it unless one of them pulls a gun on me."

"Okay," she said. Her phone was in one hand, the revolver in the other.

The first man was almost out of the car. I reached down and grabbed his arm. He tumbled out. Before he could even attempt to get to his feet, I grabbed the other hand, pulled it next to the first, and began to tape them together with the duct tape. I used the tape generously. The second man had managed to get his head through the window. I watched him warily as I taped the feet of the first one together.

I didn't see a gun, so I made sure the first man was secure, and then I helped the second one out. He tried to resist, so I slammed his face with my fist—not a gentle slam. That relaxed him, and I used more of the duct tape. Once I had them secured, tightly taped, and lying face down on the ground, I patted them down. They were both armed. I found a pistol on each of them. I relieved them of their weapons and stepped back.

"I guess you really did need that tape," Wyanne said as I stepped past her and put their weapons in my truck. Then she handed me my revolver, and I put it back in my shoulder holster. "Now what?" she asked.

"I hear sirens. I'll see if I can direct the cops here," I told her as I pulled out my phone. She still held hers in one hand. She put it back in the truck in her purse while I made my call. Then she joined me, put her arms around me, and laid her head against my chest.

"That was awesome," she said, and we both laughed.

Detective Shelburn and another deputy pulled up shortly after the local officers had arrived. "How did you get here so fast?" I asked.

"I was worried about you two," he said, "so I asked Bart to jump in with me, and we headed this way. It looks like you have things well in hand though. Are you guys okay?"

"We're great," Wyanne said as she once again snuggled up to me.

It was chilly, and we both began to shiver as we watched the officer replace my duct tape with handcuffs. "Let's sit in the truck," I suggested. "We can turn the heater on."

A half hour later, Sheldon opened my door and said, "These guys are both on parole. I'm going to go on over to Vernal and question them after we get them checked out at the hospital."

"They look fine to me," I said.

"I'm sure they are, but we need to have a doctor tell us that before we lock them up. So what are you guys going to do now? I won't be home until late and—"

"We'll be fine. I think we've got the immediate danger out of the way," I said. Wyanne and I had been talking, and we had devised a plan. "We're going to each pack a bag, and then get rooms at a hotel out of town somewhere. I'll call you in the morning."

***

We ended up in Provo late that night and booked rooms, just like we'd planned. We both had phone calls to make the next morning. Wyanne called the principal while we were eating a late breakfast. In the meantime I was on the phone with Detective Shelburn.

After we had both finished our calls, she said, "He'll have my class taken care of, and I am to take as much time as I need. I suggested a couple of weeks. He said that it might have to come out of my paycheck. I told him that was okay. He's a good man. Oh, and I didn't tell him we're getting married—just that the danger had picked up and I couldn't stay in town."

When she had finished telling me about her call, I told her about mine. "Sheldon says that the two parolees aren't talking. But they also aren't going anywhere," I said. "Since they're on parole, they are being held without bond."

"That's good," she said.

"Sheldon is going to have both of the guns checked by the lab to see if either one was used in any of the shootings. He thinks that if they are the killers, they were hired by Jarrod or his brother. He told us to be careful as we can't be sure there aren't others, but he thinks they may be the killers."

"I'm still scared, Saxson," Wyanne said, reaching across the table and putting her hand on mine.

"We'll be fine," I assured her. I knew that there could still be danger for both of us, but I wasn't nearly as worried as I had been. "The Miano brothers are in jail, and their criminal friends are as well. Those two were driving a car belonging to Micah, and it really isn't a stretch to assume one of them could have borrowed a black SUV. So the four people most likely responsible for the terrible things that happened are in jail. I certainly hope so."

Next I brought Dave up-to-date. "I'll need a little time off," I told him after explaining the excitement from the night before.

"We'll get by," he assured me. I didn't tell him what Wyanne and I had planned. I didn't want to give him another heart attack. We had agreed not to tell anyone about our wedding. Even Sheldon didn't know. All we told anyone was that we were hiding out somewhere beyond Duchesne.

Wyanne and I finished our breakfast and then spent some time taking care of important matters in Provo. We made a stop at the county clerk's office and bought a marriage license. We found a ring—not too expensive but very pretty—and I put it on her finger while we visited the grounds of the Provo temple.

Finally, we both called our bishops, and I called the stake president. We made arrangements to meet with them that evening at their offices in Duchesne. We didn't tell them what it was about, only that it was urgent. To my fiancée and me, that's exactly what it was.

***

We parked her car at Sheldon's house after we'd met with both bishops and the stake president. All three men had told us that what we were doing was highly unusual, but after we'd explained our circumstances, they agreed it was the right thing. All three men agreed that they would not tell anyone of our plans. I would have expected nothing less. They were Church leaders and knew the importance of confidentiality. Sheldon was curious why we'd come back to town, but we simply told him that we needed some things. He didn't press us. And we were glad. We wanted to keep this a secret. It was actually kind of fun.

We stayed in Provo again that night. First thing the next morning, we called the Provo temple and made arrangements to be married that day. To others, it would probably have appeared rather hasty and perhaps not very wise, but to us it was the right thing to do. I had never felt better about anything in my life. By three o'clock, we were leaving the temple, husband and wife. I had never been happier, and from the glow on the face of my bride, I could tell that she was at least almost as happy as I was.

The next few days were the best I'd ever had. Wyanne assured me that they were her best as well. We drove wherever we pleased, spent time doing whatever we wanted, and stayed in different hotels every night. On Sunday, we picked out a chapel in Idaho and attended meetings. We were gradually, in a roundabout way, heading toward the ranch I'd grown up on in Wyoming.

My wife and I were about twenty miles from my childhood home on Monday afternoon when I got a call from Detective Sheldon Shelburn. I had my phone synced to the truck, so we could both listen and talk. He asked how things were going, and I told him they were fine. He informed me that he'd visited Corporal Kingston in the hospital. I told him that Wyanne and I had as well. He asked me what we were doing. I told him I'd tell him about it when we got home. Then he got down to business and told me that the lab had ruled out both of the guns I'd taken from the parolees.

He had my undivided attention now. "That's not good."

"I'm afraid you're right. They may have used a different gun, but it could also mean that the killer is still out there," he said. "There is one positive thing though. We found a pad of paper that matches the notes threatening Wyanne. It was in the backseat of the gray Sebring. We checked for fingerprints. We found a clear one that belongs to the older Miano brother, Micah."

"So he could be the shooter?" I asked.

"Yes, he could, but we still don't know which vehicle Miss Grice saw."

That wasn't her name anymore, but I didn't correct him. I just looked over at Mrs. Cartwright and grinned. "It's got to be one that the Mianos and my two goons all had access to."

"I agree, and I'm working on it."

"Has there been a connection made with these guys and the beating of Malcom Glazebrook?" I asked.

"The cops in Salt Lake made an arrest," he said. "The suspect is a local gang member who recently got out of prison. It seems that Glazebrook represented him, but he got, to use his term, out lawyered by the prosecutor in the case. The gangbanger went to prison. He was simply getting revenge on Glazebrook, who he blames for his conviction. So that assault is not related to our cases. And Glazebrook is going to be okay."

"I appreciate the call. You're doing a great job, Sheldon," I said.

"I wish I had better news, but I'm afraid there's still more," he said. "And you won't like it."

My stomach took a turn. "Tell me," I said.

"Martin Jameson has an attorney."

"Let me guess. Malcom Glazebrook," I said quickly.

"Yup, and the report I'm getting from Detective Reeves is that Jameson is bragging that he's going to beat them, that he didn't kill his parents and Glazebrook will prove it," he said.

"Yeah, good luck on that one," I said. "Does he say who did do it?"

"Are you sitting down?" Shelburn asked.

"I'm driving," I said. "So yes. Who's he accusing?"

"His girlfriend, Wyanne Grimes," he said.

"What?!" Wyanne screamed. "I would never—"

Sheldon cut her off. "It's good to hear your voice, Miss Grimes. We know it wasn't you," he said. "But that's what Jameson told Detective Reese when he questioned him."

I was shaking my head. "What does Jameson say to try to back up his ridiculous statement?"

"He says that her father is in prison, that he's a killer and she learned from him," Sheldon told us. "Is your father in prison?"

"Yes, and he did kill someone," she said.

"I'm sorry," Sheldon replied. "Of course, what your father did has nothing to do with the kind of person you are."

"Actually, it does, Detective," she said. I looked over at her briefly and then got my eyes back on the road.

"In what way?" he asked.

"He made me want to be as different from him as I could. And I've always tried to do just that," she said firmly.

"She's the best person I know," I said, looking over at her. Then I addressed Sheldon on the phone again. "Besides pointing out that Wyanne's father is in prison, what else did Jameson say?"

"He told Detective Reese that Wyanne had gone willingly with him to Vegas and that they planned to get married there but that when he introduced her to his parents, they told him she wasn't good enough," Sheldon said. "He says Wyanne got really mad at Martin's mother and shoved her. She fell and hit her head on the corner of a coffee table, a very heavy, solid one. The fall killed her."

Wyanne was shaking her head. I simply listened, wanting to go to Vegas and punch Jameson's lights out. "What about the father?" I asked.

"Jameson says that his father knelt down beside his mother and that he joined his dad there. They were trying to help her. He says his father said something about Wyanne going to jail for what she did and that he would make sure she never got out," Sheldon explained. "He says neither one of them, Martin or his dad, were paying any attention to Wyanne at that point. Then he says she walked up behind them and said, 'I'm not going to jail,' and stabbed his father in the back with a long, sharp kitchen knife."

"Wow, that guy has an imagination," I said. Wyanne didn't say anything. But her face was red, and she looked like she was about to explode.

"Jameson claims she tried to stab him too but that he caught her hand and made her drop the knife. He says that's why he drugged you, Wyanne. He didn't want you to try anything again."

"Wow! This is crazy. So did he say I cut them up and put them in the freezer?" Wyanne asked. "While I was drugged?"

"No, he says he did that," Detective Shelburn said.

"Okay . . . and *why* did he do that?" I asked slowly.

"He claims he was going to take them somewhere out in the desert and get rid of them later. His reason was his *love* for Miss Grice. He said he didn't want her to go to prison and figured that after a while he could let her come out of the drugs and promise to marry her and take care of her and that she'd go along with it because she loved him."

"Saxson, stop the truck," Wyanne cried out. I looked over and saw that she was holding her mouth with her hand. I found a wide spot on the two-lane highway and stopped. She bailed out and threw up.

"What's wrong?" the detective asked.

"My wife is throwing up," I said.

"Your . . . your . . . what did you say?" he asked.

"Sorry, that was a slip. I'm kind of stressed." I got out of the truck and put my phone to my ear.

"Stressed as in you don't know the difference between a wife and a girlfriend, or stressed as in you guys are married and didn't want anyone to know," he said. I knew that if I could see his face right then, I would see a great big grin.

"Don't say a word to anyone, Sheldon. Please."

He chuckled. "Your secret is safe with me. Wait a minute, Counselor; you said you had an idea about what you could do to keep her safe. Your plan was to marry her, wasn't it? You said that she had to agree to whatever you had in mind. I take it she agreed."

"She did," I said. "I need to go now."

"Call me back. There's still more you need to know."

"I hope it gets better," I said and ended the call. I turned my attention to Wyanne.

At her direction, I got a Kleenex from her purse. She wiped her mouth. "Now my breath stinks," she said. "I'm sorry, sweetheart; I didn't mean to gross you out. But when he was talking about Jameson cutting those people up, it was more than I could take."

I hugged her and helped her back in the truck. "We're almost there," I said.

"I have some Certs in my purse," she said as she began digging in its cavernous depths. "I don't want to smell like puke when I meet your family."

"Let's stop and get a snack, if you can handle it," I suggested. "We're almost to town. We can take a little while before we drive out to the ranch."

"I love you, Saxson Cartwright," she said.

"Right back at you," I countered.

Twenty-Five

I CALLED DETECTIVE SHELBURN BACK as soon as we were in the truck again. "You said there was more?" I asked him.

"There is, but first, congratulations, you two. And how are you feeling now, Mrs. Cartwright?" Sheldon asked.

"I'm okay now," she said as she gave me a sharp look. "You told him!"

"It slipped out," I said sheepishly.

"I'll keep your secret," Sheldon said. "Don't get mad. Your husband's a good guy, you know."

"Yes, I know." She grinned. "Now, tell us what else you've learned, and please, nothing else that will upset my stomach."

"Okay, Mr. and Mrs. Cartwright," he said. I could feel the teasing grin in his voice. "Here's the rest. The Mianos have hired Malcom Glazebrook to defend their sons on the antics they pulled that day in the courtroom. When he called and talked to Josie in your office, I guess he told her that you would wish that you had taken the job he offered you. He told her that before he got through with this case, you'd be lucky to be able to practice law at all."

"Sounds like a sore loser," I said.

"I'll say," he agreed. "He didn't say he was going to defend your duct-tape pals. I guess they'll have a court-appointed attorney."

"We need to stop now and freshen up a little before we drive out to the ranch," I said.

"So your parents are about to meet their new daughter-in-law? I suppose they know about your little secret."

"Not yet," I said.

Sheldon laughed. "You guys are too much. Oh, there's one more thing. Glazebrook told Josie about your father, Wyanne. And he must have told someone else. Anyway, it's all over town from what I hear, and it's thanks to Glazebrook."

"That creep," I said. "Are you sure you can't tie him in to the murders some way?" I was being facetious.

"Maybe," he said. "I'm working on it."

"You're not serious, are you?" I asked.

"Very. I'll fill you in later. I'm keeping what I know close to the vest for now. And one more thing, you two; don't take any chances. I don't know that I've identified all of your enemies yet."

"Meaning what?" I asked him.

"I'll only say this much. I have a snitch in the jail, a very reliable one. He's been talking to the Miano brothers at my request."

I asked Sheldon to tell me more about Glazebrook, but he wouldn't. I finally ended the call, put the phone in my pocket, and pulled up to a gas pump.

A few minutes later, Wyanne and I drove into the yard of the Cartwright ranch. It was late afternoon, and the huge cottonwoods cast long shadows across the lane. I parked beneath one of the trees and looked over at my wife.

"This is beautiful," she said as she looked around. The large two-story log house sat behind a white vinyl fence. A short walkway led to the east of the house, through a gate, and to a spacious three-car garage. Grass and flower beds surrounded the house. The flowers were still blooming, and the grass was green and neatly trimmed. It appeared that there hadn't been a frost yet. Behind the house was a large fruit orchard. We could see part of it, but the house hid most of the trees from our view. There was also a large vegetable garden behind the house, but it was out of view from where we sat.

Near the front of the house and within the fence were several tall blue-spruce trees. Beyond the yard were barns, sheds, and even a small bunkhouse for hired hands. Beyond that were acres and acres of fields. We could see some of the cattle and a few horses. I opened my door and breathed in the familiar scent of the ranch. I walked around the truck and helped Wyanne out.

"This is beautiful and so peaceful," she said with a smile.

"It is that," I agreed.

She turned to me. "How could you leave this to go and spar with the likes of Malcom Glazebrook?"

"It does seem a little crazy, doesn't it? But I love Duchesne, and I love my work there. Duchesne is my home now, our home, but I always have this to come back to," I said. "*We* always have it to come back to," I corrected myself.

A dog barked and came running from the area of the barn. My dad's cow dog, a black-and-white border collie, skidded to a stop beside me and started begging for attention. I reached down and petted him until he ignored me and started sniffing at Wyanne. She laughed and petted him. "Can we have a dog sometime?" she asked. "We had one when I was little, before my dad came home drunk one night and hit it with his truck. I will always believe he did it on purpose."

"I'm sorry. Yes, we'll have a dog sometime," I promised.

I spotted my father walking toward us from the barn. He was wiping his hands on a rag. He suddenly sped up when he saw my truck and Wyanne and I standing beside it.

"I guess you'll get to meet my dad first," I said.

We watched as he approached. My dad still had a thick head of hair that was already gray beneath his brown felt cowboy hat, even though he was only fifty. He was a tall, solidly built man with a smile that was always available to whoever he met.

We walked past the front gate of the yard and met him near the garage. "Saxson, what a surprise," he said. "It's good to see you." He gave me a quick man-hug and then trained his clear blue eyes on Wyanne. "And this is the girl on the phone?" he prompted.

"This is Wyanne, my wife," I said with a large grin. "My father, Kendrick."

My father was not an easy man to stun, but I had just stunned him. For a moment, all he could do was stare at the two of us. Finally he said, "Am I getting hard of hearing, Saxson, or did you just say this beautiful young woman is your wife?"

I put my arm around her shoulders and pulled her close. "Your hearing is as good as it's always been," I said. "We were married a few days ago in the Provo temple."

He pulled his hat from his head, wiped his brow with a large blue bandana, and then said a little gruffly, "I suppose there's a story to go with your surprise, you two."

"I'll say," was my response. "And you'll hear it all. After you do, I think you'll understand."

His smile came back, and he looked at Wyanne again, and then he reached out and pulled her into a bear hug. "I don't know how you ever landed this guy. His mom and I had given up on him ever getting married. He wouldn't even date. Shyest kid I ever knew."

Wyanne grinned. "I helped him get over that," she said.

"Well, I'm glad. You're welcome in our family. Saxson, your mother's in the house. Let's go give her the surprise of her life." He laughed heartily. "Sonia had good vibes when she talked to you on the phone. Believe me, she is going to love you, Wyanne. I can promise you that."

We entered the house by the front door. Once inside, my father called out with a booming voice, "Sonia, we have guests."

My mother was a pretty, petite woman, who had always prided herself on looking her best. I knew her well enough to know that if she was in the kitchen, she wouldn't come out until she made sure her hands were clean and dry, her short brunette hair was neatly brushed, and she had just a touch of makeup on.

She called back, "Give me a minute, Kendrick. I'll be right there. Show our guests to a seat."

Dad waved his hand at the sofa, but I said, "I think I'll stand."

"Me too," Wyanne agreed.

Dad smiled. "I can't wait to see Sonia's face. She'll be delighted," my father said to Wyanne. "She always tried to talk Saxson into, shall we say, mingling with the girls, but he just couldn't do it."

We talked for a couple of minutes. Dad told me how the ranch was doing. He asked me if we were okay, since he knew that there had been some kind of trouble. I assured him that we were fine.

Just then, my mother walked into the living room; she took one look at me and cried out, "Saxson, you're home." Then she stopped and looked at Wyanne, a puzzled look in her eyes.

"Saxson, is this the girl I talked to on the phone?" she asked.

"Of course, Mom," I said with a grin. "Why do you ask?"

"Well, you've never brought a girl home before. We had about—"

I took pity on my mother; it was time to let her know the truth. "Wyanne, I'd like you to meet my mother," I said.

My mother stepped up to us, gave me a hug and a kiss on the cheek, and then hugged Wyanne. "Saxson has never brought a girl home to meet us before," she said, pretty much repeating what she'd said only seconds before.

"Well," I said, "this will be the only time I ever do. Wyanne is my wife."

For a moment, I thought my mother was going to faint. The blood drained from her face, and she swayed slightly. My dad put an arm around her for support. For a moment there was dead silence in the room. It was broken by the ringing of my cell phone. I pulled it out and looked at it. It was Detective Shelburn. "I better take this," I said. "Mom, are you okay?"

She nodded her head, staring at my beautiful wife.

I answered my phone.

"Saxson, you've got to get out of there!" Shelburn said urgently.

"What? Why?" I exclaimed.

"Someone's after you guys. They know where you are. Take Wyanne, and get out of there now."

"How do you know?" I insisted.

"The snitch I put in the jail. Go, and go now!"

There was no denying the urgency in his voice. Nor could I deny the fear in my wife's eyes. "Saxson, who is that?"

"It's Sheldon. We've got to get out of here. Someone has found us somehow."

She grabbed onto me. My father, never a man to stall when he knew something needed to be done, said, "Let me grab a rifle. Go out the back with it."

"I have one in my truck," I said as we all headed toward the back of the house.

I was still carrying my phone. "Saxson, take the batteries out of your phones," Sheldon instructed. "Get new phones as soon as you can and call me with your numbers."

"Okay," I said. We were on the back porch. Dad handed me a loaded rifle and a box of ammunition. He was holding another one for himself. Mom was as white as a sheet.

"They may have tracked us with our phones," I said. "We need to take the batteries out." I popped the back open and removed the battery. Following my lead, Wyanne did the same. I put mine back in my pocket, and she put hers in her purse.

"Take mine," my dad said, handing me his phone. "We'll use your mother's."

We moved quickly through the orchard behind the house, listening for any vehicles that might be coming. We didn't hear a thing. That didn't mean there wasn't someone close. My brother Cliff met us at the barn and looked at us like we were crazy. "What's going on?" he demanded. "Why the rifles? And who is this girl?"

"She's my wife, and we are in danger. Someone followed us here. My truck's in the front yard. We need to get to it and go."

"Give me your keys," he said as he pulled a set from his pocket. He was just like my dad—never one to let the grass grow under his feet. "Take my truck. It's the blue Dodge over there."

I knew his truck. We'd kidded about him driving a Dodge and me a Ford for several years. I pulled out my keys and handed them to him. "Good to meet you, Saxson's wife," Cliff called after us as we ran to his truck. This was the first time since our marriage that I didn't open the door for Wyanne. She didn't give me time.

"Go the back way," Dad shouted.

"You guys need to get away too," I called back. "These people are killers."

"The back way?" Wyanne asked as I started the truck.

"Yes, there's another way out." I handed her Dad's phone as I drove around the barn, across a cattle guard, and onto a dirt road that skirted the fields. "Call Sheldon."

"I don't know his number," she said. "It's in my phone."

"Okay, call my office. Tell them to call Sheldon and have him call the police up here. I don't know if my folks and brother will leave or not. We've got to get someone out here." I told her the number, and she made the call. While she was on the phone, I said, "Give them the number to Dad's cell phone and have them give it to Sheldon. Tell them to have him call us at that number."

We had to go through three gates before we finally pulled off the ranch and onto a graveled road. By then, my office had called back and said that Sheldon had already called the authorities in Wyoming and that officers were on their way to the ranch. "Call Mom's cell phone," I told her. I recited her number from memory as I headed east on the dirt road.

She punched in the numbers as she asked, "Saxson, isn't this the wrong direction? Won't that get us closer to the entrance to your ranch and not farther away?"

"They don't know this truck," I said. "I'll have you duck down when we get back to the pavement. I think I saw Cliff's cowboy hat in the backseat. I'll wear it and these sunglasses." I snatched the glasses from a cup holder on the console between us.

"Okay, I'll get the hat," she said, and she twisted around while holding the phone to her ear. She handed me the hat and said, "Hello. It's Wyanne. Saxson wanted me to call you."

She listened for a moment and then said, "Yes, we made it out the back way. Are you guys okay?" She listened again. Then she said, "Here, talk to Saxson." She handed me the phone.

My dad's voice was strong and clear as he said, "We locked your truck in the barn. We have your suitcases with us. We haven't seen anyone. All three of us are in my truck and headed out behind you now. We'll meet you someplace and give you the suitcases. Our hired man isn't coming in today, so we don't have to worry about him."

"Dad, I can't believe you took time to hide my truck," I said.

"Cliff got it while I kept a rifle pointed down the lane, just in case anyone showed up. And you know I can shoot. But they didn't come, and we're fine. Where are you exactly?" he asked.

I told him, and he said, "You're going the wrong way! You've got to turn around and get out of the area."

"I have Cliff's sunglasses and hat on. When we get close to the turnoff to the ranch, Wyanne will duck out of sight," I said. "I want to see if I can recognize anyone if they happen to pass us."

"Okay, Saxson, but don't be a hero. We want to get to know that sweet wife of yours and hear all about your wedding since we weren't invited," he said gruffly. But I could hear a smile in his voice.

"Sorry about that, Dad. We needed to get married soon so that I could keep her right with me," I explained. "So I could help keep her safe."

"I understand, knowing that people are after the two of you. That can wait though. Call me if you see anyone," he said.

I handed the phone back to Wyanne, and it instantly began to ring again. Wyanne said, "Hello." She listened, and then she said, "Let me hand the phone to Saxson, Detective."

"Sheldon," I said as soon as I had the phone to my ear. "Thanks for calling us back. We're fine. We're in my brother's truck. My dad, mom, and brother are behind us in Dad's truck. But they didn't see anyone before they left the ranch."

"Did you see anyone as you were driving back to the highway?" he asked. "I thought they were close."

"This is a big ranch. We went out the back way. My truck is locked in the barn," I said. "What else can you tell me now?"

"A lot. The cops are heading to your father's place, but they weren't close when I contacted them, and we don't know for sure who we're looking for or what they're driving."

"Sheldon, listen. I'm heading back toward the main entrance to the ranch now," I said. Before he could protest, I explained what I was doing and why.

"Okay, as long as you're sure you won't be recognized," he said. "Call me if you see anyone suspicious. I'm positive someone is in the area and that they are after the two of you. So don't take any chances, please."

"I'll call you," I promised and handed the phone back to Wyanne.

"That's them," she said, pointing urgently as we approached the turnoff.

"Keep out of sight," I said. "I'll give you a license number if I can get one."

Two men stood beside a black SUV. They appeared to be arguing, if their wild gestures meant anything. Then, just as I was almost to them, they piled into the SUV and drove onto our lane. I read off the license number to Wyanne and told her to call Detective Shelburn. I drove by. But after they were quite a ways up the lane to my parents' house, I turned around and drove slowly back. Tall brush lined the lane, and I could only get glimpses of them as they drove. They were going slow, and I relayed that to Sheldon as soon as Wyanne handed me the phone.

"The local cops are getting close," he said. "I told them to go silent so they wouldn't spook our suspects."

Wyanne said, "There are cops coming now. I can see them."

I also spotted them and told Sheldon. He asked, "Can those men go out the back way like you did?"

"Yeah, but I'll have my dad keep an eye back there until we can get some cops to go around."

I got out and waved the cops down as I ended the call and handed the phone to Wyanne. "Call Dad and tell him to watch the back way," I said. Then I identified myself to the deputies and told them that there were only two ways out of the ranch and that someone should cover the back road where my parents and brother would be.

I was told to wait there. They took my cell phone number, and two cop cars headed up the lane; a third headed toward the back entrance to the ranch. Wyanne and I got out of the Dodge and leaned against it, waiting. "They're probably wondering where we disappeared to," I said. "I suppose I could put the batteries back in our phones now, but I don't think I will. We don't know that there aren't more besides these two."

"Maybe we should sit in the truck in case we need to get away quickly," she said sensibly.

I didn't argue. We got back in the truck with the windows down. Not a minute more had passed before we heard shots fired in the direction of the ranch. "Oh no," Wyanne moaned. "Here we go again."

Twenty-Six

SHELDON CALLED AGAIN. "I WISH I was there," he said. "What's happening?"

"We just heard shots near the ranch house," I said. "I hope the officers are okay." There were two more shots just then, and I told Sheldon I should get off the phone in case the officers tried to call me.

An officer did only moments later. I spoke briefly to the officer and then ended the call and said to my wife, "One of the officers is injured. A perpetrator is dead. The second one is on foot, fleeing through the fields. Ambulances have been dispatched."

Before long, additional cops were involved in the search for the missing man, who was believed to be wounded. A tracking dog and his handler had been summoned. It was hard to imagine that the fugitive would be able to stay at large for long. Sheldon called and told me more about how he knew that the men were pursuing us. In short, he said that the snitch he'd placed in the jail was able to get the Miano brothers bragging.

They told the snitch, who Sheldon still didn't identify, that the prosecutor and his girlfriend were going to die. He was quite upset when he reported back to Sheldon. The detective sent him back into the cellblock to see if he could get specifics. It seemed that Micah Miano had made a phone call. He was giddy about it and revealed to the snitch that more guys had been hired and that they were following my wife and me using the GPS on our cell phones. When Sheldon called me, it seemed that the hired killers, as Micah referred to them, were closing in on my parents' ranch. Thus the frantic warning and scramble to get away.

"Do you have any idea who Micah talked to on the phone?" I asked.

"I do," Sheldon said, and he gave me a name.

"You're kidding," was my response.

"Nope. We'll make an arrest as soon as we can build a stronger case. We have the suspect under surveillance. What you've seen up there helps us build a case. I am keeping Dave Padrick up to speed," he said. "He's prepared an information and arrest warrant, but he doesn't think we have enough yet, so he hasn't yet given them to me to serve."

"How does what I told you help?" I asked.

"I ran the plates on the black Lincoln Navigator you guys saw." Sheldon gave me the name on the registration. "So as you can see, it matches what my guy is telling us."

"How reliable is the snitch?" I asked.

"Very," Sheldon said. "I trust him totally. Also, I don't think I mentioned that another attempt was made to kill Corporal Kingston. Some guy dressed as a doctor entered his room and had everyone leave. His parents and wife were suspicious and reported it to the nurses' station. Security and the UHP officer on duty there responded, and they entered Kingston's room. The fake doctor had already walked out. As a precaution they undid the IV. Kingston said the guy had fiddled with it. They got to Kingston just in time. It turned out that a poison had been introduced into the IV. They didn't catch the suspect, but a surveillance camera showed him running through the halls, going down on an elevator, and getting into a black SUV outside."

"Did they get a license number?" I asked.

"Only partial," he said. "But the numbers they did get match what you gave me for the Lincoln up there, the one that you saw go to your father's ranch."

"So it was probably one of these guys," I said.

"Probably," he agreed. "I've asked the sheriff up there to look in the SUV and see if there are any medical scrubs. They haven't had time yet, but they're impounding the Navigator. And security on Kingston is beefed up. I guess that even though the Miano case is over, the owner of the Lincoln must think the corporal might remember something about whoever shot him."

"There are some evil people in this world," I said.

"There are," the detective agreed. "Oh, and one more thing, Saxson. My snitch, even though the charges on him aren't real, hired an attorney on the recommendation of Jarrod and Micah."

"Malcom Glazebrook," I guessed.

"The one and only," he agreed.

After finishing my conversation with Detective Shelburn I relayed what I had learned to Wyanne.

She was trembling when I finished. "How many more people could there be trying to find us?"

"I hope we've got them all," I said. "All but the killer, that is."

That worried her, but I assured her that surveillance was in place, that we were safe.

"I hope so," she moaned as she leaned against me.

Wyanne and I waited until my family joined us, then we drove into town and found a restaurant for lunch. While we relaxed the best we could and shared our story with my parents, my brother, and his wife, who had joined us from their home in town, the search went on at the ranch.

We were still eating when my dad's phone rang again. I answered it when I saw that it was Detective Shelburn. "I just talked to the snitch again," he said. "The Miano brothers are talking up a storm to him."

"What now?" I asked.

"They told him about Glazebrook trying to hire you to work for his firm of corrupt attorneys," Sheldon said. "And they did use the word *corrupt*."

He didn't say anything more for a moment, and I finally said, "Come on, Sheldon, out with it. I take it your reason for calling has nothing to do with my ability as an attorney."

"You've got that right, not that you aren't a good attorney," Sheldon said with a chuckle, "because you are an excellent one. It's because Malcom knew who was behind the shootings, and he had been hired by the suspect. He figured that if he could get you working for him, he could bring you in on the case, tell you who it was, and then you would be ethically bound to keep it to yourself. Micah said he knew you wouldn't tell because you were too honest. He also said that Glazebrook knew you wouldn't quit looking for the killer as long as you worked for the Duchesne County attorney."

"That creep," I said angrily. "He needs to be disbarred."

"In time he will be. My inside man is wearing a wire. We have it all recorded," the detective said.

It was late evening before we were allowed to go back to the ranch. The fugitive had been found and arrested. He had a bullet wound in the right leg, so he was taken to the nearest hospital. I was present when a couple of officers searched the Lincoln for the fake doctor's clothing. It was wadded up and shoved under the backseat, stethoscope and all.

The injured man refused to speak to the cops following his surgery. I had hoped to be able to speak with him, but that didn't work out. As a precaution, I bought Wyanne and myself new phones. There was still a possibility that there could be others searching for us, so we kept the batteries out of our old ones.

The probability of us being targeted again got a lot higher when Sheldon called me with bad news: the suspect they'd had under surveillance had somehow slipped away and was on the loose.

"So I guess you and Wyanne need to extend your honeymoon," Detective Shelburn told me. "I'm sorry. Our guy messed up big time."

"Okay. I guess we'll go somewhere else for a few days," I said.

"You do that," he said.

***

The next day, we were in Idaho when we got still another call from Sheldon. "My snitch is out of jail. Malcom Glazebrook bonded him out."

"Why would he do that?" I asked. "Can't he defend someone who's still in jail?"

"It's not that. Glazebrook hired him to find the two of you," he said.

Wyanne and I were eating dinner in a restaurant in Idaho Falls. I put down my fork. I locked eyes with her as I asked Sheldon, "What is he to do when he finds us?"

"I think you know the answer to that. Of course, Glazebrook didn't specifically order a hit. He just said, and this is recorded, 'You are to convince them not to come back to Duchesne ever again.' This conversation took place in Glazebrook's SUV. He seems to think my snitch will do what he says."

"Are you sure?" I asked.

"He gave him $5,000 in cash and promised more after he finished the *assignment*. That was the word Glazebrook used," Sheldon told us.

"That's enough to charge him with conspiracy," I said, thinking as a prosecutor. "You need to arrest Glazebrook. I've had all I'm going to take from him."

"Don't worry; we'll get him, but we'd like something a little more specific. So here's what we'll do, if you agree," Detective Shelburn said. "We'll allow the snitch to find you. Then he'll call Malcom and see if he won't be more specific. Then we'll make the arrest."

"And how will he find us?" I asked warily.

"You can meet him somewhere. You name the place, and I'll see that he gets there," Sheldon said.

"Will you be with him?" I asked.

"If you want me to be."

"I do," I agreed. My eyes caught Wyanne's again as I asked my next question. "Sheldon, do you trust this man? I mean totally. If we're going to meet with him, I've got to have your total assurance."

"Yes, I trust him. He won't let me down, and more importantly, he would never let you and Wyanne down," he said.

"Can't you at least tell me his name?" I asked.

"His name is Anthony Green."

I looked at Wyanne. "Does that name mean anything to you?"

"No," she said. "I don't think I've heard of him. Saxson, are you sure this is a good idea?"

Sheldon didn't wait for me to answer. "You have nothing to worry about with him. And I'll be there when he meets you."

"Okay, but don't let Glazebrook or anyone else follow him," I cautioned.

"That won't happen," he said. "Trust me on this, Counselor." He chuckled. "You'll be surprised when you meet him—so will your wife."

We agreed on a time and location for the following afternoon. I got my laptop out and spent some time learning what I could about Anthony Green. All I found was a criminal record, and I wasn't so sure about the accuracy of that since I remembered Detective Shelburn telling me they had manufactured charges against him. I wondered if he had also somehow managed to manufacture a past criminal record. Wyanne and I both felt uneasy, but she said, "We've got to trust Detective Shelburn."

I couldn't disagree. But it was with uneasiness that we waited in a hotel room in Boise the following afternoon. It was an overcast day, not terribly cold but not warm like it had been for the past few weeks. No storm was forecast, so I wasn't worried about Sheldon and the mysterious Mr. Green having bad roads. Our ground-level room gave us a clear view into the parking area. Sheldon's department-issued, unmarked gray Ford Explorer pulled in and parked near my pickup.

Wyanne and I both stood at our window and watched closely through a slit in the curtain as the two men got out and walked toward the front door of the hotel. They reached the sidewalk and walked right past our window, deep in conversation. Wyanne, who was holding my arm, suddenly squeezed tightly and gave a little gasp. I looked over at her. The color had drained from her face, and her eyes were wide. She looked like she was in shock.

"Wyanne, what is it? You look like you've seen a ghost," I said.

"I think I have," she said, her eyes trailing the two men until they passed out of sight.

"Are you okay?" I asked.

"I don't know," she said.

"Did you recognize that man?" I asked.

She faced me, still pale. "I don't know. Maybe he just reminds me of someone."

"If you don't want to talk to him, just say so. I'll go out in the hallway and speak with him and Sheldon," I offered.

"No, but you answer the door," she said. "I'll stay back here."

"Are you sure?" I asked, worried about her reaction. No way was I going to let her get hurt.

She leaned against the windowsill, gripping my hand. The color slowly returned to her face. A knock came on the door. She released my hand, and I crossed the room. I slowly opened it, my senses on high alert and one hand on my pistol.

Sheldon was just lifting his hand to knock again. "Counselor," he said. "This is Anthony Green." Green was behind and to the left of the door, where he couldn't see my wife and she couldn't see him.

"It's nice to meet you," I said.

"I've heard some good things about you, Mr. Cartwright. Is Wyanne with you?"

I heard her gasp again, and I looked over my shoulder at her. Green stepped into view, and Wyanne's face again went white. She stared at the man, her hand covering her mouth. I stiffened. He stepped past Sheldon and beside me. His eyes were on my wife, and I was ready to react if I had to. Something strange was going on here. I was scared that this was another old boyfriend. My mind was in a whirl.

"Hi, Wyanne," he said. "It's been a long time." A huge smile covered his face.

She started forward. He stepped toward her. I stayed right with him. They both stopped when they were about a yard apart.

She finally spoke. "Denver?" she said, making it a question. "Is that really you?"

"Yes, sis, it's me," he said. "I've missed you."

"Denny," she said. Her eyes filled with tears, and she suddenly sprang forward and threw her arms around him. "I thought you must be dead, Denny. Mom's dead, did you know that? How did you find me?"

I knew from the exchange who this guy was. And I was sure she'd mentioned his name to me before. The two of them hugged for a long moment. Finally she stepped back, and with a glowing face and misty eyes, she said, "Saxson, this is my brother, Denver. Denny, this is my husband."

Sheldon was grinning. "I would have told you sooner, Saxson, but he swore me to secrecy. He has quite a story to tell."

"I'll bet," I said as I turned back to my wife. "So this is Denny."

"It is," she said as she rubbed her eyes. "I haven't seen him since I was fifteen. Where have you been all these years, Denny?" she asked.

"All over, sis. I've missed you too. I wrote to Mom once. I didn't want her to worry. I told her I was okay. But she probably worried anyway, didn't she?"

"Yes," Wyanne said.

"I knew she had died," he said. "I read her obituary on the Internet. I thought about trying to find you, but I was in California. And I wasn't sure you'd want to hear from me after what I did."

"I've thought about you every day," she said.

"I also know what Dad did." His voice took on a bitter tone. "I hope he rots in prison."

"He will," Wyanne said.

"When did you see him last?" he asked.

"On the night he was arrested. I wasn't strong enough to do what you did; although I would liked to have," she said with a wisp of a smile.

"I suppose I shouldn't have beaten him up," Denny said. "But I couldn't take it any longer." He paused for a moment. "So you haven't visited him in prison?"

"No. I don't want to ever see him again."

"I don't blame you. So how are you doing, Wyanne? I see you found a great guy."

She moved to me and put her arm in mine. "I did."

They talked for a minute. Then I said, "Is anyone hungry? There's a restaurant in the hotel."

Twenty-Seven

"How did you find me?" Wyanne asked as we ate dinner. "For that matter, why did you look for me?"

"Because I missed you," her brother said with a grin. "I lost my job in Ventura a few weeks ago. I hadn't done anything wrong; they were just downsizing. Not that it matters why, but I was unemployed and decided to look for you. It wasn't too hard. When I found that you were teaching school in Duchesne, I just decided to go there and surprise you."

"I'm so glad you found me," my wife said. "You're the only family I have—except for my husband."

"And except for Dad, but I guess he doesn't count," Denny said. He was silent for a moment and moved his dinner around on his plate with his fork. No one else said a thing, and finally he spoke again. "I know this sounds crazy, but as much as I despise him, I'd like to visit him."

"Really, why?" Wyanne asked, her eyes wide with disbelief.

"I was in jail for six months once. I thought a lot about him when I was locked up." He shook his head. "That was why I didn't mind helping Detective Shelburn when he asked me if I'd go in and see if I could get Jarrod and Micah to talk to me, to admit anything. Anyway, I don't know. I just guess I'd like to at least try to talk to Dad."

"That's great, Denny. It's very noble of you," Wyanne said stiffly.

He stirred his food some more. "I have a huge favor to ask," he finally said, his eyes assessing the mess he'd just made of his dinner.

"Denny, I don't know," Wyanne said.

"Don't know what?" he asked.

"You know I could always tell what you wanted, Denny. I guess I still have the gift." She chuckled and finally looked up at him. "You want me to go with you to see him, don't you?"

"Yeah, if you will," he said.

"I don't know that I want to see him." Wyanne hesitated. Then she spoke again. "Maybe I will on one condition."

"What's that?" he asked.

"Well, actually, there are two conditions," she corrected.

"Okay, hit me with them," Denny responded, looking quite hopeful.

"First, you have to cut your hair," she said.

He chuckled. "And second, I have to get rid of my tattoos," he guessed.

"That'd be nice, but I know you can't do that," she said.

"It's okay," he said. "I wish I could get rid of all but one of them." She looked at him with a question in her eyes. "This one," he said and pulled up the right sleeve of his shirt.

"Wyanne," she read, and tears sprung into her eyes. "You have my name on your arm."

"I've missed you, sis. This was my reminder of you. You were always the peacemaker in our family," he told her. "I'll cut my hair."

"I'd like that," she said.

"So it's a deal then?" he asked.

"There's still the second condition," she said with a tease in her voice. "I want my husband to go with us."

"That's easy. Of course he can come, if he wants to, that is."

Both of them looked at me. "I put people in prison for a living. He might not like to meet me, but I'll go if you two want me to."

"Thanks, Saxson. I do love you, you know," Wyanne said.

Detective Shelburn spoke up then. "I'm all for your idea, Denny, but first, we have to catch a killer. You'll need to call Mr. Glazebrook and report that you've found them and ask him what he wants you to do."

"I know what it will be," Denny said, his face dark with unbridled hatred.

"We'll record it, and as soon as he says it, we'll go after him. That man is going to jail," Sheldon said. "He stepped way over the line. Also, Denny, I might need you to go back to the jail again and see if you can get some more information." Sheldon looked at Wyanne. "He's done a great job so far." She nodded an acknowledgement.

"That's fine," Denny agreed. "But I doubt I'll get anything if the Miano guys know that Malcom is locked up."

"He'll be in custody, but we'll make sure he won't be able to contact the Miano brothers."

"Okay, but *then* I want to go to see our father as soon as we can."

"That's settled then," Wyanne said. "Now, tell me how you found me and how you came to meet Detective Shelburn."

"You tell them, Detective," he said.

Sheldon smiled and put his fork down. "I got a call from the manager of your apartment," he began. "She was really worried. She'd heard what had happened to you in Vegas or at least enough to know that you were lucky to make it back to Duchesne. Anyway, she called and asked me to come by. She said it was very important."

With his fork, he speared a green bean, put it in his mouth, and chewed for a minute. Finally, he put the fork down again. "She said there was a note on your door. She told me that it scared her. I asked if she'd touched it, because without even seeing it, I was worried. She told me that she hadn't. So I went to your door with her. And there it was. I read it, tore it down, and took it with me."

"What did it say?" Wyanne asked.

"It was addressed to you, just your first name. It read something like, 'I'd like to see you. Call me as soon as you can.' There was a cell phone number with a California prefix. It was signed with just the letter *D*."

Wyanne grinned at Denny. "I would have known who it was from. Sometimes, when we were kids, he went by D. I'm sure I would have panicked until I saw the *D*. Then I would have been excited." She looked back at Detective Shelburn. "What did you do then?"

He shrugged his shoulders. "I called the number of course. He told me who he was. Well, sort of. He told me he was a close relative of yours. He told me his name was Anthony Green."

"I used that name for a long time," Denny explained. "Everyone knew me as Tony."

Sheldon took up the story again. "He agreed to meet with me. When I told him that your life had been threatened and I wondered if he might have been the one who had done it, he told me that his real name was Denver Grice, that he was your brother. I was skeptical, as you can imagine. I didn't know you had a brother. I began to believe him after I told him that you weren't in Duchesne, that you were hiding."

"I got really angry when he told me that," Denny said. "I'd finally made up my mind to find you, but then when I found where you lived, you were gone."

"He told me he'd do anything he could to help me catch whoever was doing this to you," Detective Shelburn said. "He even agreed to be fingerprinted. And that was the thing that convinced me that he was who he said he was."

"And when I asked him if I could go to jail and see if I could learn anything helpful from any of the prisoners, he was all for it," Denny said.

"It was a great idea," Sheldon said.

"I was in jail for a while a few years back, like I told you," Denny said. "You'd be surprised about how much inmates know about things you would never suspect."

"There was no time to waste," Sheldon went on. "So I got with the sheriff and his jail commander and with Dave Padrick and worked it out in time to get him in that same night. I said nothing to Denny about the Miano brothers, but we did arrange to have him housed in the same cellblock they were in. I was hoping he would find out if *any* inmates, the Mianos or others, were talking about murders. Then I got him out and spoke with him the next morning. He'd already discovered who the Miano brothers were, and he became friendly with them. When he went back in, he knew that they were the ones he needed to pump for information. You know the rest. He may have saved your lives with the information he got."

"Thanks, Denny. There's no question that they would have gotten to us if you hadn't sounded the alarm," I said.

After we had finished our meal and were waiting for our check, I asked, "So what now, Sheldon?"

"I want Denny to call Mr. Glazebrook and report that he's found you. It will be recorded so that if Glazebrook asks him to harm you two, we'll be able to charge him and get him behind bars."

The call was made. The two of them did it sitting in the detective's car, where Sheldon had the equipment he needed to record the conversation. My wife and I waited in our room. Both of us were nervous.

After a few minutes, the two of them joined us in our room.

"What did he say?" I asked.

Sheldon snorted. "He thanked Denny for finding you and asked him to tell you that he's heard there are people who want to kill you."

Denny took up the narrative. "He specifically said that I should convince you to not come back to Duchesne, but he didn't go so far as to tell me to do anything to you."

"I don't know what you think, Saxson, but I don't see where we can charge him with anything," Detective Shelburn said.

"I'm afraid not," I agreed. "And he thanked you, Denny?"

"Yeah," Denny said. "He asked me how I found you so fast. I told him I knew people who were willing to help me. He seemed satisfied with that. But he did tell me to get back to Duchesne before I got in more trouble."

"As if he cares." I rolled my eyes. "Okay, Sheldon, what do we do now?"

"We find the killer," he said. "We are working on that. In the meantime, I would suggest that the two of you stay out of sight," he said. He shrugged. "For now, do what Malcom says and stay away from Duchesne. Denny and I will go back and see if he can learn more in the jail." He chuckled. "He's going to get in more trouble, I'm afraid. Glazebrook will like that, I think. This way, he'll be able to charge Denny more for his defense."

"Won't Jarrod and Micah get suspicious if he goes back in this fast?" I asked.

"We planned for this to happen," Sheldon said. "He'll go in and tell them he already committed another crime. We're trying to make him look worse than they are. That way, we believe he'll avoid suspicion, and hopefully they'll talk to him more."

Sheldon and Denny stayed the night. Denny and Wyanne talked for hours. They had a lot of years to catch up on. When she finally came to bed, she was happy in a way I hadn't seen before. She summed it up when she said, "I have family again." She kissed me and added, "And I have you."

***

Sheldon and Denny drove back to Duchesne the next day to fake an arrest on new charges and book Denny into jail again. Afterwards, Sheldon called. "We think we know where our killer is," he said. "With a little luck, we'll make the arrest tonight and you guys can come home."

"That would be great," I said, smiling at my wife over breakfast.

We drove around much of that day, both of us too nervous to really do the tourist thing. Finally, in the early evening, Wyanne said, "Let's drive toward home. We can at least go to Salt Lake or Ogden or someplace fairly close."

I liked her idea, so by ten that night we were booked in a hotel in Salt Lake, still waiting for the call from Sheldon. It came an hour later. Sheldon simply said, "You can come home tomorrow. Our suspect is in jail, and Malcom Glazebrook is already demanding that bail be set low. He's claiming that our case is weak."

"He would," I said. "Frankly, I was hoping he wouldn't be involved at this point in the case."

"You knew he would, Counselor. If he would have done something more when Denny reported that he'd found you, we could have locked him up for a while."

"That's okay. We'll be home in the morning," I told him.

"Don't get careless," Sheldon cautioned. "We have the right person in jail, but who knows how many others there are who are prone to violence."

"We'll stay together," I said. "When is the arraignment set for?"

"Ten in the morning in front of Judge Feldman," he said. He chuckled and said, "So is Denny's. Denny is out on bail again, but we thought it would be fun if you could be the one to make the motion to drop the charges on him."

"Okay, we'll be there," I said.

I called Dave Padrick and asked him how he was doing as we were driving toward Duchesne early the next morning.

"I was doing better," he said, "but I've had a bad couple of days. When will you be home?"

"We're on our way," I said.

"Will you be here in time to handle the arraignments for me? My doctor has some tests scheduled for me in the morning. One of the other guys could be there, but I'd rather have you do it. You've invested a lot in this matter. And I'm sure you'd like to face Malcom Glazebrook again."

He was right on that one. The man had tried to ruin my wife's reputation. He may not have known she was my wife, but nonetheless I was determined to meet him and beat him. I would start by doing my best to keep his homicidal client in jail, for I was sure Malcom would argue vigorously for a low bond. I was going to have none of it.

Wyanne and I walked into my office at 9:30 a.m. Josie spotted her diamond ring, and our secret was out. There was a chorus of surprised but congratulatory statements. She could have stayed in my office and out of the public eye while I handled the arraignment, but she would have none of it. "I want to be there," she said in a no-argument voice.

Detective Shelburn assured me that the courtroom would be secure. He told us that Denny would be there but warned Wyanne that she would need to appear not to know him.

Denny sat on the back row in the very far corner of the spacious courtroom. Wyanne sat in front of him and a few seats over without so much as looking at him. I took my place at the prosecutor's table. Detective Shelburn didn't need to be there for the arraignment, but he told me he'd like to be, both as added security as well as for moral support. I appreciated the gesture.

I was seated and reviewing my notes when there was a stir in the courtroom. I looked up just as Malcom Glazebrook's latest client was escorted in by a pair of deputies. They led her to the defense table. At that same moment, Malcom entered and joined his client. The look I received from the accused killer would have sent most people scampering for cover. I tried not to flinch. I don't remember ever looking into a face emitting more hatred than the defendant's did at that moment.

After whispering to his client for a moment, Malcom stepped over to me, stooped down, and said, "If I'd known your girlfriend was a killer's daughter, I would never have offered you the job." I held his gaze and said nothing. He wasn't finished. "Now I hear you're married to her. Word's all over the courthouse this morning. You two deserve each other." He smirked.

I still held my peace. I knew he was trying to get a rise out of me. I was determined it would not happen. I was saving my words for later, for the preliminary hearing.

He wasn't finished though. "Not only are you married to a killer's daughter, you're also married to an accused killer's former fiancée."

I wanted to shout that she'd never even been Jameson's girlfriend, but I managed to resist.

When I still didn't respond, he said with a smirk, "Before I'm through with this case, you'll wish you'd never gone to work for Dave Padrick. I would have thought he'd have had sense enough to assign a real attorney, not a buckaroo, to handle this case. You're going to get squashed like a bug before I'm through with you."

I changed my mind. I decided that I could spare a few words for Malcom. I simply said, and quite loudly at that, "To think that you offered me $300,000 a year to work for you. If I'm such a poor attorney, I wonder what you would pay a good one." My comment was heard by a lot of people, and they caused a ripple of laughter to go through the gallery. Beside me, Sheldon almost choked. I almost regretted saying those words—almost. The look on Malcom's face made me glad I had. He turned an ugly shade of purple and spun away from me, taking his seat next to his client. The stage was set for a nasty fight, and after all this man and his client had put me and the girl I loved through, I was up for it. I was even eager for it.

The judge came in as the bailiff said his obligatory, "All rise."

We rose, all but the defendant. It took a rough look and a hand on the defendant's arm before compliance was obtained. We sat when the judge told us.

Judge Feldman said, "We're here today for two arraignments."

"Malcom Glazebrook, for the defendant," Malcom said as he stood.

"Good morning, Counselor," Judge Feldman said. He looked at me. "I understand that you have a motion for the court on another matter. I'll call that case first."

"That's right. In the case of State versus Anthony Green, I move to dismiss all charges. I've reviewed the cases with the arresting officer, and I don't think we can meet the standard to convict him."

Glazebrook jumped to his feet. "He's my client," he informed the judge. "Why don't I know anything about this?"

"I just made the decision. I guess you win on this one," I said.

He smirked. "I'd have won in court, Mr. Cartwright," he countered snidely. "I was really hoping we could go to trial on those cases."

"Sorry," I said. "But if the court is willing to grant my motion, those matters are concluded."

"Your motion is granted," Judge Feldman said with a straight face. "Is the defendant in the courtroom?"

I looked back as Denny, alias Anthony, stood and said, "I'm Anthony Green, Your Honor."

"You witnessed what happened just now. All charges against you have been dismissed. You may leave now."

"Thank you, Your Honor. Is it okay if I stay and watch? I have nothing else to do right now."

"Suit yourself." Judge Feldman then called the next case and instructed the defendant and the counsel for the defense to come to the podium. Once they were standing there, he read the information charging Glazebrook's client with two counts of first-degree murder, one count of attempted murder, and several other charges that arose from the attempts to have my wife and me murdered.

There was a brief exchange in which Glazebrook stated that his client understood the charges and his client finally, after a little prodding, said the same.

"To count one of the information, murder in the first degree, how do you plead?"

From my position behind and slightly to the left of the defendant, I could see a mighty storm brewing on that already angry face. It reminded me of a time as a young man when I had failed to heed my father's warning. A Guernsey heifer that we'd bought to provide milk for our family had just had her first calf. I was helping my father that morning as we attempted to get her away from her calf and into the barn so we could milk her for the very first time.

Dad had said, "Saxson, this heifer has always been a bit of a pet, and you might think that she's gentle. But she has just had a calf. She's a new mother today. She might know you, but her instincts are to protect her young. She won't want to leave that calf. So watch her closely. If she even thinks that you might be planning to hurt her offspring, she could take off after you. If she does, get over the fence before she hurts you."

I had failed to watch as closely as I should have, and that young cow actually boosted me over the corral fence as I was frantically scrambling to get over on my own. If she had caught me before I started to climb, I shudder to think what she would have done to me.

I was thinking of my father's words as I watched the defendant. Instead of answering the judge directly, she looked back at me, and in a voice that was as full of menace as that cow had been that day, she said, "You!" and poked a finger in my direction. "Because of you my sons are in jail."

Well, that wasn't completely true. Her sons, Jarrod and Micah Miano, had played a rather large part in that. But she didn't see it that way any more than our young Guernsey cow had thought that I had no intention of hurting her calf.

"I'll see you rot for that, cowboy!" She had used Malcom's favorite slur. Beside me, I was aware of Detective Shelburn rising to his feet. I think he thought, as I did right then, that the angry mother was about to attack me.

As Judge Feldman rapped his gavel, Malcom took Mrs. Tamara Miano by the arm and jerked quite hard. She swung toward him, and he said, "Say, 'Not guilty.' And do it now."

She stared at him for a moment and then at the judge, and finally, sullenly, she said, "Not guilty."

"To the charge of count two of the information, murder in the first degree, how do you plead?" Judge Feldman said.

"I'm not guilty," she shouted without hesitation this time.

"To the charge of count three of the information, attempted murder, how do you plead?"

"Not guilty." She entered the same plea to all of the charges.

The judge said, "This matter will be set for a preliminary hearing."

Glazebrook said, "The defendant demands that it be set for a date that is not far distant."

"I'll have to defer to Judge Dunson, who will be conducting the preliminary hearing."

"That man?" Glazebrook scoffed. "He's only a justice court judge, and he doesn't even have a law degree."

"Judge Dunson is an experienced judge and has been trained and certified to conduct preliminary hearings. You will check with him and with Mr. Saxson to get a date for the preliminary hearing," Judge Feldman said in a stern voice that even Malcom Glazebrook apparently took notice of.

"Yes, Your Honor," he said.

His client, the deadly Mrs. Miano, wasn't intimidated. "You sent my sons to jail for nothing!" she yelled.

"Mrs. Miano, I'm familiar with why your sons went to jail, and it was not for nothing. You are out of order here. Any more outbursts and you will be found in contempt of this court," Judge Feldman said firmly.

Malcom was tugging at the sleeve of her orange jumpsuit. He was whispering to her but not so quietly that I couldn't hear it. He said, "Shut up! I am just about to argue for bail. Don't make the judge any angrier than he already is, or you will end up sitting back there until the preliminary hearing."

She apparently understood him, though she glared at me, at Detective Shelburn, and at the judge. She kept her mouth closed.

Glazebrook said, "Your Honor, I would like to ask that bail be set and that it be a reasonable amount."

That was my cue. I was on my feet in a flash. "Your Honor, the state requests that she be held without bail. Two of these charges are capital offenses. It is the position of the state that Mrs. Miano is a danger to society and must be kept in custody."

"That's bunk!" Malcom shouted.

"Just a moment, Mr. Glazebrook. Let Mr. Cartwright finish, then I'll hear from you again."

Malcom glared, but he let me go on. "The state also believes the defendant is a flight risk. When she somehow realized that the sheriff's office considered her a suspect, she fled the area. She was found in an old cabin that has no running water and on property that does not belong to her family."

"We're thinking about buying that property," she said. "I was simply evaluating it."

"That will be all, Mrs. Miano," the judge said sternly.

"With a bedroll and an air mattress?" I asked.

"That's enough, Mr. Cartwright," the judge said sternly.

"Sorry, Your Honor," I said. I had made my point. I could also have pointed out that she had not driven one of her luxury vehicles to the site but had borrowed an old pickup to make her trip, but I didn't need to rile the judge.

"Okay, Mr. Glazebrook," Judge Feldman said, "it's your turn now."

"She is not a flight risk; she is innocent of the charges," he said. "She could easily make a reasonable bond. The defense requests that bond be set at a hundred thousand."

"I strenuously object to that," I said.

"I've heard enough," the judge said. "Defendant is to be held without bond."

"That's ridiculous," Glazebrook said.

"I have ruled," the judge said. He had his gavel in his hand. I could see that he was ready to end the proceedings.

But Glazebrook wasn't through yet. He said, "I disagree with your ruling, and I want the record to so reflect. But, considering your ruling, I renew my request for a near date for the preliminary hearing."

"And *I* renew my order that you work that out with Mr. Cartwright and Judge Dunson." The gavel came down firmly. The next step was the preliminary hearing.

Detective Shelburn leaned over to me as I picked up my file. "There's one person who is noticeably absent today. I don't see Armando Miano."

"I wonder why," I said, looking around the courtroom. "He'll be here for the prelim, or I miss my guess."

Malcom Glazebrook watched as his client was led out by two officers, and then he hurried and caught me before I left the courtroom. "Let's go to Judge Dunson's office and get the preliminary hearing scheduled."

"Sure thing," I said.

When we left the justice court office, we had a preliminary hearing scheduled for a Wednesday morning, two weeks away. That was longer than Glazebrook wanted, but he had to settle for it. As he was leaving the office, he said, "You are way over your head, Cartwright. I'm going to play you like a fine fiddle."

Twenty-Eight

As I HAD PREDICTED, THE husband of the defendant entered the courtroom as we were waiting for Judge Dunson to take the bench. He did not, however, sit directly behind his wife, nor did he attempt to speak to her. His face was dark and brooding. I wondered what he was thinking.

I was ready for today's preliminary hearing. Basically my task today was to convince Judge Dunson that it was more likely than not that Mrs. Miano had killed Evan Morberg and Darrius Chaudry as well as attempting to kill Corporal Kingston and hiring others to find and kill Wyanne and me. I had more than enough evidence to get Tamara Miano bound over to stand trial. Of course, Malcom told me before court began that I wouldn't even come close and that his client would walk free before that day was over if the judge did his job.

My wife and her brother, who had both found the arraignment quite entertaining, were once again in the courtroom. We had become fairly well acquainted over the past few days, and I had come to like Denny very much. As in the arraignment, Denny and Wyanne did not sit together at the preliminary hearing. Unfortunately, we felt that it was best to keep up the pretext that they didn't know one another, so he'd stayed in a hotel over in Roosevelt. But we'd managed to meet up with him and spend quite a bit of time together.

There were three of us at the state's table that morning. Of course, the bright and capable Detective Sheldon Shelburn was there, seated next to me. On the far side was Marv Hanger. He had protested, but Dave had said, "I am confident in Saxson's ability, but even if I were handling the case today, I would have one of you there with me. This is the most serious crime we will ever handle. A second prosecutor should be there just to make sure nothing is missed. We must get this woman bound over." So Marv came, and frankly I was glad he was there.

The first person I called to the stand was Detective Shelburn. I walked him through the case he had established. The judge heard testimony that Mrs. Miano owned a black Lincoln Navigator. That Navigator was the one recovered on my father's ranch in Wyoming. The Lincoln's tires matched the tracks from the murder scene.

A pair of women's hiking boots had been found during the execution of a search warrant at the Mianos' home in Vernal. They were in the back of the defendant's large closet. The shoes matched footprints found at the scene of the murders. The defendant had obliterated the tracks around the bodies of both victims, but she had missed the ones at the edge of the road. That was a big element in the state's favor. Sheldon also testified regarding motive. She'd made statements that indicated that she would do anything to protect her son Jarrod who was facing charges where the second victim, Darrius Chaudry, was a key witness against him.

Sheldon introduced phone records that indicated that the man who died in the shootout at my father's ranch had received calls from Tamara's phone as had the two men I duct taped in Ballard. And of course, he was able to show that the hired killers were driving Tamara Miano's Navigator in Wyoming. He testified that the weapon used to shoot all three victims was the same one, a .45-caliber pistol, which had not been found. He was, however, able to show that the defendant owned a semiautomatic of that caliber.

Finally, and probably most damaging to the defense, was the fact that he had recovered hair samples from the back of the Navigator that he'd sent to the state lab for comparison with the victims' hair. I called a lab technician who testified that the hair samples taken from Mrs. Miano's Navigator were a DNA match to Mr. Morberg's hair in some instances and a DNA match to Darrius Chaudry's hair in others.

I was impressed that while my wife and I had been honeymooning and trying to stay alive, Detective Shelburn had been busy building a solid case against Tamara Miano. Both he and the expert witness were vigorously cross-examined by the defense attorney, but Glazebrook was unable to trip either of them up at all. I believed we had more than enough to bind her over at that point. Of course, I had in reserve Wyanne seeing the black SUV near the murder scene that fatal morning, but I had not listed her as a witness and had no intention of using her testimony unless I had to call her as a rebuttal witness.

I had also intentionally not used Denny as a witness for today's hearing, although the defense knew of his conversations with the sons of the defendant and their admissions to him in the jail. Of course they only knew him as Anthony Green. What they didn't know was his connection to me and my wife or that he'd been working undercover for Detective Shelburn. I was saving that little surprise for the trial.

There was nothing that Malcom could do to diminish the effect of the evidence I had presented. His biggest problem, actually, was containing his defendant. She shouted out that someone had stolen her Navigator and that she'd had nothing to do with the murders. The judge reminded her that she'd get her turn.

When the case went to trial, I also planned to use the man who had been captured after the botched attempt on Wyanne's and my lives. Sheldon had managed to get him to turn on Mrs. Miano, and he'd confessed that he was doing her bidding. That was for another day.

I was confident that I had enough for today and was conferring with Sheldon and Marv when one of the judge's clerks, Rosemary Rivard, came up to my table and handed me a note. "You need to read that," she whispered and then quickly left.

So I did. She had written that the defendant's husband wanted to talk to me and that it was urgent. I had no idea what that was all about, but I asked for a recess, simply stating that I needed to speak with a witness.

Malcom objected. The judge overruled him.

Marv, Detective Shelburn, and I met with Armando Miano in my office a minute later. "I want to testify," he said.

Not sure what he had in mind, I exercised caution. "I'm sure Mr. Glazebrook plans to call you when he presents the defense's case in a little while."

Armando's face grew dark. "You don't understand. I want to testify *against* my wife."

"Why would you do that?" I asked, both surprised and very skeptical. "As her husband, you can't be compelled to testify."

"I know that, but I also can't be prevented from doing so," he said. "Anyway, by the time this goes to trial, we'll be divorced. I've already filed, and she'll be served with the papers as soon as court is over."

Wow! I hadn't expected that. "Mr. Miano," I said after giving myself a moment to recover from shock. "I've already presented enough evidence to bind your wife over for trial."

"I agree," he said. "But I still want to testify. Let me tell you why." He spent the next five minutes giving me information that would, almost without a doubt, assure the conviction of his wife.

"I'll call you at trial. Right now I need you to meet with Detective Shelburn and tell him everything you've just told us so he can record it," I said. I looked at Sheldon, who simply nodded his agreement.

"Please, Mr. Cartwright. Let me testify today. I think we can end this all today if you will let me testify," he begged.

"Mr. Glazebrook will object that I didn't disclose you as a witness in the discovery process," I argued.

"I heard that he tried that on you in a DUI trial a few weeks ago and that the judge let the man testify. Shouldn't it be the same here? You need to try," he urged.

"Okay. Let's try, Mr. Miano," I said thoughtfully. "Mr. Glazebrook will put on his case, and if your wife testifies, then I could put you on as a rebuttal witness."

"He won't let her testify," he said. "He knows what Tamara's temper is like. He knows you would make her angry when you cross-examine her and she would probably blurt something out that would hurt his case."

I had to admit he was probably right. I looked at Marv, who said, "I think it's worth a try. What can it hurt?"

"All right, we'll do it," I said. "But let's take a moment and go over what I'll ask you, Mr. Miano." Ten minutes later, I had what I needed written on my legal pad. "Why don't you go out to your car with Detective Shelburn and you can give him that item. Then I'll see both of you back in the courtroom."

After he'd left my office, I said to Marv, "I hope he doesn't get up there and do exactly the opposite of what he says he's going to."

"If he does, we'll still be okay," he argued. "But frankly, Saxson, I believe we can trust him."

"I hope," I said as I rose to my feet. "Let's go see what happens. This will either be fun, or you and I will have egg on our faces."

"You'll have egg on your face." Marv chuckled. "I'm just assisting."

***

I took a deep breath when Judge Dunson asked, "Are you ready to proceed again, Mr. Cartwright?"

"I am, Your Honor," I said. "The state calls Armando Miano."

Malcom Glazebrook jumped to his feet while shouting, "Objection! I don't know what the state's attorney thinks he's doing. This comes as a complete surprise to me. It simply cannot be allowed."

"Mr. Cartwright, would you like to explain?"

"Yes, Your Honor," I said. "I didn't know about this witness until minutes ago. He can present evidence that I think you need to hear. He wants to testify against the defendant."

"There is no way I'm going to allow this," Glazebrook shouted. "He is her husband; he can't testify."

"He can't be *compelled* to testify, Mr. Glazebrook," I said. "You need to brush up on the law."

"Again, I am not going to allow this!" Malcom shouted, throwing a deadly look in my direction. He hadn't liked my barb. I smiled at him.

"It's not up to you, Counselor," Judge Dunson said firmly. "I will make the decision."

"That's what I meant," Malcom countered. "There is no way you can allow this."

"That's not what you argued in a recent case in my court when you were the one with a last-minute, undisclosed witness," the judge said with a straight face. "Anyway, this is only a preliminary hearing. If I bind this over for trial, you'll have a chance to do whatever you have to before Mr. Miano testifies again. And if I don't bind your client over, then what have you lost? Your objection is overruled. I will allow Mr. Miano to testify."

His wife screamed out as she turned and looked at her husband in the gallery, "You can't do this, Armando. You're my husband. You can't testify against me."

"Mrs. Miano, you must control your outbursts, or I will have you removed from the courtroom and we'll proceed without you," Judge

Dunson said even as Malcom was trying to rein her in. "And as to your remarks, Mr. Cartwright is correct. A husband cannot be *compelled* to testify against his wife, but there is nothing to prevent him from doing it if he so chooses. Mr. Miano, please come forward and be sworn."

After asking Armando to state his name and place of residence for the record, I asked, "Mr. Miano, have you and I or you and Detective Shelburn discussed the matters that you have asked to testify to prior to today?"

"No, sir, but I should have. It's time my wife's terrible behavior is stopped."

"Objection," Glazebrook said. "That answer is beyond the scope of the question."

"Overruled," the judge said.

"Let's start with a certain .45-caliber semiautomatic weapon that Detective Shelburn earlier testified is owned by your wife," I said. "Do you know where that gun is?"

"Yes, Detective Shelburn has it," he said. "I gave it to him a few minutes ago."

"Objection, we know nothing about this gun," Malcom said.

I waited until the judge overruled him before walking back to the table. Sheldon handed me the pistol, and I returned to the podium, holding it up. I read the serial number then asked, "Is this the gun?"

"Yes, that's my wife's gun," he said.

"Can you tell me how you came in possession of it?" I asked.

"I took it out of her closet this morning," he said. "She hid it there just last night."

"Is there any reason you can think of that would make it important that I ask the court to admit this gun as evidence?" I asked.

Mrs. Miano was mumbling, but Malcom was so far able to keep her from making further outbursts.

Her husband testified, "Yes, that's the gun she used to shoot Mr. Morberg, Mr. Chaudry, and Corporal Kingston."

Malcom objected. His client started to say something, but he silenced her. "Your Honor," he said, "there is no foundation for such an outrageous statement."

"Your Honor," I said, enjoying myself immensely. "I was about to ask the defendant to explain."

"The objection is overruled. You may go on, Mr. Cartwright," the judge said.

"Mr. Miano, how do you know this was the weapon she used in the commission of her terrible crimes?" I asked.

"My wife told me it was the murder weapon just before she hid it in her closet," he said.

I would never have believed that Malcom Glazebrook could be stunned, but he was; it was clear on his face. He remained seated and whispered something to his client. She whispered back.

I asked, "Mr. Miano, did your wife tell you *why* she shot the three victims?"

"She said she did it to protect our son, Jarrod, to keep him from going to prison."

There was a ripple through the gallery. The judge rapped his gavel and brought the court back to order.

"I can understand her morbid reasoning when it comes to Mr. Chaudry and Corporal Kingston. But you'll need to explain why she would kill Mr. Morberg. He was a juror," I said.

The expected outburst came at last. Mrs. Miano screamed, "You keep your mouth shut. I told you that in confidence. You are my husband. Jarrod is your son too. I was only protecting him."

The judge, in what I thought was an admirable display of patience, said, "Mr. Glazebrook, please control your client. Mrs. Miano, if you make another outburst, I will have you removed from the courtroom. Mr. Miano, you may proceed."

"He refused a bribe from my wife," he said. "She offered him a large sum of money if he would vote to acquit Jarrod in the automobile homicide trial. He refused, and she lost her temper, kidnapped him at gunpoint, took him to a remote location, and killed him."

I glanced back at the defense table. Tamara was seething. Mr. Glazebrook had his head in his hands, his elbows propped on the table. I asked, "What were the juror and your wife doing in Heber?"

"She told me she called him and asked him to meet her there. She didn't tell him who she was, or rather I should say she lied to him. For some reason, he agreed to drive there. She didn't tell me what story she used to get him to go there, but she's pretty imaginative, so it was probably really good. I was so disgusted that I didn't even ask. Anyway, she met him and made her bribe. He refused, and she pulled her gun on him, made him get in her car, and took him to the cabin where the officers found her when she was arrested. She said she tried to convince him that he should simply vote to let our son off. Even then he refused. So she took him to the location where his body was found and killed him," he said. His face showed anguish, not anger, at this point.

"And Corporal Kingston?" I prompted.

"She called him, made an excuse that his wife was having car problems, met him in Indian Canyon, and shot him. She thought he was dead when she left him there," he said.

"What about the second attempt on the corporal's life?" I asked.

"She was behind that as well, and she also sent those two thugs to Wyoming to kill you and Miss Grice," he said. "Oh, and she hired a couple of other men to attempt to frighten Miss Grice enough that she would forget what she saw."

"Which was?" I asked.

"She saw my wife in her car leaving the area where she had just murdered Mr. Morberg."

"Thank you, Mr. Miano. Oh, there is one more thing I'd like you to explain to the court. Why did you wait until today to come forward?"

"She's my wife. I was in love with her. I went out of town for a few days to think about what I should do. That was why I missed her arraignment," he said. "I'm sorry I didn't come forward sooner. But after what she told me last night, I felt like I could never live with myself if I let her get away with this."

I'd glanced back at his wife several times over the past few minutes, and I could see the storm brewing in Mrs. Miano's face. She finally exploded again. "He's lying!" she screamed. "Judge, put him in jail. He doesn't even care about his sons. Put him back there."

The bailiff and two other officers grabbed hold of her. She screamed at them and spit in the face of one of them.

"Remove her from the courtroom," the judge ordered with a sharp rap of his gavel. She was dragged out, screaming and swearing and making threats to kill the judge, to kill me, to kill her husband, and to kill the officers.

Mr. Glazebrook rose to his feet. The fire was gone from his eyes, and he spoke softly. "Your Honor," he said. "I'll talk to her. If you'll give us a brief recess, I'll see if I can convince her to behave herself when we come back in."

"You have ten minutes, and then we'll proceed without her unless you can calm her down and assure me that there will be no further outbursts. You still have the right to cross-examine Mr. Miano," the judge said. "But you can do it with or without her."

Ten minutes later, she was led back in, and she seemed much calmer. The judge told me to proceed. I asked the witness, who was looking thoroughly miserable on the witness stand, "Is there anything else you would like to tell the court about what your wife did or said to you?" I asked.

He shook his head then finally said, "No, I think it's pretty clear. That's all."

"Your witness," I said to Malcom.

He approached the podium while I returned to my seat. He appeared to be looking at his legal pad, but it was a minute before he spoke. Finally, he said, "You know that you will have to tell all this to a jury if the court binds your wife over today?"

"Yes, but I don't think it will be you asking the questions then," he said.

Malcom jerked. "Why do you say that?"

"You told us that we had to come up with another fifteen thousand dollars if this went to a jury. And I don't know where you plan to get it," Mr. Miano said quite softly. The witness shook his head. "I have filed for divorce. She'll be served by a deputy after court today. And I'm going to insist that the divorce move quickly."

Malcom looked baffled for a moment, but he soon collected himself and said, "You can't withhold funds from your wife," he said. "She'll pay me."

Mrs. Miano was nodding vigorously but saying nothing. "She's in jail, and I won't write you another check," Mr. Miano said. "And anyway, when the divorce is over, she'll have nothing."

Glazebrook turned and walked back to his table to confer with his client for a minute. Then he again slowly walked back to the podium. "I need to remind you that half of what the two of you have will be hers."

The defendant shook his head. "Not so," he said. "I think Tamara has forgotten about the prenuptial agreement she signed when we were married. She had nothing when she married me. The money, the property, the stocks and bonds—everything is mine. She will have nothing when this is over."

Mr. Glazebrook turned to the defense table. "I don't work for free," he said to his client.

Her head was hanging. She said nothing.

"She's on her own from here on out. I can't take any more," Mr. Miano said. "She's not getting one more dime of my money."

"Then she will have to have a court-appointed attorney," Glazebrook said. "I have nothing else to ask this witness."

"Then present your defense," the judge instructed.

"I don't intend to call any witnesses," Glazebrook said. "The defense rests."

"In that case, Mrs. Tamara Miano, you are bound over to stand trial on all counts." The judge rapped his gavel, and we were through.

***

When Malcom informed Judge Feldman of the District Court that he was withdrawing as counsel for Tamara Miano, Judge Feldman told him that he couldn't, that he had to proceed even if he didn't get paid. Malcom wasn't happy, but he said he'd see what he could work out. I could only smile.

In my office a few days later, Malcom said, "Cartwright, I guess you win. I would never have guessed you could beat me in court. But I have a proposition for you. We both know I can't win in front of a jury. I will plead my client guilty to one count of first degree murder if you'll drop the other charges."

"This is a capital case," I reminded him. "Make that two counts of murder in the first degree."

"Only if the death penalty is off the table," he said resignedly.

"Life without the probability of parole," I countered.

"It's a deal," he said.

"Will your client agree to this?" I asked.

"She'll agree," he said in a tone of voice that told me that he would accept nothing less from her. I didn't ask him how he was going to convince her.

Epilogue

SHORTLY AFTER I WRAPPED UP all of the Miano cases, the beautiful fall weather changed for the worse. For the next few months, it was bitter cold, snowy, windy, and with periods of dense fog. In my little apartment, however, it was warm and comfortable. Wyanne finally was able to teach without interruption. I handled the cases that came my way, but none were as tough as the ones I'd already handled.

It finally warmed up, and on a sunny Saturday early in April, Wyanne and I saddled our horses for a ride we'd waited for all winter. We invited her brother to join us, but he begged off, saying, "I'm not a cowboy." He had found a job in the oil field and seemed happy. I think that just having family again made his life worth living. He even attended church when he wasn't working and wore long sleeves to hide most of his tattoos. His hair was short, and he looked good whenever we saw him.

"Where should we go?" I asked my wife as soon as we were mounted and starting up the lane on our horses. We'd packed for a ride of several hours, so it didn't matter much which way we rode.

She surprised me when she said, "I didn't think I'd ever say this, but if you don't mind, I'd like to ride out to Little Egypt."

"Are you sure?" I asked, looking skeptically at her. "I was thinking maybe we could ride over to Starvation Reservoir."

"Maybe next Saturday if the weather's good," she said. "I can't explain it, but I just feel the need to ride out there again."

"All right," I agreed. "Whatever you want is fine with me."

At one point on the way, Wyanne said, "I don't suppose you have any idea what happened to Martin Jameson. I can't imagine that Malcom Glazebrook got him off."

I chuckled. "I got a call one day from Detective Reese. You remember him, don't you?"

"How could I forget him?" she said.

"Yeah, well, he called me one day and said that Jameson had heard about the Miano case on TV, and he fired Malcom and hired someone from down there. His case is still pending, but Detective Reese assured me he would be convicted."

"You haven't mentioned Glazebrook lately. Do you ever see him in court anymore?" she asked as she rode around a clump of sagebrush.

"He was disbarred," I said. "That was the only thing that could happen. He was a smart lawyer but not a wise one. Lionel Gancina runs the firm now. He doesn't take any cases out here nor do the other lawyers in the firm."

We rode in silence for a while, but when she spoke again, it had nothing to do with the Miano cases. We rode close together and held hands. We finally reached the area where the murders had occurred. She took the lead and rode ahead of me to the exact place where the corpses had been found. She pulled Raspberry to a stop and stared at the ground where she had stumbled over Mr. Morberg. For a minute or so she just stared. Then she finally said, "Let's go."

We rode on to the edge of the draw and ate lunch on a sunny ledge. "I'm so sorry about what happened to those men," she said. She took a drink from her water bottle before speaking again. "But if it hadn't been for their deaths, I would probably have never come to know you. I hope that somehow, they know that they brought us together and that we're both thankful for that."

"I hope so too," I said.

"Even though Dad died of cancer before we got to see him, I still have to thank him for the fact that I'm a teacher. And if I hadn't been a teacher, I would never have come to Duchesne. And so I guess in a way, I have my dad to thank that I have you now."

Then she suddenly started to laugh.

"What?" I asked.

"I almost got carried away. There are two people I won't thank—Mrs. Miano and Mr. Glazebrook."

We laughed together, and I took her in my arms and silently told the Lord how grateful I was for this girl who helped me through my shyness and helped me to fall in love. "It's funny how life works out sometimes," I said as I held her close.

"Mmm," she replied.

About the Author

CLAIR M. POULSON WAS BORN and raised in Duchesne, Utah. His father was a rancher and farmer, his mother, a librarian. Clair has always been an avid reader, having found his love for books as a very young boy.

He has served for more than forty years in the criminal justice system. He spent twenty years in law enforcement, ending his police career with eight years as the Duchesne County Sheriff. For the past twenty-plus years, Clair has worked as a justice court judge for Duchesne County. He is also a veteran of the US Army, where he was a military policeman. In law enforcement, he has been personally involved in the investigation of murders and other violent crimes. Clair has also served on various boards and councils during his professional career, including the Justice Court Board of Judges, the Utah Commission on Criminal and Juvenile Justice, the Utah Judicial Council, the Utah Peace Officer Standards and Training Council, an FBI advisory board, and others.

In addition to his criminal justice work, Clair has farmed and ranched all his life. He has raised many kinds of animals, but his greatest interests are horses and cattle. He's also involved in the grocery store business with his oldest son and other family members.

Clair has served in many capacities in the LDS Church, including full-time missionary (California Mission), bishop, counselor to two bishops, young men president, high councilor, stake mission president, Scoutmaster, and high priest group leader. He currently serves as a Gospel Doctrine teacher.

Clair is married to Ruth, and they have five children, all of whom are married: Alan (Vicena) Poulson, Kelly Ann (Wade) Hatch, Amanda (Ben) Semadeni, Wade (Brooke) Poulson, and Mary (Tyler) Hicken. They also have twenty-five wonderful grandchildren. Clair and Ruth met while both were students at Snow College and were married in the Manti temple.

Clair has always loved telling his children, and later his grandchildren, made-up stories. His vast experience in life and his love of literature have contributed to both his telling stories to his children and his writing of adventure and suspense novels.

Clair has published more than two dozen novels. He would love to hear from his fans, who can contact him by going to his website, *clairmpoulson.com*.